Sleight of Hand

An Amber Farrell Novel
Book 1 of the
Bite Back series

by
Mark Henwick

Published by *Marque*

Series schedule, reviews & news on
www.athanate.com

Bite Back 1 : Sleight of Hand
ISBN: 978-1-912499-13-7

First published in August 2012 by Marque

Mark Henwick asserts the right to be identified as the author of this work.

Cover design: CreativeEdge, Andrew Dobell
Cover model: Maria Askew

Author's note:

Asian names:
Throughout this series, I use the Western sequence (First, Middle, Last Name) to depict names, so as to match with the majority of characters in the books. Most Asian societies would put the Last Name first.

Chapter 1

MONDAY

It had been a couple of years and I was neither dead, nor undead, which I ranked as an achievement.

It wasn't as if I lacked opportunity. Even when I wasn't really looking for it.

I was safe at the moment. My perch among the roof beams of the Crate & Freight warehouse in the Northfield section of Denver was only fifty feet above the concrete floor. Those SCAR assault rifles down on the loading bay weren't aimed at me. No one knew I was here and it was dark in this corner. That was safe, by some definitions of the word safe. I was kind of enjoying myself.

Still, I knew what a few SCAR rounds could do to a body. The guys down there weren't carrying them for show. If they pointed a flashlight up into the gloomy recesses, they would be surprised to see their afternoon visitor from the HR department, now minus her clipboard and big square glasses, in black coveralls and toting a camera with a zoom lens.

Given what they were involved in, they wouldn't stop to ask questions.

I needed to call this in and hand it over to the police. I wasn't armed tonight and besides, I was supposed to be a discreet PI, not a one-woman SWAT team.

I didn't want to risk them hearing me call 911. And I didn't want the nearest cruiser with a couple of bored officers to swing by and spook these guys, thinking the call was some crazy woman. I wanted the Denver PD SWAT team, tooled up for the job. So I was waiting for a few of the photos to download from my camera to my cell and I would text them directly to Captain José Morales with details.

I had his contact for a completely different reason, but surely he'd thank me for this?

A noisy problem outside with the last truck emptied the warehouse, and I took the chance to climb down. Climbing urban structures was a teenage hobby of mine, so the prominent bolts and cross struts made this about as difficult as coming down a ladder.

I lurked in the shadow of a pile of pallets, waiting for my cell to finish loading.

Campbell Carter, the CEO of Centennial State Crate & Freight, had hired me on my office landlord's recommendation. He suspected some of his drivers and dispatchers were stealing from him. Nothing major, just something he wanted straightened out. Crate & Freight was an important local business in Denver and Carter the kind of man who wanted to be squeaky clean. I knew he was gearing up to run for office next year.

He was absolutely right in his suspicions—a group of drivers were skimming a margin, just enough that they thought it was below the radar. So far, so routine, so tame. But Carter's assignment had been to find out what was going on, and it turned out skimming was the least of it.

I'd worked out a cover story for the day with the Crate & Freight HR manager. She'd even given me a real HR survey they wanted done, laconically wishing me the best of luck with it. I'd wandered around the depot that afternoon with my clipboard, asking mind-numbing questions about job satisfaction.

Every stuttered answer, every shifty eye, every sweaty face, told me something was happening today.

They hustled me out at 5 p.m., and I was back, over the fence, at 9 p.m. I'd left the clipboard and the glasses behind. I was in black coveralls, black ski cap, black boots and some *real* good makeup.

The photo transfer completed and I texted Morales: *URGENT! Northfield Crate & Freight depot. See pix—large drug shipment moving NOW. RIFLES! SWAT team ASAP. Txt only. Amber Farrell.*

The text took forever to transmit with the photos, while I stared at the screen wondering how it would play with Morales. I was supposed to be low profile. I was supposed to be on call for him and not the other way around. I sighed. I'd find out soon enough what he thought about it.

Of course, I'd come straight to the place they hadn't wanted me this afternoon; the old warehouse. It was a vast building, about three stories tall, with a drive-in, drive-out loading area. It was stacked high with pallets and containers waiting for shipment. Normally, storage was all it was used for, but tonight they'd wanted to be able to load trucks with the shutters closed, away from prying eyes. Except mine. And my shutter was wide open.

I'd expected to get photo evidence of some shrinkage of the stock. Not a sign of it, at least not tonight. There were thirty-two big rigs scheduled to leave the compound before morning. So far, a dozen had been driven into the warehouse and loaded just across from my hiding place. From what I'd seen, four were just regular loads. The others were carrying something extra, hidden in a compartment between the trailer and cab. From the lengths they went to for security and the size and shape of the packages, it was both drugs and weapons.

All of the illicit stuff came from a blue box truck parked alongside the loading area. I didn't recognize the company, Ranchos Rigs, but the plates were from New Mexico. In among a lot of edgy men, the driver, Nokes, had been the edgiest. He'd stood watching the transfer impatiently, talking only to Guy Windler, the Crate & Freight driver in charge of this operation. Windler took no crap from anyone else, but he was wary around Nokes.

I checked the cell in case the vibrate wasn't working. Nothing.

Come on, Morales, the clock's ticking. Look at your freaking texts.

Given what was going on, the outer gates were locked and the eight drivers, site manager, forklift operator and dispatcher in the compound were all in on it. But you don't keep a shipping depot like this closed for long. Other drivers would be arriving. They had to get those trucks out of the depot before then. Of course, the police would be able to round them all up eventually, but who knows if the drugs and guns would still be on board. And the credit for the bust would be shared with whichever cities the trucks were bound for.

Morales, you want it for Denver PD, you come get it now.

No one had come back inside the warehouse yet. I crept out of my hiding place and risked taking shots of the box truck plate and logo with my cell camera. I sent them to Morales: *Delivery vehicle.*

I registered that the blue box truck had been closed up. The delivery had been completed, and Nokes was going to want out of here soon. Not on my watch. There was a chance he might lead Morales back up the supply chain.

I checked his doors—locked. There are lots of ways to sabotage a truck, but I needed it to be quick and quiet. I also didn't want to be obvious. There weren't many good places to hide in this depot, if someone were really looking for you. I started with a tire. Front and left, where he'd see it. I got a thin splinter from a pallet and jammed the air valve open.

I lay down to see how much of the engine I could reach from underneath. And the loading bay exit door in front of the truck started to rise.

Oh, crap.

The huge steel door would take about four seconds to get high enough for someone to see underneath. I pulled the splinter out and ran to the back, where the matching entry door was closed. Three seconds. Next to the truck entrance was a personnel door that was unlocked.

Someone had left a stockman's coat tossed on a chair near the entrance. Two seconds. I grabbed it and put it on as I opened the door. One. It was a calculated risk taking the coat, but it was what everyone was wearing outside. I closed the door gently. Zero. Through the small glass panel I watched Nokes go to his truck and stare at the half-deflated tire.

Double crap. I'd been flushed from hiding and all I'd gained was a few minutes.

Dammit, Morales, where are you?

I was on the far side of the warehouse from whatever commotion had gotten everyone outside, but there would be another truck coming around here any minute. Turning the stiff collar up on the coat was barely half a disguise. I sprinted down the side of the warehouse, trailing coat like Batman, and slid into the dark gap between the warehouse and the dispatcher's office. I made my way down to the end and peered out carefully into the central area.

There was a gentle rain falling, making blurry halos around the sodium floodlights. Mack trucks, looming blank-eyed and sinister in the dark, were lined up in rows, ready to roll. The commotion was centered around the last truck loaded. It was one of the ones carrying drugs, and there'd been a problem with the hydraulics. It looked as if the cab's steering had broken while it was maneuvering back into line. It was partly blocking the exit from the warehouse. Except for that, the dispersal might have started already. A huge lucky break for me and the Denver PD.

A group was standing in front of the faulty cab, centered around Windler. He was only an inch or two taller than my five-ten, but massively heavy in the chest and shoulders. The bulk of him, the way he lowered his head, and his dark brown, unkempt hair and beard made me think of a bull buffalo. That crazed, wall-eyed look he'd given me this afternoon during my HR rounds shouted *don't get in my way.* He'd refused my questions and I was *so* going to report him for it.

Estes, the site manager, was standing alongside him, fidgeting and looking at his watch. They'd given up on the faulty cab. Another cab had been pulled up and was sitting there with its engine idling while they transferred the contents of the compartment. Headlights supplemented the sodium floodlight on the side of the office. The dispatcher, forklift operator and one of the drivers were staying to help, but the others were starting to drift towards their own rigs. Damn.

My cell tickled. I pulled it out and shielded the screen.

From Morales: *Are you still inside compound?*

At last, and he was treating it seriously. *Yes. Trucks about to roll.*

Shouting brought my attention back to the group. Nokes had come back out of the warehouse and squared up to Windler, gesturing in agitation.

"…some fucker in here. The fucking hydraulics go on your truck and then some fucker's let the air out of my tire."

I couldn't hear Windler's response. His back was to me and he was drowned out by Nokes's panicked shouting.

"I'm telling you, there was someone in the warehouse. And they've been out here, fucking with your trucks. Shit! We're busted, man, we're busted."

So much for the lucky break. The hydraulics were nothing to do with me. He was adding two and two and getting a big number. The drivers were returning. Even the guys trying to switch the cabs had stopped and come across.

I didn't wait to hear what Windler said back to Nokes. It was time to find another hiding place.

The gap between the warehouse wall and the office wall was just right. I wedged myself in and walked my way up the wall, eased myself quietly onto the flat roof of the office. I was close enough I could hear some of what was going on, but I was well above everyone's eye line. And with all the people in the compound, hiding here would be a lot safer than creeping around. I pulled my ski cap lower and raised my head enough to see the group.

Nokes had calmed down a fraction and backed off to make a call. Windler was standing in front of the cabs, frowning.

Estes was alongside Windler, tapping his watch and talking in his ear. I could just about lip-read him. "The next batch of drivers will be here any minute. We've got to do something. Just move them out?"

Windler shook his head as if dislodging flies. He looked up and spoke to the group loudly.

"Nokes is sure there was someone in the warehouse. We can't take the risk, but we can't take the risk of someone seeing rifles either. Rack the rifles in my trailer, take the pistols instead and keep them hidden," he said, looking around. "Spread out and check this place from one end to the other. In, on, under everything. You see him, fucking kill him. We'll hold anyone else at the gate. I'll come up with a cover story."

I texted Morales again: *They're looking for me. Real soon would be good.*

Inbound, he responded. *Head down.*

What the hell had spooked Nokes? It wasn't the missing coat—he'd have said. I'd left no trace. He hadn't seen me. He hadn't heard me. Smell? I'm trained; I wasn't wearing perfume and last I checked I smelled better than the coat I'd stolen. Maybe he was just right for the wrong reasons, like he'd been about the hydraulics.

The only benefit from this was that the drivers who were looking for me weren't driving away in their rigs. But if they did a good job with the search, they'd look up here soon. It was a straight race between the SWAT team and the search party. I distracted myself by trying to estimate how long it should take those men to search the compound, and comparing it with the response time the SWAT team quoted.

It had gone quiet, except for the idling engines. I peered over the shed roof again. Windler and Estes were still there, Nokes to one side arguing on his cell. Everyone else had gone off to look for me. Nothing like being wanted to give a girl a nice, warm feeling on a cold, wet night.

Estes held his pistol up in the headlights, checked it and chambered a round. He stuck it back in the pocket of his coat, unsafed. Idiot. The pair of them wandered over toward the office.

"Don't like this," Windler muttered, not ten yards from me. "Not tonight. It's trouble."

"He's just jumpy, for Christ's sake, Guy."

Windler wasn't going to be calmed. "There's been something the whole fucking day."

"What d'you mean?" said Estes. "It's just a hydraulic pipe. It happens, man. Nokes is scared of his own shadow."

"No. Right from the start today. That fucking bitch from HR poking around. Something off about her. Trouble," he said again.

"Look, him or her, we'll find them," Estes said. "Then they'll be no trouble at all." He chuckled and grabbed his crotch. "If it's her, maybe we don't kill her right away."

Windler had started to shake his head in irritation again when there was shouting from the gates. Awesome. The cavalry was here.

Windler was the first to react. He turned and sprinted to the new cab. It hadn't been connected to the trailer yet, and its engine was running. Nokes went for it too.

No freaking way. I leaped off the roof, coat flying, and landed next to Estes.

He turned to me, shock and disbelief on his face giving way to terror. I guess it was the makeup. He started scrabbling in his coat pocket, jerking at the pistol to free it.

"Pleased to see me, are you?" I said, as I grabbed his wrist and slammed my elbow into his face.

Everything happened at once. The pistol in his pocket went off and the bullet tore through his thigh. Windler's cab started to roll. Estes screamed and would have collapsed but for my grip on him. The SWAT team opened the gates to come swarming through. *No! No! No! Shut the gates!*

"FREEZE! POLICE!" was being bellowed from every angle. Someone was yelling my name. Shots were fired. I was standing right between the cab and the gates. It was barreling down on me, twelve feet tall and eight wide, hard bright chrome, lights blazing, engine roaring, dirt and gravel spurting out the sides. I felt a stupid sense of disbelief. He wasn't going to stop.

There was no chance Estes could get out of the way.

I wanted him in prison, not the morgue. I'm far stronger than I look; I lifted him up and hurled him clear. I'm also very quick; I nearly made it, too.

So, so close.

I was diving backwards when the cab hit me and I did the old rag doll flip through the night air.

"MAN DOWN!" someone screamed.

Oh, jeez, that hurt. I know it was dark and, yeah, I was wearing coveralls and a coat, but come on, guys, gimme a break. Then the ground came up like a huge fist and punched my lights right out.

∞ ∞ ∞ ∞ ∞

Cold. Dark. Squeezed in a still, breathless space. Why was I crying? Sergeants don't cry.

I opened my eyes. Rain, not tears, on my cheeks. Hands on my face, pinching my nose, gripping my jaw. Behind that, someone loomed, inches away. *No! I won't go back to that cell.*

I sucked in a panicky lungful of air and lashed out. I caught him on the chin, and Detective Jennings grunted and collapsed backward.

"Farrell!" Morales shouted at me. "Stop!"

"Oh, shit. I'm sorry. I'm sorry." I levered myself up. Bad mistake. The world went all wobbly for a second and when it settled, I was on all fours, kneeling beside Jennings. At least he was blinking and mumbling.

A medic shouldered me aside and bent over him, muttering about friendly fire.

Morales knelt next to me, but not too close.

"You okay?" he said.

I grimaced as the fog in my head cleared out. The truck…

"Windler? Nokes?" I twisted around to look, making my head spin, and ended up slumped back on my ass.

"The guys in the truck? They got out the gate. We probably hit the driver with a couple of shots, but we didn't have time to set up a blockade. They're gone, but they won't get far." Morales reached out carefully and lifted my chin up to the lights, looked at my eyes. "You weren't breathing," he said. "No pulse."

"Just shock," I said. "It wasn't as bad as it looked." It was. Or would have been for anyone else. "Anyway, heart and lungs working now."

"You need to get to the hospital?"

"Thanks, but I don't like hospitals." I flexed my shoulders. "Nothing but bumps and bruises anyway." My shoulders twinged and I stifled a hiss. A lot of bumps and bruises, but I can't have doctors looking at me.

Morales knew some of the background on this and he was just fishing with his question. I guess I couldn't blame him. He thought I must know more about it than I did.

I wasn't a vampire. Yet. And if there was anything I could do to stop it, I wouldn't become one. In the meantime, I couldn't risk what might show up on X-rays and blood tests any more than I could risk violating my agreement with the army. And even mouth to mouth resuscitation might have been a really bad idea for Jennings to try, for both of us.

"This man has a concussion. We'll need to keep him under observation." The medic glared at me as they stretchered him away.

"I was *not* going to lie there and let him pump my chest and slobber all over my face," I said defensively to Morales. "You know why…ah, hell. Apologize to him for me, will you? I'll buy him a drink next week. And, uh, thank you too. Good timing."

Morales grunted and stood up. "Well, if you don't need to go to the hospital, do you need a lift home?"

I started to shake my head and thought better of it. Falling over wouldn't look good. "No, thanks." I got shakily to my feet. Not good, but not bad. I've felt worse.

He handed me a handkerchief. "You might want to get that muck off your face," he said. "You *will* have a full report in my in-tray tomorrow morning, 9 a.m. And you *will* be available for any further questions."

"Yes, sir." Damn, so much for sleeping in tomorrow. But at least he wasn't chewing me out for not keeping a low profile.

"Then get the hell off my crime scene." He waved toward the gate.

I couldn't resist. "Oh. That's what all this pretty yellow ribbon is for, is it?"

Chapter 2

TUESDAY

Well, unless sitting in the office was my own personal purgatory, I was still alive.

I hurt like hell, though.

I completed the report and stretched, carefully. The bruises would fade and the sprains and strains would repair themselves. I heal exceptionally quickly, but being hit by a truck is always going to hurt for a while.

Scary stuff. Just my kind of evening's entertainment.

Sitting still while typing the reports had stiffened up my back and I attempted some gentle twists. One of the problems with being five-ten; there was more of me to hurt. Still, on the bright side, a normal person would have been in the hospital, if she were lucky.

Morales had gotten his report. This one was for Carter. I attached it and a final invoice to an email, signed it off as Amber Farrell, Commercial and Private Investigator, and sent it. That began the sweet process that would end with money in my beleaguered bank account. Not a moment too soon. This case had lasted way longer than I had anticipated; the flat fee I'd agreed to had turned out to be a bad decision. It had been interesting, sure, and that was important to me personally, but it meant I had put aside the everyday work that kept an investigation business solvent.

I couldn't face the thought of that everyday work at the moment. I'd earned an afternoon off. But should I go swimming and show off the bruises all down my body, or just opt for a run to loosen everything up? Or both? That way, I could justify a steak dinner and one of Lario's legendary chocolate desserts. My mouth started to water at the thought. I'm totally OCD on physical fitness, and a girl's gotta fuel all that energy.

Before I did anything else, I logged into the bank account and paid Tullah. She had come to work for me with the clear understanding that salaries get paid when they can, but I felt guilty when it was late.

Done. I gathered the remaining notes on my desk and stuck them in the Crate & Freight folder.

I guessed Windler would be in custody by now, with a charge for attempted vehicular manslaughter added to a long rap sheet.

My cell rang and at the same time, the outer door opened. That was unusual, since we didn't get much walk-in business, but Tullah would hold whoever it was for a few moments. The caller ID on the cell showed Morales.

This ought to be good. Clearing up a major drug smuggling operation in one hit like that would look good in front of his bosses. So, a little thank you from the police captain, that would just be icing on today's cake, or Lario's chocolate dessert, whatever.

The warmth from outside had set the air conditioning off again and made me think how cool that swimming pool would feel. I needed to keep this short.

"Captain Morales, good day," I said cheerfully.

"Farrell, we have some problems."

"Hmm. 'We', Captain?" My vision of an afternoon off receded, but I wasn't going to let it go without a fight.

"Yes, 'we', Farrell, and you can put away the smartass comments any time now."

"What's wrong?" I said. "Don't tell me Windler and Nokes got away?"

"For the moment."

Despite the sour note of their escape, I still felt good about the op, but I had to get moving.

"Okay. Well, I guess you didn't call for that."

"Yeah. Look, Farrell, we've locked down Crate & Freight."

"Damn! Carter's not going to be happy." Not to mention me—my invoice wasn't going to get paid while the company accounts were frozen.

"He isn't, and let's be clear, that's an understatement. That's the first reason I called you—to give you a heads up. He's hurting and he's blaming you."

The heads up surprised me. Captain Morales wasn't ever my biggest fan. When I left the police force, I guess I could have dug my heels in and made it an issue, which wouldn't have looked good on Lieutenant Morales' watch just as he was pitching for the next slot. In the event, I had left quietly and he was made Captain a month or so later, but that didn't obligate him to call me with warnings on a matter like this. I guess this was my thank you for last night.

"Okay. Thanks for that." I hesitated. My paycheck was delayed, and I didn't want any more bad news today, but I knew there was something more here. "What else?"

"Farrell, we're talking literally tons of cocaine. This is major league organized crime. There's someone else hurting here."

He didn't need to go on. I was the cause of an astronomical loss to some crime boss. It wasn't a good place to be.

The landline phone rang and I heard Tullah pick up. Never one thing at a time. I had to end this call.

"I hear you. Thanks again, Captain. I'll be careful."

He wouldn't let it go. "Haven't you got somewhere else you could be? I'd still need to be able to—"

That plain ticked me off. Of all people, he should have had a good idea of how well I can take care of myself. "I have all this kinda stuff hanging over me already, remember, *Lieutenant*? Now, I have a business to run. Gotta go run it. Bye."

"Dammit, Farrell, the feds will want—" I hit the cut off and sighed. So, the local drug boss wanted my hide. *Take a number. See if you can find me before the vamps do.*

Tullah put her head around the door.

"Amber, there's Ms. Kingslund to see you, and a call. It's Mr. Carter on line 1." Tullah looked irritated, and I guessed that Carter was beyond being polite. If he had a beef with me, I'd take that, but I didn't want him being unpleasant to Tullah.

I sighed, and all hope of the afternoon off disappeared completely.

"Ask Ms. Kingslund if she would allow me a couple more minutes for this call, please," I asked Tullah.

"Okay, honey, I hear you," came back through the partition in a pleasant contralto. "Go ahead."

My office was a former storeroom at my accountant's. Ms. Kingslund and I were separated by the thinnest of partitions. I grimaced. Not ideal. I could have done without the 'honey', too, but this wasn't going to be the best introduction a client could have and I let it ride. I couldn't put Carter off any longer.

Steeling myself, I picked up the landline.

"Carter, it's Farrell—" I was going to apologize for him having to hold while I was on my cell, before we discussed how he talked to Tullah, but I never got that far.

"You're finished, Farrell," he shouted down the phone. "I should never have trusted you. When Greg told me you were reliable and confidential, I believed him. What was he thinking? When I'm done with you, you'll never get work again in this town."

"Whoa, Carter. Can we back up a couple of steps here?"

"Don't give me any of that bullshit. I'm not going to waste my time talking to you any longer than I have to. You betrayed my confidence by going to the cops. You exceeded your assignment. You—"

"I made the police aware of serious criminal activity," I cut across his rant. "You look at my contract, Carter. I've done what I said I would do, and you owe me my fees."

"I don't give a flying fuck what you think, you've screwed my whole company with your incompetent meddling."

I have a little demon in my throat that just ups and says things sometimes. "Incompetent?" said the demon sweetly. "I'm not the one who's been running a busted drug smuggling operation."

That was probably not the best thing to say, but we were beyond any reasonable conversation anyway, so I wasn't too upset with the demon.

"I'm going to sue you, you bitch," he screamed before I put the phone down.

"I'm not taking calls from him until further notice, Tullah, and neither should you," I managed to say calmly.

My guts were churning with anger. There was no way his lawyers could get anything to stick against me, but I really couldn't afford to waste time in court, or money on lawyers.

Taking deep breaths and deliberately not thinking about the five most painful ways to kill a man with my bare hands, I told myself it was likely Carter was just letting off steam and it would never come to a lawsuit. Or he'd take it to his lawyers and they'd talk some sense into him. Maybe, eventually, I would get my money. Maybe.

I couldn't spend time thinking about that now. I'd ignored my steady work for a bit of excitement, much good it had done. I needed a nice, run of the mill, predictable case that paid well. If Ms. Kingslund was still there, I really needed her business.

She was.

Tullah ushered her in, and my stomach did a flip. *Oh. That Ms. Kingslund.*

What with my anger at Carter, my surprise at seeing who it was, and getting out of my chair like I was suffering from rheumatism, I must have looked a sight to her. She ignored all that, walked over and stuck her hand out. "Jennifer Kingslund. Please call me Jen." She ran her eyes over the office as we shook, taking it all in. That didn't take very long, and they were back to looking at me.

"Then I'm Amber," I replied. Her eyes were the cool blue of a shirt too often washed. Nice, but wary. Not that I blamed her; she'd come to my office looking for a private investigator. The name would have told her I was female, but maybe she'd been expecting a Kathleen Turner, playing V. I. Warshawski, turned out in a chic dress and jacket. What she'd got was darker, taller and leaner, short auburn hair pulled back in a pony tail, dressed in my office clothes, also known as slim jeans and plain white T.

Oh, and with extensive bruising all down one side. Yeah, I'd have looked wary too.

"After your last call," she said, with a flicker of a smile, "maybe you would appreciate a cup of coffee over in Papa Dee's?"

"Sure, let's go across."

I picked up a blank client file, nodded to Tullah and we walked out into Denver's fall sunshine. Both of us slipped on sunglasses against the bright light. It was hot, maybe one of the last few days of Indian summer, with the heat coming off the asphalt in waves.

That Jennifer Kingslund. What the hell was she doing out here, talking to me?

Chapter 3

"I'm sorry about the call," I said as we walked. "It was just wrong to take it while you were waiting and could hear. I'm usually much more discreet with a client's business, but I didn't think he'd appreciate waiting."

"Campbell gets overexcited, and I guess this isn't a good time for him," she replied. Of course, she would have heard about the company on the news. She would have connected the dots while she listened to my side of the telephone conversation. And of course, she would know him. She waved an elegant hand. "Let's leave it, for the moment."

Jennifer Anna-Marie Kingslund was the CEO and owner of one of Colorado's leading businesses, the Kingslund Group. She owned hotels, restaurants, sports facilities and nightclubs. I remembered hearing she had diversified into PR recently.

Given her history of marriages that had come apart in public and the intriguing rumors of boardroom struggles, there weren't many people in Denver who didn't know something about her. According to the papers, she was a role model for businesswomen, or attractive and extroverted, depending on the angle of the story. She famously championed local causes. I didn't think I qualified as a local cause and had to scratch my head trying to come up with a reason she might want to hire a solo private investigator.

That, however, isn't a question you ask, as a solo private investigator.

Jennifer Kingslund could afford the best of the downtown agencies. If she had a reason to come to me, hopefully she would tell me. Even if she didn't, I wouldn't let that stop me from taking a case. I needed the money. Paying Tullah against the expectation of a prompt payment from Crate & Freight had left about sixty dollars in the account.

In the flesh, she seemed a bit taller than her pictures on the news, though still a couple of inches off my five-ten. Maybe that was the effect of the pretty Italian heels that she clipped along on. She was slim. She wore a simple red dress hanging to just below the knee. Her Scandinavian blonde hair had been done that morning by the looks of it, big and swirly. It was a color that made me think of old gold. A single, thin chain hung around her neck and she carried a little clutch bag. What with the dress and the hairdo, the bag and the chain, she was probably carrying around more value than my entire wardrobe. Sigh.

If she noticed me looking, she didn't let it show and she didn't return the favor. I guess there wasn't a lot to see beyond the casual clothes and ugly bruises. My belt and cowboy boots were top quality, but no one ever noticed them.

"Do you suppose," she said, tilting her chin up at the peculiar turrets above Papa Dee's, "that adding those ridiculous little roofs has resulted in so much as a single extra client?"

I laughed. "Maybe not, but at least everyone knows where Papa Dee's is." Then we were inside, where it was cool and dark, even with the sunglasses pushed back up.

We picked up a couple of coffees and sat in a corner. There were only a handful of customers, mainly people from the surrounding small businesses. It was late for lunch. The wooden tables were wiped down and the staff was beginning to set them for dinner. I glanced around. The music was turned down low, but the customers were spread out through the restaurant. It was comfortable and it was reasonably discreet, if that was what she had wanted.

"So, ahhh, Jen, how can I help?"

She didn't dive right in. "You were in the army for a while, weren't you?"

"Yes, that's where I learned accounting." Not a word of a lie, but not the whole truth at all. I hated being evasive, but there were things I couldn't talk about. If she picked up on it, she didn't show it.

"Some time in the police as well." That was a statement rather than a question, and she could have read that off the company website, so I just gave a little hum of confirmation. My time in the police included more things I couldn't talk about. If she was one of those clients who needed a comprehensive review of my past, I was going to have to turn this one down, but it seemed she'd just been settling herself down.

"You've been recommended to me." She saw the question forming on my lips and held her hand up to stop me. "I promised them I wouldn't tell you who it was and I take my word very seriously." Her eyes got cooler and held mine. "I expect the same level of discretion from you. I need your word that anything I say from now on is held in absolute confidence. If a situation arises like the one with Campbell's call in your office, you will find a way around it without revealing anything about me or my case to anyone else, or we can't do business."

I don't have a problem with people who state their requirements clearly, so that didn't raise any hackles. It startled me a bit that she had gone from Ms. Nice to the ice queen businesswoman in the space of a couple of sentences. It gave me some appreciation for her reputation as a tough person in the commercial world. From what I could recall, she'd inherited a small restaurant business in a mess of family shares and bad deals. She'd turned it around, paid the rest of the family off, two ex-husbands included, and made it the successful company that she owned today. I was beginning to see how.

"Agreed." I nodded and took a sip of my coffee. "You have my word."

"Good." The eyes warmed up a touch. She sat forward. I know all the body language pop psychology, but that doesn't mean I don't go along. I sat forward too, and she began to talk quietly and intensely.

"I believe my company is under attack. I don't mean in the normal commercial sense, but a systematic, criminal attack intended to disrupt my business to the point it collapses or my only viable choice is to sell. But I can't prove it."

She paused to see if I had any comment, but I just sat and waited for her to continue.

"This is the worst possible time for this to happen. You may know, my new division, Kingslund Media, has been formed from the purchase of an existing PR business, Frankell-Maines?"

I nodded; that much I knew from the papers.

She continued. "The funding came through the banks, and it's taking a lot of effort to keep it going and repay the loans while it gets in a position to maintain itself. In the meantime, my capital reserve is earmarked for a takeover bid that I'm preparing. Any damage to either operation could put the whole company in jeopardy. Just a rumor of a financial problem could start the dominos falling in this environment. I can't walk into Bell and Hewitt and get a bunch of their agents rooting through my business because everyone would know there's something up. Even worse, there might be a leak about the funding or the takeover."

I nodded. I could see the problem. Bell and Hewitt were the big downtown investigation firm, but I always got the feeling that companies used them for show rather than results. *Meow.*

"Okay," I said. "I see why you might need a less well-known investigator, and one with some financial expertise. Is that why you were advised to come see me?"

"No." There was still a wariness in her eyes when I mentioned the recommendation. It made me very interested in where this story was leading. She continued, "I'll get to that in a moment. First, I need to say that the level of attacks has been escalating. In the beginning it was just minor financial irregularities. If I'm right, it's now completely out of hand. I'm worried that a key employee may have been abducted. I'm sure that some staff who've just left, have done so because they've been threatened. I need this stopped now."

"Jen, I understand the secrecy issues, but if I'm working on your case and I discover a felony, such as abduction, we *will* need to talk to the police." I had to draw that line for her. I needed the business, but not at the expense of giving Morales an excuse to come after me.

She looked a bit unhappy about it, but nodded. My respect for her went up a notch. Faced with compromising her business operation or helping an employee, she'd gone for the employee.

"Also, I'm not the police." I tapped the table to make my point. "I can discover things for you, and maybe with that knowledge you can prevent anything further from happening. But if someone needs 'stopping', then it's back to the police again. They have the big guys in uniforms with all the guns and helmets and flak jackets."

She nodded again.

She seemed reluctant to go on with her brief, so I prodded her. "We can go into more detail on those things, and if we proceed, I'll draw up a set of tasks against them, but I need to hear the rest first."

Her mouth became set, as if she were unsure how I would react. Her weight shifted backwards. She really wasn't happy about this part.

"I have a great piece of land outside of town, out on US 285. It's called Silver Hills. I have planning permission for a resort and golf course, but I'm not building yet. It's supposed to be getting a bit of preparatory landscaping work. I've had a couple of work crews..." she stumbled a bit, broke off eye contact and then finished, "well, scared off."

I raised my eyebrows questioningly. "Scared off? How? Guys with guns or telephone threats of some kind?"

It took a while for her to respond. "No, something completely different. Wolves, pawprints all over the site, things going missing. The site getting torn up overnight. Damage to equipment."

I blew out a breath. "Well, I can't believe we've got wolves in this part of the Rockies, not this close to Denver. Wild animals, okay, maybe a bear. More likely a bunch of bored teens walking their dogs and stealing stuff. Can I be clear—I got specially recommended because something or someone like this scared your work crews?" I sat all the way back, folded my arms and just watched her. There was obviously something about this she wasn't telling me.

"Yes," she said. "I spoke to a friend about this, one with some experience in these kinds of things, and the recommendation came back that, if it involved something 'weird', then you're the person."

This didn't sound good to me. I wanted to keep the number of people who know anything about me and weird things to an absolute minimum. In my experience, weird is dangerous. I already spent enough time looking over my shoulder. But at the same time, I was intrigued and, of course, I had to think about my bank balance.

"Any weird stuff that might have happened to me doesn't make me an expert," I said cautiously.

"Do you know someone who is?" Her eyes were locked back on me and the ice queen was showing through again.

I shook my head. "No."

"Is that 'no' you don't know anyone better suited, or 'no' you won't take the case?"

I needed the business. I held up a placating hand. "How about this—I'll split the case into three and do some checking on each. The three are staff, financial and your resort at Silver Hills. I'll report to you if I discover anything significant, or at the end of the day, regardless. If I can't find anything on any one of the cases, I'll say so and you'll be able to get someone else in for that part if you want. If I do find proof of a felony, we go to the police. In between, we just proceed as seems fit."

"Done," she said quickly. There was a note of relief in her voice. I hadn't done anything yet, but it was something I'd seen before, as if just talking to someone else had shifted part of the burden.

"Can I see the contract, please?" she asked.

I passed the standard duplicate forms across and sipped my cooling coffee as she bent her head over them. She noted some stuff on her smartphone as she went. She also made some changes, initialing them before moving on. I huffed quietly. I'd have to take a look at those and I hated reading legal forms.

There was a bit of turnover in Papa Dee's clientele. A couple walked out, kissed and went to separate cars. A guy whose face made me think of an angry rabbit came over and sat one table away from us. Now, there's a convention that most people stick to in half-empty coffee shops. You try to space yourself out, you don't take a table right next to someone else. He flicked up his laptop screen and dived in. A nerd. Low level of social skills. Probably only came in for the free internet. I sighed. Nothing that set my alarms off, but we'd have to talk quietly if there was more to say.

The waiter wandered over with a coffee refill for us. He had a bit of a swagger and strong, square hands. I imagined those hands gently massaging my back and I shifted uncomfortably in my seat. A quick peek confirmed he had thick, dark hair that I could almost feel my fingers running though. And a nice smile. I gritted my teeth and closed my eyes. *Not going to happen. Not allowed. Rules.*

Back in the real world, Jennifer had signed the contracts and pushed them back at me. I hoped she hadn't spotted me eyeing the waiter. Or my reaction afterwards.

I checked her amendments. They were perfectly fair. She had emphasized the confidentiality aspects, corrected a typo that I'd kept meaning to correct, and added nothing that made me unhappy. I matched her initials, signed both copies and passed one back to her.

She fiddled with her smartphone and looked up.

"Good. Thank you. I've transferred five thousand into your bank account to cover preliminary costs. Bank details as in the agreement." She made a wry face. "Or at least, the money is wherever it goes to when it's left my account and isn't yet in yours."

I kept my face impassive and managed not to punch the air. Five thousand would take care of the bills due next week and then some.

"Thanks," I said blandly. "My reports will detail costs."

We exchanged cell numbers and email addresses, and she handed a USB drive across to me. "This contains files of my internal accounts with my analysis, a list of employees who've left recently, with contact details, and the missing man I'm especially worried about, Troy Huber. And security footage from Silver Hills."

She bit her lip and looked down at the table. "Amber, I know I sound evasive about the problem at the resort. Please, just have a look at the clip before you make your mind up. You'll understand."

As I slipped the drive into my pocket, she also handed me a photo and a set of keys. "That's Troy and these are for his apartment down in LoDo. The address is on the label."

I took them silently, glancing at the picture. I wondered how she came to have a set of keys for Troy's apartment.

"What's his job?" I asked.

"He's the head chef at the Golden Harvest restaurant. He didn't show up for work over the weekend. The police won't do anything yet. All that information is on the drive."

I nodded. The Golden Harvest was her signature restaurant and the priciest place in town. Certainly not somewhere I could afford to eat, but I had heard the chef was something special. People would notice his absence.

"Married? Partner? Local family?" She just shook her head.

"Okay. I'll start with his apartment and I'll call you."

She nodded her thanks and made a call to her driver to pick her up, before turning back to me.

"May I ask a personal question, Amber?"

I shrugged. "Of course."

"Those are really beautiful boots. They're handmade, aren't they?"

I pulled my jeans up to the tops of the boots and stretched my legs out beside the table to show her, obscurely pleased she'd noticed. "Yup. Made by a friend of mine."

"They're so soft!" She felt the supple leather. "Does he do it as a business?"

"Sure. Here, I'll give you his contact info." I fiddled with my cell and sent Werner's details to her.

"Werner Schumacher?" she asked. "Mr. Schumacher is the shoe maker?"

"Indeed he is." I laughed. "Your car's here." I pointed at the black limo and the driver shouldering his way through the doors.

She got up and took my hand, squeezing it.

"Thank you, Amber. Please call as soon as you can." She started towards the door and stopped as if something had just occurred to her. She turned back and waved at my boots. "Do you ride?"

I shook my head with a little smile. "Not unless you count a couple of hours when I was fourteen."

"Oh. Never mind. Maybe we can do some, after we straighten this business out. I have horses. Bye." And with that she was out the door.

I loved the cheerful assumption that all would go well.

I sat there, watching a car that had gone around the block a couple of times do it again, and wondered why I hadn't picked up my gun when I walked out of the office.

In between, I wondered what the hell I was getting into, let alone what I was already in. And what were the prospects for a private investigator in, say, Alaska?

Chapter 4

The fourth time the car came around, I walked out in front of it, making the driver hit the brakes.

"Hey, lady!" He stuck his head out the window. "You wanna watch where you're going."

He got points for the lady tag, even if he was shouting at me. I *had* walked in front of him.

"Sorry, just not used to cars driving around here this time of day." I wandered over to his window, standing just behind his shoulder, where it would be difficult for him to turn and fire a gun accurately. I bent down stiffly and checked out the interior of the car. There was nothing suspicious I could see, but that didn't mean anything. "You looking for someplace?" I kept my voice casual and friendly.

"Yeah, I am, matter of fact." He pushed his bottle bottom glasses back up his nose and peered at me through them. "You know where Tiley's Architects are?"

I had to smile. Paranoia might keep me alive another day, but I didn't think this guy had my number. "Sure. See the turn there, looks like it goes into the parking lot?" He nodded. "Follow it around the far side of the building. It branches off to the left and Tiley's is the building at the end."

"Ah, thanks! I've been looking for ages." He pushed his glasses futilely back up his sweaty nose. "Sorry if I gave you a scare with the car. You did kind of surprise me."

He drove off with a wave to where I had pointed. I watched him follow my instructions. It's as if men are welded to the car seat. Why can't they just get out and ask someone?

I made it back to the office without being attacked by any more nearsighted drivers.

Tullah had gone off to her classes at college. That was part of the deal we had cut, that she would only be here when she could. Sometimes her mother came in for her. She was an impressive woman, Mary Autplumes. A full blood Arapaho, she was married to my Kung Fu teacher, Master Liu Leung, hence the train crash of last names that left Tullah calling herself Autplumes-Leung.

Between Mary and Liu, I wasn't sure which one of them scared me most, but their daughter was a joy.

Except for her last name, the mixture had worked well for Tullah. She had a fresh-faced look with exotic, half-Chinese eyes and long dark hair. She was always cheerful. She was good for me and the office. I didn't look forward to her graduating and getting a real job.

Right on cue as I sat down, the cell bleeped at me. I peered at the caller ID and flipped it open.

"Colonel," I said.

"Sergeant." We weren't big on formalities or small talk. "Tomorrow afternoon, fourteen hundred, your office?"

"Okay," I said and the line went dead.

I logged in and marked it on the calendar, more for Tullah than me. I didn't forget meetings with Colonel Laine.

At that point, I finally got the opportunity to sit back and feel pissed off.

It wasn't that I had a problem with Jennifer Kingslund herself. I liked her as a person. Her story was a bit vague and she wasn't telling me everything, but I'm used to that. No, the first thing that was getting to me about taking this job was that I couldn't afford to turn it down. I hated being in that position.

Then there was the 'weird' stuff. There are whole days when I forget and act as if I'm a normal person. But I'm not, and there are things out there that aren't either.

Weird stuff had gotten close to killing me. The fewer people who could link me to weird stuff, the safer I would be. I should have run a mile. Instead, I was dying to get into the case. It would stop me from going out and doing safe, well-paid surveillance on some cheating spouse. Adrenaline is addictive.

The weird stuff started a couple of years ago. I was doing a job I loved in the army, in special operations, a covert battalion called Ops 4-10. I had a clear role and well-understood objectives in a unit I respected. I had colleagues to watch my back, friends and more. And it had all changed in one blinding, terrifying night in the South American jungle.

My hand unconsciously touched my throat. There was nothing to see now, not even scars, but still, a phantom sensation tingled the ends of my fingers, as if I could feel the wounds. According to the medic in the relief squad, half my throat had been torn out. I'd healed in five days. There were some benefits to what had happened. Among the not-benefits was waking up in an isolation cell.

I got the mirror from the desk drawer and looked at myself, touching my face, as if I expected it to feel different today. I checked my canines. Normal. No sign of the ticking time bomb in my blood.

My desk was clear except for my photos. They were there to give me inspiration when I needed it.

"Guys, I need it now," I whispered.

I picked up the picture of my Dad, Blane Farrell. He's standing in Wash Park, midway through explaining the way the latest toy works. It's some water powered rocket whose sole purpose seems to be to get everyone wet. His hair, always unruly, is having a bad day and sticks out at all angles, but on him it looks good. His handsome face is serious, because, well, toys are serious things. His shirt is caught in the breeze, flapping open with half of the collar up, half down, and the tail pulling out of his shorts. On his feet he's wearing his favorite sandals, scuffed and scratched. A gawky girl stands next to him, grinning. She's all knees and elbows, sticking out of her tomboy clothes, freckles on her too-big nose. She's turned her face up to look at him, and it's as if the first springtime sun is shining on her after a cold winter.

Dad died when I was fifteen.

I swapped his picture for the one of Top, aka Master Sergeant Gabriel Luther Wells, standing at attention with the ease of a man who has lived a long time in the army and has nothing to prove and no one to fear. He's huge, completely dwarfing the gawky girl beside him, even though she's grown some. She's standing at attention too, but she's stiff as a board, those knees and elbows tucked away in her uniform. She's scared those new sergeant stripes are going to fall off her arms, but through all that, you can see the joy shining in her eyes.

It was my proudest day.

The third I didn't pick up. It wasn't actually a photo. It was a slim rectangle of jet black granite the size of a desktop photo, polished to a sheen, with gold letters in the bottom right hand corner saying simply, *Tara Farrell*. This one was for reflection rather than inspiration.

If Dad and Top had something to say to me, I knew it would be: 'If you've got a job to do, girl, get out and do it'. I sighed. Who needs inspiration when you can have a kick in the butt? I needed to stop wallowing in self-pity, get out and do my job. And take even more care than usual.

First, I would go run. That sometimes helped with the frustrations. After that, I would start on Jennifer Kingslund's case. I pulled out the keys she had given me and read the address in LoDo, the lower downtown area, where her top chef lived.

I got my running gear from the car and changed in the office. My work clothes and laptop went into my main backpack, along with some standard crime scene gear, the apartment keys and Jennifer's USB drive.

I went to my gun safe and after a little thought, I took out the Heckler & Koch pistol and stuck it in the little jogging pack around my waist. The HK Mk 23 was big and heavy, but I was used to it and you just gotta love that stopping power. I was sure I was going to need it sometime soon.

Chapter 5

I headed down Parker Road, past the interstate and the main entrance to Cherry Creek Reservoir, to the small parking area opposite the Chambers Road junction.

I parked and sat in the car for five minutes, waiting to see if any other cars pulled in. I had an itchy feeling that I was being watched, but no one followed me.

Temporarily satisfied, I locked up and ran along the trails that would bring me to the lake, avoiding the paved tracks and cutting through on paths in the scrub that provided me with an obstacle course. The gun made an uncomfortable weight in the jogging pack, but it also served as a constant reminder that I needed to be alert. As I ran, the late afternoon sun stretched out the shadows and the heat of the day began to ease off.

About halfway around my course, at the edge of the lake, the running had eased the knots of tension. I cooled off with a walk through the cottonwoods, jumping irrigation channels and practicing vaults over a fallen tree. I stopped by some willows and did stretches in their shade, taking the opportunity to look around carefully. With the summer crowds gone, it was quiet, but the feeling of being watched remained. If anything, it had gotten worse. I dunked my shirt in the water and put it back on wet, to cool me, then started trotting off in the direction that would take me back.

I had just gotten back to the main trail when the watcher attacked.

The scrub gave him enough cover for me to get close without being able to see him and he came out at me like a cat after a bird. Unfortunately for his plan, the day had wound me up like a spring, and I was good at this.

He came in too high, going for the head. Working on instinct honed in long hours of practice, I ducked and twisted, using his momentum to throw him past me while I rolled on the trail. We came up together. He was dressed in running gear like the other park users, but his outfit was dark and had been difficult to see when he hid. Smart man. He wasn't much taller than me, more heavily built, but wiry rather than bulky. In an out and out strength contest, I knew he would beat me. I also knew he was fast, but I had learned my fighting in a very hard school.

He closed quickly, not bothering with feints, putting all his effort into getting a quick result. Too predictable. His punches went wide or were turned aside by my blocks. My single reply hit him mid-stomach and knocked him back hard enough to take out most men.

He shook it off as if it were nothing and lowered his head like a bull to come in again. This was going to get rough. This time his approach suddenly changed and instead of swinging at me, his weaker left jabbed out and took me on the chin. I had it covered and went with it to take the sting out, but I couldn't take the sting out of my own evaluation of myself. I had gotten overconfident; because he came in one way, he wouldn't come in any other way. He shouldn't have been able to land a touch on me. I was furious with myself and I was going to take it out on him.

A girl jogged around the bend about fifty yards from us.

His arm twisted, the elbow lifting as his fist relaxed. We smacked hands overhead, trail dust puffing out in a cloud.

"Shit! David, you can't do that to me!" I yelled at him, sticking my hands on my hips.

We stood laughing as the jogger gave us a wide berth and the type of look you give crazies who have been rolling in the dirt.

"Goddamn it, Amber, you're still too quick. I gotta get some advantage."

"Have you been stalking me?"

He grinned. "Nah. Parked and recognized your car. Hood was still warm and I guessed you'd do the run round the lake."

That concerned me. If he could predict where I'd be, then so could someone else. David must have seen something of that thought on my face. "Problem?" he asked.

"Oh, I don't know. Maybe. I've had a feeling someone's been watching me this afternoon." I squinted, looking up the trail and rubbing the back of my neck. "Walk and talk, or you really want to run?"

"I'm good to talk," he said easily and we fell into step. He opened his mouth as if he were going to say something more, but closed it again. He glanced up and down the trail.

"Who managed to bruise you?" he asked. That wasn't what he had started to say. I'd have to find out what that was about.

"Mack truck," I replied. He snorted.

I had met David three months previously, and he'd turned my world on its head. Not in any romantic way, though he was easy enough on the eye.

Two years ago, when I'd come around from my attack, I'd been in restraints, in an isolation cell. I still had nightmares about that. The army finally and reluctantly let me go, with conditions. Everything about my entire time in Ops 4-10 and especially what had happened to me at the end was secret—national security, special access program level secret. I had to cut off all contact with my old unit. I had to submit to regular checks on my progress. If they suspected I was becoming a danger to the public, or heaven forbid, I infected someone, I would be back in the isolation cell. Meanwhile, I was to 'seek ways to communicate with or infiltrate any community associated with the type of attack suffered'. They still couldn't bring themselves to write 'vampire'.

My one tool for my task was the knowledge that I had smelled and sensed the vampires that had stalked and killed my unit in the jungle. It was difficult to describe, but I had been certain that I would know if I were close to a vampire again. I had been right.

David was, in his words, an Aspirant, a person in the process of becoming a vampire. He smelled maybe halfway vampire. He'd become my friend. I was spying on him. It chewed my gut and I still hadn't spoken to the colonel about him in my regular meetings. That shocked me—how much I had changed in the past two years. The ingrained military obedience wasn't working any longer.

"So, how's it going?" I opened neutrally.

"It's good. Really good now." He filled his lungs and let the air sigh out contentedly. "I haven't told you before, but since I started sparring with you and taking your advice on training, I've moved up three grades. Three months, three grades."

"Fantastic!" I thought back on his description of what he was going through as an Aspirant and my heart skipped a beat. "Hold on, that means—"

"Yeah. It means I'm ready." He was looking ahead, smiling into the distance at nothing. Or at something I couldn't see. My heart went out to him. I hoped it was good, whatever it was he was looking towards. I hoped it was worth the effort he had put in, whatever sacrifice he would have to make. Above all, I hoped it was the right thing for him. But at the same time I knew, however much my view of vampires had changed since my attack, I couldn't believe it was the right thing for me.

As if he had heard my thoughts, his mood changed and he grabbed my arm.

"Amber, please, *please* change your mind. At least come talk to them."

"No." I took his hand from my arm as gently as I could. We'd had this conversation before. "I don't think I can just talk to them. And I'm not going to become a vampire. End of story." I walked on and he had to follow.

"From what they tell us, you may not have the choice. You've been bitten and you're already on the path. They say that if you change out in the community without support you'll go insane. You could die, Amber."

I sighed. "Listen, you were first bitten about the time we met, three months ago?" He nodded. "And they've told you it takes three bites to convert you?" He nodded again, his eyes losing a bit of focus. Whatever went on with the biting was having a profound effect on him.

"And the last one is due now you've passed your Aspirant training?" My heart skipped a beat again at that thought. One more bite and something dramatic might happen to my friend. "Tell me, what happens if an Aspirant doesn't pass training? Or decides not to go on? Do those people go mad and die?"

"No. I don't think so," he said reluctantly.

"It wears off. The body recovers." I wasn't pressing the point just for his sake. This was important to me. There was a flutter of worry in my stomach that I was just whistling in the dark.

"I don't think that applies to you." He threw up his hands in frustration. "I can't ask all the questions I need to. We agreed to keep all this secret between us, so it's difficult to make up a reason for asking. And even if I did get an answer, I'm not supposed to talk to anyone other than an Aspirant about it. If only you would come talk to them yourself."

I waited him out. Finally, he went on. "Our training is carefully managed. I get the idea that it's a very dangerous process otherwise. From what I can piece together, someone bitten out in the wild, by a powerful vampire, can get the full dose in one bite and is really at risk."

He was fishing. I had told him the bare minimum, but David was one smart guy and he had filled in some blanks.

I held my hand up to stop him. "Back to my point. You were first bitten three months ago. I was bitten over two years ago. I'm stable, David. It's not happening, okay?" A cold wind found me, touched my cheek and chilled the sweat from my run. I shivered. "But anyway, you watch my back, I'll watch yours. Whatever happens. Deal?" I held out my hand.

He took my hand and shook without hesitation. "Of course. But I've got them watching my back. You've just got me." I didn't challenge him on that. I didn't want to explain I had the US military watching my back. And looking over my shoulder.

We had reached the parking lot where several more cars had appeared and an enterprising food van had set up. Selling ice cream. Not fair.

I opened my mouth to speak, and he was already snickering. "Yeah, I know. Big, bad ninja lady wants an ice cream with a piece of chocolate in it. I got it."

That saved me fishing for money in my bag with the barrel of the Heckler Koch poking out, so I let him live, this time.

We stood leaning against my car to eat the ice cream. It wasn't Lario's dessert, but it was going to have to do today. David ate quietly, his eyes going back and forth.

"Look, David," I said as we finished up. "I need to say some stuff, because I'm worried about you. Promise you won't get upset."

"Shoot," he said, looking sideways at me.

We stopped talking as a couple with kids passed within earshot. We edged together and lowered our voices slightly.

"From the outside, you understand, only from what you've told me, I can't tell the difference between this vampire community you describe and a cult scam." He stirred a bit, but didn't say anything. "I'm talking specifically about the 'us and them' feeling that they're creating in your head."

"It's not like that."

"Okay. You're sure it's not like that, and you're a smart guy and you're on the inside, but I can't tell from the outside. From where I stand, it looks as if Aspirants are isolated from their old friends before they get to pass the grades. But let's park that for the moment." I took a deep breath and stopped hedging. "You've been pretty secretive, but I've picked up that you think there are a few dozen vampires in Denver. Right?"

I waited till he nodded before I went on. "I don't know how many Aspirants there are, but I'm guessing maybe twenty? With about three or four at your level, about to become vampires?"

He grunted and looked away. I knew I was close enough, so I pressed on. "And this is not a special year with a bumper crop of Aspirants? And this has been going on for a while?" He twitched; I had him now. He knew where I was going. I stopped and waited for him.

"Yeah," he sighed eventually. "Where are all the vampires going?"

"I think we'd know if vampires were being staked out in the community," I said. "So that leaves one of three things, to my thinking. One—vampires don't live for as long as they claim. Two—something's killing vampires outside of the human community. Three—and here I'm getting really worried for you—moving from Aspirant to vampire goes wrong more often than they let on. That may be one reason why they isolate Aspirants from other people."

"Or four—they move away," he said. Good. I might have upset him, but he was still thinking.

"Okay, four," I conceded. "But the description of the vampire community that I've pieced together from you suggests that's not the way. Why are they not explaining these things to you?"

Forget finding out for the army, I wanted to know for myself. It was frustrating. We had to keep our friendship secret—he wasn't supposed to talk to anyone. I was trying to watch the Denver vampires without them realizing. But this way, we'd lost the best chance of finding things out.

Most of my background knowledge on vampires, I'd put together with the colonel in preparation for being released. Vampires didn't burn up in sunlight or cringe away from religious icons. They had communities and some way to remain hidden, even with their need for human blood. It was the details that eluded me. Important stuff, like how long can you go after you're bitten before you turn? How can you tell you're turning? And, is there any way to reverse it?

"You're right," he said. "You're absolutely right. It's something I think I get the answers to before the last step." He bounced on his toes and started to warm up. I could see he wasn't ready to talk about this yet. Maybe he was like me, and he found running a good way to mull things over. His lips curved up a touch. "I'm sure they'd answer your questions if you asked them. Listen, I gotta run."

I'd said enough. I couldn't live his life for him. That cold wind touched me again. "Whatever happens, David, I'm here for you as a friend."

He stopped bouncing and looked me in the eyes. "Thanks. Look, you know, I'm really not allowed to tell you about what goes on when I meet them." I watched him struggle with his conscience. "But I was there a little early last evening. Heard something I probably shouldn't have; your name."

I raised my eyebrows and my heart skipped a beat. *What the hell?*

"There's this security committee meeting—"

I couldn't help it, I burst out laughing, which was plain rude. "Vampires have committees? Oh, David, you really are doing the full sales talk on me now."

He smiled tightly, but pushed on. "Come on, Amber, it's serious. The security meeting handles stuff like vampires who've gone rogue." A shiver ran up my spine at the word, but he didn't notice. He ran fingers through his curly black hair. "I didn't hear anything to suggest that you were regarded as a rogue, just a concern. I shouldn't be telling you any of this, but when you said about thinking you were being watched? I'd lay odds you're right."

I had mixed feelings about this. A security issue could be anything. It wasn't as if I hadn't been expecting something, sometime, as a response from the vampire community to my poking around. There was nothing I could do about it immediately, other than stay alert and be careful.

"That's why you're a bit on edge today?" I asked, and he nodded. He couldn't afford to be seen with me if I was a security issue for them. It was a remote chance, but he'd staked a lot personally on this.

"Thanks, David. I appreciate it. Next time, the ice cream's on me," I said. We bumped fists and he jogged off back into the park to do his full circuit, hopefully without leaping out of the bushes on any more unsuspecting females.

I never had a brother and I guess David filled the role. I felt very bad about not telling him everything that was going on. I needed him because I wanted information to understand my condition and maybe find a cure for it. I hated that I needed him to become a vampire to be of any use in that role.

In the end, I wished David to be happy in what he became, while trying to avoid it myself. I just hoped we would remain friends through it all.

But there was one serious incident that the vampire security committee might have found out about that could ruin that scenario; I'd killed three vampires a year ago.

While I did some stretches, I let my gaze travel over the other cars. I spotted a face that I recognized: the nerd from Papa Dee's. I had to smile. He didn't look like anyone a crime boss would hire. I didn't ignore him, but I wasn't going to lose sleep over him.

After early attempts to get me settled into a nice, safe job like accounting failed, I managed to persuade the colonel to fast-track me into the police force. That had looked good until a year ago, when three men killed a couple of police officers and took a young girl, Emily Schumacher, hostage. I was in the area and I picked up the scent, literally. It was the first time I had crossed paths with vampires since that night in the jungle. I had gotten much better at it, evidently, or they weren't up to scratch. By the end of it, all three were very dead.

What came out in the news was a fabrication that suited Lieutenant Morales and Colonel Laine, without any mention of me or vampires. The bodies disappeared into Laine's army laboratories. Morales made captain. I left the police force. Emily went home to her parents. And her father made the most beautiful boots in the world for me.

Outside the spotlight, Captain Morales, Colonel Laine and I had a long discussion.

We agreed that there had to be a hidden vampire community in Denver, but that in the normal course of events, it kept on the right side of the law and the three dead vampires were rogues. I would keep searching and report anything to the army. Laine would update Morales. I was on call for Morales and if vampires broke the law, I might have to be involved in some form.

I had lived the last year with the worry that the vampire community would discover the truth about the rogues and either take exception to my actions or an extreme interest in me. Now my name was being raised by a security committee.

Concern for David was also a big factor in my worry. Given the potential for danger to friends and family, I tried to keep myself distant from people. All my old friends in the army I was forbidden to see. I saw my family: my lawyer sister, Kath, and my mother, Stacy, but we had grown a little apart when I was in the army and I kept it that way for their safety. David was my only new friend and not only was I lying to him and spying on him, I was putting him at risk.

As for lovers, I had a possibly incurable, national security level infection and the army scientists couldn't even tell me whether it was contagious. So, despite mom's hints about marriage and grandchildren, I was permanently, frustratingly, 'between' relationships. I'm a healthy woman with healthy desires and, excuse me, no fucking outlet.

I finished up my stretches and my worrying with a sigh and when I drove out, no one followed.

I stopped at a gym back near the office, where my membership had long since run out. My luck was in, and Sol was on the door. He was so damn cute that, if it weren't for my no-touch rules, I would have enjoyed delivering on all the provocative suggestions I attacked him with. As it was, after ten minutes he let me in to shower and change, while he went and stuck his head under the cold water faucet.

Afterwards, I went by the office to check if there were any important mail or voicemails. In half an hour, I was back on I-25 and heading for the center of Denver as evening fell.

Downtown was a whole new ball game.

Chapter 6

Jennifer Kingslund's chef, Troy Huber, lived on the fifth floor of a new apartment building. It was tucked between old warehouses that were being converted to apartments, with clubs and restaurants dotted around. It was a good area. Way out of my budget, of course. I drove past and headed towards the main streets to find a parking garage.

Since leaving the office to come here, I'd had the feeling of being followed again. This was an opportunity to shake it up and see what fell out. I'm not a great one for waiting.

I parked and grabbed my backpack. Down on 16th Street, it was busy, with the tail end of people heading home after work and the start of the dinner rush for restaurants. Everyone was moving and half of them would be moving in the same direction I was, which might make it difficult to spot a tail. Operating in cities was not the particular specialty of Ops 4-10, but I'd had the basic training. Vary your walk, don't look for the tail, just look at the people and wait for someone to stand out.

It was getting chilly with the threat of rain later, but the restaurants with outdoor seating were still doing well. Another time, I might have sat and had a cup of coffee and enjoyed watching the world walk by. Denver's good for that, but I couldn't remember the last time I had been carefree enough to indulge myself.

Troy's apartment was a couple of blocks south. I headed away from it and crossed the street to a takeout restaurant, walking slowly and using the shop windows to look behind me. I picked up a burger and stood outside, taking my time juggling the sauce and salt packets and taking a few bites.

I saw him.

Without giving any indication I'd made him, I tossed the remains of the burger in a trash can and started walking again, back across the street and down towards the apartment.

Mr. Obvious was about six foot, dressed in dark brown jeans and a loose jacket. The jacket would be to hide his gun. He'd walked up the street behind me and followed me across, lingering a couple of stores away. His head jerked around when I started walking again, and he followed immediately.

After passing the entrance to the parking garage, I turned into a side alley, getting out of his line of sight, and sprinted away, thanking the stars for my backpack with my nice, big gun in it.

I wasn't intending to outrun him, even though I probably could, so I ducked behind a dumpster and got the Heckler Koch out. The safety snicked off and I strained my ears to hear the sound of his footsteps following. What had he been wearing on his feet? Running shoes? Boots? It was a stupid, rookie mistake to miss that.

The alley was formed by the tall brick backs of offices and apartments. It was used for deliveries and services, and was punctuated with rolling steel doors. Few ordinary doors and almost no windows opened on the alley. It was dark, and the occasional spotlights over delivery doors only served to make the shadows deeper. With all that featureless brick, it should have had great acoustics.

I strained to hear. Out on the main street a car door slammed. A motor started. Traffic noises seeped in. Then someone close by grunted loudly, as if in pain. I came around the dumpster in a crouch with a double-handed grip on the gun, sighting back up the alley.

Mr. Obvious was lying face down on the ground, unmoving, one arm broken. His jacket was half torn off and a pair of even bigger guys were standing over him. One was taking his pistol and the other was looking down the alley at me. *Not* police. My skin prickled and out of old habit I gave them target names. Fang 1 and Fang 2 seemed appropriate. They were dressed in matching black suits, for God's sake.

I clamped down on the hysterical giggle that followed the rush of adrenaline. The different groups on my tail were fighting over me and the two vampires stuck out, like, well, like black suits in summer in Denver. In daylight I'd have been able to pick them out across a quarter mile of city. They'd only been able to tail me by tailing my tail.

They walked slowly towards me. Fang 1 had Mr. Obvious's gun held out between finger and thumb in front of him. That's not to say he didn't have a slick move where he whipped it up and fired, all in a heartbeat, but he seemed to be trying to make it clear that he wasn't going to shoot me. I let them come. I was pretty sure that these guys were representatives of the local vampire community and that dictated that I treat them with a certain respect unless they gave cause for anything else.

At twenty yards, I spoke. "That's far enough, gentlemen."

I hadn't put my gun down and whereas it wasn't quite aiming at either one of them, it was close enough. They stopped. My nose prickled with the copper scent of vampire, overlaid with something sweet. Cinnamon?

I jerked my head at the guy lying behind them. "Thanks for that, I guess. How is he?"

"He's unconscious," said Fang 1. "I'm going to unload his gun and throw it in the trash, okay?"

I nodded, not taking my eyes off either of them. I watched him strip the magazine slowly and carefully, clear the chamber and toss everything into the dumpster.

They glared at the HK in my hands, but hey, I didn't ask them to toss the gun. I wasn't going to shoot them if they weren't armed, but I didn't want them to know that.

"Unless I'm mistaken," I said slowly, "I have just had the pleasure of being saved by two of Denver's very own fang-dangling vampires."

They didn't smile. Maybe the gun ruined their sense of humor. Maybe a vampire's smile shows the fangs and means something else.

"You're coming with us," said Fang 2.

"The old 'resistance is futile' line, eh?" I sighed. "Gentlemen, thank you for your help this evening. However, I am holding the gun and I will not go with you."

"You will, you know," said Fang 1 too loudly, but Fang 2 ruined it by twitching. I talk too much when I should be listening, but I can read a tell.

I ran; *up* the side of the brick building. Enough to give me height and confuse Fang 3 who had snuck up, really quietly, behind me. I backflipped over his head and tried to kick down with my boot. It was Hollywood style and it wouldn't have worked, but anyway, Fang 3 had already moved. Damn, but he was quick. Quick, but not quick enough to avoid tangling up with Fang 1 and 2, who'd come in like a pair of Dobermans.

I landed unbalanced, which gave them time to turn on me. The first one I punched in the jaw and he reeled back, grunting in surprise. I was punching left hand because the right was keeping my options open with the HK, but I'm strong with both hands. The second suit lashed out and half caught me in the ribs, making me grunt in turn. I whipped his face with the HK, but a third painful punch from the other side clipped my jaw and I saw stars.

If it's not working, do something different, Top would have said to me. I backpedaled to get free and brought the HK back up.

"I *will* use this if I have to," I said, aiming at Fang 1's face, and they slowed up. "Call it even, guys. Back off and leave me alone."

Unfortunately, that wasn't going to work either. Either they didn't believe me or they didn't care, which was really scary. Fang 3 started to edge to one side and in a few moments they would be spread out and I couldn't handle them like that. I had to find a way of getting them to come to me one at a time.

I turned and sprinted down the alley into the gloom. Assuming they had been together to start with, if Fang 3 had gotten in that quickly behind me, there was a way to get out quickly too. I was betting one of the few doors off the alley led into a building that was being converted. I could hear them running right behind me. I got the horrible feeling they could have run much faster if they wanted and all they were doing was herding me. That would mean there was another black suit up ahead somewhere. As soon as I thought it, I saw him come around the corner at the far end, silhouetted by the streetlights. He start sprinting towards me. One more option gone.

One of the doors opening onto the alley looked as if it wasn't fully shut and I shoulder-charged it. It slammed open and I was through. I was right, this old warehouse was being converted to apartments. Partition boards stood stacked against walls, boxes of tiles and cement littered the floor. This had to be the way Fang 3 had gotten in behind me. It was long after work hours and he must have disabled the alarm, so I couldn't expect any help. I got the door shut and slid the bolt home just as the first black suit crashed against it. The door was a temporary fixture made of plywood and it would hold them awhile, but there wasn't anything else to secure it, other than a bench, which I shoved up against it.

I ran inside the darkened building and up the stairs as a foot kicked right through the door. A hand followed and started scrabbling for the bolt. Note to self: avoid being kicked full-on by these guys.

I was going up the steps four at a time when I heard the door heaved open, scraping the bench along the ground. I reached the third floor before I spotted what I needed, some solid timber poles. I grabbed one about five feet long and another short offcut and made the next floor, checking down the stairwell. I could see all four black suits—moving shadows on the stairs, shown by zebra bars of light shining in through the streetside windows. They were eerily silent, except for the panting and the slap of their shoes on the bare wooden steps.

At least they were panting. That suggested that they could get tired.

The HK was back in the bag when they started up the last flight. I stood in plain sight, holding the long timber pole upright to one side, like a military standard, both hands on it, my weight on my back leg. I was just inside a doorway. I tried to look confident and as if I knew what I was doing, but my heart was hammering and my mouth was dry. I had no idea what it took to persuade a vampire to stop, or what it took to knock one out. All I had ever done before was kill them, which was an option of very last resort now.

Seeing me waiting made them slow down: first mistake. They came straight at me: second mistake. They came in line, one at a time: third and worst mistake. Their strength in numbers should have been used to rush and overwhelm me from different directions.

The first got the timber offcut, which had been lying across my front foot, flicked up into his face. Although there was no danger from it, he reacted and jerked his hands up to his face, leaving his front unprotected. I hit him hard in the stomach with the end of the long pole, hard enough to propel him backwards into the others. Not hard enough to rupture internal organs, I hoped. I really, really didn't want the vampires to have any more reasons for coming after me.

As he went back I saw unmistakable vampire fangs in his open mouth.

Number two got the side of the pole across his chin while he was tangled up with number one and went down with a broken jaw.

Number three managed to hit me in the face again as I launched him back down the stairs, but he took my pole with him and I had no time before the next.

Fang 3 was the fourth through the door. He was a student of Kung Fu, and a very good one. His relentless attack of twisting, snapping punches quickly started to break through my defenses. I let some land, only partially blocking them, so I was in a better position to punch back. Any body punches I landed he seemed to be able to ignore and he kept his head well protected. I was in trouble, taking a lot of pain, and I was tiring more quickly than he was. He only had to keep that up and I was finished.

Then he tried a movie-style *coup-de-grâce*.

His beautiful, graceful kick went over my head as I ducked. My ungraceful fist went straight and hard into his groin, and I swept his leg out from under him. He slammed into the floor, doubled over and making noises like a sick puppy. Well, good news! At least one of the major disadvantages of being a man transferred to vampires.

Number one tried to get back up. *Ten out of ten for effort, boy, but not when you can hardly breathe.* I slugged him tiredly and he collapsed again.

Number two was still out of it, groaning and squirming on the floor. It looked like a broken jaw and concussion. I ran down the stairs.

Number three had a broken leg and I figured he should have a concussion as well after falling an entire flight of stairs. He was lying very still. It was Fang 1. As a reflex, I checked his throat pulse, which I guess might seem an odd thing to do with a vampire. Regardless, he had a pulse of sorts and his eyes flickered open.

I stepped back. "Next time, a written invitation might be better," I said. "Then it won't hurt so much when I turn it down." I was unsure whether he was tracking well enough to take that in. He didn't laugh, anyway. I went down the remaining stairs at a run and was out of the building and away.

There was a group of people gathered around Mr. Obvious, one of them talking into a cell. I headed down the other way, trying to walk as if I were oblivious to anything else.

At the end, I turned the corner to get out of view from the alley and leaned against a wall.

I was still panting and I was nursing a whole new set of aches and bruises, but I was in better shape than any of them. I had gotten the upper hand over a group of four vampires and I pumped my fist in exhilaration. Yes! They were quicker and stronger than me, but they'd only learned to fight. I'd gone to a harder school and I'd learned to *win*.

Sober thinking quickly took over. This hadn't settled anything. It didn't mark the end of either group's intentions towards me. I was pretty sure neither group would know what I was doing in LoDo. The best place for me at the moment should be Troy Huber's apartment. I was just around the corner from it. I calmed down and walked there slowly, just another person in the night. Almost.

Chapter 7

When I reached the lobby door of Troy's apartment building my breathing was back to normal, but I opened it with fingers still shaky from the aftereffects of adrenaline. I noted the security camera as I walked to the elevator and went up to the fifth floor. I pulled some latex gloves out of my kit and snapped them on.

One hand in my backpack, holding the HK, I let myself into Apartment 503. It was dark.

"Troy?" I called out as I flicked the lights on, on the small chance that he had come back, but the place had an empty feel to it and there was no response. I locked the door behind me.

I dropped my backpack, sank down beside the door and let out a long sigh. Strangely, I felt much better now. It was like when I was in the army. I had always been stressed before an operation, but once it started, it went where it went.

I had to expect both groups to try again.

The crime boss would get a replacement for Mr. Obvious and maybe the replacement would be better at the job, or use a sniper rifle or whatever. I needed to take the initiative on that. If I could find out who the boss was, the playing field became more level. I could even get the police to do the work, if I could find some hard evidence. I'd need to start that tomorrow.

The vampires would come again. It was reassuring that they had put so much effort into capturing me, rather than killing me. If things escalated, then I guessed I would have to call in the colonel. I couldn't think of any way I could precipitate things or find out more about them in a hurry, so that was wait and see for the moment, however much I disliked that option.

Those things mentally filed away, I needed to work to pay the rent, which was the reason I was here in the first place. I took a pair of plastic booties from my kit and slipped them on over my boots. So sexy.

I stood still in the middle of the floor and surveyed the room. The apartment faced over the creek towards Elditch Park. Good living space with pale cream walls and quality wooden furniture was my first impression, immediately followed by *too neat*. Troy was a *very* tidy bachelor. Or he had a maid. Or someone had cleaned up thoroughly.

There were two bedrooms off the living area, a master bedroom with the same view of the park and a second bedroom for an agoraphobic dwarf. I started there. Troy was an avid cyclist and he kept his fancy street racer in the second bedroom on a sheet of blue plastic, along with a wall of photos from bike racing events all over Colorado. The small pine dresser held a jumble of brightly colored bike gear. Nothing seemed out of place.

The master bedroom was no more illuminating. The bed was neatly made, but only with sheets. Clothes hung in the closet, looking forlorn. I noticed jackets and pants were all mismatched and shoes were just tossed in the bottom.

"Not so neat in here, Troy," I muttered.

The storage space above the clothes rail was taken up by a couple of suitcases, both empty. I got a chair and checked if there was anything suggesting another missing suitcase, like a dust pattern, but there wasn't. There were some spare sheets in a plastic bag, but no other bed coverings.

A stack of magazines lay in a pile by the bed—a company magazine which featured Troy and the Golden Harvest, some biking and cooking magazines, and a few general interest.

His razor, toothbrush and toothpaste were in the bathroom. If he had gone on a trip without telling anyone, he hadn't used his suitcases and he hadn't taken the things you would expect.

The kitchen looked well used. Everything had been washed and put away. In the fridge, half-wilted lettuce lay next to a carton of milk with an expiration date over the weekend.

I turned back to the living area and noticed a couple of framed photographs, both of Jennifer Kingslund—one with Troy outside the Golden Harvest, and one of her alone.

A local newspaper lay on the table, open to a picture of Troy receiving an award for winning a bike race. I checked the date—last week. He wore a distinctive shirt and shorts with a large yellow and black diamond pattern. It was so distinctive, it made me go back to the second bedroom and check out the bike gear. The clothes weren't there.

I walked back. The whole living area smelled clean. Not clean in a nice way; a sterile, bleached way. I got down on my hands and knees, cursing the aches and bruises, and sniffed the carpet. Next to the coffee table, someone had washed it with bleach. It was a shade lighter and the smell was very strong.

Moving the stuff off the top, I lifted the coffee table. On the underside of the foot was what looked like dried blood, as if a little had seeped underneath before the carpet had been washed.

That did it for me. I eased myself back up and got my cell. She answered right away.

"Jen, it's Amber, can you talk?"

"One moment, please." I could hear some background noises as she finished a conversation, then she came back on. She was back in clipped businesswoman mode, despite the late hour.

"I'm listening," she said.

"I'm at Troy's apartment. Can I ask you a few questions?"

"Go ahead."

"You said he wasn't at work over the weekend. When was the last time you or your staff saw him?"

"He finished work on Friday at about 11:30 p.m. I checked with the staff at the restaurant. That's the last I know."

"Do you know if he has a cleaning service come in?"

"It's a company apartment, Amber. We pay for a cleaning service to go in on Fridays." Ahh. That's why she had the keys. That crossed one question off the list, but I was still going to have to ask her some personal questions.

"Do you know him well enough to say whether he's a tidy person?"

"Troy? No. We met at his place occasionally. It wasn't dirty or anything, but it wasn't neat. Typical bachelor."

"Jen, you may find this intrusive, but I have to ask. Is there anything between you and Troy on a personal level?"

"You mean lovers? No. Not my type and anyway, not a good idea these days."

"Okay, Jen, this is my reading, worst case. He was dressed for biking, about to go out or just come back. Some of his biking clothes are missing but the bike's here. Either someone that he knew came over, or someone very good broke in without damaging the door, and waited for him to come back. There was a struggle, some blood was spilled. Someone washed the carpet with bleach. He was carried out, wrapped up in his comforter or bedspread."

I waited, but Jennifer didn't say anything, although I'd heard her breath hiss in while I'd been speaking. I went on. "But I can read this a completely different way. He doesn't like covers on the bed. He spilled some red wine and cleaned it up. He went out for a jog instead of a bike ride. He got hit by a car and he's in a hospital somewhere."

"No. I've had my assistant check every hospital already," Jennifer said. "Nothing."

"That's good work. Jen, if this is a crime scene, the longer we leave it, the less likely it is that the police will be able to do anything. For instance, there's a security camera in the lobby. It'll take the police to get hold of the footage in a hurry. Neighbors need to be questioned, and they'll be a lot more cooperative with the police. I don't *know* that there's been a crime here, but I'm advising you to call them tonight."

"Will they take it seriously, Amber? Will they do something quickly enough?"

"A request from you to the police is going to carry some weight, but I'll be honest, it's hard for them to spend time on a missing person when they have rapes and murders to deal with." I thought quickly. "There's not enough of me to do everything, but what about I bring in another PI agency just to do a missing person check on Troy? I can brief them and keep it very separate from everything else, so there should be no problem with any confidentiality issues. They might find him, or find some clues as to what happened that might get the police to concentrate more on it."

She gave it some thought. I could imagine her sitting in her executive chair in her fancy office, and I wondered which cogs were turning in her mind—how much this was going to cost or how quickly Troy could be found.

"Okay, Amber," she said. "I'll go with it. What do I have to do?"

"Come down here. Make the call from the apartment, make the police come to you."

"On my way." She hung up.

I flipped through my contacts and dialed. The Georgia voice that answered was beautifully deep and gravelly, like smooth river rocks grinding together. We had worked with each other before and I would keep him on my list just to get that Dixie molasses poured in my ear from time to time.

"Victor! How goes it, Mr. G?"

"Well 'nuff, Amber. Whatcha doing calling me while I'm off work and restin' at home?"

I laughed. "You're never off work. And you know that little button on the top of your cell? It's called an off switch."

"Uppity like always. Whatcha need, girl?"

Victor Gayle ran the biggest small PI firm in town. His specialty was more along the lines of security and bodyguards, but I rated his team as good investigators as well.

"I need a missing persons investigation, Vic."

"Oh, you want me to find why you got no clients?"

"Ha ha, so funny, big man." I grinned anyway. "No. I'm working a related investigation and I can't quite cover this as well. The police are going to be involved but I don't think they'll treat it seriously enough unless some more evidence turns up. Or alternatively, we find the guy and we can close this part of the case."

I ran through a quick account of Troy's details, and what I had found or not found at the apartment. I could tell Victor was curious as to how this linked with my case, but he didn't pry. He said he would email me a reminder of his terms and promised to get someone on it in the morning.

Shortly after I'd hung up, the lobby door buzzer sounded. I checked the image—Jennifer and her driver—and let them in the building. It would be worth checking if the video intercom system stored images as well. I unlocked the door to the apartment.

"Amber!" Jennifer came through the door and looked at me, appalled. I hadn't forgotten the fight, but I had forgotten that I would be showing signs of it. The bruises hadn't matured yet, but my chin was raw and scraped and my lip was split.

"Ah, yes." I rubbed my face gently. "I took a short cut through an alley on the way here and a couple of guys attacked me. It's nothing."

She stared at me. "Hardly nothing."

I shrugged it off and, after warning them not to touch anything, I led her around and showed her the details I had seen and the conclusions I had drawn. I handed her back the keys along with Victor's contact information.

"Time to call the police, Jen. And time for me to go. The police may see me on the security footage and if they ask you about it, you'll have to say I'm investigating. Until then, play it that you just came here and were concerned by the things I've pointed out."

An odd little smile flickered over her face as she got her cell out.

Her call connected and she said brightly, "José, hello! It's Jen."

I did a double take. Surely, she wasn't calling Captain Morales?

"Yes, I'm fine," she said. "I'm so sorry to disturb you at this hour, I know how hard you work, but I just don't know who else to turn to. You've already helped me and I was hoping you could help me some more. I'm so worried."

It was difficult not to laugh. I happened to know Captain Morales was happily married, but that wasn't a defense against this kind of attack from Jennifer. And it showed good thinking on her part. If she could persuade Morales to send a squad car here, they would treat it more seriously than if the desk sergeant did.

Another time, I would have to find out how she knew Morales. I waved and let myself out.

Chapter 8

Back at the parking garage, I approached my car cautiously, but there was no one waiting for me. I headed back home to Aurora through the late night traffic.

Even cheap is expensive for me. Aurora is part of Denver and yet is its own whole city, with good parts and bad. I lived in a room on the side of a house in the cheaper part of Aurora. It suited me fine. There was a half kitchen, a tiny bathroom, a bed and a place to keep some of my stuff. The rest was in a storage unit.

The only drawback was that the door to my room was off the porch, and Mrs. Desiarto was reliably found on it at night. She was an old-style Italian mamma transplanted into the suburbs of Denver. In an Italian village, she would have had many people to talk to. Now that her children had fled the nest, she had me. I suspected the rent reflected this and I did try to sit and talk some nights.

However late I came home, she always seemed to be there, sitting in her cane rocking chair. She claimed she was unable to sleep due to the pain in her hips.

As I stepped up, I gave thanks it was dark and she couldn't see my face.

"Amber, you been working late again."

"Maybe I've been out with a boyfriend, this time," I replied, leaning against a post.

She laughed, which was a bit unfair. It wasn't that unlikely, surely. "You have no boyfriends, Amber. You scare them off. Look at you. I couldn't pinch so much as a tweezer of skin from you. It's not natural."

"It is for me, Mrs. Desiarto." I sighed. "But you're right, I've been working and I've still got to finish up."

"A man would think he was lying on a bed of stones with you. You need to eat decent food, take it easy. Find yourself a man. You need to think about starting a family, you know."

I made a move to my door. Once she was off on this, I would get her history of how she had met her husband and the clever way she had snared him. Unless I went now, I would be here a long time.

"I'm sorry, Mrs. Desiarto, maybe another time. Good night."

I escaped and slipped into the dark warmth of my room. I stood in the darkness for a few moments before switching on the light, and only then did I take my hand out of the backpack where I had been holding the gun.

I threw everything on the bed, sat down and wrote up the day's report on the laptop. I emailed Jennifer a brief review about my visit to Troy's apartment along with my suspicions and recommendations, even though we'd spoken.

I glanced at the clock and winced—another late night. I didn't care for the idea of looking at accounts at this hour, so instead I did a search through the USB drive for the security footage from Silver Hills.

It was a black and white closed-circuit camera time-lapse movie. The camera and lights had probably been linked to a motion sensor and timer. It started with a couple of frames showing an area with bulldozers and storage containers, in natural light with long shadows. Nothing was happening. The clock timer at the bottom showed early evening. Then there were a couple of frames where the timer had triggered and the lights came on briefly to record that nothing was still happening. The timer showed 9:30.

What showed next made me sit up in a hurry.

Between the directional security lighting and the limitations of a black and white security camera, this wasn't going to win awards for detail, but the motion sensor triggered and the camera went to full video, capturing what looked like a pack of wolves swarming over the site. I froze the playback, backed up a couple of frames and looked at it for a long time. It was blurred, but I wasn't looking to see detail.

The work crew had used shipping containers to store equipment during off-hours, a common alternative to securing the whole site. A shipping container is relatively inexpensive and fits on a truck. It's robust and secure, and it's about eight feet tall. A wolf stands about three feet at the shoulder. Either the wolf I was looking at standing next to the shipping container was over four feet tall or there was some trick of perspective I couldn't figure out. The others were as big.

Eventually, I let it play again. It lasted only a few seconds more before the screen went black and the clip ended. The timer was at 9:53.

I went back to just before the end and froze it. There was a hint of something like a stone heading for the camera lens. Neat trick for a wolf, throwing stones.

I went back frame by frame and came to the second startling image. For two frames, in the top right-hand corner, what looked like bare human legs passed at the limit of the illumination of the security lights. It was as if someone had run across the site thinking they were outside of the reach of the camera. Naked. In amongst a pack of huge wolves.

I turned it off. No wonder Jennifer had been having trouble talking about this.

There was no way that was a pack of ordinary wolves with one handy person along to throw stones. Since being bitten by a vampire, the thought of other weird things being out there had seemed a lot more likely. This raised the hair on my neck.

I would have to visit the scene. I needed to talk to Jennifer about it, but it was way too late tonight. I sent her another email saying I wanted to see the site as soon as possible.

Thinking through what else was going on, with the threat from crime bosses and vampires, I realized I would have to avoid sleeping here at Mrs. Desiarto's. I wouldn't want any collateral damage if I was attacked. Maybe I could sleep at the office or in my car, but not tonight. I was sore all over and I had been up late last night as well.

I packed away my gear, took another shower and went to bed, making sure the HK was within reach beside me.

The gun wasn't much use that night.

This one I'd had before.

I'm floating on water, staring up at a bright blue sky. I'm getting heavier, sinking. The water closes over me. The sky ripples, distorted. I'm breathing water, not choking, but not getting oxygen. It's too late to struggle. I've run out of options. I just have to give up and I'll be at peace. So easy. A couple of minutes and I can rest in the cool dark. No more striving. No more fear. Better this way.

I jerked upright in bed, lungs laboring, drenched in sweat.

Just another night in the Amber zone.

Chapter 9

WEDNESDAY

I woke early to greet the dawn, because someday there might be a morning I can't. It was especially worth it today to remind myself what I stood to lose. That army isolation cell had no windows. I had to finesse the colonel this afternoon.

I did a quick check in the mirror, and yesterday's bruises were hiding some of the previous day's. My lips were a bit fatter on the one side, but half a set of bee-stung lips isn't quite the same. I sighed.

At least the strains and sprains had healed. Sure, the body looked a little battered at the moment, but it was strong and healthy. All the exercise gave me a lean runner's build. My Arapaho great-grandmother's genes showed up in the bronze cast to my skin and a sharper nose than would be considered attractive. The Celtic side came out in the auburn hair and the green eyes. There wasn't much on the rack, but as Mrs. Desiarto noted in our last conversation, there wasn't anyone but me to appreciate the view at the moment.

But underneath? I leaned closer to the mirror, staring at the face that looked out at me.

Is this what a vampire looks like?

I pulled on my jeans and chose a man's shirt for a change. The tall collar would hide some of the neck bruising. I filled a couple of bags with clothes to keep in the back of the car and cleared out the last of the fruit to eat on the way.

At the office, I pulled the Crate & Freight file and noted Windler's address. According to the news, he hadn't been arrested yet. I wanted to see if there were any clues as to who the drug boss was and Windler's house was as good a place to start as any. Exactly how I was going to square this with Morales, I put on hold.

Then I started to go through Jen's financial files, starting at the top level and checking that everything added up and cross referenced, making notes to come back to.

I heard Tullah come in at nine and she put her head around the door at once.

"Knock, knock." She was grinning.

"Come in, Tullah."

She slid a takeout coffee across the table at me. "Wake up and smell the—oh my God! What happened, Amber?" she said.

"Oh no. Did my mascara run?"

"Amber! It's not funny, you've been hit again."

"Yeah," I said. "I took a short cut through an alley and got attacked. They regret it more than I do."

"You got attacked in an alley last evening? Wow, after a few of those, you might start to think that alleys are dangerous places that you should avoid after sunset."

I snorted. The young rely on sarcasm far too much.

"Anyway," she reached into a pocket, "a bit late for last night, but Ma said to give you this."

She dropped a bracelet into my hand. It was beautiful, made with lines of little stone beads of different types and colors and sealed with a gold clasp.

"It's lovely! Thank you. Or thank your mother. What's it for?" I looked back up at Tullah.

"It's a protection charm." She rolled her eyes. "Oh, I know, it's not as if you need protecting."

I smiled. "Not what I meant, Tullah. I meant, why is she giving me something so lovely? It's not my birthday or anything. But okay, let's talk about the bracelet first. It's going to protect me from evil or something?"

Tullah answered more seriously than I expected. "Actually, magic isn't quite like that. It's kind of difficult to define good and evil in a spell, but it will warn you if someone close by intends you harm. It'll tingle."

I believed in vampires, obviously. I was starting to believe in werewolves after last night. But I was having a bit of trouble with a bracelet figuring out people's intentions.

"I know your mother is into that. I didn't know you were." I raised my eyebrows at her. She was a straightforward Denver kid studying in college. Did she believe in this stuff too?

"Some," she said neutrally. "Go on, put it on."

I wrapped it around my wrist and clicked the clasp. I really liked the look of it on my arm.

"The pattern's a wolf's eye," she said. "The wolf is your spirit animal."

After last night's security footage, that gave me a peculiar little thrill. "Well, I'll thank her myself when I see her next. But back to my original question. Why is she giving me this right now?"

"She likes you, okay? And maybe she thinks you need it." She paused. "Don't even try to think of paying for it—that would, like, so jinx it."

My cell bleeped and I checked it. There was a text message from David: *WTF!? Urgent! Coffee shop. 30m.*

Chapter 10

There was only one coffee shop where we met, First Base, a block away from the Civic Center Park. It was quiet, with old-fashioned booths that suited us, and regular clients that made unfamiliar faces stand out. A big mirror ran along the back, giving us a view of people walking in and out. First Base roasted and ground their own beans, so the place smelled and sounded like a coffee shop should.

It was a little after ten when I slid into the booth opposite David. He'd already bought the coffee. Dressed for work at his insurance company, he looked so much more upscale than my running and sparring friend, I had to stop myself from reaching out and mussing his hair.

David looked somberly at my face and lips.

"That wasn't my punch, was it?" He glanced down. "I think I know how you got that."

"Yeah." I tried to keep my tone light. "Four guys in suits tried to kidnap me in LoDo yesterday evening. It got rough. What do you know about it?"

David shook his head. "Almost nothing, but the place went crazy last night when those guys were brought back. What's going on, Amber?"

"I was hoping you could tell me."

"Dammit, Amber, I don't know. A couple of days ago, I was motoring. You'd coached me through the hardest physical tests of my life and all you got back was some clues about your condition." He didn't like it when I called it an infection. "So what if I spoke to you and it's against the rules. It didn't seem like a big deal then."

A couple of lawyers from the firm across the road walked past our booth with coffee and pastries. David waited till they were out of earshot.

"Now, you're the main item of news. You took out four guys last night and the security committee is going to be all over you. They're going to be all over me, too, if they find out I've been talking to you. They take secrecy seriously. That was kinda emphasized all over again last night. I may be stopped at the last step because of this."

I reached out. He didn't flinch away as my fingers slid over his throat and confirmed to me what had been almost hidden from my nose by the coffee smells. David had been bitten again last night. All that remained were a couple of tiny bumps where the skin was repairing itself, and a subtle rise in the vampire scent. A tremor passed through my arm and I hid it by tucking my arms together and leaning on them.

"Third bite?" I said, and he nodded. "That's the last step, isn't it?"

"The start of the last step," he said quietly. "And no guarantee that it finishes well for me if they think I'm a liability." He paused. "Amber, from what I heard, last night was just intended to be a discussion."

"You know that? For sure? To me, four guys in suits means the type of discussion that involves being tied up and blindfolded in a soundproof room. You say they're not like that, but you don't know, David. You say they're hot on secrecy, but you don't know what it means. Imagine how much more difficult it is for me to know."

He frowned at his drink. "You're right that they're not treating this like I would expect. So, what is it I don't know? Who am I misreading, them or you?"

"I don't know." I rubbed my face and came to a decision I'd put off too long. I reached out and snagged one of his hands. "Look, David, I'm not sure I can answer your questions, but I've got to tell you some stuff. Hear me out. I'm praying it won't change anything between us."

I looked into his eyes. What did I really see—trust? Wariness, certainly. Was I about to lose a friend? I'd realized I couldn't go on without being honest with him. I had to fill in the blanks in what I'd told him, but Lord, I couldn't bear the thought that it would drive him away, even though that might be the best thing for him in the situation.

"You already figured out I was in the army." He nodded. "One of the reasons I haven't told you anything about it, was that everything I'm about to tell you is classified at the highest level." He looked uncertain how to take that, so I went on. "My life in your hands, David."

"You sure about this?" he said. I was. If I was going to tell him I was supposed to be spying on him, I felt I had to offer something in return. A hold over me that could put me back in that cell. Not a smart move, maybe.

Trust and jump. My old watchwords.

"Two years ago, when I was bitten, I was in South America. I was on a covert mission, helping local forces clear out a drug lord. The reason they hadn't had any luck against him is that he'd managed to make a deal with some vampires for defense. We knew nothing about that. My team was on reconnaissance when we were attacked by the vampires. I ended up infected. The rest of my team were dead." I had to struggle to keep my voice even as images of that night crept in. My squad. My command. My fault. "The army didn't believe in vampires before that op, and suddenly they had proof: dead vampires and me, more dead than alive. They shipped everything back and I woke up in a cell, in restraints." I shivered with a sudden cold sweat. "I can't tell you how that felt. I had to make a deal to get out of there, to stay out of there. They own me, David, they watch me. I'm supposed to tell them everything I find out about vampires."

David twitched, and my heart missed a beat, but he didn't take his hand away.

"I haven't told them about you. Please believe me."

"I do," he said quietly.

"All this—the mention at the security committee and the four goons last night—could just be the vampire community in Denver hearing about me and wanting to talk to me. Or if they know about the rest of it, wanting me to stop talking to the army."

"But it isn't just that, is it?" David was one of the smartest guys I'd ever met.

"No, it isn't. A year ago, I was a police officer." I took a sip of coffee and tried to work out the best way to say this. "Do you remember an incident in the news back then, a couple of policemen were killed and a young girl taken hostage?"

He nodded.

"The three men who did that were killed. The newspapers said it was done by the SWAT team. It wasn't." I took a deep breath and looked him straight in the eye. "Those three were vampires and I killed them."

He flinched outright this time. "Is that what you do? Are you some kind of vampire hunter?"

"No! I was just there at the time." I squeezed his hand as if I could press the understanding into him. "But they needed killing, David. You've got to understand that."

He thought that over and relaxed a fraction. His hand hadn't moved. I allowed myself to feel some hope that we'd stay friends through this. "Yeah, they did, I guess," he said, and a hint of a crooked smile touched one side of his mouth. "So, I'm not on your list?"

"No, you aren't, and I don't have a list anyway." I bit my lip.

David looked around the shop. "So, how do you find out about vampires in Denver?"

I had to smile. "It's just background work, okay? I have the full time PI job. But a couple of evenings a week, I'll trawl places where vampires might be—bars, clubs, raves. Stuff at the edge of society. Like I've said before, vampires give off a scent that I can spot, even if no one else can. Kinda coppery smell. Anyway, nothing found. Hints and rumors. A lot of wannabes."

"Waste of time," he said. "But you found me."

"That was a complete accident." We had both been on a charity run and I had spotted David struggling to get a rhythm in his running. He was going to exhaust himself long before the finish, so I had run alongside him and challenged him to match my pace. We had made it to the line together and the celebratory hug confirmed to me what my nose had been telling me for the last half of the race—he smelled of vampire. It had taken several meetings to take it beyond that with him.

David retrieved his hand. "I understand you don't want to be a vampire. I understand you want to know about them for your own personal reasons. I understand you need to pass some of that information on, and thank you for making it anonymous. But now that you can make contact through me, you have to do it."

"Can you guarantee that I'll be able to walk away from that meeting if I want to?" I put my hands out and this time gathered both of his back. I had the feeling of taking irrevocable steps, but the path I was on felt better than the one before.

I took a steadying breath and had to bite my lip again before I spoke. "David, you're the brother I never had. Next week, or whenever, if you are part of this vampire community, and you come to me and say it's safe, I'll meet one of them. Only one, with you along. My choice of meeting place."

"I swear I'll do it, if I can." He gripped my hands back.

We were silent as the waitress passed the table, hiding a smirk. I could imagine what it must have looked like, but I didn't care.

"Will you answer some questions for me?" David asked.

Our hands dropped back to the table and lay comfortably between us. "Shoot," I said.

"Why is the army so concerned about you?"

I winced. "Well, there's the risk they've taken, letting me out of isolation. And there are things I can't talk about. Things I know from my work in the army. They've never said it, but I could imagine their reaction if I became…" I felt for the right words, "anything less than reliably discreet. It would be terminal. As for the rest, well, on a physical level, modesty aside, I'm—"

"Yeah, yeah, lethal." David interrupted. "Wouldn't want that to go rogue." He was smiling again. "What's in it for the vampire community to talk to you if you're going to talk to someone else?"

"Maybe I can do some good for them. A halfway house between them and the government. A trusted party. They can't hide forever, David."

He took that on board without an argument. He would have thought about all that before setting out on the path he had. He was that type of guy.

"What about the stuff we were talking about yesterday?" I asked. "Have you found out where all the vampires are going?"

He looked disconcerted. "Amber, same as there are things you can't tell me…"

"Okay, but—"

"I can't say any more, but it's not the process of becoming…vampire. It's dangerous for you out there on your own, but not for me."

He'd been about to call it something else. I was desperate to dig, but I didn't want to risk it at the moment. I felt good about where we'd gotten to and there were lots of easier questions I wanted to ask him. The army scientists, the Obs unit, were unable to tell me anything about the progression of symptoms in becoming a vampire and I had a guy on the other side of the table who was going through it.

"Can I ask you some personal questions then?" I would have backed off if he'd looked unhappy.

He didn't need to think about it. "Can't promise I'll answer everything."

"Can I see your teeth?"

"Normal," he said, and pulled his lip back briefly.

The waitress refilled our cups. God knows what she thought this time. I read somewhere that you check horses out by looking at their teeth; maybe she thought we were fresh off the farm and didn't know any better.

At least I could stop inspecting my teeth all the time.

"Nightmares?"

"Some." He looked up. "You?"

"All the time. Really horrible."

"Amber, it really sounds as if that's your subconscious fighting the turn."

But it might be post-traumatic stress as well. It was important I didn't panic over any one symptom. Calm. There was another thing that was high on my list. I stirred uncomfortably where I sat. I had never been very good at talking about this. "Do you get urges? Really strong?"

"You'll have to be a bit more specific," he said. He was trying to look blank, but the corners of his eyes were crinkling. Dammit, he was laughing at me.

"Sex," I muttered, hunching my shoulders.

"Getting the severe hots for someone?"

"Not someone. Generally."

He laughed, a little bark of a laugh, and I realized it wasn't an easy subject for him either.

"Well, no worse than being a teenage boy. I don't know, Amber." He blew out a breath and looked at the ceiling for inspiration. "I have the severe hots for one of the Mentors. I'm told that's common. I get the impression that it gets worse before it gets better, that new vampires especially are—how would you put it—highly charged. Sex and blood go together. That's something that lasts, I think, but it's not so easy for the new ones to handle. They'll keep us isolated for a while for everyone's safety."

He checked his watch.

"You've got to get back to work," I said, and he nodded.

"I've told them I'm taking a sabbatical. Business is down, so they're okay with that. But it means I have to clear my desk."

"Boulder Charity run on Saturday?" I asked.

David nodded. "I'll be there."

I pulled a couple of new pre-paid cells from my bag and laid them on the table, one for him and one for me.

"Burn phones," he said, smiling. "Cloak and dagger!"

I nodded. "Just one speed dial number in each. Let's use them when we talk or text."

He got up and put the cell in his pocket. His hand came out holding a key with a label. He passed it to me.

"That's the key to my house. If something goes wrong. If you need to do something. You got my back, Amber."

"I got it," I said huskily, and he was gone.

Chapter 11

Back in the office, I found Tullah crying at her desk. She got up and rushed into my arms.

"Hey, hey, hey, what's up?" I had never seen her like this. She was always bouncy and cheerful.

"It's not *fair!*" she said. "They've given us notice on the office. We have to be out by next week."

She sobbed while I held her. I swore under my breath at Campbell Carter and Greg Whitman, our landlord, even though I had been sure this was coming. Carter was Whitman's biggest client. A complete bastard like Carter would seek out every way to hurt me and Whitman couldn't afford to stand up to him. Whitman hadn't even had the guts to come and tell me himself when he caved in.

Tullah was right, it was unfair. There was nothing else I could have done and I was still going to be punished for doing it.

I couldn't dwell on this. Going and shouting at Whitman wouldn't achieve anything. The best thing we could do was to make this setback meaningless. And I needed to get Tullah to do it.

"Tullah, I'm going to need you to be strong for me." I stopped. "For us, I mean, for both of us. I can't stop the work I'm doing now, so I'm going to have to rely on you to fix this."

When I let her go, she hiccupped and blew her nose. Then, bless her, she got out her notepad.

"What do you want me to do?" Her voice wobbled a tiny bit, but she was over the worst.

"First task, obviously, find us a new office. I guess we're going to have to pay a bit more. You know what the business does, you know what we can afford."

She gulped and nodded. I was taking a risk, but I had come to trust her decisions. Since the crash, office buildings were sitting vacant and she would be able to get a good deal for us somewhere.

"Then you've got to find someone with a pickup or van who can carry stuff. You'll only need one trip to move us—it's just the computer equipment, phones, cabinets and the safe. You'll need to go to the discount furniture store and buy two cheap desks and chairs."

She scribbled away.

"Go to the bank, get a thousand out. Get the phones transferred. Order new business cards and letterhead. Change the website. Write a letter of authority for me to sign." As her pen came to a halt, she looked up. "That'll do you for now. I'm in till two this afternoon. After that, if there are problems, call my cell."

I left her to it. I would tell the colonel this afternoon and Jennifer when I contacted her this evening. That would take care of the current client list.

"Tullah," I called out, "why don't you ask your mother if she'd help out, if that's not imposing too much?"

"Of course she will. Amber, that's a great idea!"

I heard her call Mary and explain what was happening.

"She'll come in this afternoon. I'll start on the new office now. How's the Kingslund case coming?" she said.

"Just getting to the exciting part. I have to call up some of her ex-employees and see if I can pick up any suspicious background to their leaving."

"Oooh, fun."

She let me get on with it. I emailed Jennifer, getting her clearance to say that I was an independent employment consultant, doing a human resources analysis for her company. Her okay came back almost immediately.

I looked at my watch. I had only a couple of hours before the colonel arrived, so I had better put them to good use instead of getting wound up. I knew this meeting with him was going to be difficult.

I dragged over the phone and a notepad and started on the numbers.

Chapter 12

At 2 p.m. exactly, the door opened.

The colonel was a throwback to old-school military. His family had been in the military even before they came to America. Since then, they had supplied sons from the War of Independence all the way to Desert Storm. He walked as if he knew they were all looking over his shoulder.

I once saw an old photo of him from his college magazine: the all-American boy, relaxed and laughing at the camera. I wondered at the process that took that and ended with this steel face and the narrow gray eyes.

He'd been one hell of an officer leading Ops 4-10. After the op in South America, he had been transferred to run the Obs unit. I guess it's like they say, when it goes bad, the blame goes up the chain. He and I had an uncomfortable relationship now. I supposed it wasn't surprising, since I was responsible for his transfer.

I was expecting him and this had become a bit of a ritual, so I walked out right away, nodding to Tullah. Colonel Laine held the door open for me like the old-style gentleman he was, when it suited him.

I dropped the shades on my eyes against the glare. The colonel's thousand yard stare just got narrower.

The van was across the street, with Private First Class No-name in the driver's seat. I had seen him a dozen times or more with the colonel and so I assumed he was in the Obs team, but I had never been introduced. There were no name tags in these units.

The colonel slid the side door open and we got in the back.

It was cramped inside, with a couple of car seats bolted to the floor, facing each other across a table. The rest of the interior was taken up with medical and computer equipment. There was a blank sliding panel to the cab. The only light came from tubes overhead. It was all bright and white and impersonal.

We slid into the seats and the van moved off.

I dropped my jacket over the seat back. I hated the van. It reminded me of the isolation cell; I felt trapped. I slid the shades back up on top of my head and folded my left sleeve up past the elbow.

"You're carrying a gun, Sergeant," he commented, as he checked the battery level and loosened the straps on the little blood test unit.

"It's gotten a bit heavy in Denver. As part of my last contract, I broke up a drug pipeline and there's trouble from the organization."

He strapped the unit to my arm. "Does that include what happened to your face?"

"More or less," I responded, my eyes fixed on the test unit. I felt the eerie touch of the micro-sensors and the sting of the needle. It didn't hurt much and it never missed the vein, but I always felt uneasy when it did that.

All the monitoring now came down to these blood tests, and every test the colonel took came out roughly the same. It measured a group of proteins in the blood called prions, rather than a virus or bacteria, as they first thought. A prion is tiny, much smaller than a virus, and isn't alive in the sense that a virus is alive. These prions were strings of protein that wrapped around each other and combined in various ways. In other types of infections, prions caused untreatable, fatal nervous system disorders. The vampire prions didn't. The tests were telling me I had a constant level of vampire prions in my blood since the attack. What level they would reach for me to be considered a vampire, the Obs team wouldn't tell me. All they would say was that, if the levels went up, I needed to be under closer observation, which was a nice way to say "back in your cell."

The important thing was the readout on top. It reached 0.42 and stopped. The number went up and down a little between tests, with no pattern I could see. This was on the high side, but all in all, I let out a relieved sigh and undid the straps.

"Can I keep this?" I held up the test unit.

"Why?"

"It may be a better way to check."

"Is there something you want to tell me?" He raised a brow at me.

"Not yet." I sat back, consciously made my body relax. "I'm having meetings with someone who smells half right and I'd like to confirm using this."

"I need details, Sergeant. Name and address." He flipped his laptop open and looked at me over the screen.

"Like I said, not yet. If I gave you everyone who claimed to be a vampire, you would be ass high in fakes." I pushed his screen down, struggling to keep calm. "Can we be clear exactly what the purpose of all this is, Colonel?"

"What do you mean?"

"The army's invested a lot in the Obs unit since I got infected. What's it all for?"

I was pushing him as hard as I dared. Who knew what instructions he had about me? He was silent for so long, I thought I had gone too far, then he sighed and sat back.

"I'm tasked with two main projects—to find out if paranormals pose a threat to the United States and to assess if there is any opportunity for the army to benefit."

"And the best way to accomplish this is for me to creep around trying to find vampires? And if I find some, are you going to ignore the constitution and grab them off the street, throw them into a cell? And if you do, where does it get you? Obs has had me for two years and can't even tell me—"

"Enough!" He held up a hand.

I realized I had raised my voice. How had my temper gotten out of hand so quickly?

"Sorry." I leaned back.

"You have a proposal, Sergeant?"

I tried to calm my racing heart. The colonel was dealing with this much better than he might have. I needed to be calm and make sense for him to justify doing it my way.

"Yes. My contact isn't a vampire yet, according to him. He's in the process. If he becomes a full vampire, he's said he will try and arrange a meeting. They've got to realize that they can't stay hidden forever. I think they might be looking for a way to talk as well." I omitted that they seemed eager enough to talk to me to warrant four guys chasing me. I just needed to be more in control of any meeting.

He grunted. "That *might* be a good idea. I would need to be at that meeting."

I looked at him. He was one tough bastard, but age slows you. I wasn't sure how he would stand up to a vampire if things went wrong. At least he was accepting there might be something in this approach.

"We can try." I tucked the test unit down by my side. He hadn't said I could take it, but he hadn't actually said I couldn't.

"What I can't do…" I cleared my throat. My heart was in my mouth. "What I can't do is spy, any more than I can go back to that cell."

He was watching me. I waited him out. I'd drawn the line. Would he cross it?

Eventually, he spoke. "You've changed," was all he said.

"I have. It feels different."

"How do you mean?"

"At first, vampires were the ones in South America, or the ones downtown last year." My hands felt sweaty. "If we had any like that here, they needed cleaning out. It was simple. But the closer I get to them here, the more I recognize that they're different."

He didn't say anything, so I went on.

"And there's me. I might be a vampire soon. I'm fighting it, but what if I'm losing? Obs can't tell me. Everything I report back, they just wave off as post-traumatic stress. They don't know." I leaned forward across the table. "What if I go, Colonel? Loyal, patriotic citizen of the USA, served my country proudly, would be proud to still be doing that *and I'm a vampire*. What's your position then?"

"You ask a hard question," was all he'd say. But it was a very big thing to me that he hadn't said I'd be back in isolation.

He knocked on the partition and PFC No-name turned the van back towards the office.

"What about other paranormals?" I said.

"Such as?"

"Elves. Witches. Fairies. Werewolves. Demons." I was watching him, but his face didn't flicker once. He was probably one hell of a poker player.

"Anything more you want to tell me, Sergeant?" he said dryly.

I shrugged and waited.

"Yes, we're investigating all paranormal activity." He leaned back. "We've got credible reports of werewolves, but no hard proof. Obs assessment is that they are extremely dangerous. Extremely." He watched me. When I didn't volunteer anything, he shrugged and pulled a note from his clipboard.

"We've monitored the internet traffic as before, and we think there's an illegal rave being organized by ZK next week. Are you still tracking this?"

I sighed. Our early brainstorming on where vampires were likely to be found had thrown up illegal raves as a possibility. I had been to enough of them to discount most of them. The one group I was still concerned about were ZK, short for Zeklesh, derived from the word for 'snakemouth' in Navajo. They were a biker gang breaking out in different directions, principally drugs. They organized raves as a cover for other things. There was an edge to them that was unsettling. If there was any connection to vampirism in the rave scene, I would stake my bet on it being through them.

"Yeah." I took his note. I would need to check my sources for the last minute confirmation of the venue.

"There's one other thing to note, Sergeant." He closed his clipboard and I got the full-on thousand yard stare. "I have a report from Morales about Crate & Freight."

Oh, crap! Morales was going to land me in it.

"He says you acted as you had to, under the circumstances," the colonel went on. I tried to hide the shuddering breath I let out. "But it was a close thing with Detective Jennings. I have to warn you, if you do infect someone, it's out of my hands." He paused. "I'd predict isolation for you *and* anyone infected. The whole thing will be kicked upstairs to the National Security Council as an emergency. Things go in there, like that, they don't come out."

He was quiet for a minute while I took that warning on board, with a mixture of dread and relief. Nothing about keeping a low profile. All about Jennings trying to give me mouth-to-mouth.

I nodded. My pulse started to edge down again.

"Did you mean it about being proud if you could still be in uniform? Would you go back to 4-10?" he asked.

"In a heartbeat, Colonel." I bowed my head and closed my eyes, caught out by the depth of the reaction his words had caused in me. "But you can't step into the same river twice."

"Heraclitus?" he said, sounding surprised.

"No academic qualifications doesn't mean I can't read." That came out sharper than I intended.

"Sorry." I couldn't remember that he had ever apologized for anything before. "Why didn't you finish school and do college?"

"Too busy being a soldier," I said. That hadn't been it at all, but I wasn't going to talk to him about the difficulties I'd had, or my promise to my dad.

We sat there in silence for the rest of the trip back, watching each other and thinking our separate thoughts.

As I got out, I told him that we would be moving the office and I would appreciate our next meeting being in the new office rather than the van. I was surprised when he just nodded.

I watched the van go and wondered why I always got the feeling that the colonel was disappointed in me. Was that because I'd screwed up in South America or was it some kind of voodoo management schtick?

In the office, there were three notes from Tullah:

Gone to look at a place with Ma, maybe move tomorrow?

Please call Captain Morales.

Please eat the food Ma brought you.

Chapter 13

I switched my cell back on, got past the voicemail from Morales and called him.

"You missed his keys under the sofa," he said without preamble.

"What?"

"Troy Huber. His keys were under the sofa, Farrell. You did okay on finding the blood and reading the rest of the apartment."

There didn't seem much point in denying that I had been there and had briefed Jennifer to report it. "Thanks. That was sloppy on the keys. How are you treating it?"

"Abduction, at the moment."

"Security footage?"

"Unexplained camera problem that day."

I chewed that over and didn't like the sound of it. "You didn't call me to talk about this."

"No, I didn't. I have a couple of things I needed to talk to you about. Firstly, I'm aware you're working for Ms. Kingslund, obviously."

"Can't discuss cases, Captain."

"I'm not discussing it, Farrell, I'm telling you. I count Ms. Kingslund as a personal friend, and I understand the sensitivity of the issues and the requirement for confidentiality. I'm just saying that we should be in contact on anything that might be pertinent."

I thought that was a good idea, but I would clear it with Jennifer before I did anything. "You didn't happen to recommend me to her, did you, Captain?"

"Can't discuss that, Farrell."

"Ouch." It had to be him, but I couldn't really swear at him for getting me some business when I needed it most. "Okay, so what was the other issue?"

"Crate & Freight. We haven't found Windler. We got the truck he drove, out on 6th Avenue, near Buckley."

"How can I help?"

"I'd like you to come downtown and take a look at the evidence files. You were watching these people and there might be something that you think of when you see what we've got."

"I'll come now." Checking on Windler was exactly what I needed to be doing for my own sake, so I treated this as a bonus.

"Bring anything you have that might be relevant."

"Will do, Captain."

Jennifer's cell was on voice mail, so I sent her a quick email simply saying that the former employees I had checked seemed to have valid reasons for leaving, unrelated to any other company. There was one that I wanted to follow up. I suggested a catch-up meeting with her the next day.

I noted there was an email from Victor, but it didn't say 'found him', so I left it for later.

I picked up the snacks that Mary had brought in for me and ate them on the way downtown. They were delicious. Two things I had to thank her for now, I thought, looking at the wolf's eye bracelet.

Morales wasn't around, but he'd left instructions with the desk sergeant, Bill Carver. Bill remembered me from my brief time as a rookie and joshed me about being a PI while he fixed me an ID card for the building. I told him outrageous lies about the kind of cases I was working on and the extravagant lifestyle I enjoyed since leaving. It felt pleasant to be part of the team again, even in a small way, and I took a smile down to the office where the evidence was waiting.

It was daunting. There was a printout overview of it and what had been checked so far. It looked complete. I picked a couple of boxes at random and did some spot checks. There was nothing that stood out. The team working on this hadn't been taking any obvious shortcuts. I guessed that with the size of the haul, this had Morales' top team on it.

I started again at the top and worked on each box in order. Most of it was the contents of Windler's apartment in Aurora, things left lying around or thrown in the trash. There was nothing I could see that hadn't been thought of.

I left my additions to the evidence in a new box, cross referenced in the original overview. I had some long distance photos of Windler and the other drivers meeting people. There was an outside chance that someone would recognize a face in there. There were some audio files from surveillance equipment I had used. They were mainly about Carter's stock shrinkage problem, but again, maybe someone would make a connection from a chance comment.

It was late and I was getting ready to go when I flicked through the folder with outside information in it. This contained the results of database searches on Windler's personal life: parking tickets, medical records and the like. I was about to toss it with the rest when a street name leaped out at me.

It was on an accident insurance form from the previous year. Windler had been parked in the early hours of the morning outside a house on the other side of Aurora from his own. It was 982 Hector Street, and a passing truck had gouged the side of his car. The truck driver had stopped and noted details—an honest man.

There was nothing else that was remarkable, but Hector Street was etched in my mind as the street where the rogue vampires from last year's incident had lived. There was no reason for any link between the cases, but it was more than I had from looking at everything else and it was on my way back.

I checked my watch. It was past eleven and it was too late and too little to warrant a report to Morales. I left a note in the folder saying I was just going to check the address where the accident happened and replaced the files and boxes neatly.

The drive took me half an hour. Hector Street was much as I remembered it when I'd walked down it a year ago, given that it had been full daylight then.

I hadn't had any plan that day. I just wanted to see where the rogues had been living. I had smelled the vampire smell from the house and passed on by, vaguely surprised that nothing else marked the place—dust gathered and weeds grew, just like everywhere else.

Hector Street was a bad area and it was midnight, but I was armed and anyway, there was no one else around.

I parked, pocketed a flashlight and some gloves, and walked slowly down the road, my boots making a soft *tock tock* on the sidewalk. The sounds of music or TV drifted out from some of the houses, but most were dark and quiet.

The rogues had lived at 1105. The house had been sold and it looked like a happier place, even in the darkness. There was no smell of vampire from it now.

I walked on, and around 990 the houses became uniform: clapboard squares with a couple of windows facing the street, individual only in the efforts to provide an off-road parking space or a neater yard. 982 was as unremarkable as the others. It was a corner lot and it had a driveway with an old Buick parked in it.

My breath plumed in the chilly air. The cross street was called Monroe and it was a step down the ladder—more cars parked along the road, narrow overgrown yards, paint peeling, unrepaired windows and doors. Still, some of these people probably owned their homes, which was more than I could say for myself.

I yawned; there was nothing here. I wanted to go to bed, if not back at the Desiartos', then in the office.

I took a couple of aimless paces down Monroe Street and stopped abruptly.

The smell was faint but unmistakable. There was a vampire here, or one had been here recently. At the same time, I also realized that the rogues last year had smelled different from the four guys I had fought yesterday. And this smell was the same as the rogues.

I slipped my hand inside my jacket and checked the HK. The textured grip, warm from my body heat, felt reassuring. I lifted it from the holster, but kept it inside the jacket as if I were keeping my hand warm as I walked down the street, trying to judge which house it was.

It seemed to be number 248. Other houses had porch lights and some had strips of light showing under poorly fitting doors, or curtains lit by lights inside. 248 was completely dark and silent. I'm not much given to flights of imagination, but it felt as if the house were holding its breath, waiting.

I slipped down the side, the HK out and the safety off. This was definitely the one. The smell was stronger, even mixed with others. Fanciful thought or not, the house gave off a feeling of cold. Hidden in the darkness by the side of the house, I put my gloves on, then followed the HK around the back.

The odor of garbage piled up outside the kitchen door deadened my nose till I could barely smell vampire any more. I edged past the pile and reached a back door. It was locked, using a standard mortice deadbolt. Any reputable PI would have lockpicks in their pocket and be through that in seconds. I went and checked the windows.

The second one was warped and popped its latch when I pressed it. I opened the window and listened for any response from the house. There were no sounds, but my nose was picking up something else from inside now—the smell of death.

I eased myself in. I was standing in a tiled eating area beside the kitchen. Even in the dark, the place looked filthy. A small, half-assembled motorcycle stood in the corner, the engine lying next to it on old newspapers. Trash covered the table and chairs: clothes, takeout packaging, leftover food and empty beer bottles.

The stench of death was nauseating, swamping everything else. Tiny sounds from neighboring houses filtered in as if they were on a different planet, but this house was still. I knew there was no one alive inside.

Leading with the HK, I made my way carefully through the kitchen. The back door key was hanging from the handle by a string. I unlocked it in case I needed out in a hurry and started checking room by room.

It didn't take long. It was a small house and the scurrying rats led me to him. He was in the living room, lying on the sofa. Judging from the rigor mortis, he had been dead about a day.

I made sure there was no one else in the house and the curtains were tightly closed before going back to him. I paused before using my flashlight. I wanted to use it sparingly because my night vision was so good, and the flashlight would reduce that. Also, there's nothing so suspicious as a flashlight in a dark house. But the main reason was that I didn't want to see him. I've seen my share of deaths, in the army and police. It doesn't get any better, and I had a feeling this would be bad.

Wrapping my hand around the flashlight head and reducing the beam to a red glow, I looked on the ruin that had been Guy Windler. It was every bit as awful as I anticipated. The guy had tried to run me down, but no one deserved to end up like that. His body had shrunk in on itself, not from decay or the normal process of death. He'd been sucked dry of blood. Then his chest had been shattered and his heart torn out of his ribcage. The rats had been at his face and the remainder of his organs. The corpse stunk of vampire.

I made it out the back door and heaved my guts out onto the dusty back yard.

When I could go back inside, I called Morales from the kitchen.

"Farrell, you know what time it is?" I could tell from his harsh whisper that he had been in bed. I heard him close a door.

"Farrell! You there? What's going on?"

"I found Windler, Captain," I managed hoarsely. I could almost feel the sleep clearing from Morales' brain.

We had some prearranged signals dating back to the cover up last year. I went on. "It's snakebite. Real bad. I need your snake experts over at 248 Monroe in Aurora. In a hurry. Don't know if someone's coming to clean up."

"You okay?"

"Yeah," I replied, but I was lying.

"They'll be there in thirty minutes. I'll be there too. Wait for me, Farrell, you hear me?"

"Yes, Captain."

The call cut off and I was left with the rat infested, choking darkness and the dead man. At least Morales hadn't wasted time asking me what I was doing out there on my own. That would come later.

I stood there and thought over the other things my brief glimpse had shown me. The wounds on his throat. The way his hands had stiffened into claws. His shirt had been torn off, and his upper arms were tattooed with rattlesnakes, open mouths and fangs framing the shoulders. That was the gang tattoo of ZK, Zeklesh, the snakemouth gang.

Morales and I had agreed on *snakebite* as a code for vampires. Maybe the association went deeper than that.

Chapter 14

THURSDAY

"Fabulous. You are my hero." I swallowed a mouthful of the coffee Tullah had brought in.

She was looking me over carefully. I guess finding her boss sprawled asleep at her desk in yesterday's clothes was a concern for her.

"At least you don't have any new bruises," she said.

"Damn, I forgot. I was supposed to pick up some more last night."

"What were you doing?"

"Long story. Long night." I stretched. "We tracked down the driver from Crate & Freight. He's dead. Killed by whoever he was working with."

"Not that he didn't deserve it for trying to run you over, but why was he killed? The police have a dozen other drivers in cells. All of them were all doing the same thing."

"Good question, but not quite accurate." I shrugged. "He was the one who was the contact with whoever was running this."

We sat and sipped our coffee. Tullah was showing a good grasp of the business for someone who I'd hired to handle the phones and filing.

Around the time I started as a PI, we'd met and sparred at her father's martial arts classes and had gotten to talking. She'd explained that she had spare time between classes during the day and didn't want to go all the way home or sit in the library. I couldn't really afford her, but somehow it worked. And she brought me coffee in the morning.

"I got your message about looking at a new office, what happened?" I said.

"Oh my God! I'm sitting here in a daze." She leaped out of her chair. "I found the right place yesterday. Umm. I had to take it then and there." She looked anxiously at me. "I've got a guy with a van coming. We're moving in an hour. If that's okay?"

I laughed. "Well, go on, tell me about it."

"It's a little bigger and it's furnished already, so we saved money there. It's not even a hundred a month more in rent. Utility bills are lower than this place. Phones will be transferred in a couple of days. Oh, and there's three months' notice either way."

"Great! Where is it?"

"Colorado Boulevard. Just south of the interstate where East Evans crosses Colorado. Is that going to be okay?"

I raised my eyebrows. That was good for a hundred a month more, and handy for the college.

"It's better than okay, it's fantastic, Tullah. I owe you, big time."

She looked pleased and started to run around, emptying cabinets into cardboard boxes. I helped, and we were finished quickly.

"I'm going to get a shower and then some breakfast," I said and headed out.

Half an hour later, thanks to Sol and the spare clothes in my trunk, I was clean and presentable for my meeting later with Jennifer.

I strolled happily into Papa Dee's. This place was good and I would miss it, I thought, looking around.

Hmm.

I picked up my order and opened my jacket so the shoulder holster would show when I sat down. Then I walked over to sit opposite rabbit face and pushed the screen of his laptop closed.

"It's rude to play with your computer at breakfast," I said, and got out my Sergeant's Smile Number 13—'Unlucky for you'.

"Are you going to tell me why you're following me or do we do this the hard way?" I said through the smile. His eyes—exactly like a frightened rabbit—made a hasty circuit of my face, the next occupied table and the butt of the HK peeking out from beneath my jacket.

"You…you can't threaten me," he stammered. "My office knows where I am."

"Oh, I imagine they do. So, I'm not threatening you. You haven't answered my question." I started working on my breakfast.

My not pinning him to the seat seemed to give him some courage. He reached for his pocket, then froze when I looked up sharply. Very slowly, he put his hand in and drew out an ID and an official letter.

"Lieutenant Henry Krantz," I read aloud. "Army pay administration. And a cover letter from the Department of Veterans Affairs. I'm so impressed. You still haven't answered my question."

"I'm checking on disability compensation payments," he blurted out.

I just looked at him in disbelief. "You're checking the couple of hundred a month that I get?"

"It adds up, Ms. Farrell," he said stiffly. "Even if I accepted the legality of your claim, I've determined that you have no lasting physical injuries pertinent to any claimed operational incidents in service. And whereas it would require a fully qualified assessor to determine your psychiatric state," he paused, glancing nervously at the gun before gathering himself to stutter on, "it would seem that you are fully and gainfully employed as a private investigator which would argue against any lasting psychiatric injury."

I could argue the 'gainful' bit, but I just ate another piece of toast and watched him. I didn't like where this seemed to be leading. Officially, I wasn't in the army any more, despite the fact I was still under orders. They paid me a retainer which they had disguised as a veteran's disability payment.

He licked his lips. "So even if I accepted the legality of your claim, I would adjudge your compensation payment redundant."

"That's the second time you've used that comment about legality. You want to tell me what that's about?"

He seemed to be getting more confident as he went on.

"Your claims are commensurate with a sergeant grade E5 at a 20% rating with no dependents."

I shrugged. I had never claimed anything, but that was the right grade and it was probably what was written in the agreement I had signed.

Krantz tried to hide his triumphant expression. "But there are no salary records for you after boot camp, no army records at all, in fact, until you started claiming. You never made private, Ms. Farrell, let alone sergeant. You were never in the army."

He sat back, satisfied that he'd nailed me.

I finished my breakfast and took a swallow of coffee. It rattled him to see my lack of reaction, but he felt secure enough in his facts to take a sip of his own coffee.

"You don't have the security clearance to see my records," I said.

He laughed and brushed my comment away with a wave of his hand.

"Ridiculous. You're claiming that you were special forces or something? Ms. Farrell, if you'd ever actually been in the army, you would know that the special forces don't recruit women. And anyway, their salary records are still available to me."

I suppressed a flare of anger. "Obviously, not all of them. Just tell me one thing, Krantz. Why would it be worth it?"

This was beyond ridiculous. The money was nothing, but it was upsetting out of all proportion with that. Exasperating.

Krantz leaned forward as if he were about to impart something profound to me.

"I've found out that you're just a small part of a large conspiracy to defraud the taxpayers and divert veterans' money from where it is needed." He licked his lips, and his little rabbit eyes became earnest. "You're probably not aware of it, and the amount may seem trivial to you personally, but I can tell you, I know that this fraud is worth many millions in total. My job at the moment is to find out how the fraud is perpetrated. I'm not really interested in your case, per se. I want to find out the person in the VA department who arranged it and how it works. I mean, how much of a cut do you take and how do you pass the rest back? Who to?"

He rocked back on his chair. "If you make full disclosure I could help. It might never even come to criminal charges."

I just looked at him.

He tried once more. "You applied to join the army once. I'm thinking that showed some patriotism on your part and I applaud that, believe me, I do. Now, think of the damage this fraud is doing to this country. Please, find that patriotism again and help repair the problem."

I jerked him across the table before he realized what was happening. His eyes bulged and he scrabbled futilely against my grip.

"Listen to me, Krantz. Maybe you have found some conspiracy with compensation payments. Maybe it is worth a lot and it needs fixing. But don't you ever come around here telling me I'm part of it, and don't you ever, *ever* dare suggest I'm unpatriotic."

I threw him back into his chair and walked out. Every eye in the place was on me. It wasn't the way I'd have wanted to say goodbye to Papa Dee's, but at that moment, I didn't care.

I walked slowly back to the office. Tullah's van driver was there getting our things loaded. She sensed I wasn't in a talking mood and just gave me the address of the new office to pass on to Jennifer.

I had to scrub this out of my mind. I needed to be thinking clearly at lunchtime. Jennifer wasn't going to be happy with what I had to say.

Chapter 15

Jennifer arrived at the new office at noon. I heard her talking to Tullah and I walked out to greet her.

"Hi, Amber!" She turned on her pin-sharp Italian heels and gave me a big smile. She was wearing another beautiful dress, medium blue this time, simple and elegant, with a plain jacket.

I wasn't quite sure whether to shake her hand or kiss her on the cheek. We had been very informal with each other, but there's a certain distance you should keep from clients. I didn't want to make any assumptions.

She solved the problem by kissing me on both cheeks, European style.

"Hi Jen," I replied. "Thanks for coming over. What do you think of the new office?"

"I like it. Nice and bright. Easy for me to get to as well."

"Thanks. It's all thanks to Tullah. She found the place and did the deal." Tullah smiled shyly.

I motioned to my office. "Let's go sit down."

"Oh, honey, I booked a table for lunch," Jennifer said.

I must have looked hesitant, because she pressed on quickly.

"It's at the Moulin. It's a booth, so it'll be private." She paused. "I thought it would be easier if I run you out to Silver Hills from there afterwards."

"Ah, okay." I hadn't dressed for lunch, I'd dressed for the office and visiting the site of the planned resort. Not really up to the Moulin, which was another of those restaurants I'd heard about but couldn't afford. I ran a hand through my hair. "Give me a few moments and I'll get some stuff."

I went back to my office and took the Walther PPK and holster from the safe. It doesn't have the stopping power of the HK, but it's smaller and lighter and it fits better under a jacket. That's the reason James Bond favors it. Then again, he wouldn't have been caught dead in the sloppy jacket I put on.

I ran a comb through my hair, made sure it was neatly caught in its tie and looked in the mirror. At least the worst of the bruising was gone. Sigh. I grabbed my preliminary notes and investigation gear and rejoined Jennifer. Tullah gave me a big grin and a wave as we left.

I expected the chauffeur to be waiting for us outside and stopped for a second to look around, but Jennifer strode briskly to another car. My jaw unhinged itself. I went over and stroked it. It was all I could do not to lick the thing, it was so gorgeous.

"Are you getting in it or getting off on it?" asked Jennifer, laughing.

"Okay, okay, I'll get in." Her laughter was infectious. "This will definitely be the first time I've ever gotten in a pink car!"

It wasn't just any car either, it was the top of the line Mercedes roadster. It was already a fun car with outrageous performance. And then Jennifer Kingslund bought one and painted it a deep and dusty pink. I slid down into the pale leather seat and wriggled with pleasure.

She gunned the engine and we joined the traffic with a little chirp from the fat tires. The roof folded away. I relaxed and enjoyed the ride. We were laughing and chatting, but she drove with precision.

Far too soon, we pulled up in front of the Moulin. Jennifer tossed the keys to the valet, grabbed my arm and marched us in.

Most of the top end, one-off restaurants in Denver are to be found downtown or around shopping areas. The Moulin had bucked the trend and gone outside the boundary of Interstate 70 to a lot with a view of Peaks Park and the Foothills Country Club.

They'd avoided making any architectural suggestion of it actually being a mill, and settled for a lovely open space format with split levels and booths on top looking out over some lawns and a garden, with the park beyond. The glossy warm ochre of the floor tiles caught the sunshine and made the place glow.

If the maître d' thought I wasn't dressed for it, he didn't even blink. His eyes lit up at the sight of Jennifer and he came out and made a tremendous fuss over her. She was obviously a frequent diner here and she spoke fluently to him in French. While his back was turned for a moment, I caught a smile from her and a roll of the eyes.

"Stop that," I whispered. "You absolutely love it."

With more commotion than I'd ever had in all my years of visiting restaurants, we were eventually settled in our booth with spritzers and two orders for light meals on the way.

Jennifer took a long drink, looking out over the tended garden. Her face became serious.

"Okay," she said. "Fun over for the moment. We need to go through how it's looking."

I nodded and retrieved my notes. I didn't normally need them, but I'd had very little time for the wide range of things I had been looking at. The financials in particular, which I'd gone through last night in a desperate bid to clear my mind of the scene at Monroe Street.

"I'll start with Troy?" I looked up and Jennifer nodded.

"Captain Morales appears to be aware that I'm retained by you. Is it okay to share information with him?"

"Of course, but thank you for asking."

I tapped the notes. "Victor's tracked down Troy's friends from the cycling community. He missed a race he was signed up for, first time ever that they can recall. He hasn't made any contact with his family back east. Captain Morales tells me that it was blood on the carpet. Troy's keys were under the sofa." I waited a beat. "I think we can be sure that he was abducted. The security cameras were turned off at the time and no one can remember seeing or hearing anything. That tells me it was planned and done professionally."

Jennifer cleared her throat. "Was this done to get at me, or is there something in Troy's background I don't know about?"

I looked at the file in front of me, but didn't open it. "Jen, there's nothing Victor found in Troy's life outside of work that would warrant anything like this. No gambling debts, no secret vices. The worst we can pull up is his father wanted him to go into the family business and there was a big bust-up."

"And?" It struck me how like David she was. She knew I had something to say and was delaying saying it.

"His friends say he was infatuated with you." I sipped the spritzer to wet my mouth. "They also believe that you used that to keep him when he got an unbelievable offer from the Jardines chain in California."

Jennifer turned a furious gaze on me. "I've told you—"

I held a hand up to stop her, and she immediately backed down. "No. Sorry, Amber. You didn't say what you believe. And it doesn't matter what you believe, it's what they believe."

"I don't think you are at all the type of person to use sex to keep a key employee from leaving," I said. "And Troy never told anyone that. Quite the opposite. But the more Troy denied it, the more his friends believed it."

Jennifer stared out at the gardens, still angry.

"So, as an outside party," I went on, "I could easily identify the Golden Harvest as your signature restaurant in your home town. If I got the mistaken impression that you were also involved with Troy, abducting him would be an easy way to cause disruption and financial damage, at least for a time."

The appetizers arrived, and we paused while they were laid in front of us. I ate and continued the briefing. God, I hadn't gotten near the hard parts yet.

"Victor's still working on Troy. But I'm afraid I have to say, every day that goes by means less hope." I stopped and saw the shadow in her eyes as she took that on board.

Looking down, I flicked the notes. "On to other staff. I've looked at the rest of them who've left. I've only managed to talk to a few, but, with one exception, I think it's a waste of my time and your money."

"So why is the turnover rate going up?" she snapped.

"It *has* gone up. I'm not sure it's *still* going up," I replied. "I would lay the blame on your HR department, and your recent takeover of Frankell-Maines."

"Blame stops on my desk, Amber. What's your reason?"

"Mixing different cultures." I was reaching here. It said private investigator on my business card, not business analyst. But as a sergeant previously responsible for getting boys and girls from different parts of the armed forces to play nicely, I had an appreciation for the flashpoints caused by even minor differences in the way things get done.

"On top of that," I went on, "there are large salary differences between the parts of your company since the takeover. The former employees I talked to were well aware of what people doing the same jobs were getting in the PR division."

Jennifer looked thoughtful and we were silent again as the wait staff cleared the first course. "The exception you mentioned?" she asked when they were gone.

"I want to talk to Geoff Hansen, who left the financial department. Just a gut feeling."

She nodded, her cool blue eyes hooded. The main course came and we ate in silence for a while. The food was excellent, much more pleasurable than the next part of the conversation was likely to be.

"Finances," Jennifer said simply and my stomach tensed. I had been given a lot of information, down to the intended target for her next takeover, Tucker Beacon, a company run by a local boy made good, Jack Tucker.

"All I have are the files you gave me, so maybe I'm missing something." I took a deep breath. "You haven't got the cash to build a resort, let alone take over Tucker's company. You can barely keep the PR division afloat in today's climate. You can't get the kind of backing you'll need from the banks without losing control."

Jennifer threw back her head and laughed.

Diners looked up from their meals. Wait staff glanced and went back to work. The maître d' beamed at us from his strangely ecclesiastical pulpit; happy eaters meant good business, and people noticing that Jennifer Kingslund ate at the Moulin was even better.

When she had the laughter under control, she leaned across and squeezed my hand. "I'm sorry, that was so rude. I'm repaid for my suspicious nature. I haven't given you all the figures, and on what I gave you, your analysis is actually right, but there should have been no way you could have been able to come to that conclusion."

She dived into her bag and pulled out a single page summary which was close to mine, except for a section under the title 'war chest'. I pulled mine out from my file and laid them side by side.

Jennifer ran through the figures and wrote in an amendment on my summary for the war chest, which raised the cash available enormously. She waited expectantly as I scribbled in the margins.

I scratched my head. This was like being back at school. "With the banks coming in at a funding you should be able to sustain over three years, you could clear the costs of your resort, but I still don't see that you can take Tucker at the same time."

She grinned. "Wrong way around, Amber."

I frowned and looked at the figures again. "No, even if you delay building the resort, you still can't take Tucker as well." I thought it through and added, "Well, not at the valuation you've quoted, unless you have a different deal with a bank or partner taking much more of the business."

"Hell, no, honey. The banks can go whistle." She finished her last bite and took a sip of spritzer. When she spoke again, it was very quietly. "I might not develop Silver Hills, but the threat of it has already knocked fifteen percent off Tucker's valuation. He put a huge investment into his resort and it's not doing well. Tucker's overextended, he's hurting and he's eager to sell. But only so long as everyone thinks Silver Hills is going to be built."

I could see the plan. Without being on the inside and having a better feel for the businesses involved, there was little I could add to this, so I just shrugged. "Okay, let's leave the big picture for the moment," I said. "On what I was supposed to be looking at, well, I need to check some of these figures in more depth and go through your analyses to see if there's been any fraud."

"I'm surprised you got this much of a handle on it this soon. It's important, Amber, but not as much as Troy." She smiled. "And there's a job for you with me if you get tired of being an investigator."

"Thanks." I filed the amended summaries away and cleared my throat. "There's something I have to ask. Why bother with this? You've spent money on a resort you don't intend to build and you're working to take over Tucker Beacon, which will stress your company finances to the limit. It's not as if they have things you don't. There's no synergy. Both companies are running lean, so you won't be able to find savings. It doesn't make sense. Why do it?"

Her eyes were icy again. "Remind me who's running the multi-million dollar company and who's running the one-woman agency?"

I held up my hands in surrender. "I've only been going a year, of course," I said by way of defense.

She laughed, the tension vanishing as quickly as it had come. "I'll tell Bell and Hewitt to watch out. Anyway, it's in motion. Jack and I made a statement this morning. I let him say we're working toward a merger, to salve his pride, but I'm buying."

We ended the meal in better humor than I had anticipated. Talking to Jennifer was like riding a tiger: unpredictable and exciting, but you wouldn't want to fall off.

She waved for the check. "Let's go see the resort."

And all the weird stuff, I thought.

Chapter 16

"You speak French well," I remarked as we headed away from the restaurant and back down to I-70. I'd been afraid that the maître d' wasn't going to let us go, he seemed so happy to speak in his native tongue.

"I was at college at the Sorbonne in Paris."

"Studying?"

"Philosophy." She chuckled. "Blame it all on that. Hell, after three years you never get your head straight again."

She didn't ask what I had done, luckily. Or maybe she already knew that I left school early.

As we turned up into the foothills along US 285, Jennifer gunned the engine and the car responded smoothly. Jennifer drove fast. If we'd had wings, we would have been flying. I loved it, but like a lot of enjoyable things, there's a law against it.

"So how much have you racked up in speeding fines?" I asked.

"Not a single dollar, honey. But I have to say, I don't get the chance to drive as often as I would like, so this is a treat for me. Thanks for the excuse."

"My pleasure," I said. The sheer exhilaration from being driven in a fast, comfortable car on a sunny day, with the roof down, had lifted my spirits.

"You know," Jennifer said, "you're the second most relaxed person I've ever had in the passenger seat."

I laughed and waved it off. "You know what you're doing." But my curiosity was aroused. "So, who's the first?"

"That was my last husband."

"He liked your driving?"

"Hell, no, he only ever came with me the once. He had gotten so roaring drunk I had to knock him unconscious and take him to the hospital."

I put back my head and laughed up at the bright blue sky. I hadn't enjoyed myself so much for a long time.

All too soon, we turned off 285 and drove a ways up a couple of small roads that became a track barred by a gate. Jennifer unlocked it and parked by a cluster of containers and temporary site buildings that I recognized from the security footage. It had rained up here last night and the ground was still soft. The Mercedes handled it well, but it was going to need cleaning when we got back. I could see a mess of prints over the muddy soil, mostly erased by rain and wind and other people.

I grabbed my evidence kit out of the back and slung it over my shoulder. Jennifer changed her heels for running shoes.

"What are you going to do?" asked Jennifer.

"Me? I'm going to see what wolves do in the woods," I said, walking off to where the incoming prints had seemed to come from or return to—it was such a mess that it wasn't possible to make out much.

They headed uphill as far as I could tell, into a green and gold wall of fluttering aspen leaves, broken here and there by bands of the darkest green pine, so that's where I went.

We walked into the woods and I filled my lungs with the sweet, clean smell of aspen and pine. I loved it. It smelled of carefree days out walking with the family. Whole bright, dreamy days when my greatest burden was mom or dad's hand occasionally resting on my shoulder. I shook that pleasant memory off. I was here to do a job and I was responsible for Jen's safety as well.

"Is it dangerous?" Jennifer didn't seem concerned. I would have been okay with it if she had stayed in the car, but I liked it that she was confident enough to come with me.

In truth, I didn't know how dangerous it was. The colonel had given me a warning about werewolves and I didn't see what else it could be, not with the size of them, the stone breaking the camera and that bare human leg. Did they prowl up here in daylight? The work crew hadn't reported anything like that, but they'd only been in one spot.

I was sure Hollywood didn't portray the werewolf any more accurately than the vampire. I'd put trust in small lumps of lead delivered at high speed to dissuade anything from bothering us. But I'd chosen the little Walther over the HK because of the shape of my jacket. Dumb decision.

"What's safe?" I said.

She gave up on that. "So, what do you mean exactly—what they do in the woods?"

"Well, everyone knows what bears do in the woods?" She nodded, smiling. "Let's see if wolves do too."

I followed what trail I could, casting around where it was lost on pine needles or rock until I found it again. Jennifer was a help once she understood what we were looking for, and she had sharp eyes and a good nose.

I scraped bark off trees where it smelled. I found pungent scat dumps and they went into my little sample bottles as well. I took photos of every paw print that was clear, dropping a little ruler next to each. For the best of the huge paw prints, I took casts with quick setting foam.

Squirrels scrabbled up trees to escape us and jays shrieked abuse down on our heads.

Further in, the woods took on a different character. Here, there were no squirrels and jays. It was sacred-quiet, dominated by pine, and the thick green foliage made deep shadows where we walked. The wind sighed. Our feet pressed silently into soft beds of old pine needles. Our voices dropped to a whisper and I caught myself glancing over my shoulder. I wasn't so much concerned with what I could see as with what I couldn't. There was something here. My estimation of danger rose with every step, and I mentally kicked myself. It was one thing to have come out here on my own, quite another to expose Jennifer to risk. I loosened the Walther in its holster.

It was a relief to see the pine finally thinning out and cottonwood, juniper and aspen coming back. As we emerged from the dark into dappled sunlight, a shadow swept over us like a falling blade. We both jumped. A hawk soared up, screaming protest at our disturbance, and we laughed nervously.

We ended up at the edge of a small cliff. The trail pointed to this rocky outcrop as a focus. I looked over the side. It was around ninety feet, not a big climb, but nothing got up here on four legs. About a mile away, I could see a dirt track an SUV could manage.

"This is called Falcon Bluff," Jen said. "The foot of it marks the edge of my property on this side."

She stood with her eyes closed for a while, the afternoon sun turning her face golden and blissful.

"So, what do you think?" she said finally.

"I think your land is beautiful, Jen." That earned me a jab in the ribs.

"Okay, okay," I said. "Maybe you were right, you've got weird. I'll know more when the results come back."

She seemed satisfied with that for the moment.

I stepped up onto the highest rock and tried to think myself into a werewolf's head. The wind brought me the dry scents of early fall with their thin promise of coming cold. Animals stirred to the change of season. Below, the dirt track wound in and out of the woods like a lazy snake in the afternoon sun. I looked down at it and imagined getting a pack of Weres to drive out there, climb up here in human form, then change to go party down where the containers were. Why?

I shut my eyes and imagined the night, the moon, the commotion of fur, the rising excitement. The call hanging in the cold night air. The heart-racing chase through the still woods.

Jennifer walked around below me. I looked down on her as an intruder, with the sun behind my head, and saw her through a wolf's eyes.

"It would be a mistake to build a resort here." I had no idea why I said that. It wasn't appropriate, even if it was what I thought.

I gave myself a little shake and got off my rock. *Where the hell did all that come from?*

Jennifer didn't notice or didn't mind. She squinted up at me. "I have no intention, really. I don't even want a cell tower out here. I just need Jack to think I'm building." I could see her face clearly and I knew this was the truth, even though she shouldn't have been telling me.

We began to retrace our steps, warily.

The sun was lower and its angle made the woods lighter. They had none of the spookiness we'd felt on the way up. Without the need to stop and keep finding the wolf tracks, we were back in twenty minutes, without any scares.

At the edge of the trees, I paused and touched the trunk of one, like my dad always had. I felt the memory of his hand ruffle my hair.

I put the kit away in the trunk of the Mercedes, looking around longingly at the wooded hills. Maybe I could get Jennifer's okay to come out here and go running.

So, it was scary. I liked scary.

For a couple of minutes, I had been vaguely aware of the sound of a pickup truck getting closer and I saw a black Dodge nosing through the gates below. I came back from daydreaming with a start. A prickle of apprehension raised the hairs on my neck and my bracelet tingled.

"Jen, is there any way they're lost?"

"No, nothing else up this road. Amber, I—"

"Get in the car! If it goes badly, if you need to, use the car like a weapon, run them down, whatever, but get away."

"Amber, what are you going to do?"

"I'm going to try and run them off. Stay with the car. Try the cell."

I shoved her towards the driver's seat and started walking down quickly. They were about a hundred yards away and I cursed when I realized that the reason they had stayed down there was to block the gate.

I had the Walther, but it was worse than useless at that distance. It would only alert them and they might have a rifle or shotgun in that pickup. What I needed to do was close with them, without them realizing I was armed. The Walther doesn't look like a gun until it's right in your face.

Two men got out, and the driver stayed in the pickup. Eighty yards. The taller of the two coming towards me had a beak of a nose, a hard, square jaw and deep frown lines etched on a heavy forehead above a tanned face. His hair was thick and black, held back in a ponytail. His eyebrows met without a break above narrowed eyes. The shorter man had the sort of barrel shape that sometimes hides great strength. His hair lay in greasy rings on his shoulders. His fingers were swollen like a drowned man and in his right hand he was carrying a baseball bat. Sixty yards.

"Hey, guys, this is private land," I called out. "I'm going to have to ask you to leave."

Onebrow was dressed in brown with a tailored jacket and city shoes, getting all muddy. Deadhand was in biker gear, black denim vest and old blue jeans tucked into big black boots. Beneath a black T, snake tattoos wound around his upper arms. Forty yards.

Their attention was all focused on me and they were grinning, relaxed and confident. Onebrow said something, pointing at me. "Too fucking flat," Deadhand shouted, laughing. "I'll hold her for you. I want the blonde." He shook out his right arm as if stepping up to bat. Twenty yards. Time to rumble. My limbs became loose and relaxed.

I heard the Mercedes snarl into life behind me and I surged forward as their attention flicked up the hill. I picked Deadhand as the closer.

"Shit!" he shouted, and swung the bat reflexively. He was quicker than he looked and he struck me a glancing blow on the top of my head as I ducked. His startled movement twisted him around too far and he was off balance when my shoulder crashed into his ribs with all my downhill momentum behind it. By the time he hit the ground I had the Walther out and pointed at Onebrow's face.

"Tell him to stay down and get the jerk out of the pickup or I'll shoot you where you stand."

At five yards, a Walther looks like a real gun, and any gun's muzzle looks like Death's own eye when you're looking at it. His hand stopped on the way into his jacket and crept back down.

"Benny, out of the truck," Onebrow called hoarsely over his shoulder. His eyes didn't leave my face.

Deadhand lurched up. I shot his knee out and had the gun pointing back at Onebrow's face before he was back down on the ground again. Benny froze where he was, half out of the pickup.

"Benny gets here in five or you lose your face," I said. "Five."

"Benny! Get here now, shithead!"

Benny scuttled over in response to Onebrow's command and made it before I got to three. He was younger and smaller than the others, pale-faced and shaking. I took this in while keeping my eyes on Onebrow. I judged him an evil bastard and he was the most dangerous of the three by far. Behind me, I heard the Mercedes come down the hill and stop. It was to my right from the sound, but I didn't dare look to see. As long as Jennifer didn't get in front of me, it was fine.

I pointed with the Walther slightly lower, at Onebrow's chest. "Now open that jacket slowly and take the gun out with just your thumb and finger touching it. Slowly. Just the thumb and finger."

Onebrow obeyed carefully while I studied him for twitches or tells. The thought that it would be easier just to shoot him had crossed my mind and he knew it.

"Hold it out to the side. Put it down on the ground, gently." It looked like a 9mm Glock. "Now, both of you, drag this heap of shit ten yards back." I kicked Deadhand where he was groaning on the ground, clutching his leg.

He squealed as they pulled him back. I'd drilled the shot right through the kneecap and any movement of the leg was going to hurt him for a long time. Good.

"Jen?"

"I'm in the car, Amber. About ten yards behind you. I didn't get a signal on the cell." Her voice was strained but steady.

"Go across to the pickup and take out anything that looks like a weapon or a cell phone. And anything else that looks interesting."

While she did that and I picked up the Glock, I made them empty their pockets.

There were four options here as I saw it. I could shoot them and leave them for the animals to clean up, but I don't work like that. I could torture them and find out who sent them. That turned my stomach even more. I could get Jennifer to drive down the road and call the police. There's no way this scum would be able to turn the legal tables on us, but pinning them down with a charge of aggravated assault would be difficult and time-consuming. Turning to the police also sent a message to their bosses, and it wasn't the message I wanted sent. I took the fourth option.

After Jennifer had finished, I had them drag Deadhand over and load him into the pickup, screeching complaints about his leg until Onebrow snapped at him. Benny took off his belt and used it as a tourniquet on Deadhand's leg, then sat with him in the back. I got Onebrow to climb into the driver's seat. He'd been quiet practically the whole time, watching me closely. I had no doubt that if I'd slipped up, he would have been on me. He was the leader of this group and looked like a man who held grudges to the grave.

I was pointing both guns at the bridge of his nose.

"You look like you've got a good memory. When you think of me, remember Death's eyes staring at you." I clicked the barrels together slightly to make the point. "You see that again, and it will be the last thing you see. I don't care who sent you or why. Tell them, next time there will be no knee shots, no survivors. Now, get the fuck out of here."

Onebrow started up and drove down the road, spinning the wheels in the mud. I walked behind a little way, making sure he could see that I was still pointing the guns at them. They turned the corner and I listened carefully as the sound of the engine faded away. No stopping.

I let the tension out of my shoulders. It was one thing to do something like this with a squad behind me and serious firepower, quite another to be facing down three guys with a couple of small bore handguns.

I turned, sticking the Walther back in the holster and the Glock in my jacket pocket. Jennifer was standing behind me, pale and shivering with reaction. I gave her a hug.

"You okay?" I said.

She nodded. "What about you? He hit you, I saw..." She reached up and touched the side of my head gently.

"Ow! Damn, more bruises." I caught her wrist. "It's okay, really, just a glancing blow."

"Amber, you were fantastic! You just walked up and..."

I touched her lips with a finger and stopped her. "It's what I was trained to do, so it's not fantastic. You haven't been, so I'm much more impressed by how well you reacted."

I turned abruptly and started walking back up to the site, embarrassed. What the hell was I thinking?

I got some evidence bags from my kit and gathered all the things off the ground. Jen had found a cell phone in the pickup and some scribbled notes which I wanted to look at. There was also a second Glock and a handful of spare ammo. The contents of their pockets included wallets and cell phones. And a photo of Jen. Until the moment I saw that, I'd had a horrible doubt they might have been after me and I'd put her at risk.

I turned all the cells off and had a look at the notes, which gave directions to Silver Hills.

"Who knows you're out here, Jen?"

"You and me. I didn't tell my assistant where I was going to be."

"You have your cell on this afternoon?"

"Not till I tried to call the police. I turned it off at the restaurant and didn't bother putting it back on. It's usually a waste up here. Why?"

I sighed and lay down to look underneath the car. "Someone tracked us."

After five minutes of rolling round and getting my jacket filthy, I spotted something out of place. There was a small box hidden above the back bumper—a tracking device of some kind.

I had Jen drive back down to the highway and away from Denver. At a truck stop, I stuck the tracker on a logging truck and we turned around and headed for Jen's home overlooking the Denver Country Club.

On the way, I called Victor and arranged for Jen to have a permanent bodyguard, overruling her arguments. The attack on her company had escalated to attacks on her. Until we found out who was behind this, we could only expect more attempts and I couldn't be there all the time.

Chapter 17

It was a little after 6 p.m. when we rolled in through the automatic gates of Jen's house. The sign said it was called Manassah.

My head was in threat assessment mode, looking at ways that an intruder might be able to get in over fences, through windows and doors, so I barely looked at the house itself to start with.

When Victor's team arrived and started their own sweep, I was able to stand back and appreciate how beautiful it was. I knew Jen used a company apartment close to the office sometimes when she worked late, but she'd mentioned it felt like staying at a hotel. Here, she had stamped her individuality on the place. This was where she would live most of the time when she was in Denver. If she entertained, it would be here. Her ranch was more a private weekend retreat.

By the end of the inspection, any thoughts of entertaining were being frowned on, and the downtown apartment was being proposed as an easier place to secure. Jen wasn't having any of that, and a compromise was reached where three guards were based on the grounds, as well as one in a control center and one on the gate. All of them on maximum six hour shifts.

I winced at the expense, but Jen signed it off.

While they were setting up, she pulled me aside.

"Amber, what's happened to cause this?"

I shrugged. "I don't know what's changed, Jen. The obvious thing is we've called the police in on Troy's abduction, so they know you're aware of them, whoever they are. I don't know why that should have escalated the situation, but clearly the threat is now being directed against you."

"I hired you. That's new."

"But no one knew that except you, me, your driver maybe. And Tullah, of course."

Two of the guards came in carrying bulky equipment and we had to squeeze together to let them pass in the corridor.

Jen cleared her throat. "They tracked us to Silver Hills."

"I've already had your other cars checked for trackers," I said. "But I guess they could have followed you the old-fashioned way to our meeting at Whitman's."

We moved into her living room and perched on a couple of chairs while the guards wandered in and out checking comms equipment and blind spots.

"You surprised me at the resort," Jen said. "I mean how you dealt with them at the end. Do you intend to call the police about it?"

"Not unless you really want to. I know, I'm not being consistent here. I told you that we'd report any felonies."

"That's okay," she said. "I trust you. I'll go with your lead on this. I just need to understand why."

"With hindsight, maybe it was a bad call," I answered slowly. "But I wanted to send a message back to whoever sent them. And I want to know who that was, not have that disappear into some legal case we can't get access to, that never gets proved, or nails some low-level thugs. I'll find plenty in the stuff we took. These are gang members, not professionals. Except maybe Onebrow."

"Onebrow?"

I grinned. "Old habit of mine. Onebrow is my name for the leader. Deadhand was the guy I shot—his hands are all puffy, they look like a drowned man's. And the driver was called Benny, apparently."

Jen looked away, as if unsure about what she was going to say. "I think you could have found out directly who was giving the orders."

"Probably. Yes. I know the techniques." I frowned. "I'm not a nice person, Jen."

She snorted. "There's a contradiction in that reasoning. Anyway, I wouldn't have stopped you. I heard what that fat bastard said. Hell, I would have helped. What would that make me? No, Amber, knowing and doing are whole different countries." She waved it off, settling back in her chair and frowning in thought, her hands running restlessly up and down the armrests.

"Can you stay here as well?" she said. "There's a guest suite just across from mine. Please?"

I had been wondering where I would be sleeping that night. I wanted to stay away from Mrs. Desiarto's, but I felt I could really use a good night's sleep, and the thought of the office or the back of my car wasn't appealing. It was an enormous temptation to camp here while I worked on Jen's case, but it broke all sorts of rules in my Private Investigation 101 book. Some of the indecision must have shown on my face.

"I would feel so much safer, Amber. I'm sure these other guys know what they're doing, but I've seen you in action. There's the most wonderful bathtub in the suite, as well. Meals when you want them. And it would make briefings easier, wouldn't it?"

I chuckled, thinking I knew how Captain Morales felt the other night. At least she'd relaxed a bit, and it would be easier operating from here.

"The bathtub sold it," I said. "I need it now. But then I have to go and sort out some stuff. I'll be back late tonight. Could your driver drop me off at my office to pick up my car, please?"

"Done." She organized keys and access codes. Her maid brought towels and a robe, and took my muddy clothes away, promising to get them back to me later.

What a bathtub! It was sunk into the floor and had lights under the water. The surrounds were Italian marble and, during the day, I would have been able to look out over the gardens through picture windows. Realizing Victor's guards were out there somewhere, I closed the blinds. The maid had the water running and added something scented and bubbly while I was undressing. I eased myself into the heat. Oh, bliss. I decided immediately that my life needed more hot baths like this.

Half an hour later, slightly dizzy but smelling so much better, I wandered back to the living room in my borrowed robe, combing out my hair.

Jen was flicking through a report, but she tossed it to one side and sprang up.

"You look almost relaxed, Amber. Your clothes will be a little while. A drink while you wait?" She arched an eyebrow at me as she walked over to a well-stocked bar.

"Rum. Straight, please," I said. "A dark rum," I added as I saw the array of bottles.

She came back with my rum and a brandy for herself. "Guyanese fifteen-year-old," she said casually, handing mine across. "Should be dark enough."

I sipped the golden brown liquor and let the smooth, warm taste run around my mouth. Heaven. It exploded across my tongue: a mouthful of molasses with a kiss of vanilla and orange peel. I closed my eyes, savoring it. Wow. I'd never realized the difference between the rum I could afford and the kind of stuff people like Jen drank.

We sat and sipped for a while, completely comfortable with the silence. I put my legs up on a stool. I was going to have trouble kicking my ass off this sofa later, but I didn't care. I had never been in such a luxurious house, but instead of feeling awkward, I felt at home, thanks to the rum, the bath, Jen herself, or the combination.

Jen took some freshly made tapas from the bar and set it on the sofa between us. I bit into a smoky stuffed pepper. Another 'wow'. The flavor was delicate and almost overpowering at the same time—it made every other stuffed pepper I'd eaten seem tasteless by comparison.

"God, these are unbelievable," I muttered.

Jen gave me an odd look. "Oh, Carmen made them. Glad you like them."

She wasn't being dismissive, exactly. She was probably just so used to expensive ingredients and a gourmet cook she'd forgotten what normal food tasted like. I needed to shut up or she'd think I lived on McDonald's. I might have gotten all defensive at that thought, but I was distracted by the piece of crispy fried calamari I'd popped into my mouth. I just managed to not groan.

"Is there any link between this attack and the weird stuff?" Jen asked, interrupting my private food orgy.

I sat up and shrugged. "Too early to tell."

"What's really out there, Amber?"

"I'm sorry, I need a bit more time."

"No, I'm not being clear. I don't mean just at Silver Hills, I mean generally. What's out there and how come you're an expert?"

I struggled. I wanted to talk to someone other than the Obs team or Captain Morales, but besides the danger of Jen regarding me as a lunatic, there was always the threat of that isolation cell back at Obs if they knew I was involving civilians in the 'weird' stuff.

As if she read the conflict in my face, Jen leaned across and squeezed my arm.

"It's okay. A woman of mysteries. I'm a very patient person, Amber. Tell me when you're ready."

I smiled my thanks at her and chased the salty garlic olives with another sip of the rum.

"You mentioned the last husband," I said to change the subject. "Do you have someone else lined up in your sights?"

She laughed. "Hell, no! After what he cost me? No way. What about you?"

"Oh, I'm between guys at the moment."

"Sounds kinky." She raised her eyebrows at me, pretending to look shocked.

"You know what I meant." I tried to glare at her and we ended up giggling, but at least that was better than my blushing.

"What about where you live?" she said. "Do you have a house?"

"No. I rent a room down in Aurora. Never thought of buying. Well, to tell the truth, I never met a banker drunk enough to lend me money, at the same time I was drunk enough to borrow."

Jen waggled the rum bottle. "I'm sure I could rustle up a banker," she said.

I sighed. "An evening getting drunk with a banker. So tempting, but no, thank you. I've got to—"

"Yes, you said," she stopped me.

The maid came in to say that my clothes were ready, except for my jacket. Crawling around on the ground had gotten stains on it, and she was very sorry, but they wouldn't come out and she was afraid it was ruined.

"I have a jacket you can use," Jen said. "It was...well anyway, never been used. Should fit you."

By the time I was dressed and back in the living room, Jen had brought it out.

"I can't take this, Jen." I held it, but couldn't put it on. It was the most beautiful leather jacket I had ever seen. It was soft brown, lined with silk and had a dramatic double collar. It had to be worth a month's pay for me.

"Of course you can," she insisted. "Your jacket got ruined on my case, so it's my responsibility. Anyway, it's too cold outside without something."

She eased it on despite my protestations and zipped it up halfway. It fit perfectly. A hesitant look crossed her face for a second, but then she smiled.

"There," she said. "Go out and do your stuff. I'll see you later, maybe."

The driver came in to collect me, and there didn't seem to be time to argue any more. I went out wondering how I was going to pay for this. I had learned that lesson early in life. There's nothing without a cost.

Chapter 18

Jen's driver was called Kingston, that much I learned on the way down to the office. Beyond that he was very quiet. Still, as he drove away, he left me feeling lonely. And cold. I was glad of the jacket.

Tullah would have called me if anything important had come in during the day, but out of habit I checked my email and messages. There was a routine update from Victor on the search for Troy. They still hadn't found him, so I just skimmed it. All it gave were a list of possibilities that they had discounted. He would be including Jen in future communications now.

I got out the colonel's information about the ZK rave and logged onto one of the announcement sites. After a couple of false trails, I tracked down the address where it was being held. It was an old shopping mall, too small and too close to the giants to survive. It had a large delivery area beneath it that was ideal for the rave. No neighbors within hearing. The police's only concern would be drugs, so they would probably take a light touch approach unless things got out of hand.

I wouldn't be leaving my car near this rave tomorrow. Besides the potential for damage, I knew the police regularly noted license plates and I wanted to keep off all those databases. The new office was two minutes' walk from Colorado Boulevard's Light Rail station, and the rave was about five from Dry Creek station. I would leave the car here and take the train.

ZK were running it, but the sound and light show were going to be from a couple of teams called Electric Breath and Beat Gear. I rubbed my head— I knew them and that combo meant a hardcore dance event. At least I wouldn't look out of place in my standard clothes. Some raves I had to look like a vampire to blend in, and the humor of it was kinda lost on me.

I closed the computer down. From the drawer in my new desk I took the blood test machine and strapped it to my arm. A couple of minutes later it confirmed to me that it had edged up another point to 0.43. It wasn't anything to get concerned about yet. I wanted to keep checking it at different times to see if there was anything I did or felt that gave a different reading.

After stripping and cleaning it, I swapped the Walther for the Heckler Koch in the safe. Along with the Walther, I put in all the things we'd taken from the three men out at Silver Hills except for the two Glocks, which I also cleaned and wrapped in plastic bags. Then I locked up and walked to my car with the Glocks in a cardboard box.

Morales wanted to talk this evening, and it wasn't too late. I sent him a text asking him if he wanted to meet or talk to me on my cell, tonight or tomorrow. He came back right away with a request to meet him at Monroe at 11 p.m. Oh good, another late night.

At least that gave me enough time to visit my storage facility, which was my other task for the evening.

I reached under the center of the dash, behind my modified GPS navigation system, and retrieved an ID card identifying me as Mrs. Abigail Welchester, along with a key to Abigail's unit at the Central Self Store down near Union Station. I'd accidentally kept some of my fake documentation when I left the army. Bad girl.

If the guy at the gatehouse wondered why Mrs. Welchester should be visiting her storage unit so late, he hid it well. My key opened the gate and he barely glanced up as I drove down the streets of padlocked containers. At the cheap end, my small unit was in the middle of a row of a dozen identical ones, only the number stenciled on the front identifying it. Damn, but it was like being back in the army.

I put the Glocks in, alongside the shotgun I wasn't supposed to have either.

It was dark and the nearest spotlight shed no light in this locker, but my night vision was good. I could see my past life, hanging or neatly folded, sealed in plastic or tidied into boxes. All done and packed away.

My army uniform hung from the rail at the top. The uniform that Krantz said I never wore, the uniform that the army said I should no longer wear, the uniform that I spent ten hard years earning. I unzipped the plastic cover and slipped my hand in to count the stripes on the sleeves and to reassure myself it wasn't all a dream.

Then I slammed the door closed and rested my forehead on the cold, uncaring metal.

There was a damned good reason I left the uniforms down here. They reminded me of everything I'd lost. On top of that, now Krantz was telling me I had never been in the army. In Ops 4-10 I'd signed up for secret operations, but I couldn't believe how much pain it caused me to realize what most people would believe: there was no record, so I couldn't have been there. Nothing left.

Give it all up, I thought. Why shouldn't I go back to Manassah and get drunk? Let someone else carry the load. I'd given, God knows I'd given, why couldn't I take now? *Because I can't.*

I twisted around and looked up at the blurry moon in the night sky. Its silver radiance was dimmed by the harsh spotlights. Above Silver Hills, it would be shining, clear and pure, and the vision of it made my heart ache. I wanted to talk to the moon without the city haze and backscatter, I wanted to sing to its cold beauty in the pristine night, I wanted my song to float on the wind, I wanted to run naked through the woods, nothing between me and the clean air.

Shit, are you ever the wrong type of weird for that, Amber! Too much rum, too little sleep.

I zipped up the jacket and got back in the car. *Enough.* I was going to be late at Monroe.

∞ ∞ ∞ ∞ ∞

Morales looked better than he had the previous night. His team had cleared an area for him in the living room of the house on Monroe and they were working in the background, still sorting, tagging, bagging and photographing. The body and the rats were gone, thank goodness, but the smell stayed on.

Morales' lightweight gray suit was store-window perfect, with pants creases that a drill sergeant couldn't find fault with. I always thought he looked as if he might be called to appear on the evening news, and with some justification. His face was square, the hard lines softened by designer stubble, and fleshier than when he'd been a lieutenant. His hair was still jet black and combed straight back, and his eyes were still sharp under the eagle wing eyebrows. He was a good face on TV and the chief knew it.

"Captain, you're looking good." I shook his hand.

"Thank you, Farrell." He stared at me, suspicious of any compliment, and jerked his thumb at a seat. His team had brought in folding director seats and a table. We sat down opposite each other.

"No cleanup crew turned up," he said shortly.

"Well, hell. The squad car outside and the yellow tape around the house must've put them off. Who woulda thought it?"

A muscle in Morales' jaw twitched. "We waited till noon. I can't sit on a murder inquiry longer than that. There wasn't a strong enough reason to wait longer."

I shrugged; it was history now. The Snakebite team had crept in last night and I had no reason to suspect they would have blown it before they had to. I waved at the mess. "Is there anything in this junk that gives us a lead?"

"Almost nothing so far. We'll need to process all the prints. Forensics have a lot to work with. According to the other Crate & Freight drivers, Windler was the key man. There's got to be something here."

We'd spoken only of essentials last night, and I was counting on getting a chewing out for going in alone. To spite me, he started at the other end.

"Definitely vampires?" He nodded at where the sofa had been last night. "Not some random psycho or gang killing?"

I nodded.

"Forensics say he was probably alive when they cracked his chest," Morales said. "Were they making a statement, or is that normal for vampires?"

Chills ran over my body. "I think it's a statement. Windler was the only one who knew who was behind this. He's been killed by vampires. Either the vampires were running it, or they worked with the person running it." I shook my head and took a deep breath. "But it seems there are vampires and then there are vampires, Captain. This group are different from the locals. So were those three last year."

"You've identified a local vampire community?" He sat up and leaned over the table. "I thought I was supposed to be kept up to date on any developments."

"You thought right, but I'm not there yet. I may," I stressed the word, "*may* have an introduction. If I do, you'll hear about it."

"I need to be there, Farrell, I can't have you going in alone like last night, I—"

I cut him off. "That's not fair, Morales, and you know it. You didn't like being woken up in the middle of the night when I found the body—how would you have felt if I had called to tell you I was coming out here on a hunch because I recognized a nearby street name from an unrelated case?"

"You could have called someone else."

"Yeah? Like who, given what's here? The desk sergeant at the local station?"

He wiped his hand across his face. "Fair point," he conceded. He picked a card out of his wallet and gave it to me. "Lieutenant Edmunds is the contact on Project Snakebite. All of these people here report to him, and anything on Snakebite is his priority. He's available on this number 24/7 until further notice. His team doesn't know anything about you except that you're a consultant on this. Use the number, Farrell."

"Thanks," I said. Edmunds had been here last night. He seemed competent and even better, he had his curiosity about me well under control. His small ambush team had been geared up for serious trouble, from flak jackets to motion sensors. They couldn't really know what they might be up against until they'd faced it, but they were well prepared. Frankly, I hadn't believed that a vampire would come back last night to clean up, or I'd never have left them.

I pocketed the card. "I'll call him if I come across anything that combines vampire and criminal. But I will not involve you in meetings with the local vampire community, if they are law-abiding, until they give the go-ahead."

I watched a vein throb in Morales' forehead, and counted out ten beats before he spoke.

"What about some kind of tracer on you, one that we can only access if things go bad? You don't know what you're getting into."

"I can't think how that might work, Captain, and it's my ass. And I do have some idea of what I might be getting into. I promise, I'll tell you what happens."

"You get away with this crap with me, Farrell, but one of these days you'll be talking to the FBI. They're getting interested in this stuff and they *will* find their way to you."

"All above my pay grade, Captain. I'll just tell 'em to go talk to the colonel. Let's see how they get along with him."

Morales almost smiled before he hid it behind a hand. He turned serious again. "What did you think of the special team last night? I mean, have we got the right gear? What will work?"

I shrugged. "If it moves, it can be sensed. If it bleeds, it can die."

"If it doesn't bleed?"

"It's already dead."

"Not entirely reassuring, under the circumstances."

I shrugged again and changed the topic. "So all we have are some signs that there's a connection between guns and drug running, which was using Crate & Freight, and ZK, and out-of-town vampires. No further leads."

Morales grunted.

"What about Nokes?"

"Ian Nokes. Contract driver for Ranchos Rigs, out of Albuquerque. That was his own truck at the depot, and he was doing his own work. In the wind."

"Who owns the house?" I asked.

"The stiff, through a shell company we found this afternoon. Your original dead end."

"Back to Crate & Freight," I said, tapping my fingers. There was something bothering me about the whole setup. "Eight drivers at least, a company that transports over the whole US, the size of that shipment, compartments designed for it. This must have been a major distribution center."

Morales nodded, his face deeply unhappy. "Drug trading in Denver is going down. Much as I would like to say it's thanks to the PD, there's some indication that it's gang-on-gang."

"Keeping the base clean for their business HQ?" I asked and Morales nodded again. "This can't be ZK, they're just the hired muscle, aren't they? They're a frigging biker gang."

"They were originally," he agreed. "They're not now, they're big-league organized crime, and I hear there's a new boss, some guy called Hoben, who's taken them up a step."

"So if they go the normal route for organized crime, they'd need a legitimate front, a reputable business." The chair creaked as I shifted. "Is that Crate & Freight?" Carter going into crime instead of politics?

But Morales shook his head. "Not big enough, and strictly transport. Useful, but not enough."

"But you'd assume that they'd want to own it as well if they were planning on using it as their distribution system. But for the main front company, how about the Kingslund Group?" I asked casually.

Morales looked up sharply. "You want to run that thought by me again?"

"You said Crate & Freight wasn't big enough. Maybe Kingslund is. What if ZK were aiming to take over Kingslund? How would they go about it?"

"They'd have to shift Je…Ms. Kingslund first. She's not the selling type. But it's the type of company they'd be looking for: big, but not too big, privately owned, lots of outlets, national profile, mixture of businesses. What are you thinking, Farrell?"

I frowned. "I'm thinking I'm glad we organized a full-time security detail for her this afternoon. Victor Gayle's crew."

Morales grunted in approval. "I know him. He runs good security. What happened to prompt that?"

We had a staring contest across the table. I broke it first. "Something has happened, and at least one of the people involved had the ZK tattoos." Morales looked as if he wanted to jump over the table and arrest me right there, so I hurried on. "If I have a provable felony that'll slam dunk in court, I'll tell you."

"Find me enough ZK members in one place and I'll pull them in anyway," Morales said.

"Sir?" One of the team opened the door and put his head around. Morales looked up. "We've just got a call, sir, the news people are on their way here. Something must have leaked."

"Okay, thanks. That was bound to happen sooner or later. I'm surprised we kept it quiet for this long." He blew out a breath and got out his cell. "I gotta go. I don't want attention focused on this."

"You want a lift?" I said. "They won't know my car."

The cogs were visibly turning in his head, but he agreed. Five minutes later, we passed the news vans. I turned up towards Colfax to take us back into the city.

As I dropped him off at HQ, I mentioned that there was a ZK rave the next night and I would be going. I said I would call him if there was anything interesting, or even a lot of ZK around, and he decided he was going to be satisfied with that for the moment.

∞ ∞ ∞ ∞ ∞

It was after 1 a.m. when I made it back to Manassah and checked that the security team had changed shifts and was alert. I spoke to each of them and went through their procedures one more time.

The living room was in darkness but I could make out that the brandy bottle next to Jen's chair was pretty much empty. That was one way to overcome the stress of the day, I guessed. I was surprised how sorry I was that I couldn't have been there for her.

I took off my boots and crept along the corridor to bed.

Chapter 19

FRIDAY

I was in the office, working on Jen's finance figures, when Tullah came in with the coffee. The new office had a small area where we could make our own, but it was still appreciated.

I pointed her to a chair in front of my desk. I'd taken the bracelet off and it was lying in front of her.

"Talk me through what this is again, please, Tullah."

She looked nervous, which for her meant she went very still. "It's a warning charm that Ma made for you."

"It works," I said. "I got a tingle from it yesterday when Jen and I were in danger."

"Awesome!" Now she looked pleased and nervous at the same time. "What happened?"

"I'll tell you later. When people give you a good luck charm, you wear it and later they try to explain any good luck that happened to you was due to the charm. This isn't like that, is it?"

"No. It's real, but…" she cleared her throat. "But you've got to talk to Ma about it. I'm not supposed to say anything. I'm sorry."

"Okay. Please tell Mary I do need to talk to her. I still need to thank her for it. And the food on Wednesday, which was damn good." I picked the bracelet up and put it back on. Whatever else it was, it was pretty too. "You do this stuff too?"

"A little. I'm not—"

I stopped her. "I understand. I'll wait to talk to Mary. Now, I've got to get back to these spreadsheets." I waved her off. "There's a package on your desk that I need to go by courier this morning. It's all addressed." It was the samples from Silver Hills for the colonel. I would need to call him about it as well.

"You look tired, Amber," she said as she went off.

I grunted. "I'll get to sleep in tomorrow," I said. As if.

I made good progress on the financial files. It wasn't so much that there was fraud, as far as I could see, as the company was overextending itself. Not unusual, but not the profile I expected from Jen's description of her strategy. There was something that didn't feel right in the numbers, but I couldn't put my finger on it.

The cell bleeped, and I answered. "Hi, Mom!"

"Amber, you didn't tell me you'd moved. I stopped in at the old office and they told me you're down near the college now."

"Yes, we moved yesterday. The landlord needed the old storeroom, I guess, and Tullah found a better place for us here." I didn't want to tell her the whole story and have her upset.

"Oh. Okay. It doesn't matter. I was just calling to get you here for lunch on Sunday."

"That would be great, Mom. Twelve-thirty?"

"Yes, that's good. Is there someone you'd like to bring with you?"

I screwed my eyes tight shut. Maybe I could get David to act the part of a boyfriend. No, that would only make it worse. "No, Mom, no one special at the moment."

She made her usual disappointed noises. I said I was busy, so she let me go.

Tullah was standing at my desk with a special delivery envelope. I opened it with a feeling that this couldn't be good. Tullah sensed it too and stayed to watch.

It was from a William Davies, partner at Weissman Porter LLP, one of the top law firms in Denver. I skimmed it. It started: *We act on behalf of Mr. Campbell Carter, Chief Executive Officer of Centennial State Crate & Freight Incorporated ("our Client"), in relation to a contract between…*

Crap. He'd convinced his lawyers to start a civil suit against me. There was no way that a court would agree with him and no point in him trying to chase me for damages, even if I didn't argue the case. It was pure spite. He wanted to put me out of business, create the maximum amount of disruption for me and make good on his threat to prevent me from ever working in Denver again.

I tossed it in a drawer. "Don't sweat it, Tullah, he's bluffing. Anyway, it's me he's after, not you."

"It's *us*, Amber, like you said yesterday."

I gave her a smile. "That I did. Okay, it's us. Still, don't sweat it. I'll handle this."

Tullah went to college before lunch, quieter than I had seen her for some time.

I put Jen's spreadsheets aside. I knew where I needed to go next on that side of things, and there were other tasks I had for today.

I called Colonel Laine. He answered immediately, as always. Sometime, I was going to call him in the middle of the night just to see how quickly he would pick up.

"Sergeant?"

"Colonel, I have a couple of things for you. Are you okay to talk?"

"Go ahead," he replied.

"I've sent a package by courier for analysis in the labs. This isn't anything on vampires."

"What is it?"

"I'm hoping you'll tell me. I don't want to influence the analysis by discussing it." I couldn't resist teasing him. He'd see what it was soon enough and I went on before he could respond. "Second thing. I had a talk with a Lieutenant Krantz, of the army pay administration."

"What on earth do they want?"

"He's investigating fraud for the army and the VA. He tells me I was never in the army and therefore any disability compensation I'm paid is being claimed fraudulently."

Colonel Laine didn't swear, but the silence was angry.

"I apologize, Sergeant. I'll deal with this immediately," he said eventually, in a tight voice. "But you realize that there will never be a record of your time that he could access."

"Of course, Colonel. I signed up for that. It's just..." I hesitated. "It's being told there is nothing. And the conclusions Krantz was drawing. Kinda hard to take."

He apologized again and when he signed off, I felt a little better. I was going to need to store that up for the next call, which I was dreading. I had to look the number up. When I thought about what that really meant, I realized it was a bad sign. At least I had her direct number and didn't need to fight my way through a switchboard.

I knew she'd let it ring for at least three rings. It was her way of saying that she was always busy. I got to four rings and I wondered whether she would just dump me to voicemail. She picked it up on the fifth.

"Hi, Kath."

"Amber?" She sounded surprised to hear from me. Fair enough—I didn't call my sister very often and we had drifted apart. We used to be close before I joined the army. Remembering that made me sad. We stumbled past the 'how are yous' like strangers, uncomfortable with each other.

"So, what can I do for you?" she said.

"I have a favor to ask."

"Hmm?" Her voice became wary.

"You've read about Crate & Freight?"

"Yes." I could tell she didn't want to be having this conversation, but I had taken it this far, I felt I might as well finish.

"I was working for Carter at the time. He thought it was just drivers skimming. I found evidence of drug running and I called in the police. He's suing me because of the disruption. I was wondering—"

"Look, Amber." She stopped me. "If you reported a felony to the police, he's got nothing, even if you didn't have a contract with him. For that matter, even if you had a contract with him that said you wouldn't talk to the police, it could be put aside by the court. There's nothing he can do." She paused a moment and I was about to leap back in when she said, "But I can't help you on this case, it's just too busy here."

"Oh."

"Amber, I really have to go. Call me and tell me how it goes. Bye."

I managed to say goodbye in response and was left holding the dial tone.

Well, there was no one to blame but myself if she'd become so distant she didn't want to help me. Now I'd have to think hard about how I was going to magic up a lawyer for free.

I took a drive around the block to pick up a snack for lunch. It gave me some time to recover and it was a good way to exercise my paranoia and see if anyone was watching the office. There was no one.

When I got back in I pulled out from the safe all the things we had taken after the attack at Silver Hills. The IDs were fake. The credit cards matched the IDs. I couriered them to Morales with a note saying I believed these had been used by ZK members. Let him work them through.

The cash in the wallets I put in an envelope and mailed it to the Volunteers of America organization on Larimer Street. ZK helps the community. Sort of.

For the cell phones, I needed some help and called Jen.

"Jen, have you got a geek who could give me a listing of every number these cell phones have called and a printout of all the texts? Without switching them on."

"I've got just the person. I'll send my driver over to pick them up now. Hold on." She spoke to someone else and then came back. "Are you okay, Amber?"

I tried to pick myself up. It said something that Jen could spot my mood over the phone less than a week after first meeting me. "I'm fine, really. What about you? Did you have a sore head this morning?"

"No, honey, I practice enough. What about tonight? Should I get hold of a banker?"

I laughed. "No, but thanks anyway. I'd rather have a drink just with you, truthfully, but not tonight. I'll be late. Maybe tomorrow." *Oh God, that's Saturday night.* "If you're not busy, that is."

"Me and my shadows out on the town? No. Amber, I know the security is a good idea, but they're like a burr up my...well, they're not great for partying. Anyway, it's a date, tomorrow night. Carmen will cook for us."

She signed off and I put the phone down, happier, if a little concerned. However well we got along, had I just agreed to a date with my client?

I pushed it all to the side and spent most of the rest of the afternoon trying to find out more about ZK and their climb from biker gang to major criminal organization.

Chapter 20

The warmth had gone out of the day when I parked by the Leung martial arts academy, the Liu Leung Wu Shu Kwan. That's a hell of a grand name for an old hall, but calling a hall a dojo or a kwan makes it special. I never failed to feel a thrill as I crossed the threshold.

I changed and wandered into the main training area.

It smelled of the oil Master Leung used on the wooden floor. And sweat of course. This was a place of hard physical work. Application. That's certainly what I was looking for— something cathartic to flush away the frustrations of the day.

Master Leung's class was assembling. It was formed mainly of guys and girls who'd left work early, with a sprinkling of energetic housewives. Hey, maybe even the odd househusband. Most of them were a bit serious about it all.

I bowed to Master Leung and nodded to the others. I might have some time with him afterwards, but I couldn't guarantee it. Master Leung was happy that I came in to practice on my own most of the time. I certainly didn't need his class. All the forms they would be doing I had wired into my muscles. Worse, the class might pair off and do some sparring, which wouldn't be good for my partner.

My stupid grin turned into a grimace as I reviewed what had just gone through my mind. What the hell was I thinking? This wasn't the way you approached martial arts. I stopped myself, returned to the front of the class and bowed to them. They bowed back. They didn't have a clue what was happening or why I did it, but that wasn't important. I did. It made a difference to me.

As well as being a very pragmatic martial arts instructor, Master Leung was a stickler about respect for others and that was one of the reasons why I studied with him.

I went and knelt in the practice area and tried to clear my mind of the sour arrogance that had filled it. What was going on with me? Why was everything getting to me so much lately? And why was I reacting like that? Was this something to do with the infection? Was it just stress?

No answers came, so I sighed and started stretching. Going through some light exercises seemed to clear me out. My mind engaged with the sensation in my muscles, the feel of a body doing what it was designed to do. I relished these moments.

By the time I was ready for some real work, I was relaxed and limber. I pulled on some light practice saps and squared up with the punch bag. My chi clicked up a notch and I focused.

I got going on straight punches at head level, concentrating on speed and balance, random combinations. Then I fed in body punches, closing with the bag and putting my weight behind them. Sweat sprang up on my forehead and my muscles burned. God, it felt good!

I switched styles: Karate, boxing, Kung Fu, Thai boxing, back again. Step off, side kicks, close in, punch combinations. I was lost in the moment; time blurred.

Somewhere in the pleasant haze of effort a stray thought brushed across my mind. I would put a better combination together if it were Campbell Carter there. Rage flared in my belly; my vision screwed down till I could only see the bag and it had his face. *You'll never get work as an investigator again in this town.* My leg snapped out and there was a satisfying thud as I connected with the bag, imagining Carter taking the blow in his side. Three more, hard and fast as I could make them, low and high alternating. Lieutenant Henry freaking Krantz. *You never made private, let alone sergeant.* I slammed a right-left combination of punches into Krantz, kicked and then closed for a blizzard of jabs and body punches which would leave him shattered. I switched stance and hammered a three-punch combination to his head, finished off with a Karate *kiai* shout. And then I realized I was visualizing Kathleen's face on the bag—*I can't help you on this case*—and I stopped.

There was a complete and utter silence in the kwan behind me.

My chest was heaving, my hands heavy beside me, rivers of sweat running down my face. The bag was just a bag, for God's sake. And how could I want to hurt my sister like this?

The touch on my shoulder was very gentle. I swung around. The class was watching me, open-mouthed. Shit, I must have put on quite a show. Unfortunately, of all the wrong things. Some of the looks were just plain scared.

Liu rested his open hand on my chest. His eyes sought out and held mine.

"We have spoken of this, Amber."

I nodded. It was as much as I could manage.

"There is a terrible anger, inside, here," he pressed against my chest, "and here." He put his hand on my stomach. I flinched. "An old anger. It must come out. But this is not the way. This is not the time. And this is not the place."

"I'm so sorry, Shi Fu." I bowed, the sweat stinging my eyes. Just sweat. Keep it formal. "I've shamed you."

"No, Amber, you have not." He smiled. "But Mr. Bag will need some time to recover. Now, go and practice the forms we worked on to promote balance and harmony. In silence." He turned back to his class. "Strive only for peace and control of the form." It might have been a general comment, but I knew it was intended for me.

I looked at the floor. "Yes, Shi Fu," I whispered. If I hadn't been red-faced from exertion, it would have been from shame. Liu's art and teaching were all about control and balance, not wild-ass kicking and thumping and screaming. I felt like a complete idiot. The ability to hit something or someone really hard is not such a great skill, and not to be admired in itself, even if it is handy sometimes. Liu said the ability to not hit someone is the true art. And even worse, the thing that Liu couldn't see—I had been so angry with my sister that I had visualized hurting her.

However it had happened, the anger cleared my mind. I returned to the practice mat and began the forms. For another hour my world comprised movements mirroring the rivers, the seas and clouds. It brought a sense of peace. Tired, sweaty peace.

I left before Master Liu finished the next class. I didn't want to talk about old angers. Bad things had happened to me, but I had buried them. They were history. None of them should be affecting me like this. And especially I didn't want him involved if this was a sign that the vampire prions were taking control.

I went back to the office and checked my prion level again. It was still at 0.43, which wasn't the highest it had ever been, but was still higher than the average over the last year or so. I sat and looked uneasily at the machine for a while. There was nothing I could think of that was causing the rise. Besides becoming a vampire. I packed it away. Maybe the stress of monitoring the prion level so frequently was sending it up.

I would never get guns into the rave, so I left them in the safe and locked up the office.

At the car, I swapped Jen's beautiful jacket for an old denim one out of the trunk and walked down to the Light Rail station. There was a feeling of being watched, but I put it down to paranoia. I couldn't jump at every shadow.

I had a rave to go to.

Chapter 21

I arrived at the rave late enough for it to be pumping. Even outside, I could feel the music through my boots. Trailered generators were lined up down the side of the old mall, running to provide electricity for the event.

I went through the doors and down the steps, and I was in a maelstrom of light and sound. In addition to the spinning lasers and tumbling searchlights, they had a burning wall set up—a huge array of plasma screens, which was providing most of the light to the dance floor. It was running a lava-sim and looked like the mouth of an angry volcano. The opposite wall was a matching array of screens flickering between video captures of the actual dancers on the floor and prerecorded dancers synchronized to the music. I hated that; it had bad associations for me.

I pushed those memories back into the dark and slid along the edge of the area until I had the video screen behind me. I stood and watched the dancers for a while.

The dance floor was roughly split between Shuffle on the left and Tecktonic on the right. Where the styles met in the middle was a heaving mass of bodies just swaying and bouncing in time.

Electric Breath was in full flow. They were two goth girls who took turns sharing the DJ work and stoking the floor with their dance routines. Beat Gear were responsible for the light show. I'd already spotted ZK handling the security. They'd gotten someone to supply drinks from a couple of bars set up at each end.

The crowd mixed goth and hardcore dance types, with a dash of bikers for contrast. The place was packed and everyone seemed to be having a good time. I relaxed and breathed deeply.

Hot bodies, sweat, dope, cigarettes, drink and perfume. A chemical edge that could have been harder drugs. A lot of people enjoying themselves on a Friday night. At some raves, breathing would get you stoned, but this was mainly the hardcore dance crowd. I shifted around the edge. Another time I might have enjoyed myself, but I was a bit strung out, even after the session at the kwan, and itchy with my paranoia. And I wanted to get to bed at a reasonable time. After all the late nights, I felt like a zombie. No, scratch that. I didn't know what a zombie felt like and I didn't want to know.

The bracelet wasn't tingling either, but I wasn't about to draw any conclusions from that until I'd spoken to Mary. I didn't know if it was a one-time warning or something that would work all the time. And what was the definition of harm for a magic bracelet? Better to not rely on it.

I tried one last pass, forcing myself to dance my way through the middle of the floor, bouncing off people. It was kinda fun, but my heart wasn't into it tonight. There was nothing new till I got to the other side. I had emerged next to the bar area and dozens of ZK members were slouching against the wall. They'd claim to be providing security, but they were just checking out the dancers. I'd lay odds they were selling too. They were the old style ZK, bikers with tattoos and colors. They weren't vampires, but there was a hint in the air. Maybe they'd been around vampires recently. I couldn't see any with obvious bites, but then, it was dark. I drifted closer, pretending to look around.

"Yo! Bitch! Find what you're looking for?" one shouted over the music.

"Yo! Bitch! No," my little demon shouted back at him. He lurched off the wall, but one of his friends grabbed his arm and he subsided.

Oooh. They were on good behavior tonight. No messing with the clients.

I'd had enough. I left the basement and headed for the fresh air.

Emerging up into the cold and quieter lobby area, I saw a group standing, sharing cigarettes, talking and laughing. I recognized one of them, a mechanic who helped me work on my car when I could afford it. We had met at a couple of raves before. He was okay. I gave him a wave and he drifted over.

"Hey, Rom! You good?"

"Amber! Whoa. Yeah. Looking good. You not staying?" We clasped arms. I used the excuse to swing around and look back where I'd come from, through the group of ZK bouncers at the doors. Nothing.

"No. Don't feel the mood tonight. Thought I wanted to dance and I don't." I stuck my hands in my jacket pockets and hunched my shoulders, looking left and right.

"That's bad, man. Tight sounds, Electric Breath."

"They are that. Go on—enjoy." I clapped him on the shoulder and started walking.

As soon as I had cleared the basement I knew I was being watched again. The familiar itch was getting worse and worse. People were still arriving at the rave, but some were leaving as well. I couldn't tell if there was a watcher in that group. I'd gotten a good look around, talking to Rom, but no one seemed out of place.

I needed my HK from the office safe. The office keys were in my car and my car was at the office. Crap. Time to haul ass.

Chapter 22

I walked towards the station. About a dozen people from the rave were going in the same direction. Clearly, I wasn't the only person who had decided not to drive. They were a mixture of everyday folk mainly, heading home after a party. From the sound of it, some younger girls were bringing up the rear. The real dancers were still going at it in the basement and would be till the morning.

The night had turned colder, and it felt damp enough that I turned my collar up. That was all I needed, some atmospheric fog to set me off even more. At the station the loose group came apart like smoke and we drifted onto the north and southbound platforms to wait.

I called Morales and spoke in Spanish when he answered.

"Hello, darling."

"Are you drunk, Farrell?"

"I missed you tonight, babe, you would have loved it, there were so many of Guy's friends there."

"Guy as in Guy Windler? ZK at the rave? Enough to warrant pulling some in?"

"Yeah, loads and loads. Y'know the place—the old mall at Dry Creek. I guess you'll want to catch up with them there later."

"Okay, I'll pull them in for holding the rave when they start to close it down and people are out of the way. We'll see what falls out." He sighed. "It's not as if I have a pile of normal police work to do or anything."

"I love you too, babe," I said and closed the cell.

When the train pulled in, I moved up to the front of the second car and sat facing the back. The train was brightly lit and warm. I tried to sit still and look calm, but whatever it was that had me jumpy was going into overdrive now.

A man got into the car in front and sat alone with his back to me. I twisted around to check him out. He was wearing a dark ski jacket, ideal for hiding a gun. He was a big man and he moved smoothly, like an athlete. His jacket collar was flipped up and above that I could see his sandy hair was cut short. He wore loose jeans and running shoes. Other than me, he was the only person who got on alone. *Him?*

Two extraordinary girls got into my car in a haze of cheap perfume and dope. The blonde looked dazed, her eyes half closed beneath her snake's nest hairstyle. She wore tall black boots and a leather trench coat, with a raised collar like a fan behind her head. Her friend was Asian, Vietnamese at a guess, and if I had to guess any further, her parents' despair. She wore a black Victorian corset, baring her neck and shoulders and showing they were tattooed with leopard skin spots. Below a leather skirt, her legs were in fishnets and she wore black combat boots. Both of them wore thick black lipstick and eyeshadow that made them look like sleepy raccoons. The Vietnamese girl had blood trickles drawn from the corners of her mouth. Seeing me looking, she stood up straight, all perky, and gave me a goofy smile and wave.

I gave her my sorry-I-wasn't-really-staring look and turned away. God, it must be chilly in that outfit! No place to hide a weapon, anyway. The pair of them went down to the back of the car and sat together, heads close, sharing earphones from an MP3 player and nodding along to the music while chatting. Good multitasking skills.

I couldn't see well into the car behind them without appearing to stare, but I did make out a tall couple getting on, hand in hand, and then the doors closed. The train started to move.

I couldn't let the paranoia take over. Nothing was going to happen on the train. I would just have to be alert when I got out.

At the second station the athletic guy from the front car got out and walked away. So much for the best suspect. A few more people got on, but I didn't bother to add them to the list. The warmth started to relax me and my eyes half closed.

Glancing back down the car, I realized the goth girls were now completely oblivious to me. Sucking face, as they say. Eeek!

While they were otherwise engaged, I looked hard at the couple in the car beyond, but they were sitting with their backs to me and paying no attention.

Colorado Station finally came and I got down, casually glancing around.

The couple from the car behind mine got out and walked off without a glance, buttoning up their long coats. So much for them too. Just another white-collar couple out for some excitement at an illegal rave.

The goth girls stumbled out and made it to a bench, where they collapsed. The blonde had her head in her hands and the Vietnamese girl was murmuring in her ear, stroking her back. I wanted to stop and check that they were okay, but if I was being followed, I didn't want to draw any attention to them.

I sighed and started walking. No one followed. I was sure that the paranoia would keep me alive, but maybe it was also going to keep me on edge unnecessarily. I walked onto Colorado Boulevard and down to Evans, then across behind the office to the car.

At the car, my nose twitched with the smell, but I was too slow. One second I was unlocking the car door, and the next I was pinned against the car. There were two of them, and they had to have been inhumanly quick and quiet to get me like this.

I wrenched to the left, intending to feint, then spin to the right and start kicking ass. The move died before it got started. It was like pushing against the side of a building. All I managed to do was bang my nose on the car. I added inhumanly strong to the list.

"Please, do not struggle. We are much stronger and quicker than you," said a quiet voice in my left ear—a female voice, a nice voice, a voice you could trust. "We have no intention of harming you."

I twisted my head around until I could glare at her. It was the woman from the couple on the train. *Damn, completely suckered. No, not a woman, a vampire.* "Then why sneak up on me and slam me against my car?" I said.

"We want to talk. Would you have just come along if we'd asked nicely?" She smiled at me, all sweet reason. And she was right. A couple of vampires suddenly up and ask me to accompany them and I'd have been running or fighting again. Much good that would have done with these two. The four in LoDo had been ordinary. These two were something else entirely.

"Maybe not," I conceded. "Going where?" This conversation was becoming surreal.

Her eyes held mine, near as I could tell in the darkness. "The Master would like to meet you," she said.

"As in the Master of the Denver vampires? And that's supposed to make me feel calmer?"

She leaned closer and I cringed. It was an unconscious reaction, but I was defenseless in their grip and she was in range to do whatever she wanted. Like bite me. As soon as she saw the reaction, she moved back.

"I'm sorry, I didn't intend to alarm you further. I assure you there is no harm intended, no violence that you do not bring," she said carefully. She thought for a moment and added, "On my Blood, I so swear."

I could hear the capital letter in her voice and strangely, that comforted me. I got a slightly better feeling about this.

I turned to the man on my right. "What about you?" I demanded.

His smile was a little tight. I got the feeling he wasn't happy with the oath. "What she says is binding for me. But there's no way that you'd know that, so, on my Blood I swear, no harm is intended to you."

I turned back to her. "Okay," I said. "I suppose I have to say something like I'll come quietly."

The grip on my left wrist eased experimentally. When I didn't move, she backed up and let me go. I glared at the man and he let me go too.

I turned around slowly and we stood looking at each other while I rubbed my wrists. They were both taller than me, dressed in long coats against the chill. I could barely make out their features.

"Your cell, please," said the man. I handed it over and he switched it off and placed it in the glove compartment.

My nose hurt from smacking against the car, and when I touched it, I came away with a drop of blood. Crap.

"I have a nosebleed," I said warily. "Is this going to be a problem?"

I could have sworn they were laughing at me. "Oh, no," the man said, "we fed before coming out." *Not a man, a male vampire.*

"Please get in the back, Ms. Farrell," the female vampire said, opening the door.

I got in. She was on my left and he went around and got in the other side, so I was trapped between them in the back seat.

"This car doesn't drive itself," I said, though what the hell did I know. I seemed to remember a Dracula movie where a horse carriage drove itself up to the castle. Again, I got the feeling they were amused.

The driver's door opened and the third vampire got in, heralded by a fog of cheap perfume and the smell of dope. No wonder I hadn't smelled anything on the train.

She sat in the driver's seat—*my seat*—and turned to look back at me over her leopard-spotted shoulder.

"Oh, your spotter. How appropriate," I said sarcastically. "Pretty tatts, Pussycat."

She gave me a cool smile with a hint of fang beneath the black lips. "Fooled you, Round-eye."

The demon in my throat snapped back in bad Vietnamese. "It won't work twice, little sister, and the only real fool is the last fool."

The eyes widened a touch and the smile went a little strained, but she didn't reply as she set about changing my seat to suit her.

The one beside me snorted in amusement. "We should not talk to you beyond the essential, Ms. Farrell. And I regret," she held up a black blindfold, "it will be necessary to cover your eyes."

I glared at her, but she let it bounce off and waited patiently, holding the blindfold. Finally, I turned my head angrily and let her fasten it. It was a good blindfold; not even a hint of light came through.

The car started and we moved off smoothly. So vampires can drive, even an old stick shift like this.

"One last question," I said. "What happened to the other girl?"

"She's fine," came from the front.

"Enough," came from my left, and I shut up.

I was stuck there, kidnapped in my car. Not exactly without hope, but Morales' tracker was sounding a lot better than it had yesterday. A bit too late for that.

There being nothing else to do, I tried my old army trick of visualizing complex movements. I mentally walked through Master Liu's forms for calmness. It helped, some.

Chapter 23

The car slowed and turned, then stopped, calling me back from my meditations. A window opened and closed. Nothing had been said. Maybe they all did mind reading or sign language. I had a feeling we had just passed through security and we were waiting for gates to be opened, but if so, they swung or rolled silently. After a short time we moved again and the sound of the tires changed; we were on a gravel driveway.

The car stopped again and the doors opened. The night air was cold but full of the scent of plants. Buddleia, like Mrs. Desiarto had. Honeysuckle and jasmine. Vampires liked night blooming plants. It figured, sort of. These vampires had no trouble with sunlight, but they seemed to prefer the night.

"Come out this way, please, Ms. Farrell." The vampire guided me out on her side, her hand on the top of my head to keep it from bumping the door frame. They were certainly showing every consideration for their kidnap victim.

"Walk this way slowly, please," she said, bringing me around the door, her hand holding my upper arm gently but firmly. "There are steps here."

I felt my way up some lipped stone steps and was guided through a door. I could feel the change in the air again. It was warmer and moister, carrying a hint of cooking smells, furniture polishes and something else. Underfoot, the floor was wood and our heels clicked on the surface. The room was large and gave a slight echo. I took comfort from the sound of footsteps departing, leaving just mine with my one escort.

On the other hand, the something else in the air was like the smell of my abductors, copper and cinnamon. I was inside a vampire house. The soothing effect from meditating in the car was gone and my fear spiked in my stomach again. I wanted to rip the blindfold off and lash out.

Immediately, her voice came quietly in my ear. "Ms. Farrell, we do not intend you harm. Please be at ease."

"That's a big ask, what with me blindfolded and kidnapped, in a vampire house."

"I understand. The blindfold will come off soon." Her hand squeezed my arm reassuringly. "May I ask you a question?"

"Sure, why not?" I recognize a distraction when I hear one, but it didn't hurt me to play along. Maybe she would drop her guard and I could test that awful strength and speed again.

"What did you do in the car?" In the pause while I tried to understand the question, she went on, "I ask because you changed."

"Changed?" I said, puzzled.

"You became very calm. I can hear your heartbeat, Ms. Farrell. I can smell the chemistry of your blood," she said. "In the car, it was almost as if you had fallen asleep, but you had not."

I shivered. "I was meditating, that's all."

"No, Ms. Farrell, that is not all. I've observed meditation before. You changed. People might express it that your aura changed. I don't like the word, but it will do."

I shrugged blindly. "If you say so, but I was just meditating."

We had reached a different part of the building, moving into a room. Acoustics changed subtly. There was carpet underfoot and it was warmer than the entrance hall. She let go of my arm, and her hands touched my shoulders and turned me around. The blindfold loosened and was taken off.

She looked different. I had seen her first in the darkness behind my office and it had made her face seem hard and angular. In the soft light of this room she was serene, beautiful and mysterious, even strangely familiar. *And deadly*, I thought, *and not human any more. A vampire. Don't ever forget that.*

If she could read my mind, she showed no sign of it, or maybe she read every word and it bounced off her like my glare did. Her face was serious, her eyes shadowed and staring into mine. Her hands were still on my shoulders.

What next, a little bite or two? My stomach lurched again, and I felt my muscles tensing up—fight or flight. I knew she was strong and she had moved so quickly when they caught me, but her colleagues were not in sight. Maybe this would be my best opportunity. I was backed up against a wall, which would give me a good platform. My eyes flicked over her shoulder to see if I could spot the way out.

"Please, Ms. Farrell. Raising your heartbeat and flooding your body with adrenaline is not going to achieve anything here. We intend you no harm."

That was the fourth or fifth time she had said it. She waited while I got all those muscle groups to stand down. If I did anything, I needed surprise on my side, and that was going to be difficult with her reading me like a book.

"You are standing on an elevator platform. This will take you down to an audience room. He will be there soon. Be calm and be careful." She paused and went on, almost sounding concerned, "Respect would not go amiss."

Before I had time to process what she had said, let alone respond, she let go of me and stepped back. Curved glass doors whispered around from behind me and shut with a snick, making me jump. The floor dropped, gently but swiftly.

I got another bolt of adrenaline. Whatever was going to happen was happening now and there seemed no way to get off this train before it crashed. I tensed up again, coming up on the balls of my feet as the elevator stopped and the doors whispered open, but the audience room was an anticlimax. It was even dimmer than the room above, but the light here was deep blue and directionless. The room appeared empty. I stepped forward and waited for my eyes to adjust.

I managed to stifle an impulse to giggle, afraid of the hysteria that hid behind it. If you thought modern subterranean vampire lair, you might well have conjured up something like this.

The floor was stone underfoot. In the darkness, I got the impression of pale lines running through it. I knelt and touched the floor. It was cold and hard; there was a glossiness to the finish and pale lines spread out like a network of veins through the blackness—maybe polished granite or marble. Slippery underfoot if it came to fighting. A horrible thought drifted through my mind—*very easy to clean and not liable to stain*. I suppressed that firmly.

I had thought it was silent at first, but I realized there was an almost imperceptible noise all around, unrecognized, yet tantalizingly familiar.

When I turned my head to try and locate a source I got a shock. My eyes, now better adjusted, could make out looming figures lining the sides of the room. I froze for a second before getting back to my feet in a rush. They remained motionless. My heart rate gradually returned to more normal ranges.

I took a couple of steps towards the sides of the room and they remained where they were. Had I just been spooked by a bunch of statues? I peered at them; they were almost human, but misshapen.

I took a couple more steps. The sound of my boots was absorbed. There were no echoes in this chamber. I could make out statues and chairs along the walls.

The subliminal noise was just perceptibly louder as I got closer to the side of the room, and I noticed there was something wrong about the walls behind the statues. I couldn't see, but I got a sensation of cold movement from it. I shuddered and edged closer.

Water? I reached tentatively through a space between the statues and touched the wall, jerking my hand back as if I were expecting to be electrocuted. My fingers were wet. I sniffed them, rubbed them together. Cold, not oily, odorless and clear as far as I could make out. I was *so* not going to taste it, but it appeared as if the wall had a sheet of water running down it and disappearing into a gap at the bottom. The noise was the water passing over the surface of the wall.

Having solved one little puzzle, I stepped back and took some deep breaths, trying to calm down. If vampires reacted to the scent of fear, the best thing for me at the moment was to be relaxed and unafraid.

Where was the master vampire? Maybe he had forgotten, I thought hopefully, which made me smile to myself. It would seem strange to have me hauled all the way across Denver and then not be here to explain why. Or maybe this was just like office politics—making me wait to show me who was really important. In any event, the wait allowed me either to get wound up worrying or to do some exploring.

I turned my attention back to the nearest statue. It was the second in the line. It was maybe seven feet tall and in this light appeared to be of black or very dark stone. It had seemed misshapen because the head was not a human head, but a jackal. I was looking at a statue of Anubis. It was seamless, fashioned from a single stone, and the craftsmanship was unbelievable. It was like Michelangelo's David moved to an Egyptian context.

The statue to the right was human and shorter, about my height, a samurai warrior with sheathed long and short blades in his belt. Again, the workmanship was superb. The clothing was real fabric, silky to the touch.

The statue to the left was also human, naked, almost as tall as the Anubis and, umm… well proportioned. An ancient Greek-style helmet with nose and cheek guards was pushed back on the head, revealing a hint of curly hair in the gloom. In the right hand was a long spear, butt resting on the ground. *How the hell do you carve that?*

It might have been the darkness, but I was sure I had never seen any work of this quality before. I reached out and touched the arm of Anubis.

"Impressive, aren't they?"

Chapter 24

I jumped like I had been stung and whirled around. "Don't freaking creep up on me like that," I yelled, my fists raised and my body unconsciously falling into a fighting pose.

There was a brief silence from the darkness at the head of the room, before the voice went on conversationally. "You know, where I come from, you could have been impaled for displaying such a lack of respect."

The demon got my voice before I could throttle it. "You know, where I come from, you could have been staked and beheaded and then left out in the sun. A bit old-fashioned, I admit, but we're traditionalists like that."

For one heart-stopping moment, my head managed to catch up with my mouth and snapped it shut. I waited for the master vampire of Denver to step down and kill me. But there was only a wheezing noise which I finally recognized as laughter. Vampires laugh? David did, but he was only on the way to being a vampire.

"Oh, dear. They did warn me about you, Ms. Farrell. But the trouble is, the more I have learned, the more intriguing you have become."

He was sitting on a chair against the wall at the head of the room. A throne might be a better description. It was raised on a dais and had a fanned back like a peacock's tail. What light there was showed him as a vague outline in the chair.

"You refused my first invitation—" he began.

"Your first invitation," I cut across him, the demon not being quite done yet, "was a gang of thugs who tried to abduct me. As an invitation that counts as pretty damn crude. They were arrogant and incompetent."

I could see his head bow. "I'll grant you that they were overconfident and unprepared. I think perhaps your treatment of them was a lesson and punishment enough in itself. I also offer my apologies, and I assure you that the sending, this evening, of a pair of my most senior and trusted associates hasn't happened in a very long time."

I wondered what a long time meant to a vampire and what the honor of being collected by senior vampires meant for me. My heart rate was inching down on the basis that it was better to be talking than fighting. I completely ignored the thought that maybe it was just that vampires enjoyed a chat before dinner.

"I should be flattered that you sent your top team? It's still kidnapping, and last I looked that's illegal here."

"Would you really have come if I'd sent you a written invitation, as you suggested on Tuesday?"

"You've got me there," I said.

There was a little silence while I glared at roughly where his face was and he sat unperturbed, as far as I could tell.

"Diana thinks highly of you," he said.

"That's the tall one or the Vietnamese with spotty shoulders?" My bets were on the tall one. I didn't think Pussycat liked me.

"The tall one, as you describe her."

"Well, I don't know what she's got to base it on. The relationship between a kidnapper and victim is damn artificial, isn't it?" That was petty, but I was angry. "But what discussion we had included her swearing on her Blood that I would not be harmed." I didn't quite have the guts to finish that and ask him if he intended to honor that.

"She did," was all he replied. Then he sighed and held up his hands. "My apologies again. I hope we will discover that this meeting is important for both of us, and that might allow you to overlook or excuse the irregularity of the arrangement. If you would permit, I would like to start again. Be welcome to House Altau, Ms. Farrell."

I shifted my weight nervously from foot to foot. If he was playing with his food, he played a long game. My heartbeat inched down again.

"Thank you," I said, trying for politeness. "If it's important for both of us, since I'm your guest here, Mr. Altau, maybe you would explain why it's so important for you first."

"I will. But first, I've lived in many cultures," he said, and I shuddered a little. Every time I got to think that he was acting almost human he said something like that. "And I am comfortable with many forms of address. But I'm American now and I should like to follow the local customs. May I call you Amber, and will you please call me Skylur in return?"

It's not a local custom to go around kidnapping people, I thought, but I managed to strangle the demon before he got to blurt that out.

"Okay," I agreed reluctantly. "Skylur Altau? Not from around here, are you? I guess I didn't think a master vampire would be a home-grown, local boy anyway, but I'll admit you're not exactly what I anticipated."

He laughed. The creepy thing was that his laughter sounded nice now, and I wondered what he was doing to my head. How was it that I was calmly, well, fairly calmly, chatting with a master vampire in his dungeon and thinking his voice and laughter sounded quite nice.

"Please don't project Hollywood onto us. We Athanate are very different from that. And as to being local, Amber, I was here before great-grandfather Farrell boarded that leaky ship in Ireland."

I let that sink in a while. He had done his research on me. Finally I went back to the name he'd used for his kind. "Athanate?" I asked.

"Diana will speak more about that with you later." He waved his hand. "It is appropriate that you have some greater understanding of us if we are to work together. But before we get diverted again, I should like to address why you're of such interest to me." He paused. "I can summarize it simply by asking 'what are you?'"

I snorted. "Like it says on my door, Skylur, I'm an investigator. I do commercial and private investigations."

"Yes, that's what you *do*, Amber, and it's of interest to me as well. But it's not what you *are*."

"I don't follow." I had an idea of where this was going and it didn't make me happy.

"Let me see." He steepled his fingers. "We'll come back to the army, but let's start closer to home. You left the police while you were still a rookie—I believe that's the term? Hardly six weeks into your rookie placement, here in Denver. Your file is anodyne—apparently it was mutually agreed that you leave. No mention of the incident in the previous week, which is strange in itself, is it not?"

"There was no need to mention it," I said, my heart sinking. It was looking as if this was about the issue I least wanted to discuss. "There was a separate report filed about it. I just made a rookie mistake and got into a situation which should have been left to experienced officers. Luckily the SWAT team was on hand in time." I had that little story down pat.

"And right there, Amber, you have just tiptoed past the truth."

I balked at replying. There was little I could say that wouldn't get me further into dangerous waters. I really didn't want to lie. If he could hear my heartbeat and smell the adrenaline spikes in my blood, he was a freaking lie detector. I was sworn to stick to the story and that seemed a good idea to me for all kinds of reasons, not least because I was standing in front of the master vampire of Denver.

"And the only lucky thing," he continued, "was that the SWAT team were there in time so that the story you and Lieutenant Morales cooked up was plausible—just."

He sat and looked at me from the shadows while I struggled to even out my breathing and heart rate and wondered what my best options were now. *Best* didn't seem to describe them quite as well as *least worst*. He hadn't mentioned the colonel, so maybe he didn't know quite as much as he thought he did, though I couldn't see any way to use that.

"You made what would have been a mistake for another rookie cop. You went into a building where three men," he held up a finger to make the point, "three men, who were known to be armed and dangerous, were holding a child hostage. Furthermore, you went in without backup. Against three men, armed with shotguns, who had gunned down two policemen earlier. You had a pistol. And they weren't just men."

What could I say? The truth was, I didn't know why I'd gone in against those odds. I could remember the smell, crouching down below the window. I could remember thinking *vampires*. I could remember knowing what they really wanted the child for, knowing that there was a very small opportunity before she died and it all went to hell. And then I heard her scream. After that, what I could mainly remember were the windows, and Emily. I went in through a window on the ground floor, and rolled. It got disjointed after that. The glass shards falling slowly, like snowflakes. Firing, just as I was taught in Ops 4-10—tap, tap, tap—chest, chest, head. The breath of a shotgun blast that missed my face by an inch. The window on the top floor. The last of the vampires went out of that window. It was the sixth floor, and I hadn't intended to throw him out. He seemed to start falling so slowly. As he fell, I could see his eyes widen, staring at me with sudden realization of what was happening, and then he dropped like a stone.

I could remember Emily, screaming when she saw me staggering back down the stairs, covered in blood. And then at the end, I could remember she held on to me while the SWAT team boiled through the building like a pack of demented black robots. The rest was blank, except sometimes in nightmares.

While I was standing there, the level of dread had eased off. Some of the remembered anger washed away the fear. And I reckoned that at rock bottom, I couldn't dig myself any deeper.

"You need to keep better control of your vampires," I spat at him.

He held his hands up as if warding off my anger. "Amber, they weren't *mine*, and I'm not condemning you for killing 'vampires'. In fact, I would like to give you my heartfelt thanks for resolving a situation that caught me off balance."

"You don't mind?" I said stupidly. "This isn't about me killing rogue vampires?"

"I'm *thanking* you for killing them. They deserved it. If we'd had more time, some warning perhaps, we would have captured them and found out where they were from and why they came to Denver. I regret we didn't have that opportunity, but, under the circumstances, it could not have gone better."

My legs felt wobbly, and the bastard was probably reading the relief flowing through me. *Careful Amber, not out of the vampire's lair quite yet.*

"I'm sorry for concerning you so. It's perfectly understandable in the situation, but please believe me, that was not my intention. This isn't about you killing those 'vampires'."

His pause was barely noticeable. "It's about how you come to be able to kill them. The point I was trying to reach was that it is not possible for a human to achieve what you did."

"But I did."

"And thus it follows that you cannot be human," he concluded.

"Or your statement is wrong," I managed. My voice sounded thin. *Not out of the lair by a long way yet.*

He just hummed before coming back. "If I were to ask about your time in the army, what might you tell me?"

Oh, God, more stuff I'm not allowed to talk about. "I enjoyed the army. They taught me discipline, made me fit and confident, taught me enough to do the job I'm doing now."

"Again!" He laughed out loud, sounding genuinely amused. "You really are a master of saying something passably true that leaves almost everything out."

I tried not to squirm like a schoolgirl in front of the principal.

"Is it not truly remarkable that there's so little to show for it? The army records are strangely silent. You were at a training camp. After that, there's not even a record of your rank and salary, if you ignore that photograph on your desk, until you leave the army as a sergeant on a disability allowance." He stopped and waited. I didn't say anything. At least he wasn't saying I hadn't been in the army.

"Something happened, Amber." He leaned forward. "Something very important happened to you in the army."

"Maybe. Can't say." I had gotten very short on words by this time. There really wasn't a lot I could say. I had signed all those rights away.

It was as if he read my mind. "They've made you sign all kinds of documents, I don't doubt. I suppose if I'm an American, I had better respect those documents. I suspect you won't tell me now much more about your past than I already know. You will in time. But there are things I need to know about you, tonight. To know if you can work for me." He stood up. "How strong are you?"

My stomach lurched. It felt as if someone was squeezing my chest and pressing on my eyes. Gray fingers sank into my skull. I stumbled back. I could sense him *inside* my head. The room had become suffocatingly dark. I wanted to turn and run, but my body wouldn't obey me. My legs gave out and I slumped down onto my knees. I couldn't see. I couldn't tell where he was. He seemed to be everywhere and in my head.

I managed to raise one hand to ward him off. "No, please." It sounded like someone else talking, far away.

"Time to come home, Amber," he whispered, startlingly close to my ear. I fell over, trying to move away. "Your Blood calls out to us. You've been too long on the path. You're lost. You're lonely. We're waiting for you. Come home to us, where you belong, Amber. You're so close."

"You promised no harm," I gasped. I tried to get my feet under me but they refused to obey me.

"I wish you no harm, Amber. Truly. I can take away the pain and the anger. Don't you want that?" He was on the other side now. "There's nothing left for you out there any more."

"No. No." I fell again, dizzy. A voice inside my head whispered *no pain, no anger, so easy, just let go.* I screamed and put my hands to my ears but I couldn't stop it. I couldn't stop it because it was part of me and it wanted what he offered. Such sweet longing. *To come home. To rest. To belong.*

"So easy," he sighed. "Such a little step. Just stop fighting. I know you want to. No more fear. Offer me your Blood and I will carry you across so easily."

Let it go, let him do this and it will stop. There will be no more fighting, no more pain, no more fear.

"NO! NO!" I screamed. I'd faced that lie before. I was sobbing, but I knew that if you had no fear, you might as well be dead. I couldn't die. I had things I had to do. I had to silence the voice in my head. I couldn't let the coward inside ever get out again. *Never.* I tried to lash out with my fists, and struck nothing.

As swiftly as it started, it was over.

I could see again, and I was kneeling on the floor and crying onto its cold, unyielding surface. I felt like I had been on the wrong end of a long, hard beating. Every muscle was in agony, every part of me felt bruised.

There was a noise behind me and, faster than I could react, hands lifted me and placed me gently in a chair.

"You bastard," I choked. My whole body was shaking.

"Yes. But better I test you first than simply send you out and risk another taking you like that. They still could overwhelm you, I suppose, but now I know that you will fight. And you will have a chance." He returned to the head of the room and sat in the shadows again.

He let me alone for several minutes.

"I have a job for you, Amber," he said finally.

"Why would I do it, after what you just did?" My lips felt numb and my words slurred, but he understood me.

"Because we will be here for you, when you need us. And you will. I can feel the pull in your Blood." He stirred in his seat, which made my heart spike again. "Do this for me and you will come to realize that we are much better than the alternative."

"What is it? Why can't you do it?" Despite feeling like crap, my curiosity got the better of me.

"Why? Because I need someone who isn't—quite—Athanate and isn't House Altau. As to what: for a start, simply attend the McIntire-Harriman Foundation Charity Ball next week, collect a message and report to me afterwards."

"Just that?"

"Exactly. You will be like a lamp to a moth." He paused and the room seemed to darken again. "Do not let him turn it around. Do not betray me."

"Stop it!" I shrank back. It was a good thing I was in a chair, and couldn't fall over. "Turn what around? What am I trying to find out?"

"Diana will explain." He stood, and made to leave.

A hidden spark of anger flared in me. "Stop! Dammit, I can't work if I'm expecting to be bitten all the time."

He nodded, a movement in the darkness. "I will put a ban on you. None of my House or those sworn to me will attempt to bite you." He pointed to the far wall. "Go up in the elevator; Diana will take you home."

The anger flared again at his dismissal and overcame the exhaustion. "What about payment? Am I expected to work for free?"

"Very well. My payment is in information, Amber. It is this: It is *vital* that you attend the ball for the purposes of your other client, Ms. Kingslund."

He was gone. I staggered to the front of the room and tried to see where he had gone and how, but it was as if he had just become part of the shadows. There was no evidence that he had ever been there. I shuddered.

I walked unsteadily back down the room, pausing to visit the statue of Anubis again. I hadn't been mistaken. The statue was hard and smooth as rock, but warm as flesh to the touch. It was as disturbing as anything else now that the vampire—the *Athanate*—master had gone. I shuffled to the elevator. I had to get the hell out of this place.

Chapter 25

Diana was waiting where I had left her, a slight frown still marring her features. And the blindfold still held in her hands.

I felt so drained, I didn't argue the point, even for form's sake. She led me, blindfolded and stumbling, out to the car and eased me into the back. Someone got in the front. I assumed it was the Vietnamese girl from the lingering smell of her dope and perfume disguise. Under that smell, the scent of copper and faint cinnamon came through clearly in the confines of the car.

I lay back against the seat as we moved off. My thoughts wandered randomly. How the hell did they come to smell of apple pie? I felt heavy, dizzy and nauseous, as if I had a hangover.

"The feeling will pass, Amber," Diana said. "Skylur was extreme in this test, but it will pass."

"I am sorry, we haven't introduced ourselves," she went on, as if we had just met at a party. "My name is Diana Ionache, and my friend is Bian Hwa Trang."

I managed a tired smile and caught the demon before it made a remark about Bian's name. Bian Hwa meant 'secret flower'.

"You know my name," I mumbled.

"Yes. I am to brief you about the job that Skylur asked you to do, but I would rather we met during the week."

"That's fine by me." I wasn't thinking clearly enough to take a brief. "Do you make appointments or just show up?" I rubbed my forehead above the blindfold. "You have no idea how strange this feels, talking to you."

I felt her hand touch my arm briefly. "I understand," she said. "I hope it will be less strange in future as you come to know us. We are not your enemies, not you as a human and especially not you as Athanate. For the meeting, I'll give you a number to call when you're ready. The ticket to the charity ball will be delivered on Monday."

"Skylur said you would tell me more about yourself. He said I would need to know about you…to be able to work with you." It was an effort to say the whole sentence. "He said you were better than the alternative."

"We are," Diana said. "There are two groups of Athanate in the world. Think of them as political parties or creeds, if you like. House Altau belongs to the Panethus creed. It is our belief that Athanate and humans should live together symbiotically, with benefit to both."

"And the others?"

"The Basilikos party believe that humans are cattle, to be farmed," she said. "The two groups have always been finely balanced. If the Basilikos were to be the sole guiding force for the Athanate, without us to counter them or keep them in check…" Her voice died away.

Run the world. I could fill in the blank. My tired brain tried to grapple with something. There was something I needed to ask about vampires—*Athanate*—something about the numbers. I tried to form a sentence, but what came out was, "Do Athanate have children?"

"No," Diana said. There was a world of pain in that one word and I shivered. "I will take more time when we come to see you. But, until you are recovered, let's start with the little things. *Athanate*. You don't speak Greek, do you? I mean what you call Ancient Greek."

I shook my head. As if. I had little enough time for reading, let alone learning an ancient language.

"Ah. Pity. It would have helped. They took so many words from us. Their word *athanatos* meant literally 'not death' or immortal. It is from our word *athanate*, which means undying. Not as later people would have it, undead. Athanate is the name for us, the people, our language, culture and institutions. Noun and adjective."

A whole people, with a culture and institutions, hidden among us for thousands of years. My mind reeled. "Is that what the Greeks called you?" I asked. "Athanate?"

I could hear the smile in her voice when she replied. "No, those Greeks that truly knew of us called us *Demos Kryptos*—the Secret People. Not, again, as it has come down, the people of the crypt. No, Amber, Athanate is what we call ourselves."

"So you don't die?"

"Athanate can die, Amber. You know very well that we can be killed, and we can die. A stake through the heart will kill us just as it would kill a human. A bullet in the vital organs would do just as well." I could hear the smile in her voice. "Sunlight and holy water will not. Garlic is only good for cooking."

Talking wasn't making me feel better, but I was thinking less about how bad I felt. "How long?" I said. "How long can you live?"

"Perhaps that is for another day. For now, just understand that we live, we are alive, like humans are." She took my hand gently and placed my fingers against her neck. Her pulse was slow and sure, like waves rushing against a beach. Her skin was warm. She lifted my hand higher and breathed on it, her breath warm and moist, before returning it to me. "And we feel, like humans do," she said quietly.

I had goosebumps. I had touched vampires—*Athanate*—before, but my mind had been on other things. Her last words had been ambiguous and I wanted to find out how she meant 'feel'. Did she mean emotions, or just the sensation of touching?

"Your bracelet is beautiful and strange," she said, interrupting my scattered thoughts. "May I show Bian?"

I shrugged, and Diana held my arm forward so Bian could see it. I felt Bian's touch, light as a butterfly, then she spoke to Diana in a language I could not recognize, quick and full of liquid sounds.

"Bian agrees, it is magic. Another word which I don't like. Is it a protection?"

The bracelet hadn't tingled once this night. But other than being bullied and terrified into a shaking ball, had anyone done me actual harm?

I sighed. "I don't know, really." I put my head back against the seat again. I still felt tired and dizzy. Being blindfolded in a moving car wasn't helping at all. "It's difficult talking when I can't see you."

Bian and Diana exchanged a couple of sentences in their language.

"You are exhausted, Amber, and hurt from the test. Lie down here. Rest your head on me and I will take the blindfold off."

I stiffened. Her hand touched my arm again, very gently. "Yes, Athanate drink blood. Your Blood calls out to me. But I honor Skylur's ban, and even if he hadn't set a ban, I'm not one who would take what is not freely offered. Neither is Bian. I will not even try to persuade you. Please, lie down."

There was no feeling of being forced and I was at the end of my strength. Maybe I could rest a while. Warily, I swung my legs around and eased myself down until my head was resting in her lap. She removed the blindfold.

"Your feet are on the path," she said. "But I will not ask you, however much your Blood calls out. It will be your choice always."

"Prions," I muttered.

"I beg your pardon?"

I smiled a little in the darkness. "No one ever says 'beg your pardon' anymore, Diana. I said prions. Protein strings in the body. They cause the condition. That's what you're sensing." I was rambling. I realized I probably shouldn't be talking about this. It was so warm, so cozy.

Bian said something to Diana and she shook her head.

"How do you know this?"

"I'll tell you when I understand the Athanate better. I'll show you something when you come to brief me." *If Colonel Laine doesn't kill me first.*

"Very interesting. You are endlessly fascinating, Amber."

"Why? Other than me just telling you something you didn't know. Or Skylur wanting me to play secret agent. Why are you interested in me?"

Diana looked down at me and stroked my head as if I were a child. It was absurdly comforting and I felt my eyelids droop. "Amongst other things, you have been bitten," she said. "Anyone in our mantle, our territory, who has been bitten, is our responsibility, wherever it happened. We are your harbor when you need it, and we will rejoice when you come to us."

My eyes closed, just for a moment.

"And you smell so freaking tasty, Round-eye," Bian said from the front, but she was just trying to wind me up. She seemed so far away.

"Hush. True, but not important at the moment. Rest," whispered Diana, her hand soft on my hair.

No way. I would get up in a second. I couldn't trust two vampires—*Athanate*—whatever they said. Just a minute more, to gather my strength. Just a minute.

Chapter 26

SATURDAY

"Ma'am? Ma'am? Are you all right in there?" Rapping on my car window.

I woke up with a start, unable to think for a moment where I was. I pushed off a coat that had been covering me. *Diana's coat.* I clutched at my neck. Nothing. *Stupid.* Going to sleep in a car with two vampires. *Athanate,* not vampire. The same thing. *Stupid, stupid, stupid.*

I opened the door and climbed out clumsily, stiff from the awkward sleeping position. The officer was standing back, hand relaxed over his gun. Yeah, crazy woman sleeping in a car, I'd probably have been using my gun to rap on the window.

"I'm okay, officer, I'm fine other than the cramp."

He came a bit closer and sniffed.

"I haven't been drinking." I rubbed my eyes and stretched. "I was working late and I just lay down in the back for a moment. Must have been more tired than I thought." I got my ID and license out and he glanced at them.

"Amber Farrell?"

"That's me."

"The name rings a bell." He scratched his head.

"I'm a PI, you probably heard something evil about me down at the station." I smiled. "Tell you what, would you like some coffee? My office is right there."

It was early and I must have looked less crazy once I was standing up. Officer Robinson agreed to coffee and I led him into the office and started the coffeemaker. I visited the bathroom and checked my teeth in the mirror. They seemed normal still. No sign of bites on my neck. At least my bruises had all disappeared, otherwise I'm sure he'd have been asking about them. I pulled my hair back into some kind of order and went back to finish making the coffee.

We sat and drank and passed a few minutes pleasantly, talking sports. He was a nice guy, even if he was hopelessly mistaken about how the Broncos should convert third downs this season.

"Look," I said, calling a halt to the chat, "I was working last night and I was on the train. There was a girl who got off at Colorado, about midnight. I couldn't stop and check she was okay, but it's been on my mind. You know how it is. She looked so out of it. Could you do me a favor—call in and see if there's been any reports about her?"

"Sure, no problem. You got the details?"

"Caucasian, maybe twenty, five-six. Long blonde hair, wrapped in braids around her head. Wearing a black leather coat with a big collar and long boots. Heavy goth makeup."

Robinson called the desk sergeant and gave the basic description. He listened briefly and ended the call.

"Nothing," he said with a smile. "Quiet night around here, thank God." He got up and rinsed his mug.

"Well, thanks for checking anyway."

"My pleasure, Ms. Farrell. Thanks for the coffee and you take a break today, y'hear."

I smiled at him as he walked out and left me sitting at my desk.

So, maybe the girl was okay. I'd chase that. I hated the idea that she'd been used as a cover by Bian to track me and had been at risk because of it, wandering around in a daze in the middle of the night. Had Bian been playing mind games on her, or was it just dope? Either way, it felt like she was my responsibility and I would have to keep an eye out for her.

I got the test unit out and ran it, fidgeting nervously as it did its thing. It had gone up to 0.45. The highest it had ever been was 0.46. I was going to have to find a way to get Obs to tell me what the readings really signified, without giving them the idea I needed to be back in the isolation cell.

I had to talk to David too, but I was due to see him in a few hours at the charity run in Boulder anyway. We could talk afterwards.

I felt I ought to update the colonel as well, but I was in less of a hurry to do that. I was still frazzled from everything that had happened, and maybe talking it through with David would settle me down.

I went back to the car. On my seat was a folded piece of paper with a cell number and a brief message—*Call when you are ready.* I retrieved my cell from the glove compartment and stored the number under Diana & Bian. I sat in my seat and put it back to where it should be.

I'd started the week feeling like life had gotten complicated when I'd had to call in the police on Carter's company. It had gone downhill from there.

Not only was Carter suing me, a crime boss was sending hitmen after me. And someone—possibly the same person—was after Jen, whose safety felt like my responsibility.

Meanwhile, the vampires—Athanate—who I was supposed to be spying on for Colonel Laine, now wanted me to work for them.

The strangest thing was, I was eager to work with them. It wasn't only that I wanted to find out more about what was happening to me. Meeting them and seeing them as people and not faceless monsters had given me some hope that I would still be me, if I changed. Even more than that, I believed what Diana had said about Basilikos Athanate. If the situation was as delicately balanced as she had said, then I wanted to be part of making that better. The thought of Basilikos growing unchecked was frightening. The vision of a dystopian world, where people were farmed for their blood to feed an elite, made me sick.

I hadn't taken everything Skylur and Diana had said as the unvarnished truth, but it felt right, and I would find out more as I went along. At some point there might be a conflict of interest between them and Colonel Laine. I'd have to deal with it.

In the meantime, I guess I had another client, even if they were dubious on the payment front, and irritatingly secretive. And frighteningly powerful.

Still, there was something I could do about at least one small part of that list of concerns.

I bent forward, my arm reaching up behind the dash. My fingers located the back of the GPS system and worked along the edge till they found a small ridge. I pressed it and with a quiet click a tiny SD drive popped into my hand. It's the sort of thing you use in cameras to record all those pictures. Or a GPS, to record everywhere you've been in the car for the last three months. In my case, this went on even if the GPS system looked as if it was turned off. I was going to be very interested to see where I was last night.

Chapter 27

Boulder's Mountain View 10-Mile Charity Run had been popular this year. I finished in a respectable position, but barely remembered to get my ticket punched before I ran back to my car through the throngs of people. David hadn't been in sight anywhere on the route.

At the car, I took out the burn phone and dialed his, but only got through to the voicemail. I tried his normal cell and got the same. This was the first time he'd ever missed a run with me. The trickle of worry became dread, but I was stuck in Boulder.

It seemed to take forever to get clear of the people and cars and I alternated between banging on my steering wheel and calling his numbers, until the marshals eventually got the traffic flowing freely.

David had given me his key and he had trusted me to watch his back. I headed for his house in Wash Park as quickly as I could and hoped I hadn't failed him already.

Washington Park was my favorite area in Denver, if only because it was where we had lived as a family before Dad died. It's a peaceful area, with tree-lined roads and well-kept yards, neat houses and tended gardens.

I had never been to David's house before. It was small, set back in a well-cut lawn, bordered with hip-high hedges. The front had a stepped, A-frame roof providing a sunlit porch with cover and space for colorful pot plants. I ran right up and hammered on the white door, calling out his name.

I was about to use the key when he opened the door. My first feeling was a huge rush of relief and I hugged him to me, ignoring his appearance.

"David, I was so worried. I couldn't get through. Are you all right?" I grabbed his shoulders and took a good look at him. He was pale and unshaven, and wearing a bathrobe as if he had come to the door straight from bed.

He managed a wan smile. "Just peachy," he said. "A bit late to ask you to come in. Close the door and help me make some coffee." He turned and walked slowly into an open plan kitchen and breakfast area.

I realized I had launched myself through his door at him. What if he'd had a friend staying? I guess I would have improvised. As it was, I got him to sit down and direct me to the right places for coffee and breakfast things. He sat, looking tired but amused, as I fixed him a very late brunch and quizzed him. I was bursting to tell him about my visit to House Altau, but I held back. I really needed to be reassured he was okay first.

"So what's up? This isn't flu or hangover, is it?"

"No. No, just another step on the path."

"Explain to me! Come on." I put his coffee in front of him and went back to the pan.

He rubbed his face and scratched his head, sending his curly hair springing up all over the place. "I need to practice using my Ath...my skills for healing myself and replenishment."

"So much clearer," I said. "And you can use the word Athanate if you want to."

He jerked upright, spilling his coffee. "How do you know that?"

"When I understand what's going on with you, I'll tell you." I smiled sweetly at him, waving the spatula. "Sunny side up?"

He looked annoyed, but at least there was some color coming back into his cheeks, and he started to speak, haltingly at first, but more freely as he went on.

By the time he had his food in front of him, I had learned that his main Mentor, an Athanate called Pia, was responsible for this stage of his development. He had to learn to heal himself, and Pia was forcing this by drinking his blood, leaving him weak and shocked. His body healed itself, replenishing his blood far quicker than an ordinary person. But at the moment, that was just in time for her to come around again. So far he was okay, even if I had caught him at a bad time. She'd come around early in the day and there was no way he would have been able to make the run.

All of which led us to a fuller description of replenishment and the second part of the test.

Accompanying Pia on her visits was another girl. Not an Athanate, a girl who was a normal human. The legends of the vampire had at least gotten part of the truth right: Athanate required human blood. The girl was there of her own free will, but bound to Pia in a way that David did not yet understand. She was there to provide blood for David.

David looked down at his food. "I have to make her come to me. It's not that she's unwilling," he added. "But I have to call her to me across the room just using a sort of mesmerism that I'm supposed to have."

I sat back and thought about it. I guess I had been aware of the need to drink blood, but actually thinking it through with David's need to drink from some girl's neck, that was plain icky. The mesmerism I assumed was some form of what Skylur had done to me. *Bastard*, I said to myself, but without much heat any more. He hadn't made me offer my neck to him, but on the other hand, I hadn't been in any state to stop him if he'd pushed the point.

"*Supposed* to have?" I asked, picking up on what he'd said.

David looked uncomfortable. "I did some tests before and they said I was developing okay. But it's not working."

I stole some ham off the side of his plate and chewed it for a second. "Tell me a couple of things—what happens if an Athanate can't get human blood at all, and what happens to you if you can't manage this mesmerism?"

David looked somber. "An Athanate without human blood will go into a coma after about a week and eventually die. For me, they won't let me die, but I'd be a cripple, I guess you would say."

"They being House Altau?" I said casually.

"Amber! What the hell?" His eyes were huge.

I went around and gave him a hug, laughing all the while, as he teetered on his stool. "Sorry, couldn't resist teasing you a little. I had an invitation I couldn't refuse this time."

"What happened? You're okay? You weren't bitten? Tell me. Please?" His words stumbled over each other to get out, making me laugh again.

He was looking much better after the food and I hauled him off his stool and into his living room to take him through the night's events while we drank the coffee. As it wasn't strictly governed by my no-tell agreement with the army, I also gave him a rundown on prions.

David was quiet and thoughtful at the end.

"Refill?" I offered, picking up the cups, and he nodded.

"I know the names of the people you're talking about—Skylur, of course, and Diana, but I haven't met anyone except my Mentors." He laughed. "I get exactly the same blindfold treatment as you, so I have no idea where we go. It's just a room with no windows. I assume it's the same place you went, but I've never heard of or seen the dungeon part of the house."

It was on the tip of my tongue to tell him that I knew where House Altau was, but I left it for another time.

I handed him his fresh coffee and sat back down.

Taking a steadying breath, I said, "Okay, David. Homework."

He looked around, his eyebrows raised.

"Practice on me, little bro. Call me on your headphone." I waggled my fingers next to my head. "Beam your commands to me." I wanted this like I wanted root canal treatment at the dentist, but David needed to be able to do it.

He cleared his throat. "I don't think we should. It could be dangerous, Amber. That's why we learn with an experienced Mentor. It can get out of hand."

"You are *so* not going to be able to bite my neck while I'm kicking your ass around the house."

"Did I mention, you're *so* arrogant?"

I laughed. "Well, teach me a lesson." I reached out and touched his arm. "I trust you, David." I had a feeling he wasn't able to focus because he didn't know Pia's friend. There was a shyness about David. It told me a lot that he hadn't even found out her name.

"Okay. I'll try." He smiled nervously and sat back, looking at me, a little frown mark appearing. I felt something, but I wasn't even sure whether it was my imagination or not. Certainly, there was nothing like the claustrophobic attack that Skylur had been able to do, not that I'd expected that.

I was relieved and disappointed. Relieved, because I really didn't want anyone else messing with my head, but disappointed too. Surely this type of communication must be easier between friends.

"I don't think you need to look at me," I said after a few minutes. "And relax. Try thinking through an exercise—say, the crane form. Then tell me to move my hands to it."

He settled back and closed his eyes. I had taught him several of the Kung Fu forms that I practiced with Master Liu. The crane wasn't the simplest, but it had very specific hand movements.

"I'm having difficulty thinking through the whole crane," he said after a minute.

"Okay, let's try something completely different." I cast around for a question to distract him. "Tell me why you wanted to become Athanate." The question popped into my head and I asked it before thinking. I held my breath. This was one of the very personal areas we had avoided before.

There was a flicker of pain across his face and I regretted asking it. He was silent so long, I thought he wasn't going to answer me. Finally, he closed his eyes and took a deep breath. "My sister, Rachel, was a couple of years older than me. She was very good to me, from when I was a child, especially when our parents died. She was always there. You know, the one I could rely on, the one who could help me when things went bad." He stopped and a sigh passed through him. "She died from a disease called Metzl-Duncan Syndrome. It's hereditary, and I've got it too. The doctors said it was possible I would die in a couple of years. They didn't know for sure."

I sat silently. He'd stopped trying to mesmerize me, but I wanted to listen to him.

"About a month after Rachel died, I was at the gym and some of us got talking. I told the others the story. There was a guy there called Paul. He's an Athanate, though I didn't know it at the time, of course. He talked to me a lot of times, and then just turned around one day when we were alone and said that there was a cure. You know, I would have gone through a lot for a cure that just left me alive, but instead there was this change that would remake me. Is remaking me." He took a sip of his cooling coffee and turned to me, his eyes intent. "I'm on the brink of something wonderful, Amber. If only I could show you."

He did. I could see the sun rising over cold mountain peaks, the promise of a glorious new day. Mists lifted from sleepy valleys and my blood rose to meet the sun. I felt I could soar into the dawn skies.

"David!" I whispered, dizzy with the sensation, and it vanished.

We looked open-mouthed at each other.

I cleared my throat. "I don't think you'll have any trouble if you can do that again," I said.

I was shivering and sweaty. I didn't know how strong it could get. David's vision was pleasant, even uplifting, but it was the same thing that Skylur had done and I didn't want the kind of mental beating that he had given me. But this was David, and I had to trust him.

Trust and jump, Farrell.

"Try it again, just for a second, just the feeling," I said and steeled myself. "Stop if I look hurt, or raise my hand."

He looked as scared as I felt, but settled down and I could see him repeating the words to himself as he turned to look at me. It took a couple of attempts before the vision of the dawn burst into my head again.

"Wow!" I raised my hand and he stopped immediately. "Well, I guess that's the first part. You can make the connection well enough."

We tried it different ways and found he couldn't connect unless he could see me and was actually looking at me. The sensation for me was vivid, but not disturbing and I found I could somehow push it down, make it less vivid.

The confidence that gave me led to the mistake.

"Okay, try making me offer you my neck," I said.

"Amber, no, this is getting dangerous. It's all mixed up—"

"Skylur couldn't do it." I smirked. "What makes you think you're—"

He looked sideways at me as if he didn't really want to, and his silent shout in my head stopped me in my tracks.

What followed was a blur. From sitting a couple of feet away from each other, we were standing face to face in less time than it took either of us to draw a surprised gasp. My hands were on his shoulders and his grasped my hips. Our faces were almost touching. I could feel his breath on my face and his body quivering with excitement and hunger. His eyes went from baffled to glittering in a heartbeat.

I had been right, it was easier between friends—much, much easier. I could feel his hunger in a way I couldn't feel Skylur's. There were no words that he was whispering in my ear or in my mind and my own inner voice was quiet. Instead of these, there were emotions, raw and uncontrolled. It didn't hurt like Skylur's had, and it wasn't just David's hunger. There was my own in there as well. This wasn't a one-way connection.

"No," I gasped. This was wrong.

"No," he replied, but we were so close, his lips touched mine as he said it, and the feather brush of lips became a fierce kiss. My mouth opened to his and a heart-stopping shock of desire crashed through me.

We weren't looking at each other anymore, but the connection was still there, ragged and flickering, as if electric charges were jumping between our bodies. For a moment, I was lost. It didn't matter that this was David. Frustrated desire raged through my body. The thought came to me that he was one person I couldn't infect with prions. What the hell if he drank my blood as well. I could feel the freaking fangs in his mouth and I didn't care.

There was a last moment of clarity, a last realization that this was a path we could not walk back up and it would change us forever. It felt like something we had been driven to, not something we truly wanted. And because of the connection, that was a thought that we shared. The sharing gave us the strength to break the embrace. We fell apart and collapsed.

"Shit! Amber, I'm sorry." David was the first to get his voice back as we sat sprawled on the floor.

"My fault," I said, my head in my hands. "I pushed you. I pushed you."

I crawled back to my chair and lay back against it, too weak to lift myself up, my breath still coming hard and my whole body trembling.

"Damn." I managed a shaky laugh. "You did say that new Athanate are highly charged. If that's an example…"

"How can you laugh? I nearly—" he shook his head.

"*We* nearly, David. But we didn't."

"It's all mixed up," he said, still shaking his head as if that would clear it. "Sex and blood."

"Must be difficult sometimes," I said, and he blushed.

"Yes. You need to understand this now, Amber, how it works all the way around. Most times with an Athanate, sex will lead to blood, and blood will lead to sex. But it's not just that. Being bitten can make you excited or scared, and in the same way, being excited or scared around Athanate can lead to you getting bitten. They—*we*—trigger on emotion. Feed on it."

I levered myself back into my chair slowly. "When we kissed, there was something else, not just the mind thing? Like the hottest feeling ever. Quite a shock."

David nodded tiredly. "We can make the experience good. Pheromones and chemical agents released in saliva or through the fangs. An exchange for the blood, making it pleasurable to be bitten. Or kissed. Or whatever." He managed a slight laugh. "I'm not controlling it at all at the moment, but with more experience, I should be able to create feelings of desire and euphoria. I'll learn to create healing agents and local anesthetic, so you wouldn't even feel the fangs and the wound will heal quickly."

"Hmm. Okay, well, I think I got the desire dosage full on." I smiled at him. I was nearly back to normal and I wanted to bring David back from the self-doubt that our loss of control had caused.

"Sorry," he said. He lifted himself into his chair and slumped bonelessly.

"No harm, no foul." I cast around for something to lighten the mood. "I'm surprised my smell didn't turn you off. I still haven't had the chance to shower after the run."

David's head was cradled in his hand. One eye opened and looked up at me. "You're wrong about that," he muttered. "That was part of the problem. Yeah, I can smell the sweat, but underneath it, Amber, since the third bite, I find your smell..." He didn't know how to finish.

"Tasty? Bian seemed to think so, although I'm not sure if she was jerking my chain."

David snorted. "Yeah. Tasty. Exactly. Must meet this girl." He paused and rubbed his mouth. "You gave me something back as well in that kiss."

"I gave you the lust cattle-prod thingy? I can do that?"

"No." He laughed. "No, you were a bit subtler than that. For once." He ran his tongue around his mouth thoughtfully and I noted his fangs were back to being normal canines. "I'll tell you when I figure out what it was."

His laughter was an improvement, the joke even more so, but I still felt the need to show that I trusted him. "Can I use your shower, then?"

David smiled and waved over at the right door. I went out and got my stuff from the car. Once out of his sight, I took a deep calming breath and willed all the shakes to stop. Yes, we'd had a scare, but we were fine. I was sure he wouldn't flunk his mesmerism test now. If the cost was the fright we'd given each other, I was happy with the price.

I got some fresh clothes and my laptop. After the shower, I was going to quiz David about the financial figures from Jen's spreadsheets, without revealing whose they were. David was an actuary, and a clever guy. I was sure he would have some useful insights.

He did. And by the time I left, David and I were chatting and joking easily again. He looked completely restored as he leaned against my car.

"One last question, David, how long does the test last—the one where Pia keeps draining you?"

He became more serious for a second. "Until I can stop her using my mind," he replied.

I nodded. "Okay. You can do it. I'll look in on you when I can. And turn your frigging cell on, bro."

He laughed and I drove away with that image in my mind, rather than the kiss I could still feel burning on my lips.

Chapter 28

Late in the afternoon, I walked out onto Jen's tiled courtyard to find her catching the last of the sun. A central fountain bubbled into a dark pool of carp, and terracotta-potted lavender and lemon trees lined the Italian stone patio. At the bottom of the ornamental gardens, past the helipad and through the larch and cypress border, I could make out the empty fairways of the golf club. One of Vic's guards moved discreetly beneath the trees, their foliage so dark a green they seemed to have leached the blackness from the deep shadows below them.

I took a deep, scented breath and listened to the fountain and the hush of the wind.

Jen was lying on a chaise, a pile of company reports to one side and a glass of something long and full of ice on the other. She smiled and waved me over. I gave her a kiss on the cheek and settled onto the neighboring chaise. Against the wall of the house behind us, a hot pink bougainvillea waved in the breeze above sprays of multicolored chrysanthemums.

"Everything okay?"

Was it?

"I'm frazzled. There are some weird—that word again—weird things happening to me." I bit my lip. "Let's put them aside for the moment and if I go quiet or moody, yell at me."

Jen laughed. "Why is it I think that weird for you means something different than for the rest of us?" She held up an elegant finger. "Don't answer that."

The maid came out with a refill for Jen and a glass for me. I sipped carefully, but it was just a pleasant lemon and lime mix, with a tang of bitters.

"I missed our Friday briefing—is there anything to report?" Jen said.

"Some. The wallets from Silver Hills are a dead end for me. All the IDs were false and I passed all of that on to the police. The cell phones, you have at the moment, or your tech department does, and I expect some useful information from them."

"A guy called Matt will come and see you with them," Jen said.

I nodded thanks and went on. "At least one of the guys who attacked us was from a criminal organization called ZK. A group of them were rounded up early this morning by the police. Foot soldiers rather than the bosses, unfortunately. I don't know what will come of it, but I bet at least some of them will be in custody for a long time."

Jen sipped her drink.

"We don't know why they might be trying to take over your company or kill or injure you," I went on. "We don't know if they've simply been hired to do a job for someone else. But between the message we sent back on Thursday, the security we've got in place around you now and Morales tossing some of them in jail, we may have bought ourselves some time to figure out what this is all about. The best result, of course, would be that we've proved we're too difficult and they'll look elsewhere."

"It sounds as if you have an idea what the motivation might be," she said.

I shrugged. "It could be that they wanted Kingslund Group as a front for their illegal activities—basically drugs. If that's all there was to it, they'll go away now that we're alerted. Or they'll stop trying to take it over but may do something for revenge."

Jen sighed. "Okay. So much on that side. What about the financial picture? Are they involved in that, or have I got two enemies out there?"

"Well, that's why I'm being careful with my analysis. It doesn't quite all fit together. It feels like two different strategies." I let my hair out of the tie and ran my fingers through it. "Anyway, I have a meeting tomorrow with the guy who left the financial department. I may have some clearer ideas after that."

We sat for a time while Jen thought that through.

"Troy?" Her voice was very low.

There wasn't any way to say this kindly. "It doesn't look good, Jen. Victor's team have found no sign of him anywhere and there's been no ransom demand to anyone that we've heard. I have to say it again: every day means less chance of finding him alive."

Jen looked down the gardens to where Victor's guard was patrolling. "Gayle's team seem competent at security. Are you sure they've done as much as they can on the investigation side?"

"I am," I replied. "I rate Victor and his company."

Jen nodded. "He runs it like an army. Are these guys all ex-military?"

"Not all of them, but Victor employs a lot of ex-service people. That's how I got to know him. The guy down there lurking under the trees is a former Marine. Victor was a chopper pilot."

"It's important to you? The ex-service thing?"

"I wouldn't recommend him just because of that, but yes, it is."

"You're an old-fashioned patriot, aren't you, Amber?" She drained her drink. "Is that why you joined the army?"

"It's one of the reasons, Jen. I think I became patriotic by doing patriotic things."

"What about the cops? I notice you're always careful to call them police."

"I've walked a mile in their shoes is all. Doesn't mean there aren't good and bad policemen and women. Does that all make sense?"

She smiled and got up. "Perfect sense," she said. "Dinner in half an hour. I'm going in to shower and change."

"Formal?" I hoped not, because I didn't have anything.

"Formal shorts and T, honey." She patted my shoulder as she passed. "You'll be fine like that. We'll eat in the living room."

∞ ∞ ∞ ∞ ∞

There are T-shirts and then there are T-shirts, I thought as we sat down later at a simple occasional table. Jen's was gold silk with large white flowers scattered across it. Elegant and beautiful as always.

Carmen brought in the dishes and set them down on a side table. It was a good selection of spicy Mexican enchiladas and beans with a salad for balance. She left us to it.

"Delicious," I said, as I sneaked a taste off the serving plate. "You don't have to take me out to the Moulin, just bring me here for meals."

"Oh, but I do. I have to be seen. Denver's a small place in comparison to New York, say. Someone's always watching. If I'm not doing what I always do, someone will notice. Could affect my credit rating." She served the food and poured us some red wine.

I smiled. "Paranoid."

"Pot, kettle, black." She waved her hand. "Anyway, that was business as well."

I raised an eyebrow.

"Hell, I'm interested in how well out-of-town places do," Jen said. "Restaurants, resorts and so on."

"But you're not going to build a resort."

"No, but I fully intend to own Tucker's and I want to be sure I can return it to profit. The Moulin does well."

"I know what you think of my business sense, but I would buy the Moulin and leave Tucker alone."

We left it at that. The food was as good as my sneak taste had suggested, and it deserved attention.

When Carmen came in to clear the plates later, I thanked her in Spanish. Jen joined in, and predictably, her Spanish was better than mine.

"French, Spanish, any others?" I asked.

"Italian," she said, and went on at my inquisitive look. "First husband. What about you, any other languages?"

Crap. I should have thought ahead, but I wasn't going to lie. "A bit of Vietnamese," I said.

She read my face and laughed. "And more stuff I'm not going to hear about in a hurry."

We moved to less awkward topics, and talked easily about everything and nothing.

Finally, Jen glanced at the clock. "Oh God, look at the time. I promised myself I would have you in bed by nine at the latest." She stood and looked down at me. "Are you okay, Amber?"

"Ah. Yes. I think I just snorted some wine," I gasped. I had slightly misinterpreted her comment, mid-swallow.

"Well, as I understand it, you only sniff it when it's still in the glass, but you carry right on, girl."

She hauled me to my feet when my spluttering stopped. "Go on and get a full night's sleep. You've been up too late too often this week."

"Pot, kettle, black," I shot back at her.

She grinned. "Okay, I'll head off too. It's been a long week for me as well." She paused. "Have you got another run lined up for tomorrow?"

"No. A family lunch."

"Oh, I just thought it would be nice and it would get me out."

"Well, we can work up to that. I'll do some exercises with you in the morning."

"Deal," she said and kissed me on the cheek.

∞ ∞ ∞ ∞ ∞

I float through Jen's house, a shadow among shadows that seep into her room. I stand at the foot of her bed, inhaling the scent of her life, listening to the sleepy thud of her heart and the rush of her breath. I can taste the rich wine we have been drinking, I can feel the pulse in her throat as if it beats against my lips. My jaw aches and my tongue explores the unfamiliar sharpness in my mouth.

She stirs and I drift away silently and merge with the shadows again.

Chapter 29

SUNDAY

Mom lived with John in one of the pleasant parts of Aurora. It wasn't up to the house we'd had in Wash Park, but it beat the trailer park. John kept the grass tended and Mom loved the flowers she had planted around the borders.

I parked under the short Siberian elm that shaded the drive. I was early, but Mom spotted me and came out to the porch. We hugged.

"Oh, Amber, I know I make a fuss and upset you and here I am fussing, but I don't see enough of you." We broke the hug and she brushed something off my jacket and turned the collar down just so. We laughed and I hugged her again. There was the hint of a tear in her eye.

She patted me nervously on my shoulder and spoke quietly. "Kathleen's brought her boyfriend."

I hadn't even known Kath was coming. Under the circumstances, I might have begged off, but instead I put on a bright smile. "That's good. It's okay, Mom." I patted her back. "I speak jock. I can talk to him."

"No, that's the problem, dear. He's not like that. All I've heard is opera and ballet." She almost rolled her eyes before she caught it.

"Oh. Well, I guess I'm ahead on opera."

"How's that?" she said suspiciously.

"I know someone called Carmen."

She bit her lip to stop herself from laughing and gripped my jacket. "Please, Amber, you know how prickly she can be about your sense of humor." She leaned closer. "I think there may be an announcement. Please, *please* don't spoil it."

"Best behavior, Mom. I promise."

"We'd better go in." She stroked my jacket one last time and turned to lead us into the house. "Lovely jacket, by the way, dear."

My stepfather, John, met us inside. John was a decent man and he and Mom seemed happy together. It wasn't his fault that he wasn't Dad. I just never seemed to get comfortable with him. I hoped I hid it well enough and gave him a hug and a kiss.

Kath and I touched cheeks coolly and she introduced me to Taylor. He was a lawyer in the same firm as her. He was tall and skinny, with close-cut, light brown hair. His gray eyes were cautious but steady and his handshake soft and quick. He seemed to choose every word with care. I was sure he was a hotshot lawyer and a smart man, but I doubted he and I were going to be friends.

Almost as soon as I finished shaking his hand, Kath clapped hers together.

"Now we're all here—" *Oh, so I was late, was I?* "—we, that is, Taylor and I, have some news." She turned to Taylor and beamed at him. He pulled a ring box from his pocket.

"Although we've known each other for only a year, Kathleen and I have become very close," he said. "Last week, I asked her to marry me and I'm very happy to say, she has agreed. We've kept this for today." He opened the box. Inside was a lovely diamond engagement ring, which Kath took and put on her finger.

"Oh, Kathleen! Oh, I'm so happy. What a lovely surprise." Mom hugged and kissed Kath.

I'm not much for this stuff, but I was impressed with the ring. Mom and I crowded her for a look, while John shook Taylor's hand and went off to find some champagne which he happened to have in the fridge, thanks to Mom.

We toasted them and asked the usual questions about dates and plans. They weren't in any hurry, and the wedding was sometime to be agreed in the spring.

I caught Mom looking at me and sighed quietly. *Not likely, Mom.*

The other news John gave us as we sat down to eat. "I've finally persuaded Stacy that we need to take a real vacation this year." He and Mom smiled at each other. "We're going down to my brother's in Florida on Wednesday."

Given everything that was happening around me, I felt a huge sense of relief that they would be well out of the way.

The rest of the table found a lot to say about the right season for visiting Florida and the best date next spring for a wedding. I didn't say much and in a lull John tried to pull me into the conversation by asking me about work.

"I'm sorry, John, but most of my work is done under a confidentiality clause. I can't say much about it."

"Nothing new about that," muttered Kath under her breath, but I heard her. I also saw Taylor's hand squeeze hers and wondered if that was a warning. Kath with a few too many drinks was a handful.

"But in general, it's busy and complicated at the moment," I finished. My promise to Mom kept me from snapping at Kath. I knew that she had always had a problem with my not being able to tell them about what I did, but I would have hoped she had other things on her mind today.

"So, business is good, then." John made it a statement and I left it there.

"Can I see your bracelet, please, Amber?" Mom came in to steer things back on course. "It's beautiful."

I undid it and gave it to her. "It was a gift. The pattern on the back represents a wolf's eye, because apparently the wolf is my spirit animal."

"Oh, yes, well it would be, dear. This is so lovely." She ran the beads through her fingers gently. Her eyes had a faraway look.

"How do you mean, Mom?"

"The wolf spirit?" She looked up at me. "Did I never tell you about your great-grandmother?"

"Well, you told us she was Arapaho, and that your mom used to argue with her when she told you all the scary Indian myths as bedtime stories."

"Yes, yes, but her name. Did I never tell you?" Mom got up and went to the living room.

"It was Sarah, wasn't it?" I called out after her.

"That was her English name." Mom came back with her old souvenir box and scrabbled around on the bottom. "And I can't remember how to say her Indian name, but it meant Speaks-to-Wolves. The wolf was her totem."

A shiver passed down my spine. She lifted an old sepia photo out of a plastic cover and passed it to me.

A stern great-grandfather Farrell looked out at me through the years, wearing a formal jacket and carrying a stovepipe hat, both of them probably borrowed for the pose. Seated in front of him was Sarah, dressed in western fashion, but with an Indian shawl over her shoulders. The pattern on the shawl was identical to the pattern on my bracelet. The faded writing at the bottom of the photo said *Padraig and Speaks-to-Wolves*.

I stared at it for an age. "Can I borrow this to copy, please?" I said finally.

"Of course, Amber. I'll put it here for you." She returned it to the plastic folder and slipped it in my jacket pocket.

I had lost the thread of the rest of the conversation at the table and when I caught up, it was veering off towards the ballet.

"Amber used to dance," said John, when he saw my attention return.

I chuckled. "Nooo. I just learned the easy parts of some Latin dances. You know, the basic steps for the cha-cha-cha, salsa, rumba and so on."

Taylor smiled politely. "Did you study it long?"

"I got lessons from a dancing teacher in exchange for babysitting. I don't think that quite qualifies as studying. I used to enjoy it, but I've never followed up."

"I'm afraid Kathleen hasn't told me very much about you. I understand you're a private investigator," said Taylor. "What did you have to study to become one?"

I groaned inwardly. I knew exactly why Kath hadn't told him much about me; I wasn't an appropriate sister with a college education and a suitable job. But there was no way to avoid his question.

"I didn't," I replied. "I left school early to join the army."

Taylor barely had time to register that before Kath spoke. "You had to leave because you did that stupid base jump off the clock tower."

"Kathleen!" Mom was shocked, and I guess I was too. I wondered how many glasses of champagne Kath had drunk. Still, I had promised Mom, and I put as good a face on it as I could.

"Yes. Guilty as charged. I did a base jump off the clock tower at South High. But I had already made up my mind I was leaving."

"Wasn't it dangerous?" asked Taylor.

"Yes. That was the point," I said. His eyes registered blank incomprehension and I couldn't quite stop mine from rising to the ceiling. That was rude and Kath didn't take my judgment of her fiancée well.

"It doesn't matter exactly why you left school, but you threw it all away so you could go off and do stupid, dangerous things for thrills. Now look what good that's done you. You're coming to me begging for help."

Mom's eyes were wide. "What's going on? Amber?"

I pushed my chair back and got up. "Leave it, Mom, I was rude. I'm sorry, I'll go."

Kath leaned forward and started to speak.

"Shut up, Kathleen! And you sit down, Amber!" I couldn't remember when I had seen Mom so furious. My legs just folded and I fell back onto my seat. Kath had gone pale as a sheet, realizing too late the drink had made her go too far.

There was complete silence for a moment, with John and Taylor scarlet with embarrassment, Kath and I ashen and stunned. How had it all come apart so quickly?

"This should have been a meal to celebrate. I hate it when you two can't get along. I hate it. You used to love each other so much." Mom spoke quietly, but there was no misunderstanding her anger. "Amber, what is this about going to Kathleen for help?"

"I have a court case coming up and I called Kath to ask for help," I said in a small voice. "Mom, leave it, please. It doesn't matter."

"It does to me! And she refused?"

I nodded unhappily. I didn't want to go here. "Please, Mom."

"Be quiet, Amber. I'm sorry, I'm going to break my promise to you." Her hand covered mine on the table. She turned to my sister. "You listen to me, Kathleen. You've got a fine job and you worked hard for it. No one can take that away from you. But you never once questioned how we were able to manage it. Never once. Well, it's time you put that intelligent mind to thinking about it. I couldn't have paid to get you through college. Even after I sold the house to pay for your father's medical bills, I was still in debt."

Kath looked shocked. She was intelligent all right, just a bit too focused on herself to think through what had been going on around her, all those years.

"It was Amber, Kathleen. All the money from her part-time jobs while she was still here at South High, and then most of her salary when she was in the army. Right up until you got your own apartment and I met John. Without her, we wouldn't even have had a place to stay."

Mom's cheeks had bright spots of anger and her eyes were full of unshed tears. "Amber made me promise never to tell you, and now I've had to break that promise. You should be ashamed of yourself for not helping your sister, even if she'd done nothing."

I got back up. I couldn't stand this. Mom tried to stop me, but I grabbed my jacket and fled the house.

Yes, I did all that, but that wasn't the way it happened. I'm not any kind of saint. It was much more complicated than that. And I remembered standing on the school clock tower, wondering if I was going to pull the ripcord or not. It wasn't a good time.

∞ ∞ ∞ ∞ ∞

The office was cool and quiet.

I sat at my desk and listened to the muted sounds of the Sunday traffic outside, feeling numb. I had tried to do some work, but there was nothing I could concentrate on at the moment. There were two missed calls from the colonel on the cell, but I turned it off.

The desk was clear, except for my photos. I took the one that wasn't a real photo and held it in front of me. Even in the half darkness, the glossy black granite reflected my face above the inscription *Tara Farrell*. No one seems to remember her any more, except me. My twin sister was stillborn, so there are no dates. No photo existed of her, but I didn't need one; she was my identical twin. I looked into the reflection and saw her as she would be. There wasn't a day when I didn't feel as if a part of me was missing, a gaping hole in my life. There wasn't a week when I didn't speak to her. She was the only one who knew everything about me.

"Tara, it's so hard sometimes," I said. I was ashamed of the tears on my cheeks, but she would understand.

I heard her voice, soothing me. "It's all right, Amber, just talk to me."

Chapter 30

MONDAY

It was just before dawn and I was in the guest suite at Manassah when I turned my cell back on.

I felt better. Talking to Tara yesterday evening had helped me. I needed to get things moving and stop worrying about things I couldn't change. There was another missed call from the colonel. That was as good a place to start as any, early as it was.

"Colonel. Sorry about the missed calls."

"Where were you?"

"It was the weekend, Colonel. I ran in the Boulder charity race, visited with friends and had lunch with my family. Okay?"

"Sergeant, these samples you sent are important—"

"And they weren't going to get any less important over the weekend. This may be the very top of your agenda—" I stopped myself. If I went on like this, I would start to whine about how little sleep I was getting and irritate both of us. I had taken time off. I didn't need to justify it. "Anyway, you just lost the opportunity to say 'what's all this shit you sent me?' And that's the question I'm wanting to ask you."

The colonel took the change in approach better than I'd have thought. It sounded as if he was smiling. "Your evidence gives us tangible proof of werewolves. It suggests that there's a large local pack where you gathered the samples from."

"Any doubt about the analysis?"

"Not unless your sense of humor's really gotten out of control, Sergeant. Wolves don't eat pizza and burgers, nor do they drink wine and beer."

"But they can tell it's wolf shit?"

"Yes. The mixture of the digested remains includes raw rabbit and deer. It's wolf scat, just with human digested food added. And, although the prions break down outside of the body, the team has been able to identify that there were prions in it."

"Same as Ath—" I caught myself just in time. "—as vampire prions?"

"No, similar but different, but difficult to tell exactly from the disassembled proteins."

"Okay, so we have werewolves." I scratched my scalp. "As to where, w-h-e-r-e, which I feel on the tip of your tongue, if these people are werewolves then they could drive to this site and change there. The site's not important and may never get used again for all we know. I have no direct contact with them yet."

"Why do I feel you're going to say the same thing as you said about vampires?" said the colonel.

"Because I am. Look, why don't you set up a three-way meeting with Morales and we can talk it through and try and set up some kind of a plan of contact which doesn't assume these people are monsters and need to be locked up. Morales is feeling left out, by the way, and it is his backyard."

"Okay. I will," he said.

We were quiet for a second. Both of us, I realized much later, trying to think how to open the next topic. I beat him to it.

"Colonel, I've got to go, but I need more information on what the readings from the blood test mean."

"How do you mean?"

"Well, what reading should I expect from a vampire? What reading do I get to before you want to have me back under observation?"

I could hear him sigh. "Well, the scientists aren't much clearer with me than they have been with you. I believe that 1.00 means that the prions have taken over completely and that level should be fatal to the host. They're currently estimating a vampire would function with a reading of about 0.8."

I ignored the sinking feeling in my stomach. I can plot a graph and I didn't like the answer that my readings were giving. I tried to concentrate on another question while he was in a talking mood. "And what level do I get to before you want me back?"

"If you're asking me personally, Sergeant, I have a respect for the opinion you expressed at our last meeting. I wouldn't want you restrained unless it's necessary. I mean unless you go rogue. But the same caveat applies on infecting anyone."

"Thanks, Colonel," I said.

"If you're asking me on behalf of the scientific team, they want you now."

"Okay. I'll need to talk to you about this when you come. I've got to go. You'll text me the meeting details?"

"Yes," he said. "We'll need to talk more next time."

Though I didn't realize it at the time, I'd hurried him to end the call, and so I was spared his news for a couple more days. I just closed my cell and sat back to think.

Had the colonel been keeping the Obs team off my back all this time? And how quickly might I move from my current level of prions to the 0.8 reading, if that's where I was going?

I was around 0.45 now, and I had gone up that 0.05 in the last week. At that rate, it gave me only a month or two before I was fully Athanate. Diana had shown me a hint that Athanate weren't as bad as I had thought, but the burning question in me was still how I could get the levels back down.

I was all questions and few answers, as usual.

Jen wasn't up when I left the house at dawn. I did a quick check of Victor's team on the grounds and then headed for the office in my car.

On the way, I stuck my earphone in and flicked through the speed dials to 'Diana / Bian'.

It was picked up almost immediately. "Hello, Round-eye," Bian said.

I smiled. "Not too early for you, Pussycat?"

"It's late, not early. You need to meet Diana this week."

"Yes. Tuesday at my office? Say 10 a.m."

"Okay."

"Should I get some drinks and snacks?"

"Oh no, just you. That'll be fine," she purred.

I laughed, a little nervously. Skylur *had* said they would be banned from biting me. I wondered what the penalties for breaking the ban were. I would remember to ask on Tuesday.

"One other thing…"

"Yes?" Bian said.

"Can you tell me the name of the girl you were with on the train?"

"You like that goth look, do you, Round-eye?"

"I'm straight, Pussycat. I just wanted to check up on her, make sure she's all right. She looked completely out of it. It's not a good thing to be walking around like that late at night."

There was a silence, then, "Mykayla. I'll text you her cell." The line went dead.

∞ ∞ ∞ ∞ ∞

Tullah came in as usual, with her gift of coffee, but she looked tense.

I gave her Mykayla's number and asked her to try it at times during the day. If she got an answer she could put it through to me.

Before she could sit down, there was a courier at the door. Tullah came back in, puzzled and then delighted as she scanned the envelope.

"Amber, oh wow! You're going to the charity ball." She jumped up and down.

I grinned. "Yeah, but I have to leave before midnight or my car turns into a pumpkin."

She laughed. "But it costs a fortune. How did…oh, of course, this is work? You have a fairy godmother that you're doing work for?"

I nodded, smiling to myself at the thought of Skylur as a fairy godmother. Tullah looked puzzled again. "But who? You haven't opened any new files. Is this from Jennifer Kingslund?" She was looking for the return address on the envelope, which of course wasn't there.

"No. I'm sorry, Tullah, I haven't started a file for this client. I'm not expecting payment at the moment, other than this ticket. I'll get around to it." *When I figure out how I'm going to write it up.*

"Okay." She turned and went back to try Mykayla's number from her desk.

The arrival of the ticket confirmed my plans for the day and made me shake my head in dismay. I had hitmen, organized crime, Athanate and werewolves hanging over me, but because my latest clients wanted me at a charity ball, I had to go out today and buy a dress. I didn't think Mr. McIntire and Mrs. Harriman would look kindly on my arriving in my office clothes and there was nothing else in my wardrobe. Outside of my uniform, that is, and that probably wouldn't go down well either.

I also had to wait for Jen's geek to show up with the information from the ZK cells and I had a couple of other things to do during the day. I was thinking about how I could do it all efficiently when my email notification flickered on my screen. Kath.

She didn't apologize and she was very busy, but she realized her obligation and so on. She would take the case, and promised to do a review for me soon. However, she was so busy that her only time off this week would be at the charity ball. I laughed. She just had to tell me that. The cost of the tickets was legendary. I responded, thanking her for changing her mind. I said I would mail the documents and signed off by telling her I would see her at the ball. She would probably dismiss that as just my sense of humor. I grinned as I visualized her face when I showed up.

I heard a motorcycle coast in outside. Not a whine or a hum, but the throaty tick of a Harley. Surely not Jen's geek? Did geeks ride Harleys?

The guy who came in wasn't a geek. He was a snowboard dude, complete with ratty jeans, bleached blond hair and sky-blue eyes. He looked nervous, his motorcycle jacket still zipped all the way up and his hands anxiously fiddling with his sunglasses and keys.

"Hi," he said to Tullah. "I'm Matt. Um. Matthew Bierbach. From the Kingslund Group. I'm here to see Ms. Farrell." He could see me through the glass partition, but he kept his eyes on Tullah.

"I'm Tullah," she replied. "What's it about?"

"It's an analysis of phone calls," he said.

I wandered in. He didn't exactly shrink away, but he seemed to be very wary of me. I looked him over for a while, leaning against the doorframe with my arms folded and legs crossed. "I specifically asked for a geek," I said. "You don't look very techy to me. Geeks don't ride Harleys."

"I'm the real thing, ma'am." He almost smiled. God, he was going to break hearts if he did.

"Jen told you to call me that?"

"No, ma'am."

I rolled my eyes. "Well, it's Amber, then. Come in and show us what you've got."

Once we sat him down with some coffee and let him load up his results on Tullah's desktop, he relaxed a bit. The job he had done was fantastic—he had created a database of every call made and it was analyzable by frequency, length and recipient. He'd tagged names and addresses against numbers, with a score indicating where he thought the name and address were fake. He'd listed every text message.

"Awesome! Can you do that on any number?" Tullah asked, pointing at the name and address information. When he nodded, she gave him Mykayla's cell phone number.

He logged onto his work system remotely and ran the number through his software. In a couple of seconds it displayed Mykayla's name and address, an apartment in a small building on the other side of the interstate, less than a couple of miles away. Easy enough to walk down to from Colorado station if you weren't high, but still not something a girl should be doing in the middle of the night. I wondered if she'd had the sense to get back on and get off at Yale station, which was closer for her.

"Wow," Tullah said, as he got his system to email the address to her.

"Matt, that's good work, thank you," I said. "I have to head out now, but this has made my job much easier, and I'll be telling Jen that."

"No problem. Thanks, umm, Amber," he replied, as he made his escape out the door. He opened it again and put his head back in. "Thanks for the coffee, Tullah." He smiled at her like a scruffy angel and then he was gone. The Harley growled and moved off quickly.

"He's nice," Tullah said, her chin in her hand, looking at the door.

Oh yes?

"Do I look as if I bite?" I asked.

She looked up at me and grinned. "Absolutely."

I got myself ready. I was carrying the HK again and was pleased it fit neatly under Jen's loaned jacket. I was going to be upset when I had to give this jacket back. Maybe I could find something to replace it while I was buying a dress today.

Tullah's eyes were on the jacket as I came out of my office. She stood and came over.

"Very nice," she said, feeling the leather, but I could see her thoughts were elsewhere. She met my eyes. "What you said before when we needed to move the office, Amber—it is *us,* isn't it, this business?"

"Tullah, one of my big worries at the moment is what to do when you graduate and get a real job." I gave her a hug. "Yes, it's us."

"Maybe we can talk about that tomorrow, if," she took a deep breath, "if everything's okay."

Why wouldn't it be?

I was going in too many different directions to worry about that now. Tomorrow would be early enough to find out. I gave her a quick kiss on her head and headed out to my car.

I had a meeting with Jen's former employee later and I had to find some time before that to buy something appropriate for the charity ball, but first, I had a far more important person to see.

Chapter 31

The shop had that wonderful smell of leather and waxes. I breathed a deep lungful as I walked in.

Werner looked up from his bench and gave me a huge smile. He dropped what he was doing and eased his bulk out from behind his work space to greet me, his big arms spread wide.

"Klara, Klara, come, it is Amber here," he called out to his wife over his shoulder before sweeping me into his embrace. "Welcome. Welcome, my American daughter."

I laughed. His big beard tickled and he smelled of his work, but I enjoyed his whole-hearted Bavarian greeting.

Klara bustled in, as petite as he was huge, and she joined the embrace to kiss my cheek. Her eyes were red. I had no doubt of some of the things going through both their minds, but Klara showed it more easily.

"I can't stay long; it's so busy," I said. "But I just had to come and see Emily."

"Of course, of course," Werner said. "Yes, she has stayed home from school today. They are very understanding, and she is okay most times," he waggled his hand side to side, "but it is difficult today. On the anniversary."

"Come, sit with us and have coffee first," Klara said. "We have let her sleep late." She fussed over Werner's bench, tidying away things he would have to get out again later, before leading us into the back. She had her percolator going and the coffee smell took over from the leather and polishes as we sat around a small table in the kitchen.

"Such a beautiful jacket, Amber," Klara said, placing a small cup of strong espresso in front of me.

"Yes, but just borrowed."

Werner tugged at the jacket and I had to surrender it to him to inspect the workmanship. I quietly slipped my HK holster off and folded it away on a sideboard out of sight.

"He is so rude," Klara said. "He has not even thanked you yet."

"For what?" I asked.

"New business! Clients!" Werner said, temporarily leaving off examining the seams. "Ms. Kingslund came in with her friends. They all are wanting the same boots as yours." He smiled and wagged his finger in the air, looking for all the world like Karl Marx lecturing students. "I told them that only you, only you, wear those, but I make for them their boots. Different, but very good."

I laughed. I had given Werner's contact details to Jen, but I'd completely forgotten about it. "It's nothing, really. She just asked me about the boots when she saw me wearing them."

"It is not nothing. It is something, when Ms. Kingslund and her friends are my clients, that is very much something."

I shrugged and smiled.

"Why so busy, Amber?" Klara said.

"Well, I have a meeting this afternoon that's important, and you wouldn't believe it, but I have to buy a dress this morning. A client needs me to attend the charity ball this week." I laughed. "I know it's a cliché but I really don't have anything."

"The big charity ball? The McIntire-Harriman ball?" Werner asked.

I nodded. "Far too expensive for me, but the client has paid for the ticket."

Werner and Klara exchanged a look, but before I could figure out what that was all about, I heard Emily's footsteps above. I stood up and Klara reached out and squeezed my hand quickly, turning away so I couldn't see the tears that came into her eyes. Exactly a year ago today, they would have been sitting here getting the news that Emily had been abducted.

I went up the stairs to the living room and met Emily coming down.

"Amber," she squealed as she leaped on me. "I thought it was you I heard. Awesome."

I chuckled and carried her a while.

"You've grown, Em," I said, putting her down, but not letting go. "I won't be able to carry you soon."

"Yeah, you will. You could carry Dad." She giggled at the image and burrowed her face against me, which muffled her voice. "Thanks for coming."

"No problem at all, sugar."

We stood there with our arms around each other and if she got comfort from it, I was happy, because so did I. It felt to me as if a strength flowed from her to me, not the other way around. In all the difficult, ambiguous things I'd done over the last few years, saving Emily was a beacon I felt I could point to and say, *that was simply right*. If there were Emilys to save, then there was a point and a purpose for me.

"How's it going?" I asked.

"Mostly I'm good. Sometimes I have nightmares or I start thinking about it and it's not good." She sighed into my shirt. "I'm not strong like you."

I snorted. "I don't feel strong sometimes, Em. No one feels strong all the time."

"You always seem like it though," she said. "How did you get like that?"

"Well, let me see. When I was a little girl, I always ate the right food, I always kept my room tidy, I always did my homework neatly and I never answered back to a grown-up."

I could feel her smiling. "What's that smell?" she asked. "Dad must have bought a bull and put it in the backyard."

I laughed. "That was a bad word you thought there, Emily Schumacher."

"But I didn't say it." She looked up at me. "If I only think it and don't actually say the word, it's not so bad, is it?"

"Oh my God, that's too difficult for me. You need to ask someone really smart that question. Ask me a simpler one."

She didn't say anything immediately, and we just enjoyed the hug. I bent my head over her and closed my eyes. There was a warm, citrus shampoo smell from her. I sighed; I needed to savor this while I could. There was no guarantee I would feel able to do this again if I became fully Athanate. Even if I felt able to do it, I didn't know whether it was something that I would enjoy. I might need this memory for comfort later. Diana had said that Athanate do not give birth, and the way things were going, I knew I would never be able to hold a daughter of my own like this.

She leaned back and looked up at me with her wise child eyes. "Something bad has happened to you, Amber."

My heart lurched. "No, I'm fine."

"I hate it when grown-ups say that to me because they don't want to tell me something."

I sat us down on the sofa so that we were more on a level. "I'm sorry, Em. Bad things happen to everyone and that includes me." I bit my lip. "Yes, some bad stuff has happened and I'm sure it'll happen again in the future. Maybe, sometime, I won't be able to be here. But I've just got to go on trying to do the right things while I can and trying not to worry about the things I can't fix."

Emily nodded and we hugged again.

"I think I would like to stop worrying about things I can't fix and go in to school now," she whispered into my shirt, and I ached inside.

I carried her downstairs on my back and Klara said she would take her in, but that she had to have something to eat first. She hurriedly made something healthy while Emily pulled faces behind her back.

I put the holster and jacket back on, feeling numb. Time to go.

But Werner took my arm. "Come. Come with me," he said, grinning. "It may be you do not need to go shopping in the expensive places."

Puzzled, I hugged Klara and Emily one last time and followed him out the door and down the street.

He guided me into a dressmaker's shop and greeted the neat little lady who came out from behind the counter.

"Lisa, this is the lady I told you about on the phone. Amber, Lisa Macy."

I shook her hand. Okay, this was a kind of a dress shop and I might as well start here as somewhere more expensive downtown, but I couldn't wait for a dress to be made and off the rack had to be cheaper.

Lisa was small and quick in her movements. Having double checked what the dress was for, she walked around me a couple of times before disappearing into the back. I looked at Werner for an explanation, but he simply made a 'be patient' gesture with his beefy hand. I was starting to worry that he wanted to pay for a dress, which I was not about to allow.

Lisa came back with a bolt of material and some sketches. The material was a dark green silk and it looked beautiful. Lisa flipped through the sketches before handing me the pad.

"The best dress for you will be this style in the green silk. With a stole and gloves."

She was a good artist, if she had drawn them, and if she could make me look like the woman in the picture, then she was a great seamstress. Or a magician.

"Oh, I love it," I sighed. "I know I can't afford it."

They smiled. Werner stroked his beard and Lisa put her head in her hands in mock despair. "Amber, you're striking, you're tall and slim and you're going to be at the McIntire-Harriman ball. Do you know how many designers would pay you to wear their dresses to that event?" Then she looked nervously at me from the side of her eyes. "I can't pay you," she said quietly.

She might have been speaking German for all the understanding I had of those statements.

"Look, Amber, I'll make the dress for you by tomorrow night, no charge," she said, misinterpreting my silence. "Please, just wear it at the ball and if anyone asks about the dress, give them my card. Then I put the dress in my shop window and hire a couple of extra workers to handle all the new business."

After my mouth had practiced opening and closing I few times, I managed to say "Okay" and that was it. Lisa whirled around me taking measurements and Werner stood in the corner with his arms folded and grinned as if it was all a huge joke.

"And I," he said, waving a finger as Lisa scribbled, "I will have some shoes for you. You must come here before the ball to try out."

Lisa started pinning together rough cut test fabric and draping me with it. In less time than it would have taken to trawl the shops for something I probably couldn't afford anyway, the most wonderful evening dress was starting to take shape. Presently, she hurried me into a changing room and had me strip so she could hang the tests on me.

I closed my eyes and shook my head. Was I dreaming? "It's all going to fall apart as the clock strikes midnight, isn't it?"

They laughed. From the sound, I knew Werner was laughing with his head thrown back. Lisa was laughing carefully, with a mouthful of pins, never stopping as she worked around me.

Chapter 32

The cell bleeping caught me as I was about to fall asleep. My afternoon meeting at the coffee shop with Geoff Hansen, formerly of the Kingslund Group's Central Finance department, had been good and I had gotten what I needed, but ending it was proving difficult, even after I'd paid the check.

It was Tullah. "Amber, it's me, I'm sorry, I need help," she said. Her voice sounded strained and panicky.

"Hold a moment," I replied.

"Geoff, thanks very much for your time," I said, standing up. "I have an emergency here." We shook and I grabbed my bag and walked. At that point, I was thinking of debt collectors or a leaking pipe.

"Okay, Tullah," I said as soon as I was outside. "What's up?"

"I'm sorry. I've messed up. I'm at Mykayla's house."

I plugged in my ear piece and started running for the car. "I'm on my way. Keep talking to me."

"I couldn't get an answer and then the phone was disconnected. It's just down the road." She stopped and I could feel her steeling herself. "They beat her up, Amber. She's hurt, she's really hurt."

"Who did?"

"I think it's that gang you've been looking into, ZK. Amber, I think they're coming back."

I slid into the seat and started the car. It was lucky I had agreed to meet Geoff at the Café Vienne near the Cherry Creek shopping center and I was only about ten minutes away from Tullah. I could shave minutes off that.

"Keep talking, Tullah. Have you called the police?"

"No. I wasn't sure if you wanted to get them involved. I'm sorry." She was so good at her job, I kept forgetting she was just a college kid and she felt totally out of her depth now.

"Stop saying sorry, Tullah. It's going to be fine. I'll be there in less than ten. Have you got your car?"

"No, I walked along the Canal Trail. It's so close."

"Okay. How badly hurt are we talking? Do you think Mykayla can be moved?"

"Uh, I think so. I don't think they damaged her spine or anything, but she's got wounds everywhere. She's passed out now."

I clenched my teeth and felt anger take over from the worry. Colorado Boulevard was moving quickly, but not quickly enough. I downshifted and passed a couple of cars on the inside before switching back to the outside. What if the traffic got worse?

"Have you phoned your mother?"

"Yes. She didn't answer. I left her a message."

I took the ramp for I-25.

"Okay, I'm there in five, Tullah. Keep a lookout while you tell me why you think they're coming back."

"Mykayla was all tied up and she was still awake when I got here. She says they just went out to get some more of them to come back and rape her."

"Okay, Tullah, it's okay. It's not going to happen. You've got the door locked?"

"The outside door is broken. I locked the door to the apartment and I've moved the bed against it. It's on the second floor, so they've got to come up the stairs. The stairs are around the back."

"Did Mykayla say anything else?"

"It wasn't very clear. She said something about wanting to be like you and someone called Bian, and that she wanted to be with Bian."

And Mykayla had started asking around, and this happened. I could see how it had gone.

"Couple of minutes, now." I said.

"Amber, I can see them," Tullah yelled. "There are a dozen motorcycles just coming off the road."

I floored the pedal and the old car responded as well as it could.

"They're in the back. Oh God, Amber, I'm so scared."

"Just keep them out for two minutes, Tullah. Keep the line open," I shouted as I headed onto the exit. At the junction, I ran the red light, crossing the traffic in a squeal of tires. Horns blared out after me and I had to repeat it moments later, threading through a gap in the cars to come off onto the side road.

Mykayla's apartment was in a dusty, two-story building of red brick with a concrete area out front and a paved track leading around the back. I shot down the side road and emerged behind the building into a dirt rectangle with a couple of old pickups parked to one side and a dozen street cruiser bikes in the middle. A ball of shouting bikers was gathered by an open doorway.

I steered at the motorcycles, then pulled the wheel around and hauled on the   emergency brake. The back end slid around and swatted motorcycles in all directions. About halfway, I slammed the stick shift into first gear and floored the pedal again. With red dirt spraying out from the rear wheels like rooster tails, the car started to slither towards the building, quickly picking up speed.

The screaming, swearing mass of bikers came apart as they dived or ran to get out of my way. I repeated the handbrake turn, spinning around in a cloud of dirt and dust. I left the engine running and leaped out, drawing the HK. I picked one of the remaining standing motorcycles and put a round through the tank so that everyone knew I had a gun.

That cleared the parking lot.

I swung the HK around and into the doorway which led immediately to a set of stairs. Coming down those stairs was the first big problem, a biker with ZK tattoos and a pistol. I didn't have time for this. Despite what I had said to Onebrow, I shot him in the leg and his momentum pitched him out into the yard. I snatched his gun, *another* Glock, and went back into the doorway with both guns aiming up the stairs.

"Tullah," I shouted at my headset, hoping she was still listening to the cell, or could hear me through the door. "Come out now, quick as you can."

The remaining two bikers who'd been trying to break the inner door came down without needing to be told, their hands raised.

The bracelet had been tingling since I arrived, almost subconsciously. Now it became urgent. One of the guys who'd taken refuge behind a pickup stood up and fired at me. The training took over and the HK came around. Tap, tap. Tap. I saw him jerk twice and then his head flicked back and he fell. I slammed an elbow into the face of the guy who'd just come out the door and thought he could take advantage of the distraction. His friend dragged him to cover while I managed to stop my finger from squeezing the trigger again.

Tullah staggered out behind me, carrying Mykayla's unconscious body to the car. At the sight of her bloodied form, the anger came back. If the bikers had been slower to get out of the yard, I might have re-thought the decision not to kill anyone unless I had to, and damn my rules.

While Tullah got in, I walked back to the car, putting a hole in every motorcycle's rear wheel with the Glock. It had the single stack magazine of ten rounds, which left two bikes, one of which had a hole in the tank. Thanks to using three on the guy who'd fired at me, I had 9 rounds left in the HK and I wanted to keep those. If they wanted to chase me on a couple of motorcycles, the more fool them.

I thought we had a few minutes before they tried to hotwire the pickups and come after us, but any one of them could have been calling his friends right now.

"Down on the floor," I said as I got in. I spun the wheels as we fishtailed down the side of the building and away.

"Are you okay?" I asked as we left the side road and merged with the traffic.

"I'm fine. I'm worried about Mykayla, though, she's still unconscious. I'm so sorry, Amber, I screwed up," she said, trying not to cry.

"You're sorry that Mykayla is alive because you took the initiative? Don't be. Even ignoring what they intended to do first, they wouldn't have let her live, Tullah. Forget sorry."

My pulse began to slow and I tried to figure out the best thing to do. I dialed Bian. We wouldn't know exactly what had happened to precipitate this until Mykayla could answer questions, but Bian was the one who got this started by picking her up for a disguise while they were stalking me.

"Twice in one day, Round-eye. People will start to talk."

"No time for that, Bian. I've got Mykayla in my car. She's been badly injured."

The banter went off like a switch had been thrown. "Where are you?"

"Heading north on Interstate 25, just coming past Veteran's Park." I knew where House Altau was, but I wanted to keep that ace in the hole. Besides, the quicker they met me, the quicker someone could see to Mykayla, so meeting halfway was better.

Bian spoke urgently to someone else in the language I couldn't recognize and then she came back on. "We'll be waiting in the parking lot of the Lakeside Golf Course on I-70."

"You'll have a doctor?"

I could hear movements in the background, doors slamming. "Someone with healing skills, yes." There was a pause while someone else spoke. "I'm on my way. Amber, thank you," she said, and the line went dead.

"Amber," Tullah said in a small voice, "I can't meet them."

"How the hell do you know who I'm talking to?"

"The speaker on your cell is on. I feel awful. I can't say anything—Ma will have to explain."

"You know Bian?"

"No. I just recognize the language in the background."

"Shit. This is going to be one interesting conversation tomorrow. What am I supposed to do with you?"

"Just take this next exit and drop me on Ohio Avenue. I'll head for the shopping center and get Ma to come out, or I'll take a taxi."

I took the turnoff. It actually made a lot of sense. Tullah would be much safer in a shopping center or a taxi than driving around with me in this car.

"Okay. Make Mykayla as comfortable as you can and get out quickly when I turn."

In a couple of minutes, I was back on the interstate, with no one to talk to but myself and nothing to listen to but my thoughts and the worrying, grinding noise from the engine.

The smell of blood from Mykayla was unsettling me, and I drove quickly.

Tullah had said *if everything's okay* this morning, meaning after I had spoken to Mary tomorrow. I'd brushed that off as a minor matter and now, that seemed hasty. If Mary and Tullah knew the language that Bian used, which I was betting was Athanate, what did they know about them? And me?

And in the meantime, what the hell had Mykayla gotten into, and was it really Bian's fault?

Chapter 33

I drove my poor misused car in through the gates of the Lakeside Golf Course. It was getting dark now, and the little raised islands of flowerbeds scattered through the parking lot each had their central, solar-charged light glowing. About twenty cars were parked, their owners lingering over the nineteenth hole, or enjoying the clubhouse restaurant. Over by the path to the clubhouse, tall floodlights shone down, but in the main parking area, the place was shadowy, almost sinister.

Looking way over to my left, I saw a tall figure wave to me and I recognized Diana. Behind her, a couple of cars and a van were grouped together and I could make out people sitting in them. The unmistakable form of Bian sashayed out from the dark and joined Diana. Did the girl have to be quite so over-the-top? Then I realized she might have done that so I could be sure it was them.

I relaxed a tiny bit as I pulled up next to them and got out.

Bian was already in the back of my car, bent over Mykayla's head. It looked as if she were kissing her.

"What—" I turned, but Diana's hand stopped me.

"Bian is a healer. In this case, the best that could be for Mykayla. This is the Athanate way, Amber."

"She's not going to bite her." I struggled, but Diana's grip was extraordinary. I'd have had to tear my arm off to get away.

"She is not biting her," Diana said. A half dozen men had emerged from the van and cars. Without actually seeming to surround us, they formed a cordon between us and any other watcher in the dark. They would appear as a group of friends to the casual eye.

"Amber, look at me."

My heart hammered in my chest. Crap, crap. What had I gotten into now? My eyes seemed to move of their own accord and I was looking up into Diana's. My head swam.

"I have given you my word, Amber," she said. "I'm not trying to control you, but it's important that you believe me."

I calmed myself down. I told myself she wasn't going to bite me. Bian wasn't biting Mykayla. Calm. Calm. Focus. The coppery scent from Diana was strangely soothing. Her eyes were gorgeous.

"Better," she said. "Now, when we bite, which we're not tonight, Athanate saliva contains chemicals. Some of these we call aniatropics. They make the body heal itself rapidly. That's what Bian is giving Mykayla, but with a kiss."

With my head swimming as it was, a giggle threatened to escape. "So the vampire's kiss is good for you?" I said. David had said something about this.

Diana smiled, and let me get away with calling Bian a vampire. "It could be. Or not."

"Why's Bian so good for Mykayla?" I said. I'd have to find out about the *or not* part later.

"Because Bian believes she is at fault here and owes Mykayla protection. Responsibility is a very strong force for her and that motivation is helping her to create the strongest aniatropics."

I let out a breath and relaxed. I did believe her, whether it was because she was messing with my head or that I simply found her easy to believe. Diana let me go and I rubbed my arm. I'd just gotten rid of the last bunch, and I really didn't need new bruises at the ball.

"We are also in your debt, Amber."

"Well, if you're offering," I joked, "a new car would be handy, at least for a while. The bikers will know the car and they'll have my license plate. And I think I've thrown a tooth on the gears."

Diana made a signal to the surrounding Athanate and, taking my arm again, gently walked me to one side.

"Tell me what happened," she said.

I went through it, from why I felt I had to check up on Mykayla, to scaring off the gang members and escaping. I left it that I'd dropped Tullah off for her mother to pick up and implied I did it for Diana's security reasons. I filled in a bit of ZK background—the connection to drugs and their interest in finding a legitimate front for their expanding criminal organization. I didn't mention Kingslund Group. I told her about the death of Guy Windler and mentioned the similarity in smell of the vampire that did that to the rogues from last year.

Diana's nose flared and she shuddered. "It begins. Soon, it will be very dangerous for you to be on your own, Amber. Keep the cell number we have given you and use it at any time. Or simply agree to live with us." She looked up at the night sky with her head tilted as if she were listening to something else, then let her breath plume out. "We need to be back at the House. Is there anything else I can offer you in thanks?"

Else?

"Yes, I want to see Mykayla, unbitten, as soon as she's well. And I want to be convinced she understands exactly what she's getting into before anything happens."

"You will," Diana said simply, as they carried Mykayla to the van. One of the men came over and offered something to me.

I put out my hand and a key dropped into it.

"It is yours," Diana said, indicating one of the cars. "I'll bring the papers tomorrow. They've moved your things across. Give Bian your keys, please."

Dumbfounded, I held out the key to my beaten-up old car. "But it'll be dangerous," I said. "ZK will be out looking for it, they'll ambush you."

"I hope they do," Bian said, taking the key from me. I looked at her and shivered. All signs of the provocative goth girl had disappeared and were replaced with something entirely feral and frightening. It could be her choice of tattoo was justified.

"Just down to Mykayla's house to clear that up and then back, Bian," Diana said. Bian's head lowered stiffly in acknowledgement.

I dived into my car—my ex-car—and retrieved the little pack of Mrs. Welchester's fake ID hidden behind the dash. There wasn't anything I could do about the GPS system, but at least it didn't have the recording disk inside.

"We will see you tomorrow, Amber," Diana said.

"Not at the office," I said. "I'm going to close that for a while."

Diana nodded. "Probably best. Meet us here, then, in the clubhouse conference room."

I looked surprised, and she smiled. "I own the club." They drove off into the night, leaving me with a new Audi.

∞ ∞ ∞ ∞ ∞

Playing with the car kept my mind occupied until I got back to Jen's. I had to get out and show myself to persuade Victor's guards to let me in, which I approved of, and I told them so.

I turned off the engine and called Tullah. She was fine and I told her that Mykayla was in good hands. I said not to use the office for the moment, and we agreed to meet her mother in the afternoon at the Café Vienne where I'd talked to Geoff earlier today.

I called David and left a short message on his voice mail. Maybe I'd have to slap him around a bit at our next sparring session to teach him that when I said leave the phone on, I meant it.

Jen sauntered out.

"Are you aiming to sleep in your new car, honey, or would you like a drink?"

I kissed her cheek and followed her in. "I'm sorry to treat this like a hotel, Jen, but dinner would be very welcome."

"I'll get it started." She pointed me to the living room. "Butt on the chair, feet on the stool, rum in the glass, I'll be back to catch up in a moment."

In less than ten minutes, Carmen had cooked me up an omelet with some delicious little tapas dishes on the side—nuts, mushrooms with garlic and tiny, salty potatoes. Between that and the rum, it felt as if the world was slowing down to a more reasonable pace at last.

Jen sat with her legs tucked underneath her and watched me eat, smiling.

"What are you laughing at?" I asked.

"I'm just enjoying watching the way you throw yourself at everything, even eating dinner," she said. "I have some news," she went on casually, "but it'll wait till I hear yours."

"That's evil, Jen." I put my empty plate on the table and slumped back in the chair. "Okay. I met with Geoff Hansen this afternoon, formerly of your finance department."

"I bet that was exciting," Jen said, and I grinned.

"Couldn't get away."

I sat back and took her through my findings. Geoff's description of the financial processes confirmed my suspicion that there was a problem, and that it was internal to the Kingslund Group. Geoff confirmed some of the issues that David had raised when he'd seen the accounts.

A company like Jen's that was purchasing a rival should have been moving long term investments into short term. The money needed to be accessible quickly and without penalty more than it needed to be getting a good return by being bound up for a long period. The reverse was happening; money was being moved into long term investments. None of this showed in the balance sheets because the investment types were no longer being broken out. The bottom line was that she wasn't in a good position to buy Tucker Beacon. And in the current climate, the banks would assess Tucker Beacon as too big a risk to get involved.

The second anomaly was that the investment documentation provided to me was false. The return on any particular investment was difficult to extract and the total amount looked good, but I had managed to find references to a specific investment that was returning a fifth of the level it should. If all the recent investments were doing the same, the total position was only being obscured by the number of new investments that were being added.

This sleight of hand was about as stable as a Ponzi scheme. At some point, the money available from new investments wouldn't be enough to mask the fact the previous investments weren't returning the right amounts. This was a short term tactic to hobble the company. Whoever was doing this would be discovered at the next general audit. So it stood to reason that whatever plan there was had to be triggered by the end of the year at the latest, probably much earlier.

I had a feeling Geoff had been getting close to finding this out when he had fallen foul of what he thought was office politics. My concern for Jen was that the person he'd fallen foul of was Jen's financial director and second-in-command, Bernard Verdoon.

Jen's eyes were hooded as I talked it through. "I can't believe it," she said. "Bernard's been with me for ten years. He has signing rights for the company, for God's sake." Her hand slapped down on her thigh.

"He's the only one with enough authority to run this."

"I'll string the bastard up if it's him. I've totally trusted him." She grabbed her phone and I lifted my hand. "What?" she said angrily, looking up at me.

"Two things, Jen. I can't be absolutely sure it's him, and I think the best course of action is to find answers. Who, how and why may tell us a great deal, while firing him may not. We need to know what's going on to stop it or at least make a suitable defense."

She put the phone down. "What are you suggesting?"

"You have a meeting with him on something else. Matt and I will look at his computer and desk files while he's busy. You should also set up an agreement with your banks that any large transfers have to be passed by you—secretly. We won't be able to keep that hidden for more than a week or so, but that should be enough."

Jen thought it through and then nodded. She calmed down.

"So much for the financials," I said. "Next, I haven't forgotten the trouble on your land. If it's linked to everything else, it gets straightened out with everything else. If not, I'll deal with it in the next week, or explain to you why I can't."

Jen stared at me with a slight smile. "It *is* weird, then. Okay." She waved it off.

I got us refills for our glasses and took my plate back to the kitchen to thank Carmen and to give Jen a little time to think everything through. I hadn't had anything to report on Troy, but Victor was emailing her directly now.

She was sitting in the same position when I returned, but had clearly put my news aside to be dealt with in the morning. I wished I could do that sort of thing.

"So," I said, "what's your news that you teased me about?"

Jen smiled lazily. "I assume you know which asshole I'm talking about when I say Lieutenant Krantz?"

Chapter 34

"Dammit, Amber, I'm sorry." Jen had her arms around me, trying to physically stop me from venting my anger on the furniture. "I didn't realize he'd gotten under your skin so badly. I'd never have joked about it if I thought you'd react like this."

I felt the anger ebbing away slowly and I let Jen steer me back to the sofa and sit me down. Carmen's head popped around the door to see what the noise was and Jen waved her away. Embarrassment took over from the anger as Jen picked up the table I had kicked over.

"Sorry," I said. "That was childish, way over the top."

Jen slid in beside me and grabbed my hand between hers.

"Tell me about it," she ordered.

I sighed. Not telling people was like pushing water uphill. If I was going to end up disappearing into the Athanate community in a couple of months, maybe it didn't matter anymore. Thinking that depressed me. I wasn't that far gone yet and I wasn't giving up the fight.

I decided to tiptoe around the edges of the agreement I had signed with the army.

"Krantz thinks he's onto a major fraud involving vets' money. I don't know. If he is, more power to him." I sighed again and ran my free hand over my face in frustration. "Because of what I did in the army, my records aren't available to him. It looks to him like I'm being paid a vet's disability compensation without ever having been in the army. That's what he accused me of, and called on my sense of patriotism. As if he had any idea."

"What are you being paid for?" Jen's business mind cut right to the heart of it.

"Think of it as a retainer. Stupid damn decision to hide it like that, but not my decision. Anyway, I don't care. I don't want the money. It's nothing. It's Krantz telling me—"

"Okay. Okay. I get that part of it, honey. He was 'officially' telling me that you had been cleared, but that he was just tying up loose ends. Trying to tell me that you were actually guilty but he wasn't allowed to prove it."

I managed to remain seated this time. "What did you say?"

"Hell, I kicked him out, of course. I think I said something along the lines of you were so patriotic you had the flag sewn into your panties, and you would never, ever be involved in anything like that. As for my contract with you, none of his damn business. I may have used some short words, and I may have shouted a bit."

"Thanks, Jen." I looked down at my lap.

"You're blushing." She laughed. "You actually do have a flag sewn into your panties?"

That made the blush worse of course, but it was sort of true, I did have a pair with a flag printed under the words 'Property of the US Army'. A joke gift from my team about four years ago, in what I was now thinking of as very long ago. Time to change the subject.

"Matt came by this morning. Thanks for loaning him to me. He's a nice looking kid. I think Tullah may have noticed."

Jen grinned, but she let me change topics. "Did he do a good job?"

"Very good. It'll save an enormous amount of time. From a glance, it looks like there will be enough leads to get the police involved in closing down ZK."

"That'll be welcome news." Jen spared a hand to reach for her brandy and took a sip.

"Do you know why Matt might be—well, scared of me?" I asked.

Jen put her glass down and went back to holding my hand with both of hers. It was all right, really, I wasn't going to get up and break her furniture again, but I didn't mind.

"Yes," she said, and a prickle of unease went through me at her expression.

"Amber," she began finally, "I'm in a very vulnerable position. In all sorts of ways." Her hands squeezed mine and I remembered doing exactly that to David in the coffee shop. I steeled myself. Whatever she had to say, I was going to face it as calmly as David had and find the good in it.

"I had Matt run full background checks on you."

I let that sink in. It wasn't so bad. If I were in her position, wouldn't I do the same thing? I put my free hand on the others and squeezed her back.

"Thank you," she said, "for taking that so well."

"Thanks for telling me," I replied. "Find anything?"

She smiled crookedly. "As you know very well, there's an eerie absence of information about you. Matt says the only profile he can think of that fits is some secret ninja assassin. That's why he's acting nervous."

I laughed. "Too much Hollywood." Jen grinned in agreement.

"I can connect the dots," she said. "And I like the picture it shows. There's no way, for example, that your friend Werner believes you were only 'in the vicinity' when his daughter was rescued last year, and I don't either."

The feeling I had from hugging Emily that morning came flooding back and lit me up from the inside. I smiled. "Werner says you've put in some orders for you and your friends."

"Hell yes! I'm sick of people complaining that there's no diversity and then shopping in national stores for expensive crap that has no individuality. I don't want to live in a cultural wasteland. Support local artists and artisans if you want your place to have its own identity. I'll never buy a pair of boots in a store again."

"Message received and understood, ma'am," I said. She would have jabbed me, but I was holding her hands.

∞ ∞ ∞ ∞ ∞

I floated above the exercise mats in the dark of Jen's basement gymnasium, a shadow among shadows as I went through Master Liu's most strenuous exercises and the puzzles of the day.

I'd told Tullah that Mykayla was in good hands and I believed it, but I would have been happier if they hadn't been messing with my head. I found I couldn't recall a single face from the group of Athanate at the golf course, other than Diana and Bian. I couldn't recall the face of the man who'd accompanied them when they'd kidnapped me either. Apparently, Athanate security concerns ran deep and their powers were even spookier than I had imagined. What else might they have done while they blurred my memories?

I *could* recall the faces of the four who'd fought in LoDo, quite clearly. Why was that different?

I spun and fought shadows until the air caressed my skin like hot silk and yet my heartbeat never reached above 120. I was quicker, faster, more Athanate with every passing day. One half of me despaired while the other gloried in the physical benefits.

I finished up the exercises and headed for a shower, a shadow passing through the silent house.

There had been a text on my cell confirming a meeting with the colonel and Captain Morales at police HQ at 9:30 Wednesday morning.

Krantz I just had to put out of my mind. Clearly, the colonel had got his leash and he was just barking as he was dragged off. He couldn't do me any more harm.

Diana had my car with my slightly unusual GPS system—was it going to be a problem if she found that I knew where House Altau was?

What was the real price of the car she had given me? It seemed an excessive payment for an afternoon's work. Had I done the right thing getting Altau involved?

Jen had suggested that I temporarily relocate my office to an unused study here in her house. She constantly referred to the guest suite as mine.

There's nothing without a cost. I was collecting a pile of debts the size of which I couldn't reliably estimate. The banks tried that with sub-prime mortgages and see where it got them.

Chapter 35

TUESDAY

I arranged for a couple of Victor's team to stop by my office very early on their way in to relieve the guards at Manassah. I met them there and loaded them up with the office equipment and mail to take in for Tullah.

Morales called me as they drove off.

"Good morning, Farrell. Up early after a busy night, or haven't you gone to bed yet?"

This was totally out of order; that sort of sarcasm was my line.

"Why, Captain, a girl would think that something happened while she was sleeping sweetly in Ms. Kingslund's guest suite, protected by Mr. Gayle's vigilant guards."

He growled something in Spanish that I couldn't catch, as I slipped back into my new car. Being a new car, it had made clever connections to my cell, and I was able to talk while driving without having a stupid plug in my ear.

"What's up, Morales?" I prompted him.

"ZK membership is dropping. Another five last night in a car accident that wasn't. A fight yesterday, near the Yale turnoff from I-25, where a lot of ZK motorcycles got trashed and a couple of people got shot, as far as we can tell."

"They are busy boys," I said. "Look, I may have something for you at our meeting tomorrow. Some insight on what's going on, and some cell tracking and texts from ZK cell phones."

"Do you remember *anything* about correct police procedure from your brief time with us, Farrell?"

I grinned. "Barely. I know you can't use this kind of stuff in court, and I'm real sorry about that. But it'll give you leads. My feeling is that ZK rank and file are amateur. Anyone you bring in will have a rap sheet, and my bet is there'll be links to convictions and unsolved crimes. The people behind it are a different story entirely, and that's more worrying."

He grunted. "I'll see you and the colonel downtown tomorrow morning then. Take care."

"Thanks, Captain, and you." I was almost starting to believe he did care.

∞ ∞ ∞ ∞ ∞

The flowerbeds made Lakeside look like a much prettier place in the daytime. I picked a spot beneath a pale bark birch tree to give me good shade for the car.

I walked into the clubhouse and the front desk guided me to the conference room, a long, bright space with a gleaming mahogany table and cushy executive chairs.

"Mykayla!" I said. I hadn't gotten close enough to examine her yesterday, but it was the last thing I was expecting, to see her here.

She stood up and smiled. She was pale and moving carefully, but there was no scarring or bruising. She walked around and awkwardly offered her hand.

"I have a lot to thank you for, Amber. You and Tullah."

I ignored the hand and gave her a gentle hug. "It's nothing. I'm so happy to see you recovered."

"Neat, huh? That's what Bian did for me." She twisted and looked adoringly at Bian over her shoulder.

Oh boy! I hoped Bian treated her gently.

Diana came from the head of the table to greet me. She wore black pants and shirt, and a pale gray jacket. Her hair was up and gold bracelets and rings completed an understated elegance.

We hugged. She kissed me, not on the cheek, but on the neck. "Athanate style," she said with a smile. A little shiver passed through me.

Bian followed and gave me an extra squeeze. "Thank you again, Round-eye," she whispered. She was soberly dressed today, in a dark blue business suit. I was glad that Mykayla, at least, was in jeans like me.

We sat down at the table. "There'll be coffee in a few minutes," Diana said and gestured to me. "I think you want to start, Amber."

"I'd like to know first what happened leading up to yesterday, if you can talk about it, Mykayla."

She nodded, sitting very still and looking down at the table.

"There's not a lot to say. I've seen you and Bian at raves." She looked sideways at Bian and smiled. "I never got a chance to meet you before. You always seemed to be passing through or looking for someone. Then last Friday, you were both there and I guess I just jumped on Bian. I was high as a kite. I don't remember much of it." She laughed.

"Then Bian had to go. I got back home, and, oh, I don't know, Bian said she would come find me when she was ready, but I couldn't wait. How could I get in contact? Well, I knew you were vamp—I mean Athanate."

"But how, Mykayla?" I asked. I didn't bother to correct her impression of me. She was half right.

"I don't know. The way you move, like nothing's wasted. So cool. And up close," she looked down, frowning. "I danced with you once, or well, next to you anyway. There's a feeling. And there's this smell of copper and stuff. I know that sounds a little weird, but you both have it." She turned and looked at Diana. "You all have it."

It gave me a little shock to hear she could sense Athanate the way I could. Damn. Was that what tipped Nokes to me at the Crate & Freight stakeout? He could smell me?

"Okay, so you wanted to get back to Bian. What did you do?"

"Well, there was talk going around. The biker guys who run those raves. I heard they were in with vamps. I started asking around."

She took a sip of water, visibly steeling herself. "The next thing I know, they're around at my place. They wanted to know what I knew. They wouldn't believe me when I said nothing. I wouldn't give them your names. They started to hit me. And they said they would get a whole group…" Her head dropped and she trailed off.

"Okay, Mykayla," I said. Bian squeezed her hand. "I think that's enough. You were incredibly brave." That sounded condescending, but I really believed it.

I gave her a minute to recover.

"What'd be good," I said, turning to Diana, "is a description of what becoming Athanate would mean for Mykayla. I get that you might normally hold some of this back, but I think she's a special case. I want her to hear all the pros and cons before she makes her mind up." I felt I was pushing it a bit, but Mykayla needed this and I wanted to know for myself.

"Very well," Diana said. "As much as we can." She got up and started pacing, trailing her lustrous red fingernails over the glossy tabletop. Bian stood and leaned against the window, arms folded and ankles crossed.

"Vamps, you said, Mykayla." Diana bowed her head and was silent for a couple of paces. "And you, Amber, behind your concern, you fear what you may become, what you may lose."

She looked up and took a deep breath. "The soul, as I understand it, is that spiritual part of the person that is immortal. I know of no reason that prolonging the life of the physical body should dilute the soul. As for the function of the soul, that isn't directly affected by the transformation to Athanate." She shrugged. "I can't measure the soul, but I am sure I am spiritually the same person I was before I became Athanate. I need and want different things, but none that would outrage my former self."

"And vampires," she turned to Mykayla. "Vampires are the flickering illusions of Hollywood and the shadows of myth. They don't exist. We do. We are the Athanate, the undying. Humanity's secret, eternal companions on this earth."

"What are these illusions? The ones you fear?" She paused. "Monsters who've discarded their souls; evil incarnate. Killers without conscience or remorse." Diana leaned on the table and stared at Mykayla, who impressed me by holding her gaze steady. "I will not lie. There are Athanate who are monsters."

Just standing there, Diana was scaring me, and I've been around many scary people.

"But where do these monsters come from?" Diana turned on her heel and picked up a newspaper from a side table, laying it down in front of me and opening it at the latest horrific murder story. "From people. People like you. I'll ask you this: is it easier to create a new monster in a human body, or free one that's already there?"

She walked slowly down the table, her fingernails hissing quietly over the gleaming surface.

"The truth is," she said to me over her shoulder, "the monster's inside you. It has always been. The Athanate powers do no more than tempt it from its lair inside your head. What happens next is up to you. Just as it has always been."

"We're human, really," Bian said, coming back from the window to stand behind Mykayla. "No better or worse, but different, and that difference has always been a danger for Athanate, so we hide. We're not a *numerous* people."

How numerous? My interest was piqued, but I didn't want to interrupt.

Bian slid a hand down to Mykayla's shoulder. "We live longer and we don't age. Our health's better. We become stronger and faster. We have better physical control. We develop telergy—mental skills—and some skills you would call magical." Her hand caressed Mykayla's neck, and Mykayla turned to kiss the wrist. "To keep all this happening, we need pure human blood. Specifically human and not Athanate. Without it we die."

Diana leaned on the table and opened her mouth, showing her fangs: beautiful, shining, ivory knives. Mykayla shivered. After a moment, Diana's fangs withdrew and became normal canines again. "The fangs manifest to bite," she said. "They siphon blood to special glands and organs in the throat that take nutrients from the blood and create pheromones and other biological agents."

She stood up.

"You both need to be aware of what it looks like when an Athanate wants or needs Blood." Diana gestured to Bian, and Mykayla and I swung around. Bian walked a little away from us, suddenly sensuous and predatory in her movements.

"Her body is being flooded with the Athanate elethesine hormone. Blood flow changes, feeding major muscles, making the face pale, the fine movements more controlled."

Bian turned around smoothly. She wasn't one to fidget anyway, but there was an eerie stillness that meshed with the oiled precision of her motion. Her eyes had gone dark and glittering.

"Her pupils enlarge, her eyes cease to blink and her tear glands compensate," Diana said.

"My airways expand, my heart rate and breathing increase," whispered Bian, her voice as smooth and seductive as her movements had been. "My senses become very acute. My fangs manifest." Her eyes fixed on Mykayla and her chest labored. "I thirst."

Diana walked around and stood in front of Bian. After a long moment, Bian blinked and turned to the window.

"Younger Athanate would not have that control," Diana said, returning. "Be extremely careful around Athanate that exhibit those symptoms."

I watched Mykayla. It's one thing to want to be a vampire because Hollywood says it's cool, or because you've got a crush on one, and quite another to start thinking about how they actually do what they do.

"I understand," she said. She looked pale, but firm.

Bian came and leaned on the back of Mykayla's chair, looking not exactly normal, but at least more like she usually did. "We can't have children," she said, her voice still low and sweet. "Something in what makes us Athanate prevents it. But we can make new Athanate. That's what we'd do for you. We think of it as fulfilling your potential. Our name for the process is *crusis*. But, it's dangerous."

"Someone picked at random and subjected to the crusis would almost certainly die," Diana said, staring at me. "When that doesn't happen, it's interesting in itself."

"In House Altau," she went on, "we're careful. We lose no more than one in a hundred in crusis. To achieve this, our first step is selection. We start with people who're more likely to survive. Being able to sense Athanate is one of the positive indicators."

"Like I can?" asked Mykayla.

Diana nodded. "Very few people can actually smell or sense Athanate like you, Mykayla. What you sense, we call the marque. Each House has its own."

She paused, sipped some water. "For selection, we also look at mental and physical health. When we've gone through that, we call them Aspirant, and assign them Mentors."

Bian took it up again. "Next, we eliminate. You have to live healthy, train hard and pass tests. No pass, no go. Your body has to be at its physical peak. You take no medicines. And no recreational drugs. Not even nicotine or alcohol is allowed."

I could see the word 'bummer' as if it had come up in lights on Mykayla's forehead. "Ever?" she asked faintly.

"Not during crusis. There's not much need after." Bian grinned and went on. "During this training, when you're ready, you're bitten by a Mentor. The agent that begins the crusis is in the bite. Our Mentors can limit it, so that it takes three bites for the full amount to be given. This gives your body time to adapt."

Diana tilted her head to one side. "Listed out like that, it sounds a joyless, soulless process. If you choose this path, you'll see it's not. The crusis and our Blood are sacred to us. The ordeal binds us together, and the act of giving and taking Blood is the core of what it is to be Athanate."

I stirred in my seat. Diana turned and looked at me.

"What about Aspirants who change their minds? Or who are eliminated, as you put it?" I said.

Diana resumed pacing. "They try again, or they stop, but remain within the mantle of the House, as kin. Almost all take one of those options. If they don't, if they wish to return to being normal humans, they wake at their home from a fever with no clear memory of the preceding events. It's the same with those who are asked and do not wish to proceed. They have no memory that they were asked. I won't lie, erasing memories is not pleasant for them, nor is it completely successful." She stopped. "Being bitten three times, however, changes the body. There's no going back then."

"And when humans stay with the House as kin, you mean they are the ones that provide the blood? Why do they do that?"

"I could simply say health and long life. It wouldn't be a difficult sell, Amber, to give some blood once or twice a month in exchange for being young and healthy for a hundred years or more. But actually, it's not like that. For a healthy group over time, one of us needs four or five normal humans for Blood. It would be dangerous for us if these weren't deep and committed relationships. Part of becoming Athanate, and part of becoming kin, includes changes to the instincts that drive relationships."

"Don't forget the pleasure," Bian said, leaning over the back of the chair and trailing fingers along Mykayla's cheek. "That's an important part of it." I didn't think Mykayla had forgotten that.

Diana smiled briefly. "Athanate Houses are like Darwinian organisms; we've evolved needs that help our survival. We need the commitment of kin and we have the means to nurture it, and, yes, that includes pleasure as well as commitment. Athanate have subconscious drives, the Athanate imperatives, to form these bonds. An Athanate without kin is a sick Athanate."

"This bond—it's due to the pheromones or agents you mentioned? Or this mental skill—telergy?" I asked.

"Telergic compulsion in any form to provide blood is banned in Altau, barring life or death situations. Pheromones or agents? Yes, they certainly start the process; the envirics that pleasure, the aniatropics that heal. They help maintain the process. But the commitment is not based on them. It's like love; in fact it *is* love, just differently experienced. Experience is the only true understanding. It's not something that can be explained. It has to be shared. The emotion is as vital to us as the Blood." Diana stood in front and stared down at me. "We need these emotions to sustain us, but also to ground us, to give us our place in this world."

She leaned again on the table, her eyes looking right through me. Her voice dropped and yet still seemed to fill the room. "The commitment goes both ways. This is the gift and the sorrow of the Athanate; to see your loves pass before you like the days of summer while your heart still beats. To keep your vigil in the shadows and rise again with every sun."

The breath caught in my throat. I was sure she had just quoted something very old, something I had never heard before, possibly something that no one besides Athanate heard, something full of grief. I had a sense of time behind Diana, like a great, dark wheel turning. Bian walked around the table and put a hand on Diana's shoulder. She shuddered and the room seemed lighter again.

I gave myself a shake and tried to concentrate. In the silence, I spoke. "Is this for Altau, or all Athanate?"

Diana shook her head. "I could have said all Houses like Altau. That is the creed of the Panethus group of Athanate. It is different for Basilikos."

"Where humans are forced to provide blood?"

Bian nodded. "Basilikos covers a range of beliefs. Milder ones regard humans as pets. The worst, as slaves, or just food. They need their emotional sustenance as well. It's just that they've found fear works too."

I would need to come back to Basilikos and understand them better, but I needed to concentrate on how Altau behaved for the moment. "So, we are a happy little Athanate in House Altau," I said, "recently converted and with kin. Nothing to worry about?"

Diana huffed. "You have to work at being Athanate. Especially in the newly converted, there are problems. Close monitoring reduces these, but the possibility of becoming rogue is highest early on. Rogues lose themselves in the sensations of being Athanate, the pleasures we take in our Blood and emotion. Even older Athanate are at risk." Diana tapped the table in front of Mykayla. "Anything that weakens control at the wrong moment is a danger. This is why we live as a community, a House—to support each other. Caught early enough, the insanity that is being rogue can be reversed."

"And if not caught early?" I asked.

"We provide a quick and humane death," Bian said. A chill went through the room again.

"Overall, from human to well-adjusted Athanate, how many do you lose?" I asked.

"About one in fifty," Diana said.

I sat back. The numbers didn't add up, as I'd said to David. I wondered if he'd gotten much further down this line, or whether Diana in her communicative mood today was the best bet to answer my questions.

"You're concerned about something, Amber," Diana said.

"Yes. Where are all the Athanate in Denver? If you lose only one in fifty in the conversion, then either you're not converting many or something's happening."

She paced over to the window and looked out over the garden and the golf course beyond.

"We lose some when their kin die." I could hear old memories in her voice again. "We lose some when the deeper skills are taught. But those are not what you've asked about. I said I would answer as much as I can, and there are some things I cannot talk about without Skylur's agreement. I can tell you that there have been Athanate wars which have devastated our people. We're in a quiet period now, a cold war, between Panethus and Basilikos."

There was a knock at the door, and Bian went over and spoke briefly with someone outside.

"I've got to go. I'll take Mykayla," Bian said to me. "I'll continue to talk to her, as we've promised. She'll be the best-informed person ever when she makes her decision."

"I've made my mind up. It won't change," Mykayla said. "But thanks again, Amber."

They left. Diana continued to stare out the window.

"How bad were the wars against Basilikos?" I asked.

"They reached a peak under the cover of the Spanish flu and the first World War. For a time then, it seemed we'd destroyed ourselves, but slowly the survivors came out of hiding. In the 1930s, the Assembly was set up and has maintained a peace of sorts since then."

"And you think that peace is at an end?"

Diana nodded.

"What a good time for Panethus to make an alliance with normal humans," I said.

Diana smiled. "You're preaching to the converted, but many of the Panethus Assembly representatives are elders that barely survived localized attempts to find an equilibrium with humans before. It's not straightforward."

I rocked back. There was a lot to think about just in what she had said and I was sure there was more underneath it all.

"Well, you can't hide forever in today's society. Not in the States. What you need is a way to control the discovery."

"My argument exactly." Diana moved from the window and leaned over me. I felt the power of her eyes like a weight pressing me into the seat. My heart stuttered. "And you wonder why you're so interesting to me, Sergeant Farrell?" she whispered.

Chapter 36

I shrank back. My guard had come down with Diana and the shock of her attack on my mind was doubled. She wasn't brutal like Skylur, but the force of her attack was every bit as powerful. I was pinned to the chair. I couldn't take my eyes from hers.

She swayed closer and her mouth opened. I realized with horror her gleaming fangs were down. They tapered to points as sharp as needles.

"Banned," I mumbled. "No." My mouth was numb and my throat felt dry. But my neck felt warm and loose. My head tilted back and my breath caught. I *wanted* her to bite me. Her fangs grazed my neck and I gasped, arching up to offer myself.

"Gods," she groaned, and shuddered. "Bian has it exactly right. You will be delicious."

Her hands grabbed my head and jerked it back upright. Her eyes glittered inches from mine. "Fight it, Amber. You can break it, if you really try."

Her fangs were inches from my neck. Why hadn't she bitten me yet?

"Not fear? What's the key, Amber?" She stroked my cheek. "Where's the steel in your spine?"

She was playing with me. A spark of anger caught in my belly.

"Ahhh," she whispered. "Anger. Come on Amber, fight me. I like it when they struggle."

She slapped me, and just as she intended, the anger exploded in my head. I could feel it pushing at the gray fingers that dug into my mind. For a second or more it held, but I fed the anger and I tore her control loose. I could move again, though I could barely see for the fury that gripped me. My hands whipped up to seize her throat. And she wasn't there.

She stood calmly on the other side of the table. Her mouth was closed and her eyes weren't glittering.

"Bitch," I yelled at her, hyperventilating. She was quicker than me. I couldn't catch her, and even if I could, she was stronger than me. All I could hit her with were harsh words and furious looks.

"Tell me, Amber," she said quietly. "When you were in the army, what was the best training you had?"

The question was so oblique, it punctured the anger that had freed me from her control. I sat down and took some deep breaths. She hadn't hurt me like Skylur had. She'd scared me every bit as much, but she hadn't bitten me. What she'd really done was teach me that I could break the Athanate mind control, and the key was anger. Well, I had lots of that in reserve.

"The real thing was the best training of all," I said, proud that I could keep my voice level.

She walked back around and sat beside me, completely unconcerned. "You have just had the best training I can provide, and in less than a half dozen seconds, once you knew what to do, you broke my control." She looked squarely at me. "You will not find many stronger than that. Congratulations, Amber, I never had so quick a pupil. That anger, however, will need to be watched carefully, during crusis."

Saying that to someone who'd been as angry as I had just been wouldn't normally help, but I had twelve years of keeping it under a tight rein, and I was ashamed I'd nearly lost it here.

A polite knock on the door interrupted us, and Diana opened it to allow a waiter to bring in a tray with coffee and cookies. It was so ordinary and everyday that I laughed. What would have happened if he'd barged in five minutes ago?

Diana smiled, sensing the joke herself. She poured the coffee.

"Along with the imperatives that change the way we behave, we have some changes to our perceptions. All the senses are sharpened. You're more sensitive to flavors, scents, colors, and sounds recently. You're seeing better in the dark, as well."

I thought of the taste of rum and Carmen's cooking, the scent of flowers at Manassah, the color of Jen's eyes, the sound of her sleeping heartbeat. I stirred uncomfortably.

"And we are strongly attracted by things that are beneficial to us." She laid my coffee in front of me and sat down with hers. "I know that there will be benefit to us in sharing, because I find your marque so attractive."

She meant sharing blood.

"The marque is more than that, though. It's a key to Athanate society. It is subtle telergy, reinforced by pheromones. It holds a House together, like a hive." She sipped her coffee and changed tack. "Now, Amber, you have something to tell me about these prions," she said.

"Yes. Skylur was right when he guessed that something happened when I was in the army. You both know I'm part Athanate, so you know what it was." *And Colonel Laine is going to kill me.* I continued regardless. "The army scientists are monitoring me, and they have identified what causes a person to become Athanate. They're tiny strings of proteins, called prions. Most prions kill the host. The Athanate prions don't. Or rather," I said, taking the tester out of my bag, "if the person survives the initial infection, then I guess the relationship becomes symbiotic. This machine measures levels of prions."

I strapped it to my arm and hit the start button. There was the familiar feel of the positioning and the tiny stab of the needle. I watched while the readout on top settled to 0.48, the highest reading I had ever had.

"Are you all right, Amber?" I looked up at Diana and nodded. I just felt numb.

"What does the reading mean?" she said.

I shrugged. "I'm not sure exactly. It's an index. The scientists say 0.8 would be full Athanate and 1.0 would be a dead host."

"You're over halfway then?"

It felt more than over halfway to me, but I nodded again and held the unit towards her. She extended her arm and I strapped it on and hit the button. Her reading was 0.79, so the scientists must have made some progress to accurately predict her reading.

"Interesting," Diana said. "These machines—"

"I need this one." I cut her off. "I'm sure they could be made available in some kind of pooling of knowledge." I returned the tester to my bag.

Diana took a sip of coffee and a delicate bite of cookie with perfectly normal-looking teeth. "I worry about the government's ability to keep matters secret," she said.

"I bet that you've been trying to find out about my army history from government databases. Have any luck?"

"Point well made." She paused to finish her cookie. "Well, time to brief you more specifically for the charity ball."

I settled back.

"The ball is unusual this year, in that Mrs. Harriman and Mr. McIntire decided to add an incentive for local businesspeople to attend. This is in the form of an international trade delegation who are also attending, looking for contacts. The organizers have been delighted at the response to their proposals; far more trade delegates accepted than they expected." She smiled. "The delegates are all bona fide businesspeople, but the majority of them are also members of the Athanate Assembly. We're a secretive people and an opportunity like this provides us with an excellent cover to meet, which we'll do next week."

Diana resumed her pacing, coffee in hand.

"The Assembly members, the representatives, will be guarded by a neutral group of Athanate drawn from both sides of the Assembly, the Warders. No one else from the Athanate community may approach the Assembly representatives. The only time this surveillance will be allowed to ease is at the ball. House Altau, as the host, and president by the way, must not be in attendance at the event. You're our secret agent. If you agree."

I joined her at the window.

"To what, exactly?" I said.

"Most importantly, to be a messenger, and to keep your role secret. Also to listen to what Matlal, the leader of the Basilikos party, might have to say and report it back to us. Skylur is right, Matlal will come to you like a moth to the flame."

"I take a message to someone?"

"No. Someone among the delegation wishes to pass a message secretly to us in advance of the Assembly meeting. We don't even know who it'll be. Simply that it relates to New Mexico. It was decided that this was the least dangerous way to deliver it. All the messenger will know is that you are the woman who'll be with Jennifer Kingslund." She cocked an eyebrow at me. "Don't have a falling out, please."

"And I'm doing this in exchange for the advice Skylur gave?"

"For that, and the reasons we gave. We will be your harbor in your need." Putting her coffee down, Diana turned to me, her face as unreadable as an ancient statue. "And I am begging you."

I stared at her. "These are really high stakes, aren't they? I'm not allowed to walk out of here saying no, am I?"

"It's worse than that, Amber," she said. "You're not even allowed to have doubts."

I could feel her in my head again. I'd realized that House Altau could not afford for this to go wrong. I didn't doubt Diana would be able to erase all memory of the Athanate from my head if she felt it necessary. And yet she had first shown me the way to stop her mental attack. She was confusing me, but however much she frightened me, I still trusted her, and I was going to do what they asked anyway. She took my hands to steady me as I looked into her eyes, and my head swam.

I didn't fight it and that made it easier. I could feel her in my head. I could feel her ask the question and my reply came from a level below conscious thought. Immediately, she was out of my head. I knew she had done nothing and looked at nothing else.

Or she's completely screwed me and just left me feeling that she hasn't. No—that way madness lies.

"Thank you, and my apologies," she murmured, when my legs felt steadier under me.

"Can I lie, like that?"

She shook her head and let me go. "There's lots more you need to know, but until after the ball, it's best we leave you as you are."

She went to her bag and brought out some documents and handed them to me. They transferred the ownership of the car outside to me.

"Just like that?" I asked.

"You rescued Mykayla. That was our responsibility. You've agreed to be our spy. I think this is appropriate payment."

I thanked her sincerely. My old car had been failing and I didn't know how I would have afforded a new one or how I could run my business without a car.

"Can I ask you about werewolves?" I said. I had told Jen that I would settle the werewolf problem, but I didn't think just showing up and waiting for them at Silver Hills at the next full moon would be the best way to approach them.

"You can, but you missed the expert. Bian's our liaison with the Weres."

"How many packs in Denver?"

"Just the one."

"How would I contact them?"

Diana turned to look at me. "Why would—" she waved her hand, dismissing it. "No time for that. I'll ask Bian to talk to you."

"Why is Bian the liaison?" I said.

"She's our Diakon, our ambassador to the outside. And she's good with them."

No doubt I would have an enjoyable time, trying to get Bian to tell me more.

But in the meantime, Diana had finished her briefing, but she was still here, pacing like a caged lioness. If she had been the type to chew a fingernail, she would have been chewing now.

"What else, Diana? There's been something else the whole morning that you've been working up to."

She stopped and leaned over me again, resting her weight on the arms of the chair. Her eyes seemed huge. My neck went all warm and wobbly again.

"I told Skylur, you're very perceptive." She took a deep breath and stood back. "I want you to open a channel through your military contacts for me to talk in absolute secrecy to the government," she said. "Without telling anyone else, Skylur included."

Chapter 37

Café Vienne was busy with the late lunch crowd, gathered in little knots around the small tables. The huge windows lit the whole place up. It was a noisy, cheerful, airy café that I liked to visit whenever I could afford it. I saw Mary and Tullah in the corner and hurried across the harlequin-tiled floor to them.

They'd nearly finished their lunches. "Sorry, my meeting ran late," I said as I sat down.

That sounded better than 'I was agreeing on the terms for a preliminary meeting between an Athanate and an army colonel'.

Tullah said hello, but sat subdued. Mary's face, dark and lined from too much sun, was politely welcoming, no more. I knew she could laugh like a horse when the mood took her, but she seemed serious today.

"It doesn't matter, Amber. It's been nice to have my daughter's undivided attention for once," Mary said. "And I know the Athanate are the devil's own when it comes to detail." She brushed her long black hair away from her face and her deep eyes looked innocently across at me.

I pushed down a spark of irritation.

"Well, it seems you know much more about me and my business that I do about you," I said. "Even the things I thought I knew, I'm starting to doubt."

Mary looked at me without changing her expression. "I will apologize only once," she said. "I find repeating the word a pain in the butt, so this one 'sorry' will have to be enough for this afternoon."

The waitress came and took my order of a light pasta and sparkling water. Mary looked out the window, as if there was something to see on the top of the shopping center across the way. When we were alone again, she began to speak quietly.

"Amber, I asked Tullah to accept your offer of part-time work because I wanted to keep an eye on you. I regret that I put her in this position. She hasn't read your emails or bugged your office. She likes you. She's enjoyed working for you and wants it to go on."

Mary sipped her espresso and watched me. I wasn't going to react.

"Even if we hadn't had the business yesterday with that girl, Tullah has been demanding that we have a talk with you and explain ourselves. She wants to do that especially because she would like to work with you after college."

Mary had my attention, but I spared a smile for Tullah. I'd never known her to be so quiet. She gave me a small smile back.

If Mary had told me Tullah was keeping an eye on me a few months ago, I would have blown a fuse. Several fuses. At both of them. But that was before I'd had to admit to spying on my friend David, before I learned, from Jen, that I can tolerate friends needing to find out things about me. And given what I'd been through over the last week, not much was going to surprise me anymore. As it was, I just kept smiling and waited for the explanation.

Mary's face was seldom expressive, but maybe the skin tightened at the corners of her eyes. Her hand reached out and touched my bracelet. I was surprised to see the clasp must have been open and she caught it as it fell. She held the bracelet up and rolled the beads through her fingers thoughtfully. I remembered joking to Tullah about not knowing if the wolf's eye was watching me or watching out for me. Maybe that was closer to the truth than I'd thought.

"This is well tuned to you now," Mary said. She handed it back to me. "If you continue to wear it, you'll notice the tingle less and less consciously. It'll become like a sixth sense for you. It can't warn you if you're about to have an accident, but it will help where someone close by is intending to harm you."

I put it back on. "You do real magic then. What do I call you—witches, *brujas*?" I asked.

"It wouldn't be the first time," Mary said, and this time she did smile. "We don't use those words, but they'll do."

The waitress brought my pasta and I started to eat. Explanations didn't seem to be forthcoming on their own. "Why do you think I need watching?" I prompted.

Mary frowned.

"I'll start from the beginning." Her hands fiddled and I realized she was a smoker, missing her cigarette.

"What you've just called magic starts with an energy, something that can be used any way at all. Everyone accesses it at some level. Some people can tap into it and turn that energy into power that can make things happen. The use of that skill leaves a mark on a person that another user can see." She paused. "You have that mark."

I opened my mouth to tell her I had no idea what she was talking about, but she went right on.

"There are three types of user: learned, guided and instinctive. *Learned* covers the folk who use mumbo-jumbo incantations, but also the Athanate skills that they could teach you. *Guided* means you have a spirit guide who will enable your skill. That's what we use. *Instinctive* is a limited use that just comes naturally. That's what the Weres use."

I had so many questions they jammed in my throat.

"You," Mary said, waving a finger at me, "have a spirit guide."

"It's a wolf," Tullah said, then subsided again at a look from Mary.

"Oh," I said, at my conversational best.

"If that were all, I'd have spoken to you long ago," Mary said. "But users can also see workings, things that are in progress that were started by others. Becoming a Were or an Athanate is a working, and I can see that in you too. The spirit guide and the Athanate are in conflict inside you. Again, if that were all…" she waved a hand dismissively. I didn't want it dismissed. If my wolf was capable of controlling my Athanate side, I wanted to help him. Her. Whatever. But Mary didn't stop.

"Other workings include things that may lie dormant, or even skip generations before they actually do something. They may be for good or evil, blessing or curse. They require a tremendous effort to set up. They are important, so important they feed on life itself. I've seen very few of them."

Mary finally turned to look at me directly. "I can see one in you. You came here wondering what we are. My question is just the same. Amber, what the hell are you?"

∞ ∞ ∞ ∞ ∞

An hour later, the waitress took my cold pasta away and brought me coffee. I was tempted to ask for a double shot of rum in it. We hadn't gotten any closer to what the hell Mary thought I was, if not plain old me with a sprinkle of Athanate and spirit guide.

Mary said that she thought the Athanate part of me was winning the struggle against the spirit guide, and she didn't know of a way to help. She'd never seen this situation before. She didn't think Athanate were inherently evil, but that the power they wielded and the span they lived meant that most ended up being evil in her eyes. An Adept, as she called herself, lived a normal human lifespan, by choice. Adepts were valued by the Athanate, and Athanate could extend the Adept's life, as they did with kin. The result of that was that most true Adepts avoided contact with Athanate. This was going to be a problem if I became Athanate, because she wanted to keep watching me.

Mary's spirit guide was a bear, and I was treated to a disorienting, private vision of a phantom grizzly looming behind her at the table. I tried looking at Tullah, but only got a dim sense of something moving in darkness.

"Tullah's unusual, in that her guide has not made itself known yet," Mary said. "She has some skill, but I've prevented her from using it so far."

I got a sense that wasn't the full story at all. While Mary was talking, I was watching Tullah's expression, and I was sure that she knew exactly what her spirit guide was. Interesting.

"I've raised that ban," Mary said, "in light of what's happening and her desire to work with you. Maybe that's what's needed to make the guide reveal itself."

"Hold on a second," I said. "You're not talking about the job she's been doing."

"Amber, I want to help," Tullah said. "Not just looking after the office. I want to help with investigations."

"You're nineteen, Tullah. No offense, you're great at what you do, but you're a college kid."

Mary leaned across and put a hand over mine. "Yes, she's nineteen. What were you doing when you were nineteen, Amber?"

A little shock of recall went through me. My nineteenth birthday, April 16, slipping out of the village. What was it called? Lung La. I never thought I would be cold in Vietnam, but I was shivering in the misty pre-dawn as we walked into the gloomy jungle, a dozen of us from Ops 4-10, another dozen from the Vietnamese special forces, a joint operation out of sight of the world, headed for the border—

"Stop!"

I blinked. Mary was gripping my hand and Tullah was looking at me with concern. I realized I must have been talking aloud.

"That was my fault," Mary said. "I intended that just as a question, not as an instruction. I leaked a bit of persuasion when I touched you. It's as if the energy is easier to reach here."

She looked around at the bustling little café and took a deep breath. "I'm just going to walk around the block," she said and got up. She lit up outside the window and moved off.

I sat shaken by the experience. It seemed this was my day for shocks. It told me a lot that the people who were supposed to be on my side were scaring me more than any enemies.

"Did that operation in Vietnam succeed?" asked Tullah.

It had succeeded, as you judge these things. Not for Joe. Handsome Joe from Nevada, with the pretty eyes and the quiet smile. I remembered the weight of his body across my shoulders, his blood mixing with my sweat as we headed back. No 4-10 bodies were left behind, ever. I carried my share. Later, as we waited for our extraction near Lung La, our Vietnamese colleagues put rice and a coin in Joe's mouth to show their respect for our dead and lined up solemnly to shake everyone's hand. A first, hidden step in rebuilding.

"Yeah," I said aloud. "That one worked." I tried to shake off the memories.

"I am my parents' daughter—I can take care of myself and I do have skills," Tullah was saying. "You're still the boss, and I promise I'll do what you say. And my courses in criminal law will be useful."

I stopped staring into the past and looked at her again. She was smart and bright and all sorts of things. She wasn't me. But maybe comparing her to me wasn't the way to look at it. And that legal knowledge would be an asset.

"We'll take things a step at a time," I said. "We're temporarily relocating to a study in Jennifer Kingslund's house down near the Country Club. That way, we get some measure of protection from the guards she's got at the moment. It would be too easy to hit us at the office, and there are too many people trying. Victor's guards have your ID and they'll let you in."

I drained my coffee while Tullah did a little jig of celebration on her chair.

"So tell me before she gets back, Tullah, what your spirit guide is, and why you don't want to tell your mother."

Tullah's eyes went wide and she looked across guiltily at the door. That was lucky enough, as Mary was coming back in.

"Can't tell you now," she whispered. "Not on the 'approved' list." She made quote signs with her fingers.

"These spirit guides, Mary," I said to distract her as she sat down again, "are they real or just something in our heads?"

"I don't know. Ask me another."

"What else is out there? Elves and demons?"

Mary shook her head. "You could create an image of anything you could imagine from the energy, but something that complex just falls apart when you stop working at it. I've never heard of real elves or demons, or any place they could come from."

She looked sideways at Tullah, and smiled. "I can see my daughter has had good news. I'm a mother, and I would say it of course, but I believe you've made the right decision. You say you're fighting against becoming Athanate, and we'll help if we can. But I warn you, if you become fully Athanate, Tullah will have to leave."

Tullah's mouth compressed into a thin line at that.

"How can I tell when the Athanate side of me starts winning?" I asked, just to see what she would say.

Mary raised her eyebrows. "The Athanate should tell you in more detail. But from what I know, the urges, what they call the imperatives, start changing your behavior. New Athanate need to be desirable, noticeable. They need to attract humans to become blood servants. At the same time, they become more secretive." She looked me over.

"So if I start spending a lot of time on my appearance, that's a bad sign?"

"It's not just that," Mary said. "It's the reveling in it. Watch them and you'll see. It's almost funny seeing them in constant conflict with themselves. The half of them that wants to attract and the half that wants to remain unnoticed. Also, it'll be more obvious at night."

"Why? Is magic stronger at night?"

"No. It's just the way people are. Everyone has some kind of connection to the energy, even if it's just in the hindbrain. In daytime, this works against a single user. A million people in the broad daylight who believe you can't change into a wolf would make it difficult for a Were in the middle of Denver. But at night, out in the woods, those certainties are weaker." She smiled.

"So my bracelet works better at night?"

"Not quite that simple. Tullah can talk to you about it sometime." She got up. "We must go. But one last thing, Amber. Adepts can sense users around them. How to explain it?" She paused and made an expansive gesture with her arms. "Imagine the energy is like a huge trampoline. Every user makes a little dent in the trampoline. When they move, you can feel them through the trampoline. Most users are small, so you barely notice it. But if a powerful user taps the energy, it's like someone really heavy walking on the trampoline."

I nodded.

"Well, there are usually a couple of very powerful users in Denver. I've always attributed that to whoever runs that Athanate House. But this week there are a hell of a lot more." She stared at me before finishing quietly. "Be careful. And don't give up hope."

I gave them hugs and we went our separate ways.

Chapter 38

I went over to Lisa Macy's and tried on a dress that was so far outside of my experience, it was unreal. It was a dark green dream of silk. I loved it. Werner came over with a pair of shoes to fit, elegant but with a strong heel. He knew I didn't do stilettos, and these I could dance in. I felt like Cinderella as I tried everything on and turned in front of the mirror. I had to get some photos from the ball for mom. She would never believe it otherwise.

Lisa hissed and tutted over a couple of details I couldn't even see, but assured me that everything would be fine. Werner insisted I come much earlier than necessary on Friday.

Jen was still at work when I got back to the house, so I sat down in the study-office and opened the mail.

The first was a letter from the Veterans' Administration. I wanted to bang my head on the desk, but it looked expensive to repair.

Dear Ms. Farrell and *whereas no charges* have been brought and they would not *venture an opinion*, I would of course understand their position that payments had to be suspended until the conclusion of the investigation. I tossed it aside.

The second was from Krantz. It said simply that my payments were no longer a matter for investigation, but that I would need to re-apply directly to the VA to claim them again.

I sat and worked through some appropriate names for him, gathered from a variety of places during my days in Ops 4-10. Then I started to laugh. I didn't want the money. The stupid bastard thought he had won some important point, but all he'd proved was that he didn't understand the situation at all.

I was still laughing when Jen walked in. "Nice to hear, honey." She bent down and kissed my cheek in greeting. "And nice to see you back before midnight."

She settled in the other seat and told me that her meeting with Verdoon had had to be moved up and they'd met earlier today. Matt Bierbach had made complete digital images of his computer drives during the meeting, and was sorting out the contents to pass to me.

"I'm sure he'll finish quickly," she said, with a sly smile. "Something about a hot date tonight."

"No! Not Tullah? They only met yesterday."

"Honestly, I don't know, honey, but that's where my bets are. They don't waste time these days."

Carmen called us in for dinner. Only half a plate of pasta at lunch, and having the daylights scared out of me a couple of times had made me hungry. That was a good thing, because Carmen had clearly decided we were too skinny and we had what looked like half a lamb between us, cooked Mediterranean style. Wondering whether I would need my new dress taken out an inch made me remember the charity ball.

"Oh, I forgot to say yesterday. A client has paid for me to attend the McIntire-Harriman ball on Friday. You're still going?"

I could see Jen's curiosity about the client, but she restrained herself. "Hell, I'm on the organizing committee, honey, so I have to be there from mid-afternoon," she said. "You wouldn't believe the hassle this international delegation have caused. I'll fix the table seating for you, otherwise you'll be stuck in a corner."

I made a mental note to make sure Victor's guards were able to access all areas in the afternoon. The actual ball itself would be safe with the number of convention center security staff on duty, and our guards could come back to pick us up at the end.

We finished the meal with Jen telling me some stories of the way some of the international delegation were behaving, which had us both chuckling. I hoped it wasn't one of them who would have the message for me.

She poured herself a glass of brandy. I turned down a rum after the wine we'd had with dinner.

She had reports to read, but before she left me, she turned to ask: "On your desk, there's a plaque. Who's Tara?"

My stomach tightened, as it did whenever people asked. "My twin sister. She was stillborn."

Jen stood in the doorway a moment more. "You see her in the reflection."

"Yes." No one had ever figured that out before.

"I'm sorry," Jen said quietly, and went.

∞ ∞ ∞ ∞ ∞

It was dark in the gym. I didn't need the lights any more.

The test machine had read 0.49 this evening.

I worked through Master Liu's forms, and my body was quicker and stronger than it had ever been. Instead of effort, there came a sensation of floating. Up above, in the daylight, I struggled against the thought that I was becoming Athanate. Down here, in the dark, the physical sensations overwhelmed the doubts.

Both Diana and Mary had said that there weren't any monsters I didn't bring to the party. I took some comfort there, as I did from knowing more about what was happening to me.

But I was still changing.

The nightmares had stopped. Or I had changed my definition of the nightmare. Last month, drinking someone's blood was a nightmare. Now blood and sex tangled together in misty dreams that shocked me with their erotic thrill.

I half believed I was sleepwalking, but I hadn't seen any evidence I'd bitten anyone. Yet.

Chapter 39

WEDNESDAY

Morales had taken us up to his office, collecting coffees on the way from a machine. The coffee tasted as bad as it always had, throughout the building. It was strange visiting this level of HQ. Up here, in Morales' office, we were at the front between the political and policing faces of the Denver PD. The total count for Denver was less than 1,500 officers, and here was where they did the balancing act to work out where their effort was best focused. Remembering that, I resolved to be kinder to Morales today.

When we were seated, Morales opened with a gesture to the colonel. "Thanks for agreeing to come here. Before we get to the main event, I'd like to start with an issue that has a bearing."

I realized he and the colonel hadn't worked out their pecking order. I hid a smile. The colonel didn't really care, but Morales was a good politician as well as a good police officer. He didn't want to ruin a working relationship, but he wanted to run the meeting.

"Of course," said the colonel.

Morales stirred some of the papers in front of him and looked up at me. "I got a briefing yesterday from the team I've assigned to the Carter case. He's in the clear and it's confirmed that ZK were organizing the illegal shipments. I'm starting to wrap up whatever I can reach in Denver, but inevitably the FBI will get involved." He shifted uncomfortably.

"You need to understand, this meeting is on my calendar as a liaison meeting with the army. Everything today is for our ears only. But when federal bureaus get involved, I will do everything by the book."

We nodded. We both understood he was in a very tight spot.

"They'll want to talk to you, Farrell. There's your initial involvement, which I guess was straightforward, but yesterday, I was told that there's a contract been put out on you."

I shrugged. This wasn't news to me, and I was doing my best to make things difficult for whoever came in to replace Mr. Obvious.

Morales' smile was humorless. "Not a local contract, Farrell. This has gone out with a tag of a quarter of a million bucks."

Even the colonel reacted to that. That was sniper rifle level. The kind of money you'd pay for a political assassination. *What the hell?*

I tried to laugh it off. "Damn, I'd shoot myself for that much."

Morales didn't laugh. "I don't know who you ticked off, Farrell, but I suspect it may be this man. He was in charge of the smuggling operation." Morales pushed a grainy photo across. "Frank Hoben. He's the boss's son."

Shit. Onebrow.

"The feds are going to see that sum as an anomaly that they want explained," he went on. "Coincidentally, a gang war seems to have broken out. ZK foot soldiers are being killed. And your car has been recorded in the vicinity of incidents. They're going to see connections whether they're there or not."

He was doing me a real favor here. I did *not* want the feds talking to me, not ever but most certainly not now. Of course, that wasn't my car any more, but unless Altau had gotten really cute, it would show as being registered to me at the time of the incidents.

With a sigh, I passed a USB across to him. "This contains an analysis of calls made on cell phones belonging to a couple of ZK foot soldiers and this man," I tapped the photo of Onebrow, and continued in my most careful police-speak. "I took the phones when the men tried to intimidate a prominent local businessperson. I believe this was to do with ZK acquiring a legitimate business front."

Morales' eyes bored into me. I didn't need to tell him exactly what had happened. I'd had a key person in the ZK hierarchy in my grasp and I'd let him go. *Shit again.*

I was going to have to tell Jen I'd screwed up on this, trying to play macho mind games.

A thought diverted me; the attack could have been to prevent damage to an existing ZK legitimate business front. Had I been looking at this the wrong way entirely? Did they secretly own Tucker Beacon? My mind darted off in a third direction—maybe ZK wanted to buy Tucker Beacon. Stopping a rival bidder would make that easier and cheaper.

Morales was looking at me to see if I would share my thoughts, but I didn't have enough to go on. I wanted to talk this through with Jen first to get her take on it. And find out whether she wanted to keep me on the case after my news about Onebrow.

Morales had put the drive straight into his laptop and checked he could read the files. His eyes widened and he grunted in appreciation as he saw the detail on his screen. "Good. Thanks for this. But now I'm going to ask you to back off. Any more involvement with ZK is going to hamper our efforts, and get the feds on your case." He indicated the files on his screen. "With this and what we have, we should roll them up quickly anyway."

I nodded, only a little reluctantly. It made sense for them to take this. If they could wrap it up, I wouldn't need to worry about an assassin stalking me. The phone records had to be a gold mine for the police, at least on the ZK operational side. My run through them confirmed to me that regardless of how the rest of ZK operated, Onebrow knew what he was doing. His cell had only been used for a restricted number of calls. My impression was that this was his ZK cell phone. He would call Daddy on another phone. The cut off in his call history also showed he'd cleared the memory recently. The others hadn't been so careful.

"You have other news, I understand," Morales said.

"Denver's more complicated than we thought," I said with a tight smile for the understatement. "When we started this a year ago, we thought we knew that there must be a small vampire community, largely keeping to itself. For the army, the interest is security and military. For the police, crime. For me," I stopped. What had I wanted? It all seemed a long time ago. "I guess, it's now knowledge about what's happening to me."

The colonel registered that with a nod.

"Not only is the vampire community more complicated than we thought, but there are other paranormals. The colonel has confirmed, from some evidence I gave him, that we have werewolves."

Morales wasn't surprised; he had been the one Jen had asked about the weird stuff at Silver Hills.

"The vampires will provide me with an introduction to the Weres. There seems to be some interaction between the two communities. I can't say any more, other than suggest someone in your department collect any police reports of wolves, big dog attacks and the like for me to review. I've no indication that Weres are any less law-abiding than most vampires."

"The vampires are helping you? Why?" asked Morales.

I shrugged. "I'm nearly one myself, Captain."

"There's no cure?" Morales had known that I had been infected once we'd had our meeting with the colonel last year after the incident with the rogues. I guess he thought, as I had, that I was handling it. That there was a way out.

I shook my head. "I've held it off, but it's advancing now. I might have a couple more months left."

That got the colonel's attention. His head jerked up.

Morales looked shocked. He got up and paced behind his desk. The wear of the carpet showed it was something he did often. "Nothing can be done? Colonel?"

The colonel gave a small shake of his head. Morales touched his shirt unconsciously, right over where a small cross on a chain would lie. "I'm sorry," he said to me.

"Like the falling man, it feels okay so far," I replied. This was the opening I'd been hoping for. "Captain, do you still trust me?"

Morales frowned. "Sure, I trust you, Farrell. Always have. You're bug crazy but—"

"But in a couple of months, I'll be a vampire. Still gonna trust me?"

Morales sat down again and thought that through. "Yes," he said finally. "And if I can trust you, why would I assume another vampire would necessarily be any different?"

"Thank you, Captain. I went through that to make my point on how I'd like to take this forward—a citizen remains a citizen whether they're vampire or Were."

The colonel stirred, but didn't say anything. He'd been very quiet today, and it was worrying me. For his part, Morales continued to look thoughtful, but didn't challenge me.

"Okay. First things first, they don't call themselves vampires. They call themselves Athanate."

I told them everything Diana had authorized me to say, which was pretty much everything I knew, right down to the tense political situation. As agreed with her, I made no mention of the Athanate Assembly next week, or the complication that Skylur had to be kept out of the loop in dealing with them. I also didn't tell them I already knew where House Altau was.

"...and so, she's asking for a meeting with the colonel to lay down a protocol for how this is going to be handled." There was silence as I finished.

The colonel broke it. "I'm flattered but I'm not senior enough," he said. "I'm not even in the right area. I'm only involved because of what happened in the unit."

"She knows that, Colonel. She's not expecting you to come up with a treaty. She trusts me. I trust you. We have to find someone we can all trust in the administration. Grow the group carefully until we reach the president."

We all shut up for a while. It wasn't that we didn't know where we were aiming for, or that we didn't realize who had to become involved in negotiating a compact between humans and vampires in America, but saying the name 'president' has its own magic.

"And until then?" said the colonel.

"Until then, I'm the go-between. Hopefully I can hold off the problems that new Athanate have. If I think I won't be able to, I'll tell you. And I'll say this at the start: I may not tell you everything I know, but I won't lie. And I'll do the same for the Athanate."

Morales was okay with not being in the meeting as long as he got a briefing. He was less happy about an open commitment not to tell anyone else until we said it was time, but he understood.

I flipped open my laptop and took some possible dates from the colonel to discuss with Diana. He leaned across and pointed them out. His finger passed over a Sunday, with one of my dark jokes—it said NAVY.

"What have the Navy got to do with it?" he asked.

"Nothing. That stands for Not A Vampire Yet. I'll change it to Not Athanate Yet—NAY."

He smiled a little. Not that I expected belly laughs from him, but my jokes obviously weren't as good as they used to be. He continued to stare at the calendar, probably looking a couple of months ahead.

"The scientists are wanting you to come back in for a checkup," he said.

"They've had their chance, Colonel. I'll never get out if they get their claws into me now."

He didn't reply.

"Tell you what," I said. "I understand you can't study this thing accurately without a full-time test subject. I can arrange that."

"How?" he looked at me, frowning.

"Bring one of the scientists here, and I'll arrange for him to get bitten."

The pair of them just looked at me. I gave up. I wasn't going to get a laugh today. Back to business. I pulled the Krantz letter out and put it down on the table.

"This worm has just discussed the case with one of my clients. I think that may be illegal. Thanks for getting him off my case, but he's interpreting that kinda loosely." I put the VA letter down beside it. "And for the record, I don't want these payments."

The colonel wouldn't have missed the thought behind that. I couldn't resign from the army because I wasn't in it any more. I was doing the next best thing, telling him I didn't feel he had control over me; I didn't work for him.

He ignored all that and picked up the letter. "If he spoke to a client of yours I can have him reprimanded and reassigned," he said.

I shook my head. That would be to descend to Krantz's level. Anyhow, he'd tried his worst and it hadn't been much. "He might be onto something with the rest of it. He can't do anything more to me. Leave him alone."

We finished up. I wasn't satisfied with the way the meeting had gone. I had a definite requirement on the meetings with Diana, and I hadn't gotten a response yet, but the colonel wouldn't be pinned down until he'd had time to think it through. Morales was trying to help and behave normally, but when he thought I wasn't looking at him, he was looking at me as if he could see the fangs. I might have more trouble coming on that side.

He walked us down to the lobby and shook both our hands. I couldn't decide whether he'd let my hand go quicker than normal, or what I should think about it if he had.

There was a moment when the colonel was a few paces away and Morales leaned in and muttered to me. "You're going to have to explain to Ms. Kingslund that you screwed up with Hoben."

I just nodded. Of course I would and I wouldn't blame her if she fired me.

Outside the building, the colonel and I paused in the cold autumn sunshine. I closed my eyes and held my face to the light. Up in the hills, the aspen would be turning. Hillsides would look as if they'd caught fire. I wanted to forget this shit and go walk through the woods, fill my lungs with clean air and my ears with the rustle of wind in the leaves.

The colonel took my arm, bringing me back down with a bump. I don't think he'd ever touched me before.

"Farrell, I should have said this when you called on Monday. It's Top."

My stomach clenched. Master Sergeant Gabriel Luther Wells was a touchstone for me, a reference point that I could turn to whenever I felt lost. If I was unsure, 'what would Top do?' was the question I asked myself. But special ops wasn't a safe posting, and Colonel Laine's tone was bleak.

Dear God, not Top.

"He's in Rooks. He hasn't got long. He asked to see you."

I stood there, wanting to scream. Rooks wasn't the combat injuries hospital, it was the veterans' terminal care hospital, where soldiers lost their last battles against enemies within. *Not Top, anyone but Top.*

"How are you getting back?" I said, blinking. My voice was calm. It felt detached from the rest of me.

"I've got a ride on a Gulfstream carrying brass in an hour. There's a seat on that. I can get you a lift to Rooks. I'll try to swing you a flight back if there's one tomorrow."

I nodded, not trusting my voice, and let him guide me to where PFC No-name was waiting in a car. An hour later, we were in the army's Gulfstream. A couple of generals sat in the big central seats and ignored us.

The colonel worked on his laptop. I stared out the window.

Top was indestructible. There's no way something like cancer could kill him, would even dare to attack him. I knew that this had to be a trick to get me on the plane. An escort of Ops 4-10 were waiting for us to land and would haul me off to a padded cell where the Obs team could keep me forever.

Chapter 40

There was no group waiting to arrest me on landing. Just a soldier tasked with taking a civilian to Rooks: the army's impersonal efficiency offered politely to an outsider. I must have said something to the colonel before he went off in the other direction towards the base. I hope I thanked my driver as I got off at Rooks. I must have gotten directions to the room. I can't remember any of it.

It wasn't him. There was no way Top would fit into that hospital bed. His huge frame should have been sprawled across it like an over-delivery of ebony timbers, badly stacked. The man in the bed was shrunken, fallen in on himself, seemingly suspended from gray monitors by tubes and wires. He was asleep. The lights were soft, the room was warm but antiseptic.

The first time I'd seen him was the evening I arrived at Ops 4-10, with twenty other raw recruits. We'd gone through nine months of a hellish training course. We'd been whittled down from over two hundred. We were fit, we were tough, we were sharp, we were the best damn recruits in the whole damn country. And we sat rigidly to attention at the back, as the remainder of the room, full of five-year and ten-year veterans from every branch of the services, mingled, swapped unlikely stories and cast a not unkindly eye over us. They were debating what to call the master sergeant who was due in. They voted for Gunny. At the back, we abstained, which gained us some nods for knowing our place. Voting rights needed to be earned in this mess.

The room went quiet when he entered. He wasn't seven feet tall, but he looked it. He probably couldn't lift a truck on his own, but no one would have bet against it. He wasn't the only African-American in the room, but it was as if his skin sucked light out of the air.

Shit, it's the Dark Lord of the Sith, I thought.

He stood at the front in parade rest and smiled. To our credit, no one smiled back.

"I understand you've just taken a vote," he said. "That's nice. We live in a democratic country, the greatest on earth. God bless America." The floorboards creaked as his weight moved to the balls of his feet.

"You are my unit and you will call me Top," he said.

"What're you smiling at, Fire-all?" His words, in a thin imitation of his voice, snapped me out of my happy memory and back to the stark reality.

I quoted his phrase back at him, and told him what I'd thought when he'd come in that evening. He chuckled, a movement of his chest.

"And you're not allowed to call me Fire-all anymore," I said.

"Oh, still sensitive?" he said. "Names like that live forever."

I'd once been put on the spot by him about which weapons to use when entering a hostile building, and had answered with the first thing that came into my head, an apparently immortal phrase—'fire all of the guns at once'.

I cranked his bed up so he was sitting a bit higher, and puffed his pillows. The how-are-you type of greeting seemed a waste of breath, so I said nothing and sat beside him.

"I've been putting my house in order," he said. "Got to say that's the advantage of this." His hand waved at the room and the monitors. "You sure know when your train is coming."

He took his time looking me over. His eyes were red and tired, but I didn't fool myself that he would miss anything, any more than he had back in the unit. "Tell me," he said. "Why did you come?"

"Top, I had to! When the colonel told me about you. And he said you'd asked." I rubbed my forehead. "I guess with the colonel arranging the transport for me, I must have a dispensation."

"What are you talking about, a dispensation?" He frowned.

I realized that he must not know. There would be no reason for him to know once I was transferred out of his unit to the Obs unit. "I had to sign an agreement before they let me out. I'm not allowed to contact anyone in 4-10."

"Who…" the monitors bleeped at him and he relaxed with a visible effort. "Who made you sign this agreement?"

I had to think for a while. "His name was Major Petersen. I guess he was from some legal department."

A nurse came in, glared at me, and took a look around. "If his signs go like that again, you'll have to leave," she said to me, before returning to her station.

Top lay back and I could see him willing the readings back down to their resting levels.

"That's all bullshit, not being able to speak to us. That's not legal department crap. That's someone making a play. I'll tell Colonel Laine. He'll clear it up." He lay silent, while the realization of what had been done sank into me. No one in 4-10 knew about the agreement I'd had to sign. Everyone would have thought I had walked away from them, assumed that I didn't care, that my life in the unit had been a lie. I felt sick with anger. No wonder I had spent a couple of years thinking the colonel was disappointed in me.

"I'm sorry, Farrell. We all thought you just wanted to cut us off. We—I—should have known better. Long before you said something to the colonel and he spoke to me."

I frowned. What was it I had said that the colonel had queried at the last meeting? It came to me. "I said I would come back in a heartbeat, but things have changed."

"Such as…"

"I'm a goddamn vampire, Top, near as."

"And? They're allowing you to walk around in Denver. You tapping people who don't need it?"

"No one who didn't need it." I sighed. "It's not 4-10, but it's a job. I just wish I could see the lines clearly. I wish I could be certain about what's happening to me."

"Tell me," he said immediately. When I hesitated, he went on, "Not as if I've got anything else to do. And I promise to take it to the grave." His chest fluttered with his wheezy laugh.

My head felt overstuffed with things I couldn't tell people. So many things I had to remember, each one labeled who I could tell it to. Some of those labels were lies, if Top was right. If not Top, then who? I knew I shouldn't, but I began to speak. As if a dam had broken, as soon as it started, the words just flowed out of me. I went through almost everything that had happened in the case and personally.

We took a break when his dinner came. I texted Tullah, explaining I was visiting a sick friend.

Then I had to call Jen. I told her where I was and explained how I had failed her by letting Onebrow go. I started to say that I would understand if she wanted me off the case.

She stopped me. "Forget that, honey. Hell, we're all brilliant in hindsight. Straighten out your business there and then get back." She paused. "I need you here."

The way she put it made me feel better. We finished up, and I grabbed a sandwich from the canteen and made my way back to Top.

The nurses didn't look happy when I went back in, but Top waved them out and I finished off the story.

At the end, Top was lying back with his eyes closed. I thought he might have fallen asleep, until he spoke, his sentences choppy and breathy. "You've got the best team available looking for this chef, who's probably dead. And the cops are looking too. You've uncovered financial problems in this Kingslund company. You got a guy going through the computers. If he can't find out who's behind it that way, you've got the finance guy himself you can question. You've identified werewolves tearing up the resort. You're getting an intro to them from the vamps. You've got a good team protecting your client. You've got powerful friends who trust you." He grunted. "Sounds good to me for a week's work. So why am I hearing it's a problem?"

"I just think it all connects and I can't see how or why. I feel stupid."

"Jesus, Farrell, you don't lose your stripes just because you take the uniform off. If this was some pissant corporal reporting to you, you'd chew him out for his attitude. All this negative bullshit, that's just energy that isn't being directed. Sure, it may be connected. Keep doing what you're doing and you'll find out."

"But I may not have time. The prion count just keeps going up."

"You talking to me about not having time, soldier?"

I shut up and ducked my head to hide my blushing. When he put it like that, it hurt.

"Ease up on yourself, Farrell. Stop worrying about what you may become. Use what you are. Use all that energy. Do what you can while you can. None of us can do any more. And it sounds like you've got some real important work ahead of you. I don't mean the Kingslund case. Sure that's important now, but this Panethus/Basilikos war is more important in the long run. Sounds like they used to keep each other in check. Keep their numbers down by killing each other. This cold war they got going must mean that there's more vamps around than ever before. I can't say I'm happy with that, but, from what you say, the worst thing is for Basilikos to win. Get in there with Altau and make a difference for Panethus."

He laughed quietly. "Wasn't what I thought I would be talking about. Vampires, witches and werewolves! Shit."

"I'm glad we did. It helped, however pathetic I'm sounding." I gave him a smile. "What did you want to talk about, Top? Saints for the Super Bowl?"

He snorted. "Not this year. Not your Broncos either. No, some old stuff. Old, old stuff. Doesn't mean it's not important." His eyes closed again and I waited patiently, cocooned by the quiet hissing and ticking of the equipment.

"When you came to us," he started up again, "you were sending all your money home. You just told me about your sister. I want you to tell me how that came about."

This was painful stuff I left buried mostly, but he knew half of it, so I might as well give him all of it.

"It dated back to '96, when my Dad got sick—"

"Blane, wasn't it?" he interrupted. I nodded. Whatever else was failing, Top's memory was as good as ever.

"He got sick and the insurance wouldn't pay. We were broke. We'd moved into a bigger house in a good area with a mortgage, now we had healthcare bills and then lawyers' fees. Just Mom's income to keep us going. We kept all that from Dad." I looked, unseeing, at the window. It would have been a day like today in the autumn, in a room like this at home, filled with equipment we couldn't afford, and Dad lying sleeping. "I was home from school one afternoon, doing homework, sitting with him in case he needed anything. He was dreaming and he was smiling."

I felt Top's hand come to rest on mine. It felt like old paper, dry and light.

"When he woke up, I asked him what had made him smile, and he said he'd been dreaming of us graduating from college. He made me promise it would happen. I guess everything afterwards went towards that. But we did it, only way it could be done, Kath graduated and I helped make it happen."

"But you've given up on that promise then."

"No, Top, it wasn't possible to get us both through college. It had to be done that way."

"I'm not talking about back then. I'm talking now."

"I can't go to college now."

"Not today, not tomorrow, but sometime. You're a vampire now, you got more time." He chuckled throatily. "But you gotta promise me."

I couldn't say no.

"Good," he said. "Then, when I see Blane, I can tell him his daughter honors his memory by keeping her promise."

I looked down and screwed my eyes shut. There was something I had to ask him.

"Top?" I said. "Athanate have this stuff that heals people. I could—"

"No, Farrell. Sounds like you got enough debts you can't clear. And I don't want it anyway. I've made my peace. I'm going soon."

I dropped my head again. I'd had to try. I'd known what he would say, but I'd had to try.

"I'm not finished yet," he said. "And this one is tougher. I should have got to it much sooner." He cast his eyes slowly around the room before coming back to me. "You know, Farrell, you were on point down in South America because you were the best. And because of the job you did that night, our casualties were half of what they would have been. And it was still the worst we ever had."

"Thanks, Top." I'd still messed up. My squad. My responsibility.

"I told you that because the next part is going to be hard. You nearly weren't there at all."

I looked at him and waited. Top had a reason for doing and saying everything. I couldn't think he would have been saying things now that weren't important, however painful they might be for me.

"You only saw me once you'd joined 4-10, but I personally selected every single last one of you. And it was my name against every one that failed too." He wiped his mouth with his hand, the unshaven beard rasping under his fingers. "Your instructors filed requests with me to wash you out of the advanced training four times in the first two months."

He paused again and took a sip of water. His hand returned to mine.

"I had your files from basic training and I had the recruiter go talk to your school. I know what went on."

My stomach clenched.

"As far as they know it, and that wasn't far, was it? They knew you did that crazy jump off the clock tower. They knew you were working nights and giving your Ma the money. They knew lots of things, but they didn't know why you made that jump, did they?"

"No, Top," I whispered.

"You weren't sure about pulling the cord, were you?"

"No, Top."

"And that's what your instructors thought too." He thumbed imaginary files and read from them. "The most able recruit in the group, smart, strong, fast." He stopped as if at the last page. "Just not sure whether she wants to live or not."

I couldn't say anything. He was right. It had taken months to imprison the coward where she wouldn't ever get out again. I showed her that I was not her. Fear was the key. When I felt fear, I knew I was alive, and I knew she was locked away.

"And I'm reckoning it was your promise to your Pa that kept you going."

I jerked my head.

"Look," he said gently. "A girl comes to basic with her hair hacked off like you had, doesn't look at a man for the first couple of years, throws herself into every dangerous thing there is…I know what happened, Farrell. Not the detail. And I'm not going to give you any bullshit about knowing how you must have felt. But it made me ache to see, and I tell you this: I have never felt prouder of a soldier in my squad, than when you went on and made sergeant."

Sergeants don't cry. They're not even really permitted to bow their heads, so I raised mine and looked at him again, but I still couldn't say anything.

"Now the really tough part," he said, his voice hoarse. "You've buried it. My guess is, you use it. But you haven't fixed it. That and something else is chewing your gut. I don't know what that something else is, and I'm not sure you do either. But these things have a way of coming out when you don't want them to."

His voice was getting fainter.

"I was gonna suggest you talk to the colonel. He's better at that stuff than you might think. He's on your side. But the way you're talking, I'm thinking some of your new friends will be the ones." His eyes lost focus for a minute and he was quiet. I had to lean forward to hear his next words. "You're confused about a lot of things, what's happening to you, what's happening to your body, what you're feeling. But underneath all that, it's still you. You hold to that, you can't go far wrong."

His hand gripped mine, surprisingly strong still. "You listen to me one last time. You got to play the hand you're dealt."

A nurse came in behind me. "You really have to leave now, it's far too late." She started to note down readings from the monitors. "Only family are supposed to be here." She stopped suddenly and looked at me. "You aren't family, are you?"

Top laughed his bubbling, wheezing laugh. "Family? This paleface squaw! Nurse, can't you see, I'm a Dark Lord of the Sith." We laughed together, even harder at the blank incomprehension of the nurse.

"Goodbye, Amber," he said.

"Goodbye, Gabriel," I whispered.

Chapter 41

THURSDAY

I walked back to the airfield. There wasn't any other place I was going and it only took me a couple of hours. Luckily, down here, the weather was milder than Denver. It took me almost as long to get into the base as it had to walk there. The guards on the gate checked my ID about a dozen times before letting me through.

Once I was inside, the loadmaster confirmed I had a ride on a Hercules transport leaving at 8 a.m. I made myself useful to the loadmaster, and at 8:05, I was dangling on the webbing in the belly of the beast.

I felt dazed and remote from everything. There was no one I could talk to about Top. No one who could replace him. No one who could share my grief. But the world kept turning and I hadn't slept that night. Sitting in the webbing listening to the thunder of the engines was like coming home and I fell asleep till we landed at Buck field early in the afternoon. A series of hitches and walks eventually got me back to my car and I drove back to Jen's.

Tullah sent me off to shower and change, refusing to talk to me about anything until I had, and so it was almost 5 p.m. before I got an update.

Matt had stripped the data from Verdoon's computers and passed them along. Tullah had worked through the files during the day, calling Jen to ask questions about names of people and companies. I noted Jen had taken Tullah's involvement as a given, which had worked out well.

There was no smoking gun. I guess that would have been too easy, and whoever was behind this and however they had done it, it had been managed very carefully. It was clear from the data that Verdoon had been the person to sign off every single major money movement in the last month. What was not clear was why.

There were encrypted files in his personal area that Matt hadn't been able to break into. Tullah was disappointed, but I knew that the 'military grade encryption' that even cheap software offered was extremely strong. This wasn't TV, where the wiz in the lab complains when the boss only gives her an hour to decode the files. A supercomputer might crack those files by brute force in a few years' time. For us, either we found a Post-it note with the password, or we found something in Verdoon's personal life that gave us a clue. Matt was working on that, indexing Verdoon's files and trying out words found in them as passwords.

I took a USB from Tullah with a copy of Verdoon's emails to take a look at later.

"Tell me, Tullah," I said, changing the topic. "Why is your spirit guide not on the approved list?"

She looked around the study.

"It's private enough here," I said.

"No. I can't explain. Umm, let's walk in the gardens for a while. I'll show you."

Her face was carefully impassive, but for some reason, I had the sense that there was a mad glee boiling underneath the surface. I felt my eyes wanting to roll again—I was about to get another secret that I couldn't share with everyone. I was intrigued, even though the thought of keeping secrets from Mary made me nervous.

We went through the living room and out through the patio doors. It was cold—just this last weekend, Jen had been sitting here in the sun, but the temperatures had taken a dive, and now it felt as if snow might be just around the corner.

We walked past the helipad and continued on down until we were among the larches. I loved them for being different, looking like pines but turning gold and dropping their needles in the fall. Jen's garden had them hedged by spreading cypress. Our footsteps crunched on dry needles.

Once I was sure we were away from the patrolling guards, I asked, "What is the approved list?"

"Oh, the predictable animals—the known qualities. Standard spirit guides like the bear and the cougar, the wolf and the eagle. Adepts like them because they're safer. You know what you're getting."

"You've got something no one else has?"

"Hmm. Think so. Around here anyway." She pushed her hands deep into her coat pockets.

"Okay, Tullah, we're alone out here. I know you're itching to tell me. Remember, I can't promise I won't tell Mary."

Tullah made a small pouting expression. "Ma'll find out sometime. If she just looked hard enough, she'd know now. I just want to show she's not dangerous first."

She stopped and turned to me, a huge grin breaking out. "It'll be easier to show you."

I stood there in the whispering gloom underneath the larches and waited. I sensed something stir in the air around Tullah's shoulders. She put her head back and laughed, reaching up with her arms. "She's shy. Come on baby, it's only Amber."

Baby?

There was a gleaming movement like a section of river running past Tullah's head, and then another running in front of it, in the other direction. Suddenly, there was a tower of them, sliding past each other, and a looming sense of a huge golden body stirring, uncoiling. Atop it, a massive eye opened and looked down at me from beneath an armored brow. A head as big as a truck emerged and swooped towards me, a mouth opening like a trapdoor to hell.

"Oh. Shit!" I fell on my butt and thrust my hands out uselessly in front of me. My heart forgot to beat.

The head stopped and turned to let one huge ruby eye inspect me closely. A tongue like a forked red towel flicked out and tasted the air around me. Then it withdrew. For a second the whole glittering, scaled body stretched up into the evening sky, with wings spread, before it dissolved into a twinkling of lights that fell to earth and disappeared like fireworks.

My last glimpse of the face showed the same mischievous, self-satisfied smirk that Tullah wore. She knew exactly what reaction she'd wanted from me.

"Shit!" I said again. "Baby? Tullah, that's a freaking…"

"Dragon. Yes. She's so pretty isn't she? See why I couldn't show you indoors?"

When Mary had made her bear guide visible to me at the restaurant, she'd been able to restrict the sight of it to me. Tullah hadn't gotten that control yet. A guard wandered down to ask about the fireworks he had seen. We pointed off into the distance beyond the Country Club and shrugged. I hoped it was dark enough he couldn't see us trying to stop giggling.

As we got back to our study-office, a text came in from Jen. She was going to be busy till late with the organization of the ball. Tullah was headed home, enormously pleased with herself, and I decided I needed to be out and about, doing things.

The drive down to Mrs. Desiarto's was familiar, and yet it felt strange. I hadn't been here in over a week, but it felt much longer.

A lot of things change in a week, I guess. Mrs. Desiarto wasn't pleased with me. First no boyfriends, she shouted, then I go off for a week without telling her and then I have the wrong sort of boyfriends around in the middle of the night. Two of them! Two! The shame of it, the noise, the rudeness, what was I thinking?

"Mrs. Desiarto, I don't have one boyfriend, let alone two. And I haven't been back since a week yesterday."

She blinked at me as if I were speaking a different language, then resumed where she'd left off, not to be distracted from her stream of complaints. I imagined the real problem was that I hadn't been dropping in and giving her the chance to talk for the last week.

It was time to move somewhere else. Diana certainly expected me to take up residence at Altau House soon. I was at Jen's for the moment, even though I felt uneasy about taking that for granted.

Mrs. Desiarto grabbed the keys from my hand. Part of my paranoia had always been that only I would have the keys to my room, so she hadn't had the opportunity to sneak a look at it, and see what destruction such a perverted orgy might leave behind.

She turned the key in the lock and I finally started thinking again. I lunged at her, too late to stop her from opening the door.

Chapter 42

The blast was small and directed. If they heard it, the neighbors probably thought it was a car backfiring.

Mrs. Desiarto didn't hear anything. She assumed I had attacked her, and she had one defense—her voice. She screamed as loud as she could, which as it turned out was like an ambulance siren.

It was only the second time I'd ever seen Mr. Desiarto. He stumbled out onto the porch, expecting bodies lying in the road and the tangled wreckage of at least three, maybe four cars. As it was, Mrs. Desiarto was lying on the porch unhurt except for a few bruises. I had landed on top of her. I wanted to kid myself it was a protective action on my part, but I think I was just tired of carrying bruises all the time.

As for me, I was kneeling beside the door, peering around. The door itself was a ruin, shredded by gunshot. There didn't seem to be anything else about to blow up, and I cautiously made my way in.

The box was nailed to the floor. It was a simple design, an electrical connection broken by the door opening, which triggered a circuit and cooked a couple of shotgun shells held in short iron tubes. Simple, effective and lethal. A sweet feeling of relief flooded through me. If Mrs. Desiarto hadn't come to complain at me, I would have walked through that door.

The iron tubes were stuck through the eyeholes of a skull mask. Death's eyes. This was Onebrow's work.

The apartment was ransacked. I hoped once my landlady recovered her wits, she would see that not even the most energetic of orgies could have been responsible for the devastation inside. Every item of furniture had been taken apart, every drawer emptied, clothes torn, books torn. The mattress was ripped open, the small fridge emptied over the floor. My panties were pinned to the mattress with a knife.

What were they looking for? Why the messages? The mask and the panties? Because there was a good chance I wouldn't have been killed by this. Onebrow wouldn't have known I had the only keys to the apartment. As far as he was concerned, it could have been Mrs. Desiarto, and in that case, he wanted me to know he'd been responsible and what he'd do if he got his hands on me.

I backed out without touching anything.

"Mr. Desiarto." I grabbed him and lifted him away from his wife, who had subsided into a plaintive wailing. I showed him the device and the damage. "These are dangerous men and they may be back. It's very important you get inside and stay there. I'm calling the police."

He looked at me wide-eyed and open-mouthed as I shepherded the pair of them back inside their house.

I closed the door to my apartment and held it in place by moving a porch chair in front of it. Then I called Lieutenant Edmunds on the number Morales had given me. This might not be quite what the Snakebite team was intended for, but I'd ask forgiveness rather than permission.

Edmunds was as rapid as before. He and a small team made it there in half an hour.

After telling Edmunds what little I could, I tried calling Morales, but could only get his voicemail.

Edmunds chased me out and told me he'd talk to Morales.

"We don't know what the hell's going on, Farrell," he said, out of earshot of the others. "But Morales has assigned us to be available. If this isn't vampires, it's still a crime. Guess what we spend the rest of our time doing?"

He made sure he had the right contact details for me. "Morales trusts you. You're on the side of the angels, eh?" He smiled, a bit lopsided. "And if the devils are trying this, you must be hurting them. Go on, nothing more you can do at the moment."

"Take care," he called after me.

What had I done to deserve this kind of backup? I drove away praying that they would find something significant that would wrap this case up before a trick like that caught me.

That definitely did it for staying at the Desiarto's. I was angry and shocked, of course, but I felt sick that the trap could have killed Mrs. Desiarto.

I would pay for the damage somehow and I'd have to find somewhere else to stay. Jen's was the obvious place for the moment, and hopefully after I completed her case, it wouldn't be so dangerous to get an apartment again. I felt uncomfortable about being dependent on her in the meantime. Even if I was only staying a couple of days, I'd have to talk to her tomorrow, if there was time.

As to the rest of it, well, it wasn't so bad. I had half my clothes lying destroyed on the floor at the apartment and the other half split between the trunk of the car and Jen's guest suite. Luckily, everything I really needed I had with me. I'd lost my books, but I could buy them again. Not a material girl, me.

I turned towards Wash Park and put it behind me. Time to kick little brother's ass.

His car wasn't outside and the lights were off in his house. I knocked anyway, but it was all quiet. I checked both cell phones and got the voicemail. In the end, I let myself in.

It was clean and tidy, except for the unmade bed and a pile of laundry. There was nothing to suggest any problem, and there was a limit to what I could do. I left a grumpy message on the table, and headed back to Jen's.

She was still out, busy with the ball committee I guessed.

Frustrated, I changed and took a run, down Takayama Park and along the trail through Glendale and as far as Judge Joseph Park. The gun made the jogging bag uncomfortable, but running still eased out the tensions. At Judge Joseph, I turned and sprinted back. The whole way.

I felt strange back at the house. Tired of course, but not as much as I should have been, and all overlaid with a mixture of equal parts despair and elation. Normal fitness can only go so far. There should have been no way I could sprint the three miles back. This sort of performance could only mean that I was further down the track to becoming Athanate.

Within a minute of getting back, my heart rate had fallen to a resting level. In the bathroom, I stripped down. I was hot and flushed and sweating, but my breathing had fallen almost as quickly as the heart rate. I looked at my body in the reflection from the full-length mirror. I opened my mouth and looked at my teeth. I wanted to see something different, something I could point to and say, *that's changed,* but there was nothing.

I rested my forehead against the mirror.

"This is what a vampire looks like, Tara," I murmured.

"Not quite yet," she replied.

After my shower, I did as Top said I should do and put everything else aside while I thought about Jen's case again.

I sat in the living room, wrapped in the bathrobe and balancing my laptop on my thighs. I alternately flicked through Verdoon's emails and the financial spreadsheets for the Kingslund Group, concentrating on the cash assets. A little of the Guyanese rum warmed my stomach and oiled my thoughts.

When I was finished, there were two new things which had emerged.

Firstly, whatever game of hunt-the-lady Verdoon was playing with his shuffling of the Kingslund Group's cash assets, it had to end soon. He was running out of reserves to shift. Even as the financial controller, there was a limit to what he could hide.

Secondly, there was a hint about where the key to his behavior might be coming from. Verdoon's private and business lives were well separated in most aspects, and his emails from his work computer were mainly to do with business. The personal emails that caught my attention were from hospitals. Someone was extremely ill and there were regular account statement emails copied to his business address. I guessed Verdoon was paying the bills. None of which would have been particularly significant until the name of the hospital changed to one down in New Mexico, shortly before the Kingslund money started to be moved into new deposits. It was the smallest hint of a connection, but it felt right.

I emailed Jen with my notes, avoiding saying why New Mexico made the connection for me. I then emailed Victor, asking him to look into the hospitals and find out who was being treated.

I went to bed.

I was asleep later when the bedroom door opened a crack, waking me. I tensed, but it was only Jen. She peered into the darkness and then the door closed quietly again. She was checking that I was in.

My heart began racing and my jaw started to ache. I clenched my teeth together and waited for the sensations to pass. My prion reading had reached 0.5 this evening. Maybe staying here wasn't going to be possible, for Jen's safety. I couldn't ever go back to Obs now. I'd be back in that cell. My options were shrinking all the time.

We are your harbor when you need it, Diana had said.

Chapter 43

FRIDAY

Whatever the worries of the night before, I liked my short commute in the morning.

I was on the phone confirming Victor's team's access to the convention center when Tullah and Jen came into the study, laughing. Tullah had wanted a tour of house, and Jen had been happy to oblige.

"You're welcome to use the gym or the pool, of course," Jen was saying to Tullah. "Amber's using the gym, and it's good to see."

I hung up and offered them coffee. Tullah had brought the new business cards from the printers and I opened the packet.

"Perfect timing," Jen said. "You'll need them tonight. You should have received a welcome packet with your tickets which tells you to bring cards and exchange them with everyone: dance partners, people at your table and so on. Ethel—Mrs. Harriman—is big on everyone mingling and making contacts."

I got the cards out and kept my face carefully neutral. Tullah had gone way overboard on this. The background color was a skin-bronze gloss. Along with the tag line *'Reliable – Efficient – Discreet'*, the contact information was written in black in the bottom right corner in a languid italic font which I recognized with a start.

"I copied the font style you used for Tara's plaque," Tullah said. "It doesn't seem to be a standard font so I just made up the letters I needed. Is that okay?"

I'd designed the font at school when I'd first thought of getting the plaque made. I could remember thinking, *this is how Tara would write*. Tullah had got the style exactly right.

"It's fine, Tullah," I said. "Just a bit of a surprise."

"The color is your skin tone," Jen said, holding one against me, and she was right, it was close.

"They're beautiful," I said to Tullah. "Possibly not quite what's expected of a PI."

"Don't be stuffy," Jen said. "Oh, look at the time, gotta go. See you at the ball, honey." We kissed cheeks and she went off in a rush.

"They're good, really, Tullah," I said. "Thanks for getting them done."

"It's a pleasure." She looked around the study. "Jen's really nice. The house is awesome."

"This office is just temporary, until we wrap this up."

She settled down and started working through the emails. "Yeah, but it's still nice of her to let us use the place. She likes you."

"Yes. You seem to get along well with her," I said noncommittally.

"Yes, but—"

"And Matt too, from what I understand." *Bullseye!* Tullah actually blushed.

She hurriedly changed the subject. "I meant to say, if you want, I'll help today, I'll do the driving. I really want to see the dress."

I grinned. "You're on. You'll have to bring your camera. My mom is going to need pictures to prove it's real."

∞ ∞ ∞ ∞ ∞

I can sense the sun slip down, not in the failing light, but in the weakening of the million certainties that have kept me at bay. Under the cold stars, jabbering hindbrains let me be.

How does it FEEL? It is the adoration of multitudes, it is strength, it is the desire of strangers and the fear of those that know. I catwalk to the reception area, enjoying the heads that turn. The midnight green silk billows with my movement.

The doorman is too stunned to take my ticket. I press it into his hand and run a shiny green gloved finger down his slack jaw. It has a nice line.

I pass through the scanners, but my weapons are not metal.

Inside, Jen turns to me, blue eyes wide. "Amber," she says, and that's my name, but is it who I am?

It's not a cheek she's offering and I kiss the soft tension of her neck. I can hear her heart leap to my touch and her pulse beats like a butterfly against my lips.

What am I doing? Stop it!

"Hi Jen, how's it going?" I managed to wrench it back.

She gasped and pressed her hand to her chest. "You gave me such a shock," she replied, blinking. She took a step back and looked me up and down.

"Oh, my God, Amber," she said.

"You like?" I smiled, held my arms out and turned slowly on a heel, trying to shed the über-vamp aura. That poor doorman. Poor Jen, for that matter.

"Amber, I like. It's divine. No, it's—"

"It's not fair, because you always look so elegant, and all you've ever seen me wear is jeans and a T." Jen was wearing a strapless red silk dress—a simple, classical look that she made special. "You're looking wonderful."

I'd left a kiss of peach lipstick against her neck, but I noticed she wasn't rubbing it off.

"Who did your hair?" she said. My hair, normally simply tied back, was too short for anything elaborate like Jen's Grecian pile. It had been left straight with a slight curl to frame my face.

"Klara—that's Werner's wife—and Tullah. They fussed over me the whole afternoon."

"It works well," Jen said. Someone came up and murmured to her.

"We're sitting together at dinner," Jen said, "so I'll see you shortly, but I've got to welcome the delegation. Oh, if anyone asks, just say you're doing some security consulting for me."

I squeezed her hand and made my way in, leaving my stole and slinky gloves at the coat check.

From my bag, I took a small headset. It looked like a cell phone system, but it was a comms link to Victor's guard outside. I'd been so fixated on my effect on the doorman, I hadn't looked around to check he was in place. I flicked the switch and carefully looped it over one ear, avoiding the earrings I had borrowed from Lisa.

"Reynolds, this is Farrell. You awake out there?"

"Yes, ma'am." I could hear the smile in his voice. "Nice entrance. Very discreet."

I chuckled. "Guilty. I'll check the comms from time to time. Talk to you later." I slipped it back into my bag.

My sister was standing with her back to me, talking to a group near the bar with Taylor beside her. I had said I would see her before the ball, so I walked across.

The silence and turned heads alerted her. She swung around, her face as blank of recognition as Taylor's.

"Hello, Kath," I said.

"Amber? Christ! You…oh, everybody," she cleared her throat, "this is my sister, Amber."

"Just Amber," I said to the man on her right, who had put his hand out in welcome. "Not Amber Christ." He laughed. Obviously, not a bad guy if he liked my jokes.

Kath recovered the situation with introductions all around, and then made an excuse and led me away.

"What a surprise. Amber, I haven't seen you in a dress since high school. You look good."

And you haven't said that to me since high school, I thought. Something seemed to have mellowed her attitude a little.

"I promised you a quick review of your case." She looked down and frowned. "I think Carter is an ass. His lawyers think he's an ass. About now, even he's starting to think he's an ass. He'll be looking for a way out, but the easiest solution would be if you backed down and then he can be magnanimous. If we don't give him that, he'll withdraw the suit anyway in a week or two. Just leave it to me, and whatever you do, don't talk to him. He'll be here tonight."

"Okay. Thanks," I said, "and thanks for taking it."

"Yeah. Sorry about that, and lunch. I guess Carter's not the only ass." She gave me a quick, uncertain smile.

I felt a flicker of hope that, after this was over, we could behave like sisters again. I didn't know what demands being Athanate might have on me, but surely, I would be okay for that.

"You've been under pressure. I understand," I said.

"You don't know the half of it." She glanced around to make sure we were out of earshot from anyone. The rising buzz of conversations from people at the bar gave us complete privacy. "I'm being evaluated for a partnership."

"Kath, that's fantastic news." The firm she worked for was about as crusty as they come out here. For Kath to be considered as a partner with only six years' service was unprecedented.

She grabbed my arm. "Please, don't spoil it for me. All the partners are here tonight."

"I'll avoid them. And if they talk to me, I'll be demure. But honestly, what could I say that would hurt your chances?"

Kath's eyes swiveled. "It's your sense of humor, Amber. Remember the pastor? The frogs in Cassie's bed? Or what about Mom's boss at the barbeque that time?"

"Oh yeah. I had forgotten them. Oh God, that was fun!"

At Kath's glare, I quelled the giggles and looked solemn. Well, I had only been fourteen.

The sound of a gong interrupted us. The crowd around the bar went quieter and started to drift towards the escalators to the ballroom. Jen was ushering people in and waved at me.

"Keep away from Kingslund, she's trouble," said Kath.

"Don't be silly, she's just a bit of an extrovert. Anyway, I'm temporarily renting an office from her in her house next to the Country Club. I'm advising her on security."

She looked surprised, but before she could say anything, I went on, "I just wanted to say, you look good, too. You look like a partner in an awesome legal firm, sis. I'm proud."

Kath smiled her thanks at me as Taylor appeared at her side to whisk her off to impress the hell out of the partners. I was happy for her. I'd rather clean sewers than work in a legal firm, but Kath loved it, she worked hard at it, and this was her due reward.

I focused on the fiery red of Jen's dress and made my way to her side.

The attendees were arranged at round tables with about a dozen people for each. Jen and the committee had worked hard to spread the international delegation throughout the room, and to seat them with people who had an interest in whatever industry they represented. A hum of conversation built up quickly.

I had come doubting that anyone would really be interested in a private investigator and intending to spend my time scanning the international trade delegation for my Athanate contact. As it turned out, the people to my right were fascinated by what I did. Without telling them any complete lies, I did my bit for the investigation industry. Jen sat at my left and entertained her side of the table with an update on her plans to set up a Quarter Horse race track just outside of town.

Opposite us sat the delegate from Malaysia, a businessman specializing in manufacturing plastic fasteners. I would have been hard put to tell if he was Athanate across the width of the table, but he didn't seem to be.

Halfway around the table sat Jack Tucker. He was quiet, other than to support Jen's ideas about the race track.

After the dessert, Lloyd McIntire and Ethel Harriman stood and made a brief shared speech, thanking everyone for their contributions, welcoming the international visitors and outlining the ways the money raised would be spent.

The mayor said a few words on how wonderful Denver was.

The guest speaker was an international businessman and CEO of a mining company. He spoke well and praised Denver for its workforce and the positive attitude of the business community. Mercifully brief.

As the applause died down, the band started to play.

Jen grabbed my hand, grinning. "I know you can dance." I had told her about the dance lessons I'd had, mentioning that as the tallest girl there, I had generally had to dance as the male partner. "Committee members have to lead by example."

She hauled me off to the dance floor. The band wasn't particularly expecting anyone out this early, but they'd started with a simple cha-cha-cha, thank the stars. Unfortunately, we had the floor to ourselves.

I was here on a job, and the person who was going to be contacting me knew only that I was the woman with Jennifer Kingslund. I guessed this was a good a way as any to advertise that. I was going to have to make a bit of a spectacle of myself anyway, to give everyone in the delegation an opportunity to pass the message to me, so it might as well be by dancing.

At its simplest for the man, the cha-cha-cha is a basic, three-step dance and serves to provide a muted background for the woman to show off her skills. Of necessity, that's the way we played it with me as the male lead. I decided my advice to all men wanting to look good on the dance floor was to get a partner who can really dance. Jen could really dance.

Thankfully, a few others took the hint and some couples joined us. I relaxed and started to enjoy it, and we laughed as I nearly missed passes here and there. By the end, it was probably looking quite natural and I was immersed in my role. Part of which was, of course, to kiss my partner's hand.

I bent my head and our eyes met. The room seemed to recede and her eyes widened a touch. A little shock traveled down my body and settled in my stomach. *Whoops.*

At the same time, I smelled Athanate. Close.

"Jennifer, would you introduce me to your partner, please?"

"Luc, hello," Jen said, recovering herself. "This is my friend, Amber."

I turned to find a tall man standing behind me with a pleasant smile and raised eyebrows.

Another man swooped in on Jen and her eyes met mine again for a second before she was whisked away.

"Luc, pleased to meet you." I shook his hand. Diana had briefed me well enough. So this was Luc Matlal, the leader of the Athanate Basilikos party. He didn't let go of my hand. I thought for a moment he might even kiss it.

"And I am enchanted to meet you, Amber. You lead well. However, may I lead this dance?" His eyes sparkled with humor. He looked fortyish, slim with a sharp face and black hair combed straight back.

I cocked an ear to the band. They would stick with whatever made people dance, so I imagined it was going to be Latin dances for a while.

"A salsa. Yes."

We danced. The salsa is not designed for talking to your partner, more a way to show your intentions with your body. I had no intentions towards Matlal, other than to listen to what he might say to me, but the dance has a life of its own. Matlal's eyes grew very intent.

As the music ended, we were at one side of the dance floor and this time he did actually brush my hand with his lips. A little shiver ran down my spine, but it wasn't pleasure.

"Have you ever been to Mexico?" he asked.

"No," I replied, retrieving my hand.

"I will enjoy showing it to you. I will show you a side of Mexico that tourists do not see."

I bet he would. Not necessarily a part that most would want to see. "I think you're getting ahead of yourself, Luc."

"I will arrange it. An exchange between Houses in good standing with each other. I will insist." He paused and frowned a little. "Forgive me, I thought I knew the marque of every House, but I cannot place yours."

I knew exactly what he meant, but I just looked blankly at him. "I'm sorry, I have no idea what you're talking about. Excuse me." I turned to leave. Whatever Skylur had hoped I might learn from talking to him had been lost.

He grabbed my arm and his face was angry now. "I did not give you permission to leave. I can smell you, little Aspirant. Tell me what House you belong to."

I turned back and broke his grip. He was very strong, but he retained just enough sense to not start a struggle on the dance floor.

Then I got in his face. "I don't need your permission. And the thing that bit me died from it."

He glared at me, not backing down. "You will tell me your House." I felt the probing gray fingers of an attack. I didn't need to reach any depth at all to find anger to fuel my defense.

"Now, Senor Matlal, you know my rules." Rescue, in the unlikely shape of Ethel Harriman, appeared at my side. "One dance at a time."

Matlal's face underwent an immediate transformation, painful as it must have been for him. "Have you come to claim a dance with me, Mrs. Harriman?" He was charm itself, despite the anger that remained in his eyes.

"Thank you, no. My dancing days are long gone. I want to take Amber off the floor for a while." She turned to me. "I simply must know where the dress has come from, my dear."

She took my arm and steered me away. "I hope you don't mind my familiarity. I know we haven't been introduced but Jen told me your name. Please call me Ethel."

"Thank you, Ethel," I said and left it as to what I was thanking her for. I took some deep breaths and forced the anger back down. Ethel's face was calm and composed, but I suspected there was little her sharp eyes didn't see.

"I know Senor Matlal does good work with his orphanages and so on, but I find I can't warm to him." She shrugged. "Now that dress, my dear. Jen tells me it was made in Denver."

We were close enough to my table, so I retrieved some cards from my bag.

"I don't like people complaining there's nothing different here and then shopping in national stores. Rather than live in a cultural wasteland, I believe we should support local enterprise. Lisa Macy made this for me and I think she and others like her deserve our encouragement." I thought that summarized what Jen had said to me about local causes, and Ethel certainly liked it. She asked for two of Lisa's cards and took one of mine.

"Oh, I love your card too. It's quite outrageous. The sort of thing that gives Lloyd conniptions. I look forward to showing him later." She chuckled and folded her hands in front of her, looking at me quizzically with her head to one side. "Why haven't we met before, Amber?"

"Well, as it says on my card, part of my business is being discreet, and this sort of occasion isn't." We both laughed. "Very enjoyable though. Then, as well, I'm…" I struggled with how to put it. "I'm not well placed financially at the moment."

"Oh my goodness, dear, none of us are, at the moment. We're all poor as church mice." She laid a bejeweled hand across her chest. "Wall Street! Simply appalling!"

"Yes," I agreed weakly, struggling with the images of Mrs. Harriman being poor and my owning shares. "The stock market. And so on."

"Well," she said, patting my arm, "no matter. I knew if you were friends with Jen, you'd be sharp. Here's my card and I hope you'll be able to be less discreet in the future. You may not have a choice after tonight, my dear. Eligible bachelors will be all over you." She smiled coyly, eyes seeking out Jen. "If they get a chance. And speaking of bachelors, here's young Alex Deauville. I'll leave him to you." She sailed away like a galleon.

I turned. *Oh yum! Hot, hot, hot.* Alex Deauville had swagger and a lot of looks.

"I heard Ethel introduce me," he said, holding out his hand. "Alex."

"Amber," I replied and smiled at him, shaking his hand. He was about six-two, strongly built, with broad shoulders, and his light brown hair was a bit long. His eyes were an uncertain color, between gold and green, and something untamed looked out at me through them. *Double yum.*

"Shall we dance?" he asked, with an undertone that suggested there might be other things we could try.

The demon leaped up. "I'm not sure. My last two partners have set a very high standard." My eyes were saying yes, if he could read them.

Apparently he could read my eyes. He took my hand and, lifting it, led me back formally to the dance floor.

The band had suddenly decided to take a small break from Latin, and instead we had a waltz. I gritted my teeth and kept smiling. Alex's hand came up into the small of my back and we stepped out. *One-two-three* I counted in my head until the body fixed on it and moved of its own accord. Not my best dance, but not what was uppermost in my mind either.

Hot I'd called it when I saw him, and hot he was; a heat that flowed out from him and collected in a pool in my belly. He smelled so good; beneath a dash of some cologne and male warmth, he made me think of pines and mountain meadows. Something inside me was sitting up and really taking notice in a way it hadn't for far too long.

It was just a shame I wasn't going to be able to do anything about it, without risking infecting him.

We didn't speak. At first, I was pleased he was giving me an opportunity to concentrate on getting the steps right. But then once I had relaxed into it, he could have started to talk and he didn't. I'd never danced a slow dance without talking before. Our eyes met. I think we both looked slightly surprised and the silence took on a shared quality that neither of us wanted to break. I was startled when the music ended and we came to a halt.

"Was that acceptable?" He grinned at me.

"Quite," I replied, putting my hands behind my back like a teenager. "Ethel says we must exchange cards." *Gimme your card, bad boy.*

"Later. After our second dance."

The demon wouldn't let him get away with that. "If I'm not too busy." I smiled over my shoulder at him as I walked back to my table.

Oh gods, dances with Jen, Matlal and Alex. I needed to sit down for a moment.

Jack Tucker was alone at the table. I snagged my drink and sat next to him.

"Mr. Tucker, good evening. I'm Amber Farrell."

He grunted. "It's Jack. Pleased to meet you, Amber. Are you enjoying the ball?"

"Very much. You're not a dancer?"

He shook his head. "I'll stay with what I'm good at." He raised one brow at me. "You're the Amber Farrell that's just stuck it to Campbell Carter?"

"Not my intention, but yes." Tucker would know Carter, of course. I steeled myself.

"Calling Carter an ass is libel against perfectly good donkeys."

I laughed in surprise.

"Carter's got such a hard-on for politics, he's lost touch with his company. It's not your fault that other people took advantage of that." His mouth twisted in a bitter smile. "It's typical of him and his type. The old-money set."

"Well, it's refreshing to hear your view. I expected to have to listen politely to a defense of poor, maligned Campbell."

"You might yet, from others. Make no mistake, your actions have caused me considerable trouble. Considerable. But that wasn't your intention." He shrugged. "You're obviously very skilled and maybe those skills might be put to use for me. I have lots of opportunities for a person who can stand up to a man like Matlal and provide security for someone like Kingslund." He didn't sound as if he liked either of them, and clearly, he hadn't missed my turn on the dance floor.

Tucker took a long swallow of his wine and gave me a sideways stare. "You probably think I've got a chip on my shoulder about old money. But that Alex Deauville you were dancing with, he's old money and I've got a lot of time for him. He tell you he's a fully qualified doctor?" He snorted at my blank look. "No, didn't think so."

"What happened?"

Tucker shrugged. "Chucked it all and set up a trucking company. Parents disowned him. I liked his guts. Gave him his first contract. And you won't find his drivers cheating him like Carter's were."

A banker I'd seen in the papers, Scott Borders, joined us. He and Tucker started arguing about business, which gave me an opportunity to study Tucker a bit more. Top of the list, my nose told me Tucker was spending a lot of time around Athanate. I couldn't tell if he'd been bitten, but it wouldn't have surprised me.

As far as I could tell, Borders was trying to get Tucker to take Lloyd McIntire onto his board. Tucker wasn't having it and started to sound more and more extreme.

"This financial crash is what the world needed." He stabbed a finger at Borders. "A wake-up call to get rid of these parasites and knock down the house of cards that they built. They'll find all this inner circle shit won't turn into credit when they want it. You think you're in with them, you think you're accepted, but you never are, never will be. Time has come to take sides."

"You make it sound like the revolution is just around the corner, Jack," I said, trying to calm it down.

He snorted. "I probably do. Now I'm afraid you'll have to excuse me. The one good thing that Matlal's brought north with him is Inez, my fiancée, and she's just arrived."

I turned to see a dark-haired woman talking to Matlal. "You do business with Matlal?"

He snorted again as he got up. "Only because I have to. He's not the cooperating kind, if you know what I mean."

"Isn't he old money, Jack?" Borders asked.

"You would think so to look at him, but he's not. Born in a slum and made every single dollar himself." He looked at me, his eyes turning cold. "Not like Kingslund. Take a word of advice, don't ever need something from her. Might cost more than you can afford. And don't ever make the mistake of thinking you know where you stand with her. A turn on the dance floor is fun, but you'd be well advised to keep away from her. Starting right now."

I frowned. "That's the second time someone has said something like that to me this evening. I'll make up my own mind."

Tucker's face closed. He turned on his heel and walked away without another word. The woman looked around as he approached. She was pretty, with Spanish eyes and skin, and demurely dressed. An incongruous gold crucifix hung on a chain around her neck. She smiled at Tucker, then her eyes slipped past him and caught mine. I felt a little jolt, like when I looked into Diana's eyes. There was no need for her marque to tell me she was Athanate.

Matlal looked past Tucker at me and the anger was still there. I turned away.

Interesting, Tucker working with Matlal and warning me away from Jen.

"He's getting crazier by the minute," muttered Borders.

I didn't have time to think much more about it. I had a job to do and I didn't want to sit around and give Matlal an opportunity to come after me again. Making my excuses to Borders, I started to work my way through the trade delegation, luring as many as I could onto the dance floor and giving them plenty of chances to pass me a message. About half of them were Athanate, and the majority of the delegates were men. It turned out that a number of the men had messages for me, mainly about how nice their hotel suites were. Some of the women seemed a little flustered at being asked to dance, but I got few refusals. There was definitely something to this dressing up. Even more than that, I got the feeling that all the Athanate were attracted to my marque, though none were as blatant about it as Matlal.

Despite Werner's custom-made shoes, my feet were hurting by the time I was dancing with Arvinder Singh, the delegate from India. I was becoming anxious that the messenger had decided it was too risky to talk to me.

"I think I am letting the side down if I do not offer to show you my suite," Arvinder said with a grin, and I laughed. "But indeed, it was amusing to see you dancing with Jennifer Kingslund. I was saying to my companions at the table, it is like a boat in a whirlpool, port and starboard, port and starboard."

"Yes, the dress colors. We didn't pick them for that, but…"

My words petered out. I could feel a pressure in my head, not exactly like Skylur or Diana. I stumbled and tried to get a barrier up. The pressure disappeared immediately.

Arvinder laughed as if I'd said something funny. "Please keep talking. I have a message for Diana and the best place for it is inside your head. It will not harm you, and I will not attempt anything else, on my Blood, I swear. I didn't think you'd even notice."

My mouth was dry. I wish I'd had better preparation than this. I had expected a note, a USB drive, something out of James Bond. Athanate didn't work like that. But my instinct was to trust Arvinder.

"Okay," I said, trying to smile. "Go ahead."

There was the pressure again for a second and then it was gone. In its place was a presence, closed and cool and smooth.

"I am sorry to use this method without warning," said Arvinder, "but it is very secure. Only Diana will be able to unpick this lock. You must understand, what I am doing is dangerous for my House." He smiled pleasantly. "Please accept my apologies."

I huffed. I was a bit upset, but at least I had gotten the message. All I needed now was to get back to Diana.

Arvinder did his best to entertain me for the remainder of the dance with deliciously barbed comments about the other delegates.

I kept going for another half-dozen dances, then I sat down, determined to get the weight off my feet for a while.

Alex came and sat beside me, bringing champagne in long flutes.

I smiled my thanks and our hands touched as I took one flute from him. *Purr.* Little thrills all over.

"Such an unusual bracelet," he said. "Arapaho Wolf Clan style." I held my arm up and his fingers traced the design. A slight frown creased his forehead, and I wanted to reach up and smooth it out. Or kiss it better.

"It's a wolf's eye," I said. "It looks out for me."

At that exact moment, it tingled.

Chapter 44

I snarled. The stupid bracelet thought Matlal only wanted me to play pony, now it was telling me I was in danger. Who? Carter? *Alex?*

I swiveled my head, but there was nothing I could see except a ballroom full of people enjoying themselves. Jen was standing with her back to me, talking animatedly with three men not forty feet away. I couldn't see Carter. Matlal and Tucker were standing arguing on one side, oblivious to me. The only person looking my way was one of the security staff. And Alex.

"What's wrong?" he asked.

"My bracelet…no, nothing." I shrugged it off and leaned towards him. "Jack Tucker tells me you were a doctor, then gave it up to run a trucking company. That's interesting."

Alex laughed. "Yes, Jack's an original, isn't he? But I'll give him this, he sticks with you. He started me off with my first contract, and I'm still handling his shipping."

I frowned. That hadn't been quite what Jack had said to me, surely?

The bracelet tingled again. I groaned inwardly and looked at my watch. Just before midnight. I'd better check on security.

"Alex, I'm sorry. Just a moment."

I lifted the comms unit from my bag and flicked it on.

"Reynolds, you still awake?"

There was compete silence from the headset. I checked the tiny LED, which showed the battery was good. I called him on my cell. Always good to have a backup when electronics are involved. The call went to voicemail. Shit. This might be a technical hitch, but suddenly I was believing my bracelet.

"Alex, I have a problem here." I grabbed a card and thrust it in his hand. "I've got to go. Call me. I mean it."

"Can I help?"

I smiled as I gathered Jen's bag and mine. "Thanks, I appreciate it, but this is my line of work."

I came up behind Jen. She was waving her arms as she described something to the three men. I looped her bag over her arm and pulled her close, gently taking the drink from her hand and passing it to a waiter.

"Jen, stay calm, but I think we may have a problem," I whispered into her ear. "We need to go *now*."

She froze for a second and then giggled. "Hell, if you put it like that, honey," she drawled. "Gentlemen, excuse me, I'm called." She gave them a crooked smile and nodded to them, touching the nearest with one elegant finger on his lapel. "Carl, we're good on that deal, send me the contract."

We walked, and I set the pace fast but not fast enough to attract attention. I decided I would come back for the stole and gloves some other time.

"What's happening?" she said.

"Reynolds isn't answering. Could be a malfunction, but if it is, we can come back. It's too early for the others to be here. Call Kingston, please."

Jen tried her driver and got voicemail. She started to look nervous.

"What about Victor? The police?" she said.

"No time. We've got to get out of here first." I was uncomfortably aware how many ways there are to kill someone in a crowd.

The doorman had changed. It was entirely possible that they worked shifts, but I didn't like it. There were three cabs by the door and he waved us to the middle one. There were people in the first one, but it wasn't going anywhere. They appeared to be arguing.

I took the third cab. There were too many people standing around watching us. There was something staged about this, and I didn't even have the Walther. The doorman was moving towards us, shouting and pointing at the middle cab. Others started to gather. Something was going down here.

At that moment, Alex appeared at the door with a couple of friends. He had gotten drunk and very loud over the last two minutes. He was waving a bottle and draped his arm around the doorman, swinging him back away from us. Eyes left us and focused on him.

"You gotta go in that cab." Our cabbie turned in his seat and was pointing us to the middle one, and I knew then there was no way I was going in it. I jerked him back straight in his seat, grabbed his hair and held his head still. I pulled my lipstick out of my bag and shoved it into the back of his head.

"This is only a .22 but it'll make a good mess of your head if you don't start to drive. Now."

Alex had passed the doorman to one of his buddies and was leaning into the middle cab. He came out waving something and roaring: "This one's no fucking good, the key's broken."

Alex's other buddy had opened the door of the front cab and was dragging the cabbie out. I really hoped none of them were real cabbies.

Our cab pulled out. The man's hands were trembling. If this was ZK, they must be down to the bottom of the barrel, but how had they mounted such a complicated attack?

"Keep your hands on the wheel and the speed down to thirty," I said, as I patted him down. I pulled a pistol out of his jacket pocket.

"What a surprise, a ten-round Glock, no serial numbers." I put my deadly lipstick back and replaced it with the Glock. Things were looking up. Thank God for Alex.

I spared Jen a quick glance. She was looking pale and worried, but steady. I had to remind myself that, even if this was what I did for a living, it was new and frightening for her.

"Slow down. Turn here," I said to the cabbie.

"It's an alley," he complained.

I stabbed the back of his head with the Glock and he turned obediently.

"Stop. Put it in park. Open your door. Hands back on the wheel." I got out and stood behind him. "Now get out."

As he got out I hit him over the head with the butt of the pistol and he sprawled onto the asphalt. I reached across and took the keys out of the ignition.

"Come on Jen, my car's in the garage." I hurried her out of the alley and we trotted across the road in our party heels. The late night traffic ignored us and it was freezing cold in my dress.

"Amber, what the hell's going on?" Jen said as we got into my car. I started the engine and turned the heat up.

"I don't know. I thought Morales was winding up ZK and things would be safer. There's no point in them coming after you other than for revenge. Any takeover of your company now would come under too much scrutiny to be any use. But this is way over the top. I'm missing something."

"What were they trying to do tonight?"

I had come out of the parking garage and was heading south for Speer Boulevard. As we pulled away, there was a muffled thud of an explosion and a bright flash from the alley where we'd left the cab.

"They were trying to kill you, Jen," I said as she twisted around to look open-mouthed at the alley. "At least two, maybe three fake cabbies. Cars wired to blow if things went wrong. Replacement for the doorman and front desk security staff. Someone to take out Reynolds and Kingston. I'd lay bets they even had someone inside the ballroom."

"Stop the car, please," she said, gripping my arm, her eyes wide.

I pulled over. She scrambled out and was sick on the sidewalk. I mentally kicked myself. I kept forgetting that years of people trying to kill me made me casual about it, but this was all new for Jen.

She got back in and turned to the front. I could see her make an effort to calm herself.

"Thank you, Amber," she said finally. "Tonight's the second time you've saved my life."

I gave her a smile as I pulled away. "You'll have to thank Alex and his friends as well this time. That was a fantastic diversion that let us get away."

"Deauville? That was an act?" I nodded. "Did you ask him to do it?" she asked.

"No. I guess he just saw something going on."

"Oh. I thought he didn't like me."

I smiled to myself. Maybe it was me he liked. In the meantime, I'd better get my head around what this latest attack meant.

"Jen, what happens to the Kingslund Group if you're dead?"

"Bernard has signing rights," she said slowly. "My estate would have the benefit of course, but the whole nine yards would be up for sale. At a price he would set."

Well, that took care of the motive for killing Jen. We just needed to find out who. My cell rang. It was Victor.

"Amber? You okay? Ms. Kingslund?"

"We're fine, Vic. We're on the road in my car. The cab we took was blown up a couple of minutes ago. What happened?"

"Don't know yet. Reynolds and Kingston down. Door security at the ball down. Hold off goin' back till I check the place an' double up. I'll call you." He kept it short and to the point.

"We'll hold off, Vic, but I'm turning off these cells. I'll call you on another line."

"Shit, woman, you thinkin' traces as well?"

"Could be. Don't want to give them any edge."

"Okay. Try in an hour. Be careful."

"I hear you, Vic." I hung up and turned the cell off.

"What does he mean—down?" Jen said, turning her cell off as well.

"Don't know what it means yet, Jen. Just out of action for the moment."

I headed south off Speer, down Logan. If ZK had gone to all this trouble to get Jen at the ball, then they might have a backup plan at Jen's house. I was confident that Victor would check the place over thoroughly. In the meantime, we needed to be somewhere unpredictable.

I retrieved my burn phone from the bag and called David.

Chapter 45

David opened the door for us and beckoned us inside.

He looked awful, as pale and sick as he had last weekend. I felt guilty that I hadn't checked on him, but there hadn't been any time this week, what with my unscheduled trip to Rooks. I'd hoped that he was over the worst after our last meeting, but it was clear he wasn't. We couldn't discuss it in front of Jen, so I just gave him a hug and asked if he was okay.

He nodded and offered to make us coffee or hot chocolate. Jen made him show her where everything was and then herded him to the living room to sit.

I knelt close to him and spoke quietly. "What's up, David? I thought you were going to kick ass after last time."

"Got the first part done okay. It's just Pia giving me a hard time. You know, what doesn't kill you..."

"Yeah, I know the saying, makes you stronger. So long as it doesn't kill you. What's she doing?"

David was wearing a roll neck shirt. He eased the side down and I could see multiple bite wounds healing. "Just lots of it," he said. His voice was tired.

Jen came in with the chocolate and I sat with her on the sofa.

I managed to get David to talk about running a bit, and Jen and I told him a little about the charity ball, without mentioning the way we had left it. The conversation limped. David seemed to swing between half asleep and manically awake and focused on us.

I called Victor at 2 a.m. and he gave us the all clear to head home. I hugged David as we left and promised to look in on him soon.

"Ex-boyfriend?" Jen said as we pulled away.

I smiled. "No, more a little brother."

"Is he doing drugs or is he sick?"

"Neither. Really, he's just going through a bad patch. It wasn't a good idea for us to show up like that. I'll have to drop in on him this week and make sure he's okay."

It took us only five minutes to get from David's house back up to Jen's. Victor had doubled up the guards and they got us off the quiet streets and out of sight quickly.

We met with Victor in the living room.

Victor's news was better than it might have been. Reynolds and Kingston were both found unconscious and tied up in the limousine, parked in the center's parking garage. They had been injected with general anesthetics. Alongside them, in a van, were the half-dozen of the center staff who had been on door security, similarly drugged and tied.

Alerted by the failure of Reynolds to respond at about the time we were getting out, Victor had called the police in. The fake door security team and cabbies had long since disappeared, and as I had predicted, a couple of inside security staff were missing as well. The mayor had demanded it all be kept low key, and few of the attendees at the ball had noticed anything wrong.

"It feels like desperation to me," I said as Victor wound down on the events at the ball. "Too many things to go wrong, too many people involved. And blowing up cabs as an attempt at a fail-safe method, for God's sake." I turned to Jen. "What's happened or is happening over the next couple of weeks that's so important?"

Jen shrugged. "I don't have anything major planned immediately. There's the bid for Tucker Beacon which could go in once the quarterly financials are done. That'd be sometime over the next month or so. I'm finalizing a partnership purchase of land for the Quarter Horse race track next week."

"No, something triggered this. Silver Hills was half-assed, like it was done in a hurry. But tonight was planned. If you had died this evening, who controls the company? Verdoon. And they control him."

"But there's nothing planned," Jen said. "And what about Troy?"

Victor shifted his bulk on his seat. "Differen' strategy. Plain disruption. Whatever the reason, the main plan now is to kill you. So we ain't gonna let that happen."

"Vic, if they're really desperate," I glanced at the windows. "RPG, sniper, bomb—there's too many ways to hit us here."

He nodded. "Gonna ask you to move around over the next few days. Ask you to limit contact with anyone who could be involved."

There didn't seem to be much more to say about attacks, so I asked if Victor had tracked down Verdoon's background for clues. Jen had known about the hospital bills—they were for Verdoon's daughter.

"Don't know what to make of it, Amber," Victor said. "Verdoon's wife, she's saying that the move saved her daughter's life. She was in critical up here, they thought no more than a few weeks left. Then she was moved down to New Mexico and it seems she might be comin' out soon, fully recovered. Can see that would be a powerful incentive, just don't see how you could do it."

I did. Athanate healing. I didn't know how or why, but I was starting to be sure that Matlal was somewhere behind this.

Victor headed off. Jen went to bed. I sat and nursed a rum.

I was operating blind. We had been lucky, and whoever was after me and Jen only needed our luck to fail once. I had to find the source. What was it that I was missing?

Something had happened last week that changed the enemy's strategy from loosely connected financial, kidnapping and disruption to attempted murder. If I could figure out the key, I was sure I would know who it was.

I couldn't get any further.

As I soaped up in the shower I thought about the look Jen had given me on the dance floor. How did I feel about it now? I knew damn well how I'd felt about it at the time. It wasn't fair for me to lead her on, but her desire was darkly addictive.

And then there was Alex. I didn't know him yet, but what I had seen, I liked. Very much.

Which did I want more? That was a little like asking if I preferred Lario's steak or his chocolate dessert. It was a pointless question anyway. I couldn't take it any further with either of them. Even if I didn't infect them with the Athanate prions, I would end up wanting to drink their blood.

A shudder ran through me. Not a shudder of disgust, but a reaction to the startling premonition of how erotic I would find it to *bite*. I began to shiver. I used to think it was disgusting, didn't I? Surely, I could remember thinking how disgusting it would be.

But if I had, that was now erased by the intensity of the thrill at the thought. I turned the shower to cold and stood under it. The prion reading this evening was over .56—I wondered how much longer I had left.

Top's advice seemed bleaker now. *You gotta play the hand you're dealt.*

Chapter 46

SATURDAY

In the morning, we moved Jen's base to her downtown apartment, but Jen herself was booked into a hotel under a false name, with the whole corridor taken up for security.

We called in at police HQ to give our version of what had happened the previous evening and I handed over the Glock. I also managed to speak to Morales for a few minutes to update him. While Jen was driven back to the hotel, I took some time out to divert to the convention center to pick up the stole and gloves. I returned them with the beautiful green dress and earrings to Lisa.

When I walked through the door, she threw her arms around me. Ethel Harriman had stopped by earlier and asked Lisa to put on a private fashion show for twenty of her friends in time for the Christmas season. Lisa wanted me to keep the dress, but I told her to put it in the window as she had suggested and if I ever needed it again, I would come calling. As much as I loved it, it was no use to me at the moment, and I didn't even have an apartment of my own.

As I was making my way out, she stopped me. "Oh, I nearly forgot. There was a call for you as well." She smiled and handed me a note with a number and an address. "A gentleman called Alex. You gave him the wrong business card. He said it's *very* important." She waggled her eyebrows.

"Just one of the bankers," I said. "Short and smelly. Cross eyed. Hair growing out of his ears."

"And so important that you should talk about your bank balance on a Saturday?" She laughed as I left.

I tucked the note into a jacket pocket. Plenty of time for that later. It wasn't as if I could do anything about it. I couldn't go around infecting people with Athanate prions. How would Hollywood put it? My libido was writing checks my rules wouldn't let me cash. The trouble was, my libido was up when the sun was down and I wasn't sure my morals were strong enough when the Athanate inside got the upper hand. Still, it felt nice.

When I got back to the hotel, Jen was arguing for a trip down to Browns hotel. There was a committee meeting there to finish up on the charity ball, and even though she was excused, she wanted to drop in. Knowing her, I suspected a fancy lunch was on the cards as well.

Jameson, the head of Victor's security detail today, wasn't happy. To placate him, I scouted through the sports shop down the street, coming up with some Lycra cycling outfits, running shoes and helmets for both of us. I got a red fright wig I used for raves out of my car and we put wraparound shades on as well. Dressed like that, Jameson had to admit that neither of us looked like ourselves. He agreed we could go, providing I went with Jen, and there would be three guards in the building, including himself. No lunch.

At Browns, Jameson and the others spread out through the atrium, keeping visual contact with each other and their comms units active.

Browns' conference area was being transformed for a meeting on Monday that seemed to be a convention of flower sellers. Every walkway and every flat surface had exotic displays of flowers and shrubs. It was like being in the botanical gardens.

I saw Jen into one of the small meeting rooms where the rest of the committee were talking. I stayed outside, strolling back to check the guards every few minutes.

An hour later, Jen felt she had done enough and we were walking back to the escalator.

"Crap!" I spotted Carter at the bottom of the escalator. "Kath said whatever I do, I shouldn't talk to him."

Jen giggled and pulled me aside, squeezing us between two of the huge plant displays and up against the railing. The plants hid us. Even if he looked through, he wasn't going to recognize me from the back with my bright red wig sticking out from under the bike helmet.

I could hear Carter talking to his companions as he reached the top of the escalator and then moved off toward the offices.

"Well," Jen said, very close to my ear. "Not quite where I had in mind, but about time."

I was suddenly and uncomfortably aware of how close we were pressed together. And the feel of Jen's hands on my hips. Time to cancel that check.

"Jen, I'm straight," I said. *Am I? Why am I enjoying this so much?*

"Course you are, honey," she murmured. "Knew that right off, first time I saw you. I'm good like that."

Her breath was tickling my neck. "I'm good like this too," she whispered and kissed my neck. Only fair, given that's what I'd done to her last night. My legs felt wobbly. Her lips brushed against my chin. In another second we would be kissing.

I grabbed her and held her away.

"No!" I said. "Stop. Please, Jen, you don't know what you're doing."

"I know *exactly* what I'm doing, honey."

I had to turn my head away. Staring into those blue eyes, I would have lost it. I took one look down at the base of the escalator and I wrapped her back in my arms and pulled her to me.

"Change of mind, honey?" She chuckled, her arms slipping around me and pulling right back.

"Shh. Just stay there. It's Onebrow and Tucker, coming up the escalator."

She froze. "Shit! Together?" she whispered.

I nodded. "We need to be out of here as soon as they're gone. There's half a dozen others with them."

They were arguing.

"This is too public," said Onebrow.

"No one's listening," grunted Tucker. "Plain sight—best place to hide. And anyway, he said he had to meet us here."

"I don't like it. I don't trust him. And what is it with the plants?" Onebrow's hoarse voice asked, and my blood froze. What if he wandered across and took a look where we were hiding?

Tucker replied too quietly to hear and the footsteps moved away.

I let out the breath I'd been holding.

Jen pushed my frizzy wig away from her face and peered out.

"Gone," she said. We eased out between the plants and ran down the escalators.

As soon as they saw us coming, the guards hurried across and I told them who had just passed us. Jameson looked worried and started talking on the comms. The car came up right outside and we jostled across to it, with the three guys around us.

I ditched the itchy wig and helmet and called Morales to tell him that Frank Hoben was at Browns with Tucker. He swore and told me he'd get back to me.

Once I ended that call, I turned to Jen. Jameson and I were sitting in the back with her between us. She looked pale, but angry rather than shaken. Her body had gone stiff and her mouth was set in a hard line.

"Jen?"

"Tucker. It's been Jack Tucker all along, hasn't it?"

I sat there thinking. What would Tucker have to gain? Kingslund was the only company that was willing to buy him out of his problems.

"The merger announcement," Jen said. "He pushed for it to be called a merger and we made the press release the day you and I went to Silver Hills."

"Yes, but—"

"If he's got Verdoon doing what he wants, and I'm dead, he can make Verdoon sell my company to him for peanuts. Ordinarily, that would be too suspicious. But if everyone thinks it's part of a merger process that's been agreed, he can just bluff it out."

"He never wanted to be bought." I thought it through and the connection fell into place. "Oh my God! He can't let himself be bought."

Jen looked blank.

"That's what I couldn't understand about what Tucker and Alex said last night. Alex told me he ran Tucker's trucking contracts."

"He does," Jen said.

"But Tucker said I caused him a lot of trouble when the police locked down Crate & Freight. I thought he meant Carter was running his trucking. He didn't. That was his frigging shipment that got seized. He can't let anyone buy him—they'd see what he's been doing."

"He's running drugs to keep his business afloat?"

"Yes." And weapons. What else? And who were they meeting? I wanted to say Carter, but it didn't add up. That left Matlal.

Chapter 47

Morales called to say Onebrow wasn't in the center when the police arrived. I left Jen talking to him and Victor about our suspicions on Tucker. There was nothing more that we could do without proof. There was no way Morales could move on someone like Tucker without slam dunk evidence.

There was one person who had to know about this and I had to go and see him anyway. Skylur's payment for me when I agreed to attend the charity ball was the information that it was vital for Jen's sake. Obviously, he must have known about the attack. And if he knew, how difficult would it have been to give me the details and stop the whole thing?

Once I was away from the hotel and wouldn't give the location away if I was being traced, I turned on my cell. There were a host of missed calls. I picked out Bian's ID and returned the call.

She answered immediately. "Amber, are you okay?"

"Why, Pussycat, I might think you cared. My cell's been off because it may be being tracked. I'm turning it back off and coming in."

"We'll pick you up where we last met." Bian caught on quickly. A cell that might be tracked might be listened to.

"Don't bother, I know where to come. And I'll meet him upstairs, not in the basement." I turned the cell back off before she could respond. It wouldn't be fair to take out my anger on Bian. I had the impression she was fairly high up in the hierarchy at Altau, but I wanted to save it all up for Skylur.

I headed out of town, taking a couple of extra turns to check that I had no tail. I'd already searched for trackers like the one they used on Jen's car.

Half an hour later, I was driving along Bear Ridge. It wasn't a ridge and there were no bears, but I guess people with this amount of money can call their road anything they damn well please. I drove along slowly. Oak and ash trees lined the road, planted in well-tended grass verges. Small, elegant signs gave the names of the houses. I got the briefest glimpse of houses themselves, every one set back in acres of landscaped garden and surrounded by walls and gates. The house at the end didn't stand out particularly, and it wasn't called House Altau of course. It was called Haven. Indeed. I shivered. I might call this place home soon.

I had been expecting a reaction at the gate and I got it.

The gates were recessed and out of view from the road. Once I was in front of them, there was a *thunk* sound and six-inch spikes emerged from the ground behind me, angled forward. There was no way back and with the gates still closed, no way forward.

To the left and right were curving brick walls which looked very decorative, except for the black slits. Behind those slits I got the sense of metal and movement. I knew I was between two heavy caliber machine guns. If it were me, I might have gone for a flamethrower as well, and there was nothing to say I was more paranoid than them, so I sat very still and waited for instructions.

"Open the trunk and doors, get out of the car and stand in front of it with your hands on the hood."

I complied and a couple of guys with ugly, stubby Herstal P90 guns walked out and checked the car over. I refused to get embarrassed when the one checking the trunk snorted. Doesn't everyone keep half their clothes in the car? Along with a bright red wig.

A third guard, a female, came and frisked me thoroughly and impersonally, taking my boots away for checking and leaving me standing on the gravel barefoot, leaning against the car. The gates opened behind me.

"Well, Round-eye, you sure know how to cause a fuss." I heard Bian walk up and I watched the effect on the guards with interest. They all but came to attention.

"I just came to deliver a message and trade some information, Pussycat. Can I stand up?"

"Yes, and put your boots back on." The female guard held them out to me. I took a good look at her and a sniff as I took them. She wasn't Athanate, but I could see faint healed scars on her neck. Part of some Athanate's family. Kin.

"Let's walk. They'll drive your car around," Bian said, taking my arm. The house was about a hundred yards further on and we walked across a lawn which was bordered by a huge circular gravel drive. A large oak dominated the lawn and the outer edge of the drive was defined by flowerbeds with an array of scented plants. Buddleia, honeysuckle and jasmine, just as I had smelled on my first visit.

"How did you find the address?" asked Bian.

"Maybe I'll trade that with Skylur," I said.

She snorted and shaded her eyes against the late afternoon sun as she looked sideways at me. "A word of advice, Round-eye. A bit of humility might be a good idea today."

"Diana said something very similar during my first visit. Didn't seem to do me much good. And you know, I just have a problem seeing you in that position."

"I don't think you showed any humility at all on your first visit. And as for how I behave, I'm not about to try and explain to Skylur how I come to be in possession of an Altau secret. *No* outside parties are allowed that knowledge. Think about that."

She held open the front door and I walked into the reception area.

On my last visit I had been restricted to the information from my ears and nose. I had been right about the wood floors and the size of the room. The floor was tiled in warm blond oak, making a large bright area bordered by twin curving staircases of dark redwood coming down from a gallery corridor. Opposite us, an archway led to a corridor and I could see a living room and library off that.

The whole place spoke of enormous wealth and restraint.

In this area, the one piece of ornamentation was a huge carved eagle mounted on the balustrade of the gallery. It had its wings spread and its eyes covered by a cloth.

Bian saw my eyes on it. "That's the symbol of the Hidden Path," she murmured, as we passed underneath. "The path so secret, even the eagle cannot see it. Our path."

The corridor ran most of the length of the house from what I could see. I assumed that the little room with the elevator down to the dungeon was behind one of the doors. Bian stopped so suddenly, I nearly bumped into her. A figure in a black robe, face hidden by a cowl, passed silently along the corridor.

"What was that?" I said, but Bian was moving again. She led me straight across the corridor into a library.

Above us, a wooden ceiling arched, illuminated by hidden uplighting. A large stone fireplace dominated one side and the other side was given over to bookshelves. Comfortable, high-backed chairs were arranged around the fireplace. The far end of the room was a huge bay window looking over formal gardens at the back of the house.

"Come in and sit down please, Amber," Skylur said, from one of the chairs with its back to me.

Chapter 48

Bian left and I sat down opposite him. I suppose I shouldn't have been shocked that I suddenly recognized him. He had been the man accompanying Diana when I was kidnapped, whose face had disappeared from my memory. He had the kind of looks you might pass over in a crowd as you walked by, dark-haired and handsome, but not exceptional. Until you looked at his eyes—a hard, shocking blue. I hadn't seen them the first time we'd met. In the parking lot, the light had been bad and in the dungeon, it had been dark and he'd been playing tricks with my head.

"Are you going to screw with my memory again when I leave?" I said.

"*If* you leave, no." He let that hang in the air.

"What's so important about keeping this place secret?"

He sighed. "We're at war, even if it's officially peacetime. The Basilikos party will not hesitate to attack this house if they discover the location. When we host the Assembly next week, every member will arrive here blindfolded—that's the level of care we take. The only people who know this location are completely loyal."

"And you're saying I'm not. What does it take to prove I won't give this location away? Diana read my mind."

"She was looking for a specific thing—that you would go to the ball and get the message for us. Loyalty is a much more complex matter and the answer isn't yes or no."

"So how do you know those guards out there are loyal?"

"You'll understand the kin bonds when you become fully Athanate. When you stop fighting it. Now, my question which you *will* answer. How did you find the address?"

"Let me say first that no one else knows. What'll you trade for the answer?"

"This isn't a trade. It would be much easier to just keep you here." He glared at me.

Fortunately, at that moment, Diana arrived and distracted us. I knew that Skylur was stronger and quicker than me. I suspected he could break through my mental defenses. But something made me keep challenging him.

"Amber, hello. Lovely to see you."

I got up and remembered the formal Athanate greeting kiss—the neck and not the cheek. We parted and Diana's lips pressed into a lazy, predatory smile which made me sit down again in a hurry.

"You have the message?" Diana said.

"I want the answer—" Skylur began, but Diana cut him off.

"She'll tell us when she's ready. I will vouch for her. And we owe her for putting her in jeopardy." Skylur looked angry, but didn't say anything. Diana didn't play fair. I had a lot more difficulty arguing against her approach than Skylur's.

"Yes, I have a message from Arvinder Singh." At the name, both of them started and they exchanged looks.

"This is good news," Diana said. "If it's Arvinder who has changed allegiance, then Basilikos has serious internal problems. What's the message?"

I looked at them blankly. "I don't know. He put a coded message in my head. Isn't that how you were expecting it?"

Before I could blink the pair of them were looming over me, holding me down on the chair. My heart stopped and then went flat out. What the hell had I just said? Despite my previous experience trying to fight them, I struggled, which did me no good at all.

Diana was behind my chair, reaching over. Her hands gripped my head like a vise and tilted it back until I was looking up at her.

"Amber, please trust me. Stop struggling," she said. Her voice was so reasonable, so calm. Her eyes held mine until my heart started to slow and I subsided.

"I can do this because you *do* trust me. This does not mean anyone else can. You can fight Matlal or any other Athanate who tries to overcome you mentally. Do you understand what I'm saying?"

My head twitched in her hands.

"What Arvinder did could be used to do other things, things you wouldn't even realize. I need to check. You have my word, I will look only where I need to. May I?"

I twitched my head again. I had a feeling she could look whether I wanted it or not, but I did trust her and I relaxed as much as I could. There was a feeling of panic as a gray *otherness* seemed to sink into my head, and she murmured something soothing. My eyes closed. Like a film reel, the charity ball unwound in my head: the feeling while I was walking to the door, Jen's red dress, the taste of the food and wine, Matlal, the dances, my feet aching, Arvinder, the smell of Alex, Tucker's rant, the fake doorman.

It stopped and I drifted back to find myself sitting slumped in my chair. Skylur was back in his and Diana sat on the arm of my chair, one hand resting on my shoulder. She and Skylur were speaking in Athanate.

When she saw that I was back, she squeezed my shoulder. "Nothing was done to you," she said. "It was just a message from Arvinder to us."

She cleared her throat. "Amber, now that we've got the charity ball out of the way, we're going to have to formally recognize you before the Assembly next Wednesday."

"What does that mean?"

"Athanate are very concerned about knowing where everyone fits in. Matlal is already lodging complaints that an unregistered Athanate was at the ball. That's one step from rogue. You need a status that will be understood and will give you a measure of protection against other Athanate Houses. It will also protect us against claims that we are not policing our mantle correctly. There are two alternatives."

I looked up questioningly.

"One, you become part of House Altau, acknowledging Skylur as your Master. There is a ceremony and an exchange of Blood." Her hand gently squeezed my shoulder again when I started to protest. "As I felt that this is not something you want yet, there is a second option of alliance. You form House Farrell and swear allegiance to Altau before the Assembly. It's customary, but not necessary, to go through the exchange of Blood."

I laughed. "A House of one? Without a physical house either?"

"For the moment," Diana said.

"This is ridiculous," Skylur said to Diana. "We go through all this for simple requirements—to protect her and ensure our safety. The easiest way is to keep her here until after the Assembly at least. I'm strongly against establishing another House in Denver. It has no rationale."

"And it's your decision," replied Diana. "But my advice is to proceed this way. It does us no good to keep Amber here, and it may actually harm our interests."

Skylur leaned back in the chair, and made a dismissive wave with his hand. I took that as his reluctant agreement.

I turned to Diana. "Other than the Blood, what's the difference between the two options?"

"In protection, nothing. Harm done to you is harm done to Altau. Which won't keep you safe in itself, but will make Athanate think twice before trying anything. In responsibility, it's quite complex. As a member of a House, the bond is very close. As an allied House, you're much more independent unless you break Athanate law, and then discipline and reparations are Altau's responsibility. You are responsible for your House. Only you at the moment, but that would change. As a member, you wouldn't be expected to attend the Assembly. As a new House, you must, to give your oath."

"There's no way I can understand what I need to in time for the Assembly if you're expecting me to attend. Is there any possibility of an advisor?"

Skylur and Diana looked at each other for a moment and Skylur nodded. Diana turned to me. "Bian will help you. This is not a temporary reassignment; she will remain Altau, but she will advise you."

I would have preferred Diana, but I guessed I would find a way to make it work.

"Now, tell us how you came to find where this house is," Diana's grip on my shoulder added an unvoiced *please*.

"You need to know this for your legitimate security reasons, and I'll tell you," I said. "But I need to know things for my legitimate security reasons—how you knew there was going to be an attempt to kill Jennifer Kingslund at the ball."

"We have a spy in their camp," Skylur said. "Are you aware of the link between Tucker and Matlal?"

"Tucker's fiancée works for Matlal. There's some commercial cooperation."

Skylur snorted. "Tucker's fiancée is House Matlal, and looks on him as a future blood slave. And it's more than cooperation in the businesses. Tucker has crushing financial problems and Matlal is now a shareholder in Tucker Beacon. Tucker's caught. Just think of him as another commercial arm of Matlal. One that gives Matlal an excuse in front of the Assembly for visiting Denver and interfering in our mantle. Our spy knew that an attempt would be made at the ball. It was Tucker's last opportunity to get the Kingslund Group and wriggle away from Matlal. That failed and now he'll never get away."

I nodded. My sympathy for Tucker's predicament was very limited. He had tried to recruit me and then to kill me. And if he had recruited me, Jen would have died and it would have become my fault. That, I couldn't forgive. "Why couldn't you have said earlier?"

"There was a chance things might have gone differently at the ball. We didn't want to reveal that we had a spy in their camp," Diana said. "For that matter, we have been unsure how reliable this spy is. We still don't know their identity, but this message is genuine."

This wasn't proof about Tucker that I could take to Morales, but at least I understood a little more about what was going on. In the meantime, Skylur wanted his answer and I could sense his angry impatience wasn't going to hold much longer. "I had a GPS system in my old car, the one you used to drive me here. I had it modified a while back to allow it to store coordinates every couple of minutes even if it looked switched off. I pulled the track off the next day."

"Who else might have seen this information?" asked Diana.

"No one. I did it alone, on Saturday, and the file is encrypted."

Skylur and Diana did their eerie wordless stare, but they seemed satisfied with the answer. Diana left the armrest and sat in her own chair.

"For the moment, please do not breach our systems any further," she said. "Don't find out the names of Athanate here, where they come from, what they do outside—anything. Don't discuss a word about the Athanate with anybody outside. We need to keep this in place at least till the end of the Assembly this week. Once we've got rid of all the Athanate visitors in Denver, then things will change. In fact, I'd like you to conduct some tests on the security and defense systems here."

I nodded while thinking *what about knowing David?* I decided I needed to warn David first before I told them.

Someone I didn't know entered the library behind me and Skylur looked over and got up. "I have a call, I must go," he said. "I'll amend the Assembly agenda to include the oath, and I'll see you then, House Farrell." He strode out. I couldn't quite tell if he was joking or not with the title.

Diana sat, lost in thought for the moment. I took the time to look around the library and the gardens outside. It was very quiet in the house. It had a feeling of emptiness and I wondered briefly where everyone was.

I decided to use the opportunity of having Diana there to answer questions.

"Can I ask—how much am I a risk to other people?"

Diana looked over at me. "How do you mean?"

"I have Athanate prions in my body. I understand from the scientists that the prions don't survive outside of the body, but can I infect someone just by kissing them, for example? Or do I have to bite?"

She stirred in her chair and got up. "If kissing were a reliable method, we wouldn't use fangs," she said and shrugged. "Once you gain full control of your powers, then you'll do what you intend to. If you want to turn someone, you'll turn them, but you would use fangs to be sure. If you want to heal, or bind, that would be different. But at your stage, yes, there is a small risk, even with a kiss."

I got up too. "So, sex is out for the moment."

Diana smiled. "Except with Athanate."

It had been a long day, a long week. My belief in my own humanity and sexuality was being challenged, and Diana just seemed to crystallize it in that one casual comment.

"To hell with the damned Athanate," I said angrily, getting in her face.

She didn't reply, she didn't step back. Her expressionless face turned aside, but not before I caught a glimpse of pain in her eyes. My tantrum evaporated and I realized how stupidly I was behaving.

"I'm sorry, Diana. I'm a complete asshole sometimes. It's...I..." I thought of all the excuses I could give, all the reasons I had for my hair-trigger temper. They were all crap and I swallowed them. "No excuse," I forced out.

Diana turned her face back, her expression still unreadable. Her eyes looked huge. They weren't glittering. They were dark and secret as space; they were great, black moons pulling at my tides. I felt dizzy. She wasn't even trying and she was mesmerizing me.

"You did a good job bringing me in the first time around," I said, and made myself go on, steeling myself to stand straight and keep looking into her eyes. "You've been careful and patient with me and I pay it all back by getting angry and saying stupid things. Please believe me, it isn't how I really think. I don't want to be your enemy. Forgive me."

I touched her on the shoulder and a little shiver rippled through her, startling me. Moving slowly and deliberately, she gathered my hands between hers and held them between us.

"Forgiven," she murmured, a hint of fang at the edge of her mouth. "When your time comes, I would be very honored to be your Mentor."

Fear and excitement tingled up and down my spine. "I don't want..." I began, but my mouth slowed and stopped. I didn't know what the hell I wanted at the moment.

"I understand," she said.

Her eyes flickered to the left and a second later Bian came into the library. She stopped, looking at us. Our hands dropped and I stepped back, my breath easing slightly.

"Did I miss something?" asked Bian slyly, raising her eyebrows.

The demon got my throat. "Darling," I drawled, "you missed *everything*."

Bian's face went closed. Her eyes got a gleam to them, not quite the glitter of blood hunger.

"Bian, Amber is leaving," Diana said. "Would you ensure that the guards are informed, please?"

We walked together to the front door. Bian went out with a glance back and began to stride to the gate. Diana tucked a piece of paper into my jacket pocket.

"I almost forgot. That is the contact information for the Weres in Denver." She smiled secretively.

"Thank you for that," I said, "and for the loan of your coat last time. I've got it in the car."

"I have to go and speak to Skylur now. Give it to Bian, please." She was still smiling as she turned away. "She will make you pay for that little joke, you know."

I drove to the gate, got out and passed Diana's coat wordlessly to Bian while the gates started their slow, silent opening.

The guards had changed, and at her shoulder, I recognized one of them. It was Fang 3, from our little battle in LoDo. He had been the one who had been beating me with his Kung Fu technique until he got too showy. I wondered how this would go, but there was no way I couldn't say something.

"Feeling better?"

He grinned. "All fine, except my pride." His smile was unforced and I found myself smiling back and enjoying it.

"Tell me it wasn't your idea—the black suits?" I said.

"Nah. That was—" he stopped himself, his eyes not quite flicking towards Bian. I got it. No names, no background, as Diana had said. "That was the dork you sent down the stairs," he went on. "He takes everything too seriously."

"The rest of the posse okay too?"

"Getting so. We heal easily. Shame we don't get any smarter."

I laughed at that. "Well, can't help with that, but what about a return match? Maybe we could do some sparring sometime?"

His eyes lit up. "Ma'am, yes ma'am."

No one says that any more, even in training, but there was a sense about this man that I thought I recognized from my days in Ops 4-10. I would lay good odds that he was a former Marine.

"Semper Fi?"

I saw his lips shaping to answer with the marine cheer of 'ooh-rah' when Bian leaned forwards slightly, all five-five of her coming up on the balls of her feet. Despite her lack of height, she still managed to loom. His eyes swiveled to her and then back to the front and he stiffened to attention, the smile gone. When they said no information, they meant it.

I turned to Bian. "You know, it's true what Diana said about you."

She leaped into my trap. "What's that?"

"You are *no* fun at all." I climbed back into my car. Fang 3's eyes were bulging as if he had just seen something he admired, but had no wish to do himself, like dragging a leopard by its tail. Pussy.

The gates had completed their silent opening and I started my engine.

Bian's face appeared at my window, and I lowered it. She rested her elbows on the sill.

"I am *so* looking forward to introducing you to Athanate rules and customs," she said, and her tongue ran slowly along her upper lip, pushing it back to show her fangs, pale in the lights. "Diana didn't say anything about fun, but what she did say was true…I *will* make you pay."

I drove out, laughing. Damn, but I was starting to like this girl.

Chapter 49

SUNDAY

On Sunday morning, Jen went into the office to strip Verdoon of any position of responsibility in the company.

I drove away from the hotel to check calls on my cell. I still wasn't sure whether I was being tracked through the cell or not, but I wasn't going to take a chance. I had my burn phone, which was probably okay for a couple more days if I needed to make outgoing calls. I used it to call Tullah and warn her away from work until I cleared it.

There was nothing in my usual cell's call logs I needed to deal with until Monday. But there was one text message from last night: *Mike 6 call Bravo 5* and a cell number.

I had parked on the road while I was checking. I was next to the Capitol and I managed to walk around the building to sit down. My hands were shaking. I'd turned the cell off, but the words kept rolling around in my head. Mike 6 was my call sign on the mission in South America. My last mission.

I sat down heavily on the steps to the Capitol.

It's nighttime. Rising above the jungle and blocking out the stars in front of me is the darkness of Hacha Del Diablo, the Devil's Axe. I'm dizzy. Angry. I touch my neck and know again I am going to die, arterial blood pulsing over my hand. The fetid stench of death assaults my nose. My fist cramps with the grip I have on his hair, but I'm not going to let his head go, and the blood drips from the severed neck over my boots. There's blood over my face, down my chest...

"Missy, no call to be sitting on them cold steps."

I blinked. An old man, hunched over a walking stick, shuffled by and gave a smile, weak as winter sun.

Denver. Here and now. I got up and walked. No one outside of 4-10 knew the call sign. Bravo 5 was from the backup team: Sergeant Alverson. Keith. Oh God. Keith. I called the number on my burn phone.

"Keith? You in town?"

"Amber. Yes. I—"

"Keith, it's dangerous. Meet me at the Longhorn Bar on 16th. Take time to check for a tail. Thirty minutes?"

"Will do."

I put the car out of sight in a parking garage. Then I made my way down to the bar, circling around and looking out.

Almost exactly on the half hour, I spotted him. He hadn't changed a bit, but I guess it was only a couple of years. I watched him check around, double back and slip into the bar as if it was an afterthought. I watched the street for another five minutes before following him in.

He was sitting in the corner. I bought a coffee and walked across to sit beside him, so I could see the door as well.

It was strange. We just sat there looking at each other for a minute.

"You haven't changed," I said.

"You have." He took a sip of his coffee and sighed. "Amber, it's about Top."

I didn't trust my voice, so I nodded. I thought it had to be something like that.

"Yesterday morning," Keith went on. "I was there on Friday and he was going fast. He felt he'd straightened everything out as best he could, and the rest was just hanging around. Not his style."

"No, it wasn't," I managed to say and swallowed hard. "Thanks for coming to tell me."

"He said to tell you he enjoyed your visit. He couldn't have gone without talking to you. But I didn't come just to tell you. Amber, he asked me to put together some things for you. For emergencies, he said. It's in the storage facility where Mrs. Welchester has a unit."

I sighed. "I guess it was stupid to think that name wouldn't come up on 4-10's radar."

Keith shrugged. "No one looked until Top told me to. No one else knows, and I'm not saying." He passed me a key. "Unit 438. It's prepaid for a year."

"Thank you, Keith." I closed my hand over the key. "I don't know if I can make the funeral. There's an agreement I had to sign—"

Keith cut across me. "We know about it. I think Colonel Laine will have it torn up in a week or so, but maybe it would be better to stay away."

I raised my eyebrows in question.

"Petersen isn't a major any more, and he's making a big move to take over the section. Not just 4-10, but Obs and a couple of others as well." Keith paused and looked at me, his mouth twisted. "He's got a very simple attitude toward vamps. Kill them. Not much better than his attitude towards women in 4-10."

I got a cold feeling in my stomach. "Can't someone kick this upstairs?"

Keith shook his head. "4-10 isn't the regular army, Amber. There's no general sitting there with direct responsibility, no official recognition. It's the ultimate, deniable, operational unit. The entire budget is overspill, and the rule seems to be to work out problems on the base."

I nodded. "Thanks again, Keith." If Petersen had that attitude, Keith would need to be out of here and away. It also seemed that Colonel Laine had a difficult job, to work out a route for Diana to speak to more senior officers. I might need to think of a second option for that.

Keith didn't seem to be in a hurry. He just sat and looked at his cup, his hands curled around it. I'd spotted the ring, of course.

"Who's the lucky girl?" I said brightly.

"We thought you were dead, Amber. Then, you know, changed." He didn't meet my eyes. Didn't answer my question either, but I guess I didn't really need to know.

"Yeah," I said.

"What's it like, Amber? Are you a vampire?"

I took a long breath. "Not yet, but I guess it's one way traffic on this road. Most times, I don't feel different. I'm faster than I was, stronger. I see better in the dark." I looked at him. "I don't drink blood."

"Can you be a vampire and not drink blood?"

"No. From what I hear, when the change is complete, then it's drink or die. It doesn't mean killing people though. Vampires that kill people to feed are outlaws in their community and their law is pretty terminal in that sort of case."

He nodded. "What'll you do?"

"I don't know, Keith. I'm still me. I'm just playing the hand I was dealt." I cast my eyes around the bar. "You think Petersen will send someone after me?"

"It wouldn't be anyone from your time, but we've had replacements. It's possible he'll use them, or another unit he's got."

He needed to be well clear of me. I got up and leaned on the table, putting my hand over his. He'd always had such beautiful hands, even when they were callused and scarred from work. They were strong and gentle, and I'd taken comfort from them, many times. They felt achingly familiar and strange at the same time, the hard, smooth edge of the ring alien to my touch. You can't step in the same river twice.

"Keith, if I'm still me, and I need killing, then anyone he sends will be far too late." I stopped and waited till he nodded to show he understood that I would kill myself rather than go rogue or step outside my boundaries. "In any other situation, whoever comes had better know what they're doing and why."

I walked out and took a position across the street where I could watch the door without being seen. Keith came out alone. I wanted to run back and hug him one last time. My old life that I'd kidded myself I could return to, somehow, some when, was finally slipping through my fingers and away. It was time to acknowledge we'd all moved on. The wind blew a bit of dust in my eyes and his figure blurred. He turned away without seeing me and walked off. If he was being followed, I couldn't see them. That didn't mean a lot, and I was careful making my way to my car.

I hadn't thought through what I'd said to Keith before I'd said it, but sometimes you only realize the decision you've arrived at when you're on the spot. I meant it. I'd kill myself rather than become Basilikos Athanate. But I was changing. My body was giving me lots of information about how different it was going to be as an Athanate. How could I be sure that my mind wasn't changing as well? Top was gone and with that, I'd lost my absolute, my reference and my measure. I was adrift, liable to take any direction.

∞ ∞ ∞ ∞ ∞

Mrs. Welchester made a visit to her new storage unit.

Top had managed to get me issued with standard mission gear, and then some. Whatever I had told him about the situation here, he expected me to need some serious firepower at some point. I now had the MP5 submachine gun partner to my HK automatic and a number of grenades—flash bombs as well as the lethal variety. Which third world army did Top think I had to take out?

The real prize was in the back. Top hadn't forgotten my favorite weapon. Officially, it was the Variable Choke Tactical Assault Weapon. In essence, it was an oversized, overpowered, short-barreled, custom shotgun. In the unit, we just called it the BFG. It kicked like a cannon and sounded like the devil himself knocking on your door, but it could clear a room or punch through steel plate. Not a subtle weapon. I loved it.

Also hidden in the back was my batsuit and brake, I guess in case I wanted to go base jumping again. Totally against the Ops 4-10 rules, I had personalized it with a label on the slick chest—TaJ. *Trust and Jump.* My eyes misted up again. Happy times.

Tucked into the webbing was a letter, addressed to me in Top's handwriting. I pocketed it. There was no way I would be able to read it now.

I transferred the Glocks, ordinary shotgun and my specialist surveillance equipment from my old storage unit into the new one, leaving the old one for my uniforms.

∞ ∞ ∞ ∞ ∞

I drove down to Jen's house. Despite moving away for the moment, Jen had left guards on the gate. I wanted to check that everything was okay, and run through any emails and messages without having to talk to anyone.

I'd barely started on the emails when they buzzed me from the gate. Apparently my sister was there, wanting to see me. I went to the main door and switched on the video feed. It was Kath in her car. I called them on the intercom to let her in and opened the door.

Kath drove up to the entrance. Even inside the car, I could tell she looked like hell. It was barely lunchtime. Had she been drinking already?

"Kath, hi, what's up? Are you okay?"

She got out of the car with a folder, her face pinched with anger. "We need to talk," she said.

I led her to the study and tried to get her to sit down. She wouldn't. She threw the folder on the desk. Clipped to the top was a formal letter saying she withdrew from handling the case.

"Kath, what's happened?" If Carter had been threatening her, I would kill him.

"You've happened! Again. Every time I think I've got my life straight, you do something and ruin it." She balled her hands into fists and hit the desk. "What did I ask on Friday? Don't ruin it for me. What did you do? Danced with that Kingslund woman when everyone would see. Had a scene with that Mexican businessman. Then you worked your way through every trade delegate. And to cap it all, you leave with Kingslund and cause another scene at the door."

"It wasn't like that—"

"It's never like that for you," she shouted. "There's always a reason you know about and no one else does. The partners wanted to know all about you, why I never mentioned you. What could I say? I don't know what my sister did for ten years!"

Tears were streaming down her face. I tried to hold her, but she struck out at me and moved away.

"It's not as if I even know what you're doing now," she said. "You can barely make ends meet, but look at you. You have a new car," she gestured angrily out the window. She grabbed Jen's jacket off the hook where I'd left it, and shook it in my face. "You wear designer jackets costing five thousand dollars. You have custom-made boots. You show up at the most expensive ball of the year wearing a designer dress. Even your card looks more like a whore's than a PI's."

"Kath, stop it! You've got it all wrong."

"I've got it all wrong? Lie to me one more time, Amber. Tell me what you were doing when you left home."

"You know that. I joined the army."

"No, you didn't," she shouted. "You washed out of boot camp. And you just couldn't come home, could you? Not after making your grand exit."

"How could you say that? I was in the army until a couple of years ago."

"Not according to Lieutenant Krantz. He came to see me yesterday and told me all about you."

Krantz. If he had been in range at that instant, I would have killed him without a moment's hesitation. But I needed to concentrate on this first, stop Kath in her tracks. It felt like trying to climb sand.

"Krantz is just full of shit, Kath. You can't listen to him."

"Why? He's in the army. He should know if you were. He told me you would claim you were in the special forces. But they don't take women." She stabbed at me with her finger. "I know. I called and asked."

I was crying by this time. I can take a lot, from a lot of places, but not from my little sister.

"Look at you," she said. "It's pathetic. You're living here as Kingslund's whore, aren't you? Is that how you made the money you sent home? On your back?"

I tried to hold her again. She grabbed my arm and shock fought with anger on her face.

"Oh my God, look at your arm! I should have known. You're on drugs. Look at it, it's like a fucking pincushion."

The fold of my elbow showed the number of times the test unit had found the vein there. I heal quickly, but there were marks from the last few days. It wasn't a pincushion by any stretch.

She wrenched away from me and angrily flicked open the folder on the desk. Inside was a large check. "That's for paying for my education," she said. "We're even now. For God's sake, use the money to get yourself booked in a clinic."

She swayed as she stood there glaring at me and panting, cheeks wet with tears. She turned one last time to the desk and pointed at the photos. "You know, that says it all. Nothing of me and Mom. Nothing but lies and people who are dead or were never alive." She pointed at Tara's plaque. "You love her more than you ever loved me." She lashed out, sweeping them onto the floor. "I never want to see you again," she said, and ran out to her car.

I picked my photos up and carefully set them back on the desk. Dad, Top and Tara. And me. And the tears streamed down my cheeks.

Chapter 50

I left the house about an hour later. I didn't have anything planned; I just drove down to Wash Park and walked, zipping Jen's loaned jacket all the way up and raising the collar against the cold wind. I had Tara's plaque in the inner pocket.

How could I get the truth through to Kath? How much of it was my fault? I'd come back from the army and I'd tried to keep everyone at a distance. But the reason I had done that hadn't gone away. In fact, the prion count was telling me I didn't have much time left. Once I was Athanate, how much would I be able to be involved with my family?

In the middle of my circuit around the park, Jen called on my burn phone. She'd been warned by the guards that something had happened and she wouldn't stop until I told her what had gone on with Kath, at least in general terms. I didn't go into Kath calling me her whore.

Jen focused on what she could do. "Amber, put all that legal situation out of your head. I'll get my lawyer onto it on Monday." She cut across my protest. "I'm not discussing it. It's just going to happen."

I let that sink in. How could I accept this and at the same time argue against what Kath had implied? I couldn't just take it, but I needed help, and I couldn't deny it made me feel better. "Thanks Jen. I'll pay you back."

"De nada. We *do* need to talk." She paused for a second, and as she continued, she faltered a bit. "It's not one way, honey. Hell, there are some stupid things I've done, which I need to fix."

"Okay," I said. Possibly she was getting upset again about doing a search on me, or something similar. I shrugged it off. "I'll be back later. I've had some other bad news as well. I just need some time now."

We signed off and I did another circuit of the park, then sat on an empty bench. Jen's call had jumbled everything up in my head.

I pulled out Tara's plaque and ran my fingers over the glossy surface.

"Is it some Athanate thing, Tara?" I said. "Am I just looking for blood and sex?"

"Blame it on the prions, eh? Don't think so, sis. Sounds like you're looking for reasons not to go ahead, to stay safe."

"It's not my decision to go ahead anyway. If I tell her or Alex what they're risking, they'll run a mile."

"You think?" said Tara. "What is it really? Not sure about the physical side of it with Jen?"

"No. Yes."

Tara chuckled. "This is the girl who thought sex with boys would be icky too. Got over that, didn't you?" Her voice went serious. "You got over much worse as well."

I sighed and got up. I wasn't going to go there. There was a coffee shop just a couple of minutes from the park and I walked to it.

Sitting with a latte in the warmth, I remembered the note from Diana with the details of the contact for the local Weres. I pulled it out of the pocket and found I'd mixed it up with Lisa's note giving Alex's information. I dived back into the pocket and my fingers froze on the second note. It wasn't Lisa's writing on the first note, it was Diana's. I pulled the second note out—Lisa's note—and put them side by side. The information was the same. Alex Deauville.

Well, well, well; the wolf was at the ball. I couldn't remember that happening in any fairy tales. His address was a couple of blocks south of the coffee shop. If he was home, I could walk there. Maybe I could get the issue of Silver Hills settled. And whatever. Something to cheer me up today. If not, it was a only a block more down to David's house; I could go check on him.

I called Alex on the burn phone. He was there, and five minutes later he opened the door for me. He looked a bit startled.

"I did say five minutes, didn't I?"

"Oh, yes. No, it's not that. Come on in." He stood back and waved me into the living room. "Would you like some coffee?"

"Just had one, thanks." I was disappointed and I wondered what had happened. The Alex at the ball would have used the opportunity to kiss me. At the very least on the cheek.

The house had a split level towards the front, with a kitchen and dining room above the entrance hall. The living room took the whole back of the house. We walked in and sat down.

"I—"

"Thanks—"

We both spoke and stopped at the same time. At least that got a laugh and the awkwardness seemed to lessen. Grinning, he ducked his head and held his hands up. "You first."

I shifted in my seat. His smile had sent delicious little shivers up my spine. I forced that to the back of my mind. I had business first.

"I just wanted to start by thanking you for running interference at the ball," I said. "And thanks to your friends as well."

"My pleasure. It was the least I could do when I realized what was happening."

I looked sharply at him. "Other than me saying something had come up, what made you realize what was happening?"

"It wasn't what you said. It was the adrenaline charge you got when your security didn't answer. And the conversation you had with Kingslund."

"You could hear all that? You can tell when I've got adrenaline overload?" He nodded. I took a deep breath. "That's a wolf thing, isn't it?"

He smiled again, and I saw I'd gotten it right the first time I'd seen him; there was something untamed in his eyes. *Woof.* He didn't seem at all concerned about my comment. "I brought a couple of the pack with me to make sure you got to a car. Then I saw the doorman and I realized what was going on."

"Maybe I will have that coffee," I said. "I think this might be a long conversation."

We moved up to the kitchen and I sat on a stool at the central breakfast bar. I enjoyed the show, even moving his computer equipment out of the way to ensure my view was unobstructed.

"I called your dressmaker yesterday—"

"Sorry about giving you the wrong card," I murmured. *My dressmaker!* He made it sound as if I would only wear clothes that had been handmade for me.

He waved it off. "I wanted to call you and..." He slowed up. I leaned on the breakfast bar, resting my chin on my hand and giving him my undivided attention. I wished I had put on a button-up shirt rather than the T I was wearing. Much better for leaning forward, even for me. "I wanted to call you *and* I wanted to talk about what happened," he finished.

"Okay. Let's get what happened out of the way first."

He put the coffee in front of me and sat down on the other side of the bar. "My haulage company handles Tucker Beacon. He's been my largest client, ever since he was my first client. He asked me for a favor, and I agreed to help him out against Kingslund a few weeks back," he said.

"You're talking about scaring off the construction crew at Silver Hills."

Alex looked startled, then he nodded. "You obviously know about it. We didn't want a resort there. Jack didn't want the pressure on his resort. The pack went up to Bitter Hooks and we had a little fun. No one got hurt. The construction's been delayed or canceled. I was fine with that."

"But Jack's still under pressure," he went on, "and I think he's got Matlal putting even more pressure on him. I know the fake doorman. He's Tucker's fixer for dirty problems, and when I saw him, I knew this went way beyond what I was willing to be involved in. Hearing that the cab blew up later just confirmed that.

"I've got nothing you could go to the police with, but I wanted to warn you and Kingslund and tell you that I'm out of it. What I did on Friday night was the least I could do to make up."

I nodded. "Bitter Hooks?"

"Silver Hills is just a marketing name. It was called Bitter Hooks. That's derived from the old Arapaho name—Spirit Wolf." He smiled. "It's a special place for us and we like that name."

"So do I," I said. "Well, anyway, thank you, on behalf of me and Jen."

What had I said? Alex's body language had suddenly gone cold again.

"You seem okay with me knowing you're a werewolf," I said.

He looked surprised. "I thought all you vamps were told about us. You act as if it was a secret."

"Ahh. Okay. I'm Athanate, but I was solo. I only made a connection with House Altau in the last week or so."

His eyes widened. "A solo vamp? Jesus! How does that happen?"

"It happens sometimes. It's a long story. For a long fall evening in front of the fire maybe. With a bottle of wine."

Alex rocked back on his stool. *Was that a bit forward of me? Bad girl.* But then he grinned again.

"What about you?" I said. "How did you become a Were?"

He ducked his head a little. I'm not subtle, but I'm not insensitive. He didn't want to talk about it. "Oh, it involved researching the Arapaho wolf clan and not understanding the risks." He refilled our cups. "Details will only be divulged if you hold my feet to the fire. Or hide the wine."

"Deal. But we were interrupted at the ball. I'm even more interested now to hear why you gave up being a doctor. Was that a wolf thing too?"

He nodded. "I'm okay in everyday medical situations, but I was in emergency care. There's two problems with that for a werewolf; the sheer amount of blood is unsettling, and obviously, I was concerned with the possibility of accidentally infecting someone."

"So you became a werewolf and joined the local pack?"

He nodded again. "That's about it. It's not so well ordered as you vamps, but at least I knew what was happening. I was able to change successfully on my own and, like vamps, we can sense other Weres, so I found the pack." He sipped his coffee. "I'm trying to find a way to help those who can't change and make the process a little smoother."

"Some werewolves can't change?"

"Yes," he said, and something passed behind his eyes. "And it's eventually fatal, a bit like vamps not drinking blood."

"You said there was a chance of infection if you worked as a doctor. So you can pass it on if you just nicked your finger and you were working on someone?"

He grimaced. "Yeah, it's possible. It would be unlikely in any one case, or a hundred cases, but working in emergency care, it would happen sooner or later. The infection passes in blood, or any other fluids," he said casually. Typical doctor, making it all sound icky. "Not that you should be concerned of course, as a vamp."

He registered that my mouth was open.

"You didn't know?" I just shook my head dumbly. Suddenly, *maybe,* I wasn't playing just for a bit of a thrill. If he couldn't infect me…

"Weres and vamps can't infect each other," he said. "Look, I've made some assumptions and maybe it would be better to go back to the beginning and start again." He paused. "You're a new Athanate and you're part of Altau, but you haven't gone through their Aspirant process?"

"Not so new," I said. "The process has taken a long time with me, otherwise yes."

"But at the ball, you knew about me?"

I shook my head. "I asked House Altau for a contact in the local pack." I pulled the stuff out of my pocket and with the papers came the photo of my great-grandparents that I still had there from last weekend. I sorted out the two notes. "They gave me this one last night and Lisa gave me this one. You can imagine, I was kinda surprised when I looked at them side by side a few minutes ago."

Alex barely looked at the notes. He picked up the photo.

"Who are they?" His brow creased.

It didn't say Farrell on the photo. "My great-grandparents," I replied.

"Can I scan this, please?" he asked. "I'm interested in local history. And of course the Arapaho Wolf Clan reference is intriguing."

"Sure." There was more than that, I was sure, but I'd find out in due course.

He flipped open the laptop and slid the photo into his combo printer-scanner. "Okay. And what did you want to talk to me about?" He smiled. "Me as in your local furry contact."

"Jen's resort. I'm working for her. Stopping the disruption." Jen had asked me to keep things confidential, but I had to tell him that much.

"Just working for her? As in security and asking local werewolves to keep off her property?"

He'd flipped again. I started to get angry. "What are you saying, Alex? We were getting along well at the ball, and today, every other thing I say, you seem to be taking some hidden meaning. What is it?"

"I take it back," he said. "I guess you really don't know."

"What, for God's sake?"

"Well, when you showed up on my doorstep, I made an assumption that you...ahh...belong to Kingslund." He reached over and touched the arm of the jacket Jen had loaned me.

"What the hell do you mean? The jacket? What about it?"

"If I just say, you won't believe me." He called up the image search engine on his laptop, typed in Jennifer Kingslund, and thumbnail photos started to fill the screen. He swiveled it towards me. A cold, painful anger settled in my chest. About every fifth picture of her showed Jen out somewhere with a friend, male or female, wearing the same jacket as I had. All of them were attractive and clearly with Jen. 'With' as in holding hands or arms. Or kissing.

"She gives one to all her, um, companions," he said carefully.

∞ ∞ ∞ ∞ ∞

The guards must have called Jen when I returned to her house. I had finished clearing my stuff from the guest suite when she arrived. The office I would have to leave for Tullah to clear. I was outside, throwing the last of my clothes into the trunk.

Jen's face was pinched and anxious. She hurried towards me, not looking at all the confident businesswoman that I knew. She looked afraid. Under the anger I felt sorrow, and stamped on it.

I thrust the leather jacket at her. At least she didn't deny it.

"Amber, please, I'm so sorry."

"How could you do that to me?" I yelled.

"It was stupid. It was just to cover the fact you were a PI. Everyone would just assume..."

"Everyone would just assume I'm your whore."

Tears began to run down her cheeks. "No. I didn't mean it like that. I didn't think—"

"No. You got that right. You didn't think." I got in and slammed the door. "Tullah will clear the office and I'll put in a final statement covering everything. Including use of that jacket."

"Amber, please—"

I drove away. I hated the way I sounded, what I'd said, how I felt. I'd known somehow when she'd loaned me that jacket and offered me a place to stay that there was something there, and I'd taken them anyway.

Why did I have to be in control of everything? How had I felt when Kath drove away refusing to listen to what I tried to say?

My last, blurry, view of Jen was in the mirror, holding the damn jacket like it was a comforter.

Chapter 51

I pulled up outside David's house, just behind his car. I closed my eyes and rested my head on the wheel for a minute. It had been one hell of a day and I was so tired. I wanted to curl up somewhere and cry myself to sleep. I didn't feel up to checking if David was okay, but his appearance on Friday night had been worrying. I had to.

Eventually I dragged myself up his front walk and knocked on his door.

The house was dark and silent. I made sure that it was his car in front. It was too late for a walk. I stood there, undecided. He could be asleep. Or maybe he'd been picked up and taken to Haven for something.

Anyhow, I had his key. I let myself in quietly and stood next to the door, testing out the air with my nose. The place reeked of Athanate, and of blood and sex. I felt a prickle of concern in my chest. I tiptoed through the living room and the rest of the house, but there was nothing there. I ended up outside the bedroom door.

He'd told me it was usual for Aspirants to get the hots for their Mentors, and that Pia was biting him a lot. I guessed that meant a lot of blood and sex. What if I went in and they were in bed together? Exactly how would we explain what I was doing here to Pia?

Only one way to find out. I opened the door quietly. He was naked and alone in the bed. If I thought the rest of the place smelled of blood and sex, it was nothing to the bedroom. The bed was a wreck, pillows and sheets tossed aside and the mattress skewed on its base. I grinned; great sex, clearly.

But the stillness of his body, the darkness around his neck, the discarded bedclothes and the cold in the room suddenly didn't add up. I hit the light switch in a hurry.

David lay sprawled on his back, his neck a mess of dried blood. His mouth was open with his fangs down and dried blood on his face, but I couldn't see or hear breathing. I touched his face and tried to find a pulse in his throat. His body was freezing and limp, his pulse barely there and far too fast. I grabbed his hand and squeezed the end of a finger. The finger was already pale, and remained pale after I let go.

I was all too familiar with blood loss injuries from my time with 4-10, and this was as bad as I'd seen anyone. I tore his cupboards open and found blankets, which I heaped on him. I found an electric booster heater and turned it on full. In the kitchen I turned his kettle on, found some soup and put that on to heat as well.

Warmth and fluids would help, but he needed blood as well. The hospital was out of the question with the state he was in. The quickest Bian, or anyone else from Haven, could get here would be forty minutes. David didn't have that kind of time.

I trickled warm soup down his throat and washed his face and neck with hot water. The wounds gaped but barely bled. His heart was racing—he had a few more minutes like that and it would give out. As an Athanate, his ability to heal himself was incredible, but he'd been bled too much.

He'd given me his key. *If something goes wrong. If you need to do something. You've got my back, Amber.*

"Shit. Shit. Shit." I knew what I had to do. I knew what the risk was. Intentionally or not, his bite would release his prions into my bloodstream. That might tip the balance and finally make me Athanate. But if the choice was between David dying and me holding onto being human a bit longer, David won. And at least it wasn't as if I had such great ties to being human any more.

Trust and jump.

I pulled off my shirt and joined him under the blankets, trying to force my warmth into him. It was like lying on an ice pack. I pulled his mouth open and shifted till I could feel his fangs touch the side of my neck, sharp as needles.

"This had better work, David," I whispered and closed my eyes. I worked my hand beneath his head and pulled him up hard against me. I could feel his fangs break my skin and sink into me. I gasped and blood started to drip down into his mouth.

My eyes felt gritty when I opened them. At the edge of my sight, the pale green numbers on his alarm clock seemed not to change. I could hear the frantic patter of his heart, the sigh of air in his lungs. Somewhere there was the whir of the heater and the occasional murmur of cars passing by outside. All so far away.

Was he warmer now? Was his heart slowing down? Should I have called Bian as well?

"Feed and heal," I muttered.

I was so tired. My eyes closed again.

"There's nothing left for you out there anymore. Come home to us, where you belong, Amber. You've been too long on the path." Skylur.

I had screwed everything up, and not just today. I'd failed. I couldn't hold down a real job and I'd made a mess of being an investigator. My whole life was one damned train crash. My heart ached for my dad, for Jen and Alex and Keith and Kath and Top, and soon it would ache for David too. Then I'd go to Haven and maybe my heart would stop aching forever.

"I tried, Top. I really did."

"You're not here to try," he shouts in my ear. *"You're here to succeed."*

My eyes flew open. My head jerked and David's fangs cut cruelly. I grabbed his head. "David," I shouted, anger boiling up in me. "Feed, damn you. Feed and heal."

He twitched and his mouth closed convulsively on my throat. I could feel the first hint of a gentle pull. Blood flowed into his fangs. Then he pulled harder and I could feel his body, all of it, stir beneath me.

"Feed!" I could feel his hunger now. His Athanate pheromones started to kick in. I felt dizzy as I fought them off and held his mouth against my neck. One minute I wanted to tear my clothes off and ride him raw, the next I was whimpering with fear. But I didn't let go.

He started to struggle feebly, not to push me away, but to pull me closer and, at last, the mad seesaw of pheromones began to cancel each other out.

I finally let my head drop again, but this time in elation. I had dragged him back from the brink. And the price was acceptable, just something I'd been holding off for no good reason.

His body had started to warm up at last. I forced his jaws open and pulled him away from my neck. He thrashed, trying to hold me back. I slipped out of the blankets, wrapping him up in them, and managed to trickle some more warm soup down his throat. The horrible pallor had gone from his skin.

It seemed that we stayed like that for ages. I was lightheaded from the exhilaration of saving him and from all the stuff he'd pumped into me while he was fastened to my neck, so I wasn't tracking the time too well. Eventually, I started to see the awareness seeping back into his eyes and his struggles calmed down.

"You back, David?"

He nodded slightly, and I propped him up and made him drink water. His eyes were looking at my neck. I had stopped leaking and it was healing already, but it had to look a sight.

"What happened?" he whispered.

"You got drained. You lost too much blood."

"But your neck?"

"I couldn't call the hospital, David. You were lying there with your fangs out and God knows what questions they'd have been asking. Don't think Skylur would have been happy. And I didn't think Bian could get here in time. I didn't have anywhere else to turn."

"Oh God, I'm sorry." Even in his state, he knew what his bite could do to me.

"It's done." I patted him clumsily and changed the subject. "What the hell does Pia think she's doing?"

"We fought." He frowned as he tried to reconstruct what had happened. "Remember I said that you'd given me something in the kiss?"

I nodded.

"I've been thinking about what you were saying about prions. They must be like Athanate DNA." He sighed and I gave him some more water to sip. "But they also take over the immune system. That's what makes us so healthy. And the immune system fights to reject anything foreign, even other Athanate prions."

"Okay," I said. "I can see that. What's it got to do with Pia?"

"She says I smell wrong." He gave a breathy chuckle. "Seems your prions are stronger than Altau prions, and you're not even full Athanate. I smell too much like you and not enough like Altau. You know, the marque. She said she had to get me back into line. She wanted to know where it came from. I wouldn't say."

He did smell different. Pressed up against him, breathing his scent in, I could tell. The copper and spice smell like Altau was there, but with something else, something sharp and fragrant. Damn! This was my vamp scent. This was the marque of House Farrell. For the first time, I really registered what Skylur and Diana had said. I was starting an Athanate House. A shiver of fear and pride went through me.

But there were some steps to get through first. "We're going to have to 'fess up, bro."

He nodded weakly. "I suppose so. But not a good time now," he said.

"No." I could imagine the disruption that hosting the Athanate Assembly was going to have on House Altau. They could do without this distraction. Maybe we could just drop out of sight, a hidden House Farrell.

I rubbed a hand across my mouth and then took a sip of David's soup. I'd lost a lot of blood to him, but I felt okay, just tired and aching. In fact, I was feeling good.

"We'll work it out. S'okay," he mumbled. "Work it out with Pia."

No, we wouldn't. She would come back and bite him again. My jaw began to ache in earnest and my eyesight flickered. I wouldn't let her. He was mine, he was House Farrell. He needed to understand that. He needed to understand he was mine.

"Amber?" He felt my body tensing.

I leaped off the bed and stood beside it, quivering. My skin felt too small for me, as if something inside was struggling to get out. My tongue felt a strange pressure and there was a shiver of terror and delight as I felt the sharpness emerge in my mouth. I needed to bite. David needed to understand.

No. Stop.

"David," I said. It felt as if my voice came from a long way away. He jerked up in bed, his face slack with surprise.

Shit, but I had pulled a compulsion on him. All it needed was for me to push his head back and feed. He wanted me to feed. He wanted to be House Farrell. I could feel the potential building in me like a head of water behind a dam. I was sucking power out of the night. I could make this so.

No.

Tara's voice? The feeling burst like a bubble, taking all the energy away and I staggered.

"I can't stay," I gasped and grabbed my shirt, turning away. "Rest. I'll come back."

"Amber?" he said again, but I was out of the room, out of his house before he could call me back. He would be okay. What he didn't need was for me to bite him. And I didn't need it. Or I did. I swung wildly between the two.

As soon as I was out of his house, I realized I couldn't drive anywhere. The feverish Athanate high I'd experienced started to wear off, leaving me freezing and barely able to walk in a straight line. Everything seemed blurred. My head was spinning, my throat was dry and my stomach heaved.

I couldn't go back to David's—I'd bite him or Pia might show up. I couldn't go to the hospital. I couldn't stumble around Wash Park looking like I was a drunk reject from a Halloween party. And forget the people out there trying to kill me, I was having a good shot at it myself. It only dawned on me that I'd crossed a road when a car went past blaring its horn. I didn't even know where I was any more.

Another car seemed to come straight at me, and then turned away. At least its lights had showed me the road sign. I fumbled and managed to get the burn phone out. Four in the morning. I couldn't think of anything else, so I hit last number redial. Oh God, how to make an impression.

"Amber?" His voice was blurred with sleep.

"Sorry. I'm in trouble. Blood loss. Kentucky Avenue gate, Wash Park."

"Just stay there. I'll be there in five minutes." He'd woken up quickly. No hint of anger, no questions about the time, no sense that I was asking too much. It gave me a tiny feeling of pleasure in the middle of the sickness. Just five minutes.

I wasn't counting the minutes. I slumped down and tried to fend off the blackness that threatened to take me. A car pulled up and I felt a figure looming over me. It could have been anyone. It could have been the assassin that ZK was hiring, or only the local rapist. I couldn't even see. I tried to get up. At that point, the lights went out completely.

∞ ∞ ∞ ∞ ∞

I came around as he carried me into his house. My face was warmed by his chest and I breathed in the sweet smell of pine and mountain meadows. And, underneath that, like a shadow passing in the forest, I recognized wolf. It was like a balm to me. I stroked his chest and he snorted.

He did the basics as I had done for David. He wrapped me in blankets on his sofa and fed me warm soup. I was a long way from being bled out as David had been, but walking around in the freezing night had been idiotic. I knew that because Dr. Deauville told me so, very clearly, several times.

Well, I had certainly made a good impression. *Damn.* On the grounds that it couldn't get much worse, I took advantage of him bending over me to snag his head and pull him down into a deep, sensual kiss as I slipped back into unconsciousness. A girl could dream. A girl could dream.

∞ ∞ ∞ ∞ ∞

It's dark in the tepee. There are embers in the middle of the floor. A thin coil of smoke winds up like a serpent, catching the moonlight.

The form opposite me leans forward. Light makes a patchwork monster; an ear here, a furry flank, the gleam of an eye, a row of huge, pale teeth. But because it's a dream, I know who it is.

"My, what big teeth you have, great-grandmother," says my demon.

Speaks-to-Wolves turns her head, raising it. If she were still human, she would be rolling her eyes.

"You always were irreverent. Your mother is a Christian saint for putting up with you. Perhaps Old Man Coyote would have been a better spirit guide." I hear her voice in my head.

"Are you my spirit guide?"

She sneezes amusement.

"Thank all the gods, no. But I've been helping your guide guard you against the snake spirits."

The shadows beneath her split and a small wolf cub totters out. Her feet are too big for her and she's tripping over them as she makes her way around to me. Her eyes are very bright and a little anxious as she looks up at me. I gather her warm bundle into my arms and she licks my face. I laugh in delight.

"This is my guardian?"

"She's helped keep the vampire from the door for two years, but she's not supposed to be a guardian, she's supposed to be your spirit guide."

"She's very young." The cub nips my jaw gently in protest.

"Guides appear that way to begin with."

"I love her. Can I speak to her like I speak to you? What do I call her?"

"Her name is Hana. It means sky. She will speak to you soon."

"When?"

"When your spirits are in balance." I feel her pity like a heavy hand. "Child of two peoples, daughter of two spirits, woman of sorrow and anger, cursed and blessed. You tread a difficult path, Amber. You are none of the things they will think you are. In the end, you will have no guides but yourself. But Hana will talk to you when your spirits balance."

"How do I find a balance?" I ask.

I sense laughter. "You've already begun."

There is light in my face, blinding me to the textured darkness. I can't see the tepee any more. I bury my face in Hana's fur to hold her to me, and breathe in the scent. It speaks to me of forests and meadows, the joy of running through the autumn sunshine. The rush of wolf in my blood.

A quest for balance.

I woke clutching Alex's blankets to my face.

Chapter 52

MONDAY

I unwrapped myself from the layers of blankets and I let them go reluctantly. They smelled of Alex and Hana. I wanted to be warm and safe in the tepee, but I was too full of energy to lie down and go back to sleep on the sofa.

It was later than normal for me. The workload had taken its toll, but even though I had only been asleep for a few hours, I felt clearheaded and bursting with energy. I did some stretches. I wanted to storm into Alex's room and wake him up, but I restrained myself and went tiptoeing around the house. I would go in later, with coffee as a peace offering.

I liked his house. He was heavily into timber beams, pioneer-style wood and leather furniture, fireplaces, rugs and big windows. It was on the sexy side of bachelor. He didn't have a library, but his bookcase in the living room showed a wide interest. There was a whole shelf on the Arapaho and Cheyenne peoples. Even his old medical books were there.

And there was a picture of a girl, bronzed and raven-haired. Much prettier than I am. I walked away.

I checked myself in the bathroom mirror. The skin around my neck looked red and sore, but there were no wounds visible.

I went up the split level to the kitchen and started to make the coffee. I was looking in the fridge for a clue to breakfast when he wandered in sleepily, dressed in sweats.

"You're up," he said, with a smile. "And you look better in the morning."

I huffed, punched him on the shoulder and then kissed it better. And suddenly, we were standing there in the kitchen with our arms around each other. I hadn't felt this way in far too long. And at least this morning, I didn't pass out when he kissed me.

I leaned back against the railing above the hall, pulling him close. My heart was trying to hammer its way out of my chest, but he just stood in front of me, looking vaguely puzzled.

Come on, wolfy. How many neurons does it take? Boy, girl…

"You've changed," he said.

"I guess I'm feeling unstressed today, yes. I feel better."

"It's not that," he said. "Well, there's that too. But it's your scent."

"I haven't had a shower this morning, maybe we should share —"

"No, not that. Your vamp signature, your marque. It's weaker." He looked even more puzzled as his brain processed all those clever nose signals. "And instead, you smell like pack."

"I've been sleeping in your blankets, Alex. Of course some of it will rub off on me."

He nuzzled against my neck and inhaled. My skin rippled with goosebumps. He growled and when his head came back up, his eyes had become more gold than green, very focused and bright. It was deliciously scary.

I pulled him harder against me. The heat blazed off him and seemed to seep into my bones. My legs went wobbly, and it was a good thing I was caught between him and a hard place. Actually, I was caught between two hard places and I was just fine with that.

"I seem to have trapped you," he murmured. "Should I be a gentleman and offer you the chance to surrender?" He bent forward again.

"On the contrary." I sighed, leaning my head back so that his kisses unfolded like tiny blossoms on my neck, all the way up to the tickly, sexiest bit just behind my ear. "I've got you right where I want you."

I spoke the literal truth. I could feel him through my jeans and his sweat pants and he was on the exact spot. Talk about pressing my buttons.

"*Right* where I want you," I repeated, my voice becoming hoarser. I clutched his shirt and rocked him against me. Exquisite tremors coursed up through me. It had been so long, and Lord, I had missed it so much. His teeth grazed my neck and I groaned.

He seemed to understand. I wouldn't have minded at all if he'd carried me off to the bedroom, but there was something exhilarating about the unplanned position and something deeply, wildly sexy about him holding back and urging me on.

His hands snaked around my back, caressing and massaging. His mouth came down on mine again and my feelings ran out of control. Everything was moving so quickly.

I tore at his shirt frantically, and when that ripped, I grabbed his butt and pulled him against me. I broke the kiss, flinging my head back and grinding my body against him. It felt like my body caught light and I screamed out as my climax came crashing through me in waves.

"Oh my God, Alex," I gasped, as I clung to him, panting.

He was chuckling, holding me gently, still pressing, but so lightly. "Been holding back a little recently, hot stuff?" he said into my ear, and kissed it.

I smacked his shoulder, bare now that his shirt was in tatters. Seeing the damage made me laugh. "Sorry about your shirt."

"Obviously not a very good shirt," he said, his lips tracing lazy patterns down to my throat.

"Get me naked, boy, or I'm off again," I murmured, digging my fingers into the solid muscle of his back and playfully nipping at his jaw.

My cell rang.

I snorted and nuzzled his neck. This was me-time. I'd turn it off in a second.

"You'd better check it."

I couldn't believe it. "The wolf is telling me to be responsible?"

"Sometimes," he growled and retrieved the phone out of my back pocket. I suspected that was just to get a chance to grab my butt, and I wasn't complaining, but anyway, I ended up with the cell in my hand, and a smile on my face, briefly.

"Shit." The caller ID showed Jen.

"Go on. Answer it." He reluctantly disengaged and headed for the coffee. I felt chilly without his furnace heat pressing against me. I wanted to drag him to his bed for wild, wolfy sex. I answered the phone instead.

"Yes?" I said.

"Amber, help. Please." Jen's voice sounded fragile, and it brought the ache crashing right back into my heart.

I sighed and closed my eyes. I really didn't need this now, whatever it was. But I couldn't end the call. I'm not made like that.

"Talk to me, Jen," I said.

"Bernard. Troy. Oh, God, everything, Amber." She was close to tears.

"Calm down and tell me."

"I got a letter this morning, like Victor said might happen. A ransom demand for Troy. I was just about to call José—Captain Morales—when he called me. He said Bernard had asked to meet him. José was trying to tell me something and then there were shots. The call cut off. Now, I can't reach him or Bernard."

"Who have you spoken to?"

"Just Victor. He was here anyway. I wanted to talk to you. I mean, I know…"

She faltered and stopped. Yes, I'd sort of resigned yesterday. But I felt the weight settling on me again, and this morning I felt stronger. I'd been in the wrong with Jen. Morales, Verdoon and Troy needed me. They weren't innocents in the way Emily had been, but if I wasn't about doing what I could for these people, what was I here for? I was going to see this through. Top wouldn't have wasted time thinking about why, once the decision was made. Neither would I. My mind clicked into work mode.

"Jen, first off, call the police on your landline." I gave her Edmunds' number. "Explain to Lieutenant Edmunds that I believe that this is related to the other incidents we've worked on together. Tell him I'll be calling him as well. While you're doing that, pass me over to Victor."

"Thank you, Amber." I could hear her take a breath to say something else, but nothing came and she handed me over.

Victor's basso rumble came on. "This's not lookin' good, girl."

"I hear you, Vic. Look, I just know this all ties up with Tucker. I have a feeling that if we find Troy, we'll find Morales as well. Have you got anything, any suspicion, on where they could be holding Troy?"

"Yuh. That's what I was here for. Was going to talk to you." He paused and I could hear Jen's voice in the background talking to Edmunds. "Y'know Tucker's business center down in Meridian?"

I knew the place. It was a complex which offered virtual offices, private meeting rooms and temporary office suites, just the other side of the toll road from Arapahoe County Airport. "Yeah, I know it."

"Well, I been casting my lines wide and I got a bite down there from one of his workers. Main building top floor's been cut off, and half the offices below. My information says there's next to nothin' going on up there. Cleaning crew been locked out. Delivery area been closed down at odd times for special deliveries. And someone carried a long package in a couple of weeks ago. A package that looked like it was movin'." He sighed. "I wouldn't go to the cops with that, but it was the best I got. Timing was right for Troy and there's something off about that top floor."

"So you thought we'd need to take a look. What did you plan?"

"Hold on, got something on my cell." There was silence for a minute, and then he was back.

"Amber, listen up. There's more activity down there now, maybe more special deliveries." He paused. "When this was the chef, that's one level of bad. They got Morales there as well, that's a whole different game."

"What did you plan, Vic?" I repeated.

He grunted and blew a breath out. "I got a couple guys in there rentin' a temporary office. They're there right now, just called in. But everyone who visits goes in through scanners—like an airport. They make a thing about security. We got no weapons inside, but I thought maybe we could go in and see if we can look around."

"Vic, I'm going in there. I'll call you back in fifteen and we'll discuss how. Keep this cell free." I ended the call and looked up. Right into Alex's eyes. My stomach lurched. How many times could I get away with jerking him around?

I started to apologize and he waved it away. "You go fix what needs fixing, whatever it takes. Then we'll sit down and, yeah, we'll talk."

I grinned—that kinda talk, oh yeah. I had half turned to go when he growled, caught my hips and spun me back. It was so fast, so shocking, that my hands came up automatically to push him away. But he was grinning back at me, and he just kissed my nose. The unleashed wolf looked out at me with his eyes—hot, hungry and promising. This was going to be *so* interesting later. I kissed his nose back. Must be a wolf thing.

He let me go and I ran out of his house and back to my car, still parked outside David's. It wasn't even four hundred yards, however difficult it had seemed last night.

Once I was in and driving, I called Edmunds and filled him in on Tucker's building, as quickly as I could. He agreed to get a SWAT team on a training exercise at Lincoln Station, next to the business park. If it came to it, and there were more ZK people than they could handle in the building, they would do containment and a bigger team would be called in. All of which we agreed we didn't want to do until Morales and Verdoon and any other potential hostages were out of the building. The increasing desperation of the behavior didn't sound like we wanted to be in a hostage situation. Edmunds asked how sure I was that this was where Morales was. I had to admit it was our best guess at the moment. He just grunted.

I signed off and said a quick prayer of thanks for whichever guardian angel had sent Edmunds my way.

I called Tullah and told her briefly what was happening. I promised to update her when I could. Then I called Victor back and told him what I wanted.

He didn't like it at all.

Chapter 53

A little after 10:30 that morning, I trotted up the steps to Tucker Beacon's Nexus Office Complex.

The building's wings looked like some enormous layer cake, alternating brick and reflective glass. I was interested in the main block, the five-story office complex centered around an atrium and hidden from the outside by a sheer cliff of smoked green glass.

I was dressed as a courier and I was carrying the fourth package of the day for Victor's fake company, who were renting an office suite on the second floor. Every package had come in on a chain of custody signature form, and had to be signed for by the recipient in person. After arguing about the first and getting someone to come down, the door security had let the other couriers in, content to put the packages through a scanner and let the couriers take them up.

"Jaysus, another one," said the guy on the door. "Here, Frank, gimme the last pass."

He handed it to me. "You'll need this for the elevator and the door to the wing where the office is. Second floor, office 209."

I nodded thanks and squiggled an unreadable name in their log. The package went through the scanner and I walked to the elevators.

A glance around showed me nothing that was out of the ordinary, and the relaxed guys on the door were just everyday guys you'd find in half the office buildings in Denver. Either they knew of nothing going on in the building, or they were top actors. Security was a bit stronger than other companies like this, but that was their marketing angle here.

On the second floor, there were locked doors leading to the corridors. The pass opened the right-hand door and I walked down to 209, looking outwards into the central atrium. I could see a couple of people walking along corridors on the third floor, but there was no movement on the fourth and fifth.

The door was opened as soon as I knocked, and Victor's team looked the part with reports, plans and flow charts on the desks. They had their jackets off and their ties loosened. They introduced themselves as Steve and Bud.

I grinned at them. "Good businessmen, guys."

I took Victor's comms device out of my pocket and clipped it over my ear. "Vic, I'm in."

"Good," he grunted. "We're in place and ready."

I covered my courier uniform with maintenance coveralls and Steve changed into a courier uniform, both having arrived in an earlier package. I fitted a Kevlar vest beneath the coveralls, something that Victor had insisted on.

Bud opened his briefcase and took a pass card out of the machine in there. "Your friend Matt says that should be good for all floors and it'll give you access to the service stairwell too. We haven't seen any maintenance people in the customer elevators, so the stairs would be better."

"You on the comm, Matt?" I asked.

"Yeah," he came back immediately.

"Any problems you can see with the pass card?"

"It's difficult to tell, Amber. If I were designing this coding system, I'd make readers able to take the code out of the standard sequence."

"In English, please, Matt."

"I'm sure it'll work for the service doors on your floor. It may trigger an alarm on the fifth floor."

"Roger that and thank you. Stay off the comm now—it's for Vic and me."

I turned back to Steve and Bud. Steve was checking their diversion and Bud gave me the last package, a set of folding steps made of plastic. He tore the SAMPLE stickers off it. Beneath the stickers it said MAINTENANCE. A few tools in a belt completed the outfit.

Steve looked up and nodded. "We're good," he said, and they both shook my hand.

We left the office together. They turned towards the elevators and I turned the other way. If their timing was right, they would arrive in the lobby just as an incoming group started an argument over reservations.

I was on my own now. The adrenaline started pumping. I looked at my watch: 10:52. The door to the service stairwell opened to my pass and I heard no alarms.

"I'm good. Wind it up, Vic," I said to the comms unit.

"Roger," he replied, and added something under his breath that might have been 'crazy woman'. I turned the sound down. The gravelly voice was comforting, but I didn't need a distraction.

Getting to the fifth floor was easy; I simply went up the stairs. Getting into that corridor was my worry. I had some fallback options, but I really didn't want any alarms raised until I was ready.

I stood in front of the doors. Behind me, the bare concrete stairs went on up to the roof and down to the basement. Deliveries came in to the basement and these stairs would provide a way to bring in things that they wouldn't want anyone else to see. If I were running something in this building, I would have the electronic locks set up differently top and bottom.

I shrugged and set the steps out. This was an office building, not a bank. If you can't go through a door, go over it.

Above me the ceiling was a high spec office structure, with a metal crawlspace providing maintenance access for the air conditioning units and a lightweight grid to hold square ceiling panels. I was in luck. I pushed the panel out of the way and climbed up onto the crawlspace, hooking the steps with my foot and hauling them up after me. With the panel back in place, there was no sign that I had been in the stairwell.

It was dark and dusty, full of the quiet hum of venting systems. I didn't need light; I could see down the corridor in the gloom. Assuming that there was an air conditioning junction for every office, I could make out the approximate layout of the offices.

It was too easy. I knelt there in the crawlspace and peered into the gloom. I was on a tight schedule, but setting off alarms wouldn't help at all.

My eyes picked out a regular pattern of boxes attached to the main supporting columns, with wires traveling down, the nearest one between me and the first office, pointing at a matching box fixed on the outside wall. I gathered up some dust from the crawlspace and blew it towards the box.

The dust glittered as it passed through a beam. I checked again until I was satisfied that there was just the one beam and then I carefully clambered over it and crawled down to the next one. I should have taken time to change into sneakers rather than my boots, but it was too late now. I'd just have to be careful. I left the steps behind. It limited my options if I went down into the offices, but it saved time.

Luckily, each office had just one beam. My eyes adjusted and I could almost see the beams.

The first section was a row of empty offices. I turned the corner and started working my way along the base corridor, sweating and aching from the cramped position. It had taken fifteen minutes to get this far and I didn't want to get Victor to stand down yet, but things could overheat if it took too long. I began to feel uncertain; maybe this was just an empty office floor and we were in completely the wrong part of town.

Victor's voice came through my earpiece asking for a check. I clicked the mike with my nail in the agreed signal, and he acknowledged.

I passed two more offices before I heard voices.

The expensive office suites of the base corridor were on either side of the elevator section, and each was comprised of two interconnected offices and a storeroom. The voices were coming from the middle one—suite 502, I estimated.

I crawled carefully till I was over the storeroom for 502. I reached down and eased up the edge of a ceiling panel. It was dark and the door to the office was closed, possibly locked, so there was no way to sneak in, which is what I had been hoping for. I was about to drop the panel back when I realized there was something wrong. There was someone in the room, and I could smell blood. Very slowly and quietly, I lifted the panel a little more. I could see three people, one chained to a bed, two tied up on the floor with bags over their heads. At a guess, it was Troy on the bed, Morales and Verdoon on the floor. Both men on the floor had been bleeding. Damn.

I let the panel slip quietly back and sat up. I clicked the mike with the signal, three clicks, pause and repeat, three times.

Victor's voice came back, the stress blurring his voice. "Confirm you have sight of hostage or hostages?" I clicked once. "Confirm to roll?" I clicked once again. "Rolling."

I checked the time: 11:16. I had between five and ten minutes before all hell broke loose. The countdown clock was up and running in my head and the adrenaline started up again.

I crawled along until I was over the main office. The heating fans were running in this office, which gave me some cover for the noise as I lifted the edge of a panel near the air vent junction.

I could see two men in the room. One sitting in an easy chair at the break-out section, with his feet on the coffee table and a gun on his lap, the other at the desk talking on the phone. It was his voice I had heard and he was still speaking, quietly but forcefully.

"I understand, Mr. Tucker, really. However, the deposit is not refundable, even if you cancel. It doesn't matter to me if you authorized it or not."

There was a pause. "No, I'm not here to do that. You've got people here to do that for you. I'm here to take out Farrell, and if you're canceling that, I'm gone."

Another pause. "She's not with Kingslund and basically you have no idea where she is. So I'm here because, from what your son told me about her when he hired me, this is where she'll turn up."

Tucker's son? Shit. That had to mean Onebrow, Frank Hoben, was Tucker's son. I couldn't see any other way around it. The whole damn thing revolved around Tucker.

Victor's voice came over the earpiece, harsh against the deep thumping noise in the background. "Amber! Group with Tucker goin' into the delivery area now. SWAT will engage in sixty seconds. Expedite. Confirm."

I clicked the mike once and crawled over above the desk. The guy in the easy chair had a gun, but there wasn't a crawlspace on that side. The other guy might have a bazooka for all I knew, but I couldn't tell and I had to get the show going. Everything was moving. My gut feeling was that Mr. Hitman there was dead when Tucker's men got up here from the delivery area, but the same feeling said that so were the others in the storeroom. Not something I could risk. I felt my chi gather. I became intently aware of the two men and my muscles lost their cramp. My whole body felt loose.

At the desk, Mr. Hitman stood and motioned the other guy over. "Your boss wants a word with you." He handed the phone over.

"Yes, sir? All of them?" His eyes flicked to the side and I knew. "I understand, sir."

He put the phone down and started to lift his gun. At that point, the hitman punched his larynx and I dropped through the ceiling on him. Life's like that sometimes.

The guard collapsed, but his gun had fallen beneath the desk. I didn't dare go for it after I'd seen the hitman's move. This was someone who knew what he was doing. I vaulted the desk and got into clear space.

He was big and strong. It had been difficult to gauge him from peeking around the ceiling panels. He was very big, very strong. Within reach of his arms I would be dead, and we both knew it. I moved my position from standard attack to a more balanced form where I could get the hell out of the way quicker.

His lip curled as he watched me move and he didn't bother looking for the gun beneath the desk.

He strolled forward, not bothering with any defensive posture, not even bothering with any preparation, his eyes narrowed, absolute confidence in his steps. The sheer size of him meant that he was going to be able to meet anything I threw at him and brush it aside. Then, once he was close enough, those plate-sized fists would crack or crush and end it. That was his style, the way he fought, overwhelming through his bulk and relying on his huge strength.

Except that his overconfidence might make him vulnerable.

"You know Tucker's got men downstairs now," I said. "You're not going to make it out of the building alive."

He ignored me. I edged around and away, overplaying the Kung Fu moves. His lip curled more, but he didn't otherwise respond except to follow me until it was too narrow to get past him and there was no way out behind me. He knew that.

With him barely a step away, gunfire sounded from below just as I feinted a punch at his face. He lost concentration; the gunfire distracted him for the smallest moment. He blinked and raised his hand to swat my fist away. All his weight was coming down on his left leg. That was all I was going to get and that was all I needed.

I went low and hard with my boot, nothing fancy, nothing in any pretty style of martial arts and too low for him to block. A simple way for him to discover suddenly that my toecap was much stronger than his kneecap, and just like that, he was down to one working leg.

To give him his due, he realized immediately he was in trouble and lunged forward off his good leg with his arms spread wide to sweep me up into his grip, where I would die.

But he lunged to where I had been, and unfortunately for him, I was a step and a half to the side already. With his arms out to try and grapple with me, he left his whole side unprotected, and this time I did Master Leung proud. A perfect, full side-on snap kick, with all my force concentrated into the small, hard hammer of my boot sole. I yelled out as it went home and felt his ribs splinter like rotten wood. He screamed and went down hard, hands flailing, too late to protect his ribs or to catch my foot. His face hit the floor with a sickening crunch.

He was tough. Even with a busted knee and broken ribs, he tried to get up. Just the ribs must have been excruciatingly painful, let alone any other internal damage. For a moment I regretted that I'd never had him in my squad, but he wasn't that kind of guy and I didn't have a squad any more. I broke the hat stand over the back of his head and he collapsed like a poleaxed bull.

"Amber, what's goin' on?" Victor said in my earpiece.

"Dealt with guards, back to you in one."

I got the gun from beneath the desk. Yup, another Glock. Tucker must have gotten a real bulk discount on them. I checked the guard, but with his windpipe and neck arteries crushed, he was already dead.

There were keys for the storeroom on the table.

Morales blinked as I pulled the bag off his head.

"Farrell?" he groaned, trying to sit up. The movement opened a stomach wound and started it bleeding again.

"Lie still for now," I told him, and cut the rope tying his hands and feet before checking on the wound. It wasn't as bad as it might have been. It was in and out on the side and it would hurt like hell, but he could walk.

Verdoon had no bullet wounds, but they'd worked him over. His face was broken and bleeding and starting to swell. He could barely speak. His leg was broken.

The man chained to the bed was Troy, still in his cycling clothes, and thankfully he seemed unharmed.

"Oh Lordy, have we been looking for you, Troy," I said as I ran through the keys until I found the right one and unlocked his chains. "Are you okay?"

"Yuh," he said weakly, swinging his legs around and wobbling upright. "Dizzy. I thought they were going to kill me. Thank you. Thank you." He was trembling and tears ran down his cheeks, but, other than that, he seemed steady. I was impressed. "I'm not hurt," he finished.

"Good man," I said. "Now, I need your shirt, please."

He frowned in confusion, but took off the smelly yellow and black cycling top. I used it and Morales' shirt to create a basic compression bandage for Morales while I spoke to them. "Guys, we need to go. There's a SWAT team outside, but there are armed men in the building and I think their orders are to kill you. Bernard can't walk, so I'm going to need you two to help him. We've got to get down the corridor and up the stairs. Let's move."

Morales seemed most in control of himself, but he was limited in what he could do. Troy had been a captive for two weeks and would be disoriented and weak. Verdoon was going to be unable to help with anything. But I had to be free to keep Tucker's men away.

"Victor," I said into the mike, "I have Morales, Verdoon and Huber. Two wounded. No sign of anyone on this floor yet, but I can hear gunfire below. We're moving now."

"Roger that," he replied. "We're ready for you. SWAT team engaged in delivery area, holding for reinforcements before coming further in."

I stuck my head out the door. There was still nothing on this floor, though I could hear shouting below and the firing continued. I risked a quick look into the atrium. People were running around on the other floors, trying to get into the elevators or down the main client stairs.

We headed for the service stairwell, limping along at the pace the three of them could make while I kept a lookout.

The door at the end was locked. Rather than try my pass, I broke the nearest fire alarm. Bless those building regulations; the doors opened and we were through into the stairwell.

"Up!" I caught them, turning to go down automatically. "Up to the roof."

Morales understood and Troy followed his lead. I waited on the landing, looking down and listening. Our luck had run out; there were people coming up the stairs. Not as many as there would have been without the SWAT team in the delivery area, but there was only one of me.

I dived back into the corridor and retrieved the fire extinguishers stacked beside the door. In the stairwell, I checked out the types and got the foam one ready.

Troy came back down from the roof. "The door up there's locked," he said.

I tested the door behind me to the corridor, and that had now locked as well. Someone had overridden the fire precautions and we were trapped in the stairwell with the bad guys only a floor or two away.

I thrust the spare fire extinguisher into his hands. "Use that to break the lock." It was a CO2 extinguisher for electric fires, smaller and lighter than the foam one, but I needed that. He stumbled back up while I waited for the first person to come into sight.

Tucker's lead man was trotting up the steps, panting and waving his gun around. They hadn't realized the hostages had escaped yet, but the point man recovered quickly and fired wildly. I shot him, a single bullet through the chest, and then I walked down the stairs, firing into the group behind him. Men in suits. Tucker's elite troops rather than his ZK muscle.

There were screams and someone more alert than the others started firing back. I heard the vicious sound of the ricochets off the walls behind me. In my left hand I triggered the foam extinguisher, pointing it down into the mass and following it with another shot.

"Amber, sitrep," called Victor.

"The hostages are trying to break out the roof door," I shouted. "I'm in the stairwell, engaged. Where are you?"

"Comin' in on the roof," he said over the thudding of the chopper blades.

"Freaking A, Vic," I whispered as I retrieved guns from the first two bodies on the stairs and retreated back upwards. Someone was firing up blind, which was a smarter move than it sounded like. In the cramped concrete stairwell, ricochets were as deadly as straight shots. Something smacked into the wall right next to me and I felt a sting of concrete chips across my cheek.

I ran up, followed by shouts and more bullets. The foam was slippery and had caused confusion and panic when they were bunched up, but it wouldn't keep them back now.

Troy was doing a good job breaking the door—he was almost through. Morales was holding up Verdoon. I pushed Troy aside and shattered the lock with a kick.

The doors opened and slammed closed again as the downwash from the chopper caught them. I forced them back and pointed at the chopper. "Go, go, go," I screamed over the noise, grabbing Morales' shoulder and jerking him towards it.

Someone came around the corner below and I fired at him. Another followed him and I fired again, emptying one gun and swapping it for another. I was stuck; I couldn't break off to get to the chopper, otherwise they'd have a clear shot at it while it was at its most vulnerable.

"Victor," I yelled. "Take off as soon as they're aboard."

"Shit, woman, no one's leaving you here."

"Just do it, damn you. Go!"

The firing from below redoubled and again I felt the sting of chips gouged out of the walls. Then a ricochet hammered into my chest and knocked me down. Only the Kevlar vest saved me. *Thank you again, Vic.*

As I struggled back to my feet, they took the opportunity to sprint up the last few steps. I shot the first one and grabbed the second in the doorway, blocking it for the others behind. I heard the chopper wind up behind me and the downwash buffeted us as we struggled. A bullet raked along my leg. My gun went off again, into the stairwell, and someone yelled. Getting purchase on the doorframe, I managed to shove them back inside. Behind me, the chopper was gone.

The stairwell was a confused melee, and someone swore in panic. I heard a sound that made my blood freeze. Some idiot had dropped an armed grenade onto the concrete floor and it was the distinctive *ching* of the metal safety lever springing out. I tried to struggle free, but I was pinned where I was.

The stairwell exploded. The blast hurled me against the doorframe, tearing the gun out of my hand and the comms plug out of my ear. Everything went black and distant.

The place was a charnel house filled with smoke and dust. I had a dozen splinter punctures and my face and hands were leaking blood, but that was better than the guy I'd been wrestling. He'd taken the main force of the blast on his unprotected back. I shoved his tattered corpse off me and tried to get up, coughing. The others on this level were dead or badly injured as well.

A figure loomed through the swirling smoke, pointing a shotgun at my head. His foot stamped down on my chest and pushed me back.

"You should have agreed to work for me at the ball. It felt right, you know. You'd have done well." His voice was hoarse, strained. "Now it's your fault it's all fucked up."

"Tucker," I croaked, and spat dust out of my mouth. "It's over. The SWAT team are all around this place and your hostages are gone."

"Except you," he said. The edgy businessman from the charity ball was gone, replaced by an angry maniac in torn clothes. His eyes were like staring holes.

"They won't do you a deal for me."

"They won't, but she will. I saw her car. That's her helicopter that just left my roof." He laughed, sweat glistening on his face. "I know all about you two. Half of Denver knows about you, after the ball."

He pulled a cell from his pocket and dialed.

"Kingslund," he yelled. "I've got your whore up here on the roof. You can pick her up off the ground or you can give us a ride in your helicopter."

I shouted to stop him from hearing an answer. "You're not getting away, Tucker. You'll die in here."

"I don't care anymore. See?" He tore his shirt away from his neck, and I could see the mark of fangs. He'd gotten the full dose and he wasn't in any fit state to be able to stand the crusis. But he didn't know that. "I don't care if I die today. Inez has bitten me, and if I die it just means I'll return stronger." He was exultant, laughing, his eyes staring and completely mad. "I just don't fucking care anymore. You caused all of this, you interfering bitch. If you hadn't cracked our operation at Crate & Freight, I'd have bought Kingslund out and Matlal wouldn't have any claws in me. Now it's all gone. And you and your Altau friends will pay for it. Matlal will make sure of that."

The pieces kept falling into place. Matlal was cutting his losses. Tucker was a liability now. The bite was a deliberate move to force him into crusis. He was slipping into rogue behavior already. Flecks of foam had appeared at the corners of his mouth.

"Sir, we gotta get out of here," one of his men shouted in panic up the stairwell.

He bent over me, not quite close enough for me to grab him. And the shotgun was shoved in my belly. "Tell me," he whispered. "What's it like? To die and come back like a god?"

Outside, I heard the sweetest sound, the thudding of blades as Victor brought the chopper back in. But I also could hear the sounds of fighting in the stairwell coming closer.

"It's not like that, Tucker," I said.

He wasn't listening. "Kingslund," he screamed into the cell. "Decision time, bitch."

"Shit, Tucker, Matlal's screwed you," I shouted. "That bite will kill you. Dead is dead. I don't know what she told you, but that's not how it works."

Tucker didn't believe me. He laughed. He closed his eyes, put his head back and roared with laughter. The shotgun waved away. And I pulled the extinguisher out from beneath me, ripped the pin and set it off.

CO_2 comes out of the extinguisher like jet exhaust but *cold*. The nozzles have double insulated layers to stop your hand from freezing solid on them. Tucker's hand didn't have that protection. It froze to his shotgun. The firing mechanism of the shotgun froze. I lunged up as his head snapped back upright. He gasped in pain, dragging the vapors in. His lungs and his face filled with a freezing cloud and his mouth opened in a silent scream as his men arrived.

I kicked his body towards them, turned and sprinted for the sound of blades.

Victor was holding the chopper about ten feet away from the roof. He didn't dare land back on the roof, but he was giving me a chance. Even with Tucker dead or dying, his men were still trying to kill us. My back tensed as I ran, waiting for the blow. The Kevlar wouldn't stop a rifle bullet. With horrible clarity, I saw holes appearing in the skin of the chopper.

I launched myself off the roof. For a heart-stopping second I fell through the air, a hundred feet above the ground, sure I had misjudged. Then my hands closed around the chopper's skid bar. I hung on, swinging wildly while the chopper twisted on its side.

But something had gone wrong. The engine was screaming and we were falling out of the sky.

Chapter 54

We plummeted down the side of the building. At the last minute Victor slowed the fall, converting all that rotor energy into speed and we raced away, close to the ground. He'd flown the best route to get away from anyone firing at us off the roof. Not the best route for my stress levels, but I'd take that over a bullet any day. The parking lot flashed beneath me, followed by an ornamental pond and lawns, before we eased up over some trees, slowed down and then sank towards the command center we had set up.

I let go and fell the last few feet onto soft grass. Victor landed twenty yards away. The scream of the turbine and thudding of the blades changed as the chopper started to windmill down. The adrenaline subsided, leaving me feeling drained. A medic came and knelt by me, but I waved him away as I heard the yelling.

"Amber! Shit! You crazy woman." Victor hauled me to my feet. "You did it."

"Right back atcha. We did it, Vic," I yelled back at him. "You crazy bastard. We did it."

Well outside the reach of the blades, we came together to jump and bump like a pair of hotshot wide receivers celebrating in the end zone. Given our size difference, there was only one way that was going to end. I ended up sprawled on the grass again, weak from laughter.

"You okay?" he said, suddenly worried as he saw the amount of blood covering me.

"I'm freaking A-okay, man." I sat up. "Most of it's not mine. I think." I ripped the coveralls back and hauled off the Kevlar vest.

"Amber!"

Jen was running towards me. She skidded to a stop, unable to take those last few steps, unsure of my reaction.

Yes, she'd made a mistake and hurt me, but I had behaved like an ass. We both had some talking to do, but I had to be willing to listen. Part of the problem was that I was afraid of that, of where it might lead. And while I hesitated, the look in her eyes was like sandcastles crumbling before the sea.

"You have about a second to fix this," said Tara inside my head.

I closed the gap and hugged her to me.

"I'm sorry Jen," I whispered in her ear.

"No. No. It was my fault. I messed it up."

I closed my eyes. It felt so good to hold her against me, to ease the pain I'd seen in her eyes. And it felt good for all sorts of other reasons. What about Alex? Oh gods, this was complicated.

"We need to talk, even more than before. But not now."

She nodded jerkily, her face against my neck. Exactly what was I going to say to her? And Alex?

Victor gave me a thump on my shoulder and returned to the chopper to make sure everything was shut down and secured.

Jen leaned back and looked at me. "Please, honey, listen to me a minute. I'm not proud of the game I played with those jackets, but it stopped a long time ago. Believe me, I never thought of you like that. I know I should have said something. It just never seemed to be the right time." She took a deep breath and visibly forced herself to go on. "I'm sorry. I want to make it like it was."

"We can make it like it was, Jen." I sighed.

Morales interrupted us. He came over, stumbling in pain and fighting off the attentions of the medical teams. He had gotten a comms unit from somewhere and was patched in to Edmunds. Troy and Verdoon were already on their way to the hospital, but Morales wasn't ready to go yet.

I made him sit down at least, which got me some thanks from the medics. Jen and I sat by him while we followed the sounds of Edmunds and his team working their way through the building.

Whoever had closed down the central stairwell doors to trap us had also saved the other people in the building. Tucker's men were all in the service stairs or on the roof and everyone else had left the building through the main client stairwell. A SWAT chopper was coming in now and the roof would be cleared very soon. The building was surrounded. Everything had been contained.

As the operation finished up, I took the comms from Morales and told Edmunds about Tucker and the two who had been on the fifth floor, the hit man and the guard.

"Correction," said Edmunds. "Tucker's COD looks to be self-administered gunshot to the head." I nodded somberly. Tucker believed, *really* believed, what he'd been told by his fiancée. He must have come around from my attack and thought this was his magic way out. I wondered what forensics might turn up.

As I handed the comms set back, Morales took the opportunity to take my hand and squeeze it gently.

"Thank you, Amber," he said. "I wasn't expecting to get out of there." He glanced aside, almost shyly. "I'm sorry, at the last meeting with the colonel, that your news made me so uncomfortable. That was unfair of me. I should have known you better. Trusted you. Thank you again."

I felt Jen stiffen in interest, but he didn't elaborate.

"No problem, José." I smiled a little. I must have been moving up in the world—first name terms with the police captain. "Can you brief us on what Verdoon was telling you?"

"Yeah, of course. Verdoon came to me as soon as he heard what happened on Friday night. He handles all the financial contributions to the police charities from Ms. Kingslund, so we meet regularly, know each other well. He'd been down in New Mexico over the weekend and he hadn't seen the weekend news until early this morning. He called me as I was on my way in and I went to his house."

"We can all be on first name terms, José," Jen said. He nodded.

"I couldn't understand exactly the hold Tucker had over Verdoon. It was to do with his daughter's illness and I guess something weird was involved." José raised an eyebrow at me, and I nodded. "Anyway, he'd agreed to tie up all the cash assets of Kingslund Group. But then he caught up with the news about the ball. Well, he knew the position he would be in if Jen had been killed and he was certain it was Tucker behind the attack. That's where we got to. I put in an urgent request for his daughter to be taken into protective custody. I was calling Jen from his house when Tucker's men broke in and the rest of that you know."

He pulled a piece of notepaper out of his pocket and passed it to Jen. "He said he'd kept your options open. The real financial agreements on all the cash assets are in encrypted files on his computer, and the money can be pulled out without penalty. This is the password."

"That must be why the rates are so odd," I said. "He put them in long term with an option for early retrieval. But all Tucker would see was Jen's purchasing power tied up."

"So Tucker's been funding Beacon secretly from his criminal organization," Jen said. "And when Amber broke up their Crate & Freight smuggling operation, that put him in such a bad position his only way out was to kill me and take over my company by making Verdoon sign it over."

"Kidnapping Troy was just his first attempt to try and get you to sell," I said. "When the drugs were seized, his options came down to killing you or losing everything to Matlal."

The comms unit squawked and I could hear Edmunds saying the building was secured.

"Edmunds is good," I said to José. "He's seemed more than willing to go the extra distance on trust."

José smiled. "You wouldn't have recognized him under the helmet, but he led the SWAT team last year."

"Emily Schumacher?" I said, and José nodded.

The medics had left us alone for a few minutes, and he leaned over, wincing with pain.

"Look, I'd really appreciate a full report from you, but you probably want to get out of here right now." He glanced at his watch. "I've lost sight of you in the confusion. I'd give it another ten minutes and the FBI are going to be all over this place."

I'd gotten all relaxed in the glow of a successful mission and that woke me up. He was right, I didn't want to talk to the FBI right now. I had a feeling that when I did, I'd be their guest for a while.

"I'm gone," I said. "I'll send you a report."

Jen walked with me to my car.

"Thanks for the loan of the chopper," I said awkwardly. "I'm sorry about the bullet holes."

"I don't care about the helicopter. I care that you got Troy and José and Bernard back. Most of all, I care that you came back," she said, blinking. "I realize I have to rebuild. But I mean it when I say your suite at Manassah is there, always."

"Jen, we'll work it out." I opened my arms and she flowed in like she was meant to be there. "I have some stuff to do now. 'Weird' stuff. I don't know exactly when I'll get back. There are things going on this week, but I promise, I swear, we'll talk after that. I'll answer any questions you ask." *And risk losing you.*

We parted and I drove off before the FBI could grab me.

I'd cracked Jen's case. Tucker was dead, Jen had her company back under control, Troy was safe, the Weres would leave her alone and, between Morales and the FBI, ZK was finished. True, Frank Hoben was still out there and I would sleep easier when he was caught. But he was more my problem than Jen's and I had no illusions as to who was the bigger threat between him and Matlal.

Somehow, I had to get back to earning money doing everyday investigations. Sigh.

On a personal level, I had to find out what it meant to balance my spirits, what that would make me, and why I was none of the things they would say I was. I had to work out what it meant to be Mistress of my own Athanate House, including getting David through crusis. And, in the long term, I had to figure out how to get Diana in front of the president.

But I knew, long before that, things would come to a head with Matlal at the Athanate Assembly. And it would get bloody.

I wasn't, yet, what I might become. What I had feared, I no longer fought.

It had been a couple more weeks, and I was still neither dead, nor undead, which I still ranked as an achievement.

I'd be happy if I could say the same in a week's time.

Printed in Great Britain
by Amazon